Path of the Swan:

THE MAITREYA CHRONICLES PART 1

Charu Singh grew up in Chandigarh and spent her vacations at Kathgarh, in her grandparents' fort in the Shivalik Hills. After completing her post-graduation from Panjab University she moved to the North East with her husband and worked there as a freelance researcher for Unicef, before turning to journalism. She has since worked for the *Asian Age, Frontline* and *Tribune* besides contributing articles to many leading news-magazines and papers. Charu is also a classical dancer trained in Odissi and Kathak and is deeply interested in the spiritual, having explored Buddhism and Hinduism as well as other religions. After having lived for a substantial time in the North East – including Sikkim, Assam and Manipur – she came to New Delhi, where she now lives with her husband and son.

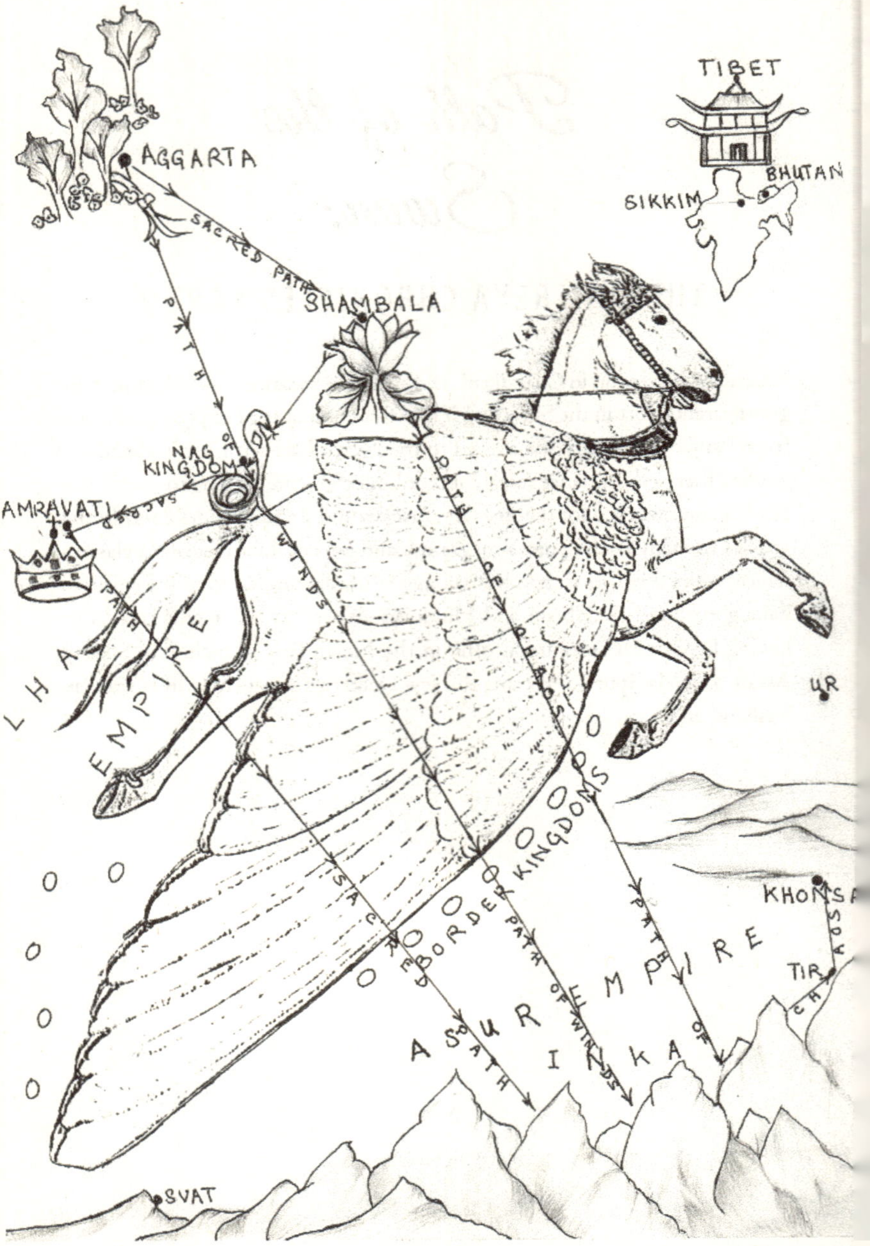
AGGARTA
SACRED PATH
PATH
SHAMBALA
TIBET
BHUTAN
SIKKIM
NAG
KINGDOM
OF
AMRAVATI
SACRED
PATH OF CHAOS
WINDS
LHA EMPIRE
PATH
UR
BORDER KINGDOMS
KHONSA
PATH
ASUR EMPIRE
TIR
SACRED PATH
PATH OF WINDS
INKA
SVAT

Path of the Swan:

THE MAITREYA CHRONICLES PART 1

CHARU SINGH

hachette
INDIA

First published in 2014 by Hachette India
(Registered name: Hachette Book Publishing India Pvt. Ltd)
An Hachette UK company
www.hachetteindia.com

SRD

ISBN 978-93-5009-673-4

Hachette Book Publishing India Pvt. Ltd
4th/5th Floors, Corporate Centre,
Sector 44, Gurgaon 122003, India

Typeset in Centaur MT 10.5/13.5
by Saanavi Graphics, Noida

Printed and bound in India
by Manipal Technologies Limited Manipal

MIX
Paper from responsible sources
FSC™ C104740

To the silent hand that guided me to write.

To the perfection behind all existence.

SONG OF MAITREYA

Two shall come by the path of the swan,
From the world of men in the fourth age –
When truth lies raped, and the word is forgotten.
Two shall come by ancient paths,
Led by neglected gods to the centre,
To the axis mundi,
To the holy isle,
Thus reversing the age,
By fire and storm,
By battle and sacked lives,
By divine rage and terrible unrest.
Let the men of the fourth age learn the ancient lesson.
Let the first stone be laid for the churning of the ages,
Let the terrible conch be blown for the new age that is come.

So shall the teachings of fire pass again into the world of men.
So shall the word be made manifest again.
So shall a new age be born on the blood and debris of the old.
So shall the vessel of truth,
The hope of the age,
The perfect one,
The child of light,
The Maitreya, come to be born in the world of men.

Chapter 1

WHERE LIES PEACE

I

A sky so blue it was unreal swooped to meet the unbroken line of black junipers that bordered a distant mist-shrouded wood of silver fir and exotic maple. Warm sunshine dappled the surrounding meadows and cast golden glints on the wood. Silence reigned. A few high-mountain goats grazed on the slopes, the snow peaks of the eastern Himalayas fanned out in an arc – lonely, forbidding, glorious.

A broken footpath wound through the glossy black junipers into the tree line. Over the fragile pink heather, concealed in the shadow of the thicket, his maroon robes strewn with leaf-bloom and dust sat Lama Nyima Ozer – upright, awake and lost to the world. Black eyes under thin, almost stencilled, brows gazed into eternity. A rosary of dark brown beads strung on an orange thread hung limp from delicate hands. The lama's slight body rested in peculiar inertness, his cheeks, crowned with violet blooms were strangely flushed and warm; despite the absence of breath, his otherwise lifeless body seemed full of a strange vitality.

The languid air of that afternoon high in the mountains was suddenly rent by loud calls as young Tashi Thendup ran from under the line of the gentle woods, looking for his teacher. Deeply agitated, he searched the far horizon, missing the bramble of glorious blooms that concealed Ozer's unmoving form. *'Why did I let the lama go out alone today? Why?* A crazed anxiety gripped him as he desperately searched for the lama. The sun had started to sink; a chill wind rose, sweeping across the eastern Himalayas and over all of Yumsemadong, in the high alpine ranges of Sikkim.

It was at that precise moment that Tashi, agonized and exhausted, chanced on his aged master's inert form. Trembling with anxiety, he knelt by the lama and shivered as the evening chill seeped through his clothes. Untying a narrow yak-hide flask from his waist, he proceeded to wet the lama's lips with a droplet of water. Bending his ear to Ozer's chest, Tashi sighed in relief when he heard the faint whisper of weak breaths.

Swiftly untying the blanket on his back, the boy picked up the frail husk that was Ozer's body, wrapped his master in it and tied him to his back. With practised care, Tashi picked his way through the rhododendron-lined meadows, merging into the backdrop with the routine of habit so that even trained mountain eyes would not have spotted him. As he made it to the line of silver firs, the ritual icy blast of evening from the snow-crowned mountains assaulted his face and hands. Yearning for strong butter tea, Tashi began the laborious descent from the meadows into the woods and from there to Demazong Gumpa, the hidden monastery. Time and again, the standing orders of the Head Lama reverberated in his ears: he was not to desert duty and under no circumstances was he to be outside the monastery after three in the afternoon.

Lithe and assured, Tashi's steps effortlessly negotiated the wood. Even now, with the darkening night sky overhead and the freezing wind in his path, he did not disturb a single twig or bend a blade of grass. His dark robes aflap in the rising wind, he made his way through the woods till he came to a rope bridge that spanned a turbulent green stream with no name. Made of hemp, the bridge was both resilient and virtually invisible. Stepping forward, Tashi instinctively placed his foot on the exact spot where the bridge began over a gaping chasm.

The wind howled in the mountains and sighed across the trees to slap Ozer's cheeks, drawing low moans from the monk whose intent remained unintelligible to Tashi. The bridge ended where the steep face of a mountain cliff began. Stone crumbled into pebble and gravel in Tashi's hands as he groped for the opening. Feeling his way through, he steered the lama and himself through the face of the naked cliff, crossing into a small tunnel invisible to the human eye. They had reached the 'Beyul' of Demazong – the hidden vale.

A cluster of stars studded the heavens. Thickets of wild white rhododendron bordered the silver stream cutting through the valley. On the far end, rising from within the thickest clump on a small hillock was the Demazong Gumpa, the hidden monastery. A small, modest-sized edifice, with a distinctive, curved structure that merged into the night sky. Tashi quickened his pace into a fast lope.

Ozer stirred weakly, the movement bringing him alive to the necessity of stealth. Discovery would mean too many questions at the monastery, followed by punishment. Cutting his arms and legs in the thicket, Tashi chose to go in through the monastery's side entrance, making for the lama's quarters in the northern corner.

Flickering lamplight greeted Tashi in the corridor. An old nun crossed them, head bowed over her rosary, as he evaded discovery and made it to Ozer's apartments. He laid the lama out on his wooden cot by the window and proceeded to heat some yak oil over a kerosene burner; he would need it to revive the monk.

'It must have been a deep trance for it to have lasted so many hours,' Tashi said to himself. 'Yet he should be out of it any time now; his breathing has normalized and his tongue has unlocked.' The warmth of the flame melted the yak oil in the steel cup and as Tashi did the ritual stirring, the door opened and the shadow of a small, curly head filled the room. Eleven-year-old Karma Lachengpa's mischievous eyes took in the scene.

'I saw you entering with Lama Ozer from the gumpa's windy side. Need any help with him? Should I keep the oil heated as you massage the lama out of his trance?'

An anxious Tashi replied, 'Dinner must be over. Run along, but keep it quiet and rustle up some soup for the lama. He will be in need of it. And save some for me too.'

Karma took one worried look at the monk and scampered off.

Tashi took Lama Nyima Ozer's frozen hands in his own and slowly started massaging them, smoothing the golden oil lightly over his arms and face. A muffled groan filled the air, as Ozer emerged weakly from the trance. His dark eyes came alive with intelligence, even as his tired limbs automatically uncrossed, coming out of the meditation posture.

'Boy, help me up,' said the lama as Tashi rushed towards him.

'Lama, you need refreshment,' the boy murmured. 'I have asked for a bowl of soup for you.'

'You have done well,' Ozer told him. 'Set it out and then inform Lama Jamgon that I must have an audience with the Rimpoche right now; it is a matter of urgency.'

As commanded, Tashi crept along the now freezing corridor, making for the Rimpoche's apartments on the first floor. The smell of incense hung in the air. A turn of the corridor, a flight of stairs and Tashi was outside the Rimpoche's quarters, softly knocking on the door. The bespectacled Lama Jamgon stepped out of his apartment.

'What are you doing here at this time, boy? You should be saying your night prayers. And incidentally, I did not see either you or Lama Ozer at the evening prayers. Where were you?'

'With due respect, Lama, I apologize for disturbing you at this hour, but Lama Ozer has sent me here with a message for you. The lama has just come out of a trance and desires an appointment with the Rimpoche right now on a matter of some urgency. He has asked me to take back your reply.'

'Please wait here,' said Lama Jamgon.

After an interval of perhaps twenty minutes, Lama Jamgon returned and said, 'Inform Lama Ozer that the Rimpoche will see him now and awaits him at his pleasure.'

Tashi ran through the corridors to Ozer's room.

A revived Lama Ozer was waiting for him.

'The Rimpoche awaits you at your pleasure, Lama,' Tashi announced. 'It is as you wished.'

'Leave, then, boy. I have sent word to the kitchens to give you your dinner, and tomorrow you may rest. Today, I fear, has been quite tough on you.'

II

Rimpoche Gyaltsen was in the pink of health; his robust cheeks, bright eyes and rotund belly added to the general sense of vitality that pervaded his environs. His tonsured head – bare as an eggshell; pale cream flesh peeping from beneath the dark muffler he had wound around it – complemented his physique. Few would have guessed that Gyaltsen was about to complete his hundred and fifth summer. In contrast, Lama Nyima Ozer looked pale, gaunt, and somewhat frail.

'Greetings, Rimpoche!' said the lama, folding both hands before Gyaltsen.

'Ozer, what brings you here today? It has, indeed, been several months since you sought me out,' said the smiling Rimpoche. 'Some tea, perhaps?'

The Rimpoche gestured to the lama who served as his attendant. Several minutes of contemplative silence followed; outside the window, the silver stream glistened in the night.

'Ah! There is much peace here; the beauty of the silver stream is beyond compare,' sighed the Rimpoche.

'The Rimpoche always knows; even my straying glances do not escape him,' said Ozer, his black eyes gleaming sharply in the night.

Two young monks clad in maroon entered, bearing a teapot and cups with a Tibetan motif, bowls of cashewnuts and biscuits.

'Is it silence you want?' asked the Rimpoche.

'You know, as always,' replied Ozer.

The Rimpoche waved away the young monks serving the tea.

As they withdrew, silence fell. The wind blew in fresh from the silver stream carrying the perfume of the night.

'So, what grace does this lonely night bring, Lama Ozer, that you have chosen to come to me?' asked the Rimpoche.

'Do you remember, Rimpoche, the fatal signs displayed in March of 2001 and through fall and winter that year, their portent in consonance with the Kalachakra prophecy?'

'Who can forget that, Lama, or what it means? The sentinels of Bamiyan fell, blown up by the collective violent karma of the age!' grimaced the Rimpoche, his thoughts on the great twin Buddha statues that had been destroyed in Bamiyan, Afghanistan.

'And Rimpoche, you still talk as crisp as ever, though I place a riddle before you. For six thousand years and four more has Demazong awaited the fulfilment of prophecy, the ancient summons,' said Lama Ozer.

'Awaited and awaited, yes, summer to fall and into winter, and the wind blew, the stream sparkled and Demazong stayed aloof in endless loneliness,' said the Rimpoche, a faraway look in his eyes. 'Yes, Lama, it is so, but the summons never came. The seasons came and went, but we stayed aloof, hidden and mysterious.'

'Rimpoche, have you noted the feel of the outer world this year? Summer breathes fire in the plains of the east; more than ever before, winter wreaks havoc in the countries to the north. Floods, famine and earthquakes ravage the earth. The oceans rage, their wrathful waters frothing; plague and terrifying diseases, many unknown, stalk the nations.' Lama Ozer sighed as he spoke.

'And more than ever before, Rimpoche, have you observed the shimmering rage in the people of the Crescent, the naked wrath? War clouds darken the Shomali plains under the shadow of the Zanskar range; the clamour of battle rings out of the nations of the West, even as nameless fears grip their souls. The plains of Iraq lie drenched in blood; the sons of Moses tighten their girdles in their daily clash against the Arabs; flaming hatred on both sides. Even history forgets to distinguish the belligerent from the wronged.

'In the Far East, fear and opportunity divide the nations as they sense a change in the balance of the world, a building shift and perhaps a Great War, or worse, catastrophe coming, the peace of the world stands shattered. Yet again, civilization seems ripe for a Great War. Rimpoche, I have a surprise for you – the summons has come; we await no longer!' Lama Ozer's voice was calm.

Rimpoche Gyaltsen's rotund features paled dramatically. 'The summons has come? How?' he asked.

'Today, towards mid-morning, I had left for a stroll in the meadows up yonder, as is my custom,' Ozer began. ' A powerful unease possessed me and overcome by a strange weakness, I sat down in the shade of a bush. Then sleep overtook me. Was it sleep? I do not know but somewhere in the middle I passed beyond the shadow of this world. The trance was very powerful, unlike any I have experienced before.

'Then, Rimpoche, the summons came from the unspoken land of Olmo-Lungring, that which in this deteriorated age is called "Shambala". A silver voice rang out in the silent space: "To the ninth realm are you summoned, man of Demazong, to fulfil ancient vows and bring prophecy to fruit. The sentinels lie scattered; the Crescent has risen in rage; the world drifts towards evil and terrible war. We summon thee at the soonest to the mystic realm, to the world axis, to the land of the Kalachakra, to the abode of the gods – ancient Olmo-Lungring – in all earnest."'

Silence followed the lama's account. The thoughts of both men focused on the mystic realm that exists in the material world, but lies far beyond the pale of humanity.

'It has come, then,' said the Rimpoche in a voice that shook with emotion. 'I thank you for informing me, old friend, but where is your guardian? For it is said that none can enter the sacred realm without a divine protector.'

'The guardian shall await by the Green Lake, the emerald waters of myth lying in the shadow of the sacred mountain, holy Kanchendzonga,' the lama replied. 'So I was told, old friend, and so I will depart. The time nears.'

'After all these years, strange are the deeds of this day, stranger still and much awaited the tidings you bear,' said a visibly shocked Rimpoche Gyaltsen. In a halting voice, he added, 'Of course, I shall give you the rosary of Demazong, such medicinal herbs as you will need for such a journey, and any of the young lamas you may choose to take along as an escort for this journey.'

'Spare me as little as you can, Rimpoche, but the ancient and blessed rosary will be most welcome and I shall not need any escort, but will proceed alone,' answered Lama Ozer.

'Is that wise, travelling alone? You are frail in health and one or two lamas would come in handy during the journey.'

Opening a silver chest of drawers, the Rimpoche pulled out a small wooden box wrapped in a length of maroon cloth and tied with an orange thread. He undid the thread and pulled off the cloth. Opening the box, he picked out a small bundle and unwound the faded cloth to reveal a rosary of jade beads.

'This is the legendary rosary of Demazong,' said the Rimpoche. 'Care for it well, my friend, and bring it back when your deed is done.'

From the silver chest, he next pulled out old, dried banana leaves strung together by a thread.

'Here, Ozer, are medicinal herbs I myself prepared with intensive incantations of healing mantras from dried rhododendrons and other forest herbs. They will help in illness and in severe cold. May the Goddess Tara bring grace on your journey,' smiled the Rimpoche.

'Yes, Rimpoche, I shall need her grace to go where I am summoned and I thank you for all these offerings and will guard them well. Also, my friend, I mean to leave with the first light of dawn. Please do not press me to accept an escort, for I am firm that no one should accompany me,' Ozer declared emphatically.

'Then it will be as you ask. You have the blessings and good wishes of all of Demazong as it travels with you,' smiled the Rimpoche.

'May I have your permission to retire, Rimpoche?' Lama Ozer asked.

'You have it. Amazing grace has visited you, my friend.'

As Lama Ozer retreated from the Rimpoche's quarters, young Tashi tossed in his bed, strangely restive in his sleep. Outside, the snow wind blew and smiled over the peace of Demazong.

III

The seven sisters shone brightly in the ageing night sky as Lama Nyima Ozer prepared for the journey ahead. He packed wheat pies, along with packets of paddy and noodles, into his brown leather sling bag. Into the inner pocket of his jacket, he put the packet of herbs and the rosary. Last of all, he picked up his new staff, only recently hewn by Tashi from the bark of a wild cherry tree.

As Ozer stepped out of the monastery into the freezing dawn, Rimpoche Gyaltsen stood waiting for him.

Hands outstretched, the Rimpoche approached the lama and said, 'I would not have let you leave, Lama Ozer, without a proper farewell. I will recite the morning prayers and invoke the Goddess Tara and the Lord Buddha to bless you with a fair and smooth journey.'

Hands folded, Lama Ozer replied, 'You should not have troubled yourself, Rimpoche.'

'It is the least I can do for you, old friend, the least, believe me, but there is one thing that troubles me greatly. At the very least, Ozer, take one of the younger lamas to assist you during what is going to be a very perilous journey. Your health is so frail, I would be very troubled to see you set out alone today.'

Lama Ozer held up his hand. 'Rimpoche, I well understand your concern, but the very nature of this journey makes it impossible for me to take anyone with me. '

'Still, friend, you will need somebody, you will,' insisted Rimpoche Gyaltsen.

'They summoned me, Rimpoche, and a guardian will be there near the Green Lake. You know well that few have travelled the road to the mystic realm; fewer still have made it back. The ways of Shambala are strange; some say the passage lies beyond death. How can I take another on a journey beyond any parallel of human experience, on a journey that will take me beyond life, beyond even death, to the mystic realm, wherever it is? No, my friend, no, my Rimpoche, forgive me, but this once, I will disobey you. '

'If that is your decision, so be it,' said Rimpoche Gyaltsen. 'I have already sent word to the Lachen Monastery that you will be passing through and may halt there tonight. They will be awaiting you.'

'I could not have done better, my friend,' said Lama Ozer. 'Indeed, halting at the blessed monastery in Lachen was my plan for tonight. I intend to hold consultations with the Head Lama there on the road to the Green Lake.'

'Then on this note we part, my friend,' said Rimpoche Gyaltsen. 'Let the dawn prayer begin and may the Goddess Tara and Lord Buddha shower their grace on your journey.'

His voice rose in the time-honoured prayer as Lama Ozer folded his hands and closed his eyes in worship. With his hands joined, Rimpoche Gyaltsen invoked the guardian deities, the Goddess Tara and the celestial Buddha. Lama Ozer bowed before Rimpoche Gyaltsen and then set off on his travels. Gyaltsen watched Ozer's receding form for a long time, until it had disappeared into the dawn and merged with the skyline.

Far, far away, the wind blew over the peaks of Mt Kanchendzonga, heralding the morning.

IV

A shivering Tashi woke up in anger, astonished at having spent such a restless night after the exhaustion of the previous day. However, there was that one saving grace: Lama Ozer had given him permission to rest today. He would like nothing better than chasing the snow pigeons at their games and observing the butterflies' flight across the meadows.

Yet, there was a sour taste to this morning, a taste of unfinished goals and hasty decisions. As Tashi completed his morning ablutions and found his way into the kitchen for some thick noodle soup, an extremely harried-looking Lama Jamgon accosted him.

'There you are!' the lama declared. 'I have searched for you everywhere, from the hostel to the grounds, and I find you in the kitchen. Get up and run to the Rimpoche. His Grace himself has summoned you – not that you deserve it!'

Tashi scrambled to his feet. *This day just does not feel right; I hope nothing is amiss,* he thought as he rushed through the corridors.

The door to the Rimpoche's apartments was open, but nobody was there. 'Where is His Eminence?' Tashi asked a lama standing by the door. 'Is he expecting me?'

'He is outdoors, telling his beads,' replied the lama. 'You will find him near the apple orchard.'

Tension seemed to have lent Tashi wings as he sped out of the building and into the open. Clear April skies met his gaze and he sighed, seeing his free day go waste. He hurried into the shade of the apple trees with their spreading branches, sighting the Rimpoche in his chair.

The Rimpoche eyed the boy as he approached, swiftly sizing him up. He liked what he saw; there was an aura of strength around him. His face reflected innocence; and yet there was something there – a steadfastness of character. He was short of stature, but sturdy of build; his arms and legs were well muscled. The Rimpoche sighed; this would have to be it.

'Boy, we have been waiting for you,' he said. 'There is a duty I will entrust you with today, one you have to fulfil in this life and beyond.'

A shivering Tashi stood in silence, his head bowed.

'Your teacher, Lama Nyima Ozer, has left on a great mission, the nature of which I cannot reveal,' said the Rimpoche. 'You, young Lama Tashi Thendup Bhutia, I entrust you with the duty of protecting and caring for Lama Ozer till such time as he chooses to return to Demazong. You are ordered to follow, escort and protect him, abandoning him under no condition, even if death overtakes you. May the Buddha lend you steadfastness.

'You will find the lama making for Lachen village. From there, he will take the high mountain route to the legendary Green Lake at the base of Mt Kanchendzonga, the holiest of holy mountains. Tonight, he will halt at the monastery in Lachen. Make straight for the monastery, boy. Make haste, do not tarry anywhere and take such help as you will find on the road in terms of transport. The lama left at four a.m. and now it is already six-thirty a.m. Stand by him, boy, no matter what. I have asked Lama Jamgon to prepare such supplies as you will need. Meet him right now at the main gate.'

The Rimpoche smiled at him.

A dazed Tashi bowed low and found himself heading towards the main gate. The sun's harsh glare threw the expression of irritation on Lama Jamgon's face into sharp focus as he handed Tashi a backpack and a bedroll. Still confused, the boy strapped the bedroll to his back, securing his backpack with it.

'Leave, boy! What are you waiting for? The Rimpoche's errand takes precedence over all else!' Lama Jamgon snapped.

Before Tashi could fully digest the import of his new responsibilities, he had taken his first steps away from the safe environs of Demazong and into the unknown.

V

Two hours of strenuous walking through the light, fir-clad wood saw Tashi in good humour and on the outskirts of Yumthang Valley. In the distance, an emerald stream, the Lachung Chu, glistened in the morning light. The prospect of travelling far and seeing distant places invigorated him. Handed at birth to a nun who had brought him to the monastery, Tashi had never set foot anywhere beyond the wood surrounding its sacred premises and the higher meadows of Yumsemadong. The reality of going far away from the confines of the known filled him with jubilation.

Tashi estimated that Lama Nyima Ozer could not be more than an hour and a half's walk away. The morning was still fresh and the beauty of Yumthang Valley was a joy to behold. As he walked on, however, the rumbling in his stomach reminded Tashi that he was hungry. He took out a strip of *churpi* – yak cheese – and sucked on it. As he rounded the hill, the entire valley came into view. In the distance, he saw a vehicle approach. A jeep was taxiing down into the valley. Tashi flagged it down.

'Travelling to town?' Tashi asked the stout Nepali driver with oily, slicked-back hair.

'Yes, Lama, and from there, I will make for Lachen village,' the man replied and offered, 'I can give you a ride.'

'Thank you,' said Tashi immediately, climbing into the vehicle.

The wind ruffled his hair as the jeep picked up speed and it was only then that he turned around and looked directly at the other passenger – his travelling companion. Astute grey eyes stared out of a weather-beaten face; silver-grey hair messed with the wind. Tashi beheld his first foreigner and stared at him with avid curiosity.

Neil Hammersmith and Lama Tashi Thendup Bhutia made incongruous travelling companions, each a relic of a world that was no longer relevant. Neil, a one-time cold-war operative of the CIA, now turned passionate mountaineer, and Lama Tashi Thendup, member of a secret religious order brought up on a world philosophy that had been extinct for several millennia. But then, the times were strange.

VI

Sensing the young lama's keen interest, a sleeping Neil was now fully awake, his hand automatically reaching under his jacket for the security of his Browning Magnum, made long ago to his specifications in an era now lost in the quagmire of history. A gulf of many decades separated Hammersmith from his murky past; yet this habit had not died.

It was over thirty years ago that Hammersmith had enlisted in the US Marine Corps. A stint with the Marines in the South-East had resulted in a quick pick-up by the CIA. For the next couple of years, Hammersmith had run a sensitive intelligence-gathering operation in Korea. In the 1970s, he was involved in covert operations across the Iron Curtain. Later, he would be routed to Pakistan, operating in Afghanistan through the course of the Mujaheedin war with the Soviet Union.

Hammersmith had earned the reputation of a legend within the covert circuit and was known as a master strategist and expert saboteur. There was none to rival him; nobody could be as coldly ruthless in attitude, clearer about objectives or more brilliantly ingenious in achieving them. And then, suddenly, in October '93, Hammersmith simply disappeared. The most sensitive tracers were sent out to locate him – to no avail. Reluctantly, the intelligence community in Washington and all over Europe gave him up for dead. Except for Garry Hawksley, a retired American diplomat living a reclusive life in the Alpine snugness of Lugano, Switzerland.

Hammersmith's practised gaze sized up Tashi in seconds. He was strangely touched by the open innocence radiating from the young boy. Any human presence was welcome after eight months of rigorous trekking in the winter desolation of the eastern Himalayas. Still, he instinctively felt something missing, something strange. It was the slightest of feelings, but important for a man who had survived this long by living off his instincts.

'Lama, you look like you are journeying afar today?' he said in Nepali.

Tashi looked back at him, wide-eyed. 'Yes,' he replied. 'I have been travelling the whole day, but will break journey at the monastery in Lachen village tonight. It is there that I hope to meet my senior lama and together, we mean to journey far into the mountain wilderness beyond Zema Glacier.'

Hammersmith found himself smiling. *How typically Oriental,* he thought. *Ask a simple question and get the life history.*

'That is a most pleasant coincidence, Lama, I myself am travelling to Lachen and from there to Zema and beyond.'

Tashi clapped his hands in delight. 'The ways of the Goddess Tara are divine!' he exclaimed. 'Here I was, worrying about making my first trip so far out alone. And now I meet a fellow traveller bound for the same destination.'

Hammersmith smiled, his eyes turning the exact shade of steel. 'If I can be of any assistance, Lama, let me know,' he murmured.

Tashi looked into the distance. Evening was falling in waves over the countryside that swept past as they drove by. 'Our journey to the Green Lake is a quest I cannot talk of,' he confided. 'And more I do not know. I simply accompany my lama.'

Hammersmith shook his head. 'It will be night soon. I hope you do not mind, Lama,' he said, indicating the cigarette he was rolling out.

Tashi looked away; the jeep was rattling through the tiny Lachung hamlet as mist rolled down the surrounding mountains, and the failing light of evening set ablaze the forest of a thousand hues that surrounded Lachung. Ahead, the steep mountain road unwound like a ball of wool untangling haphazardly down a cliff.

Neil tucked his hands behind his neck, amazed at his own circumstances. He remembered travelling to Gangtok, the capital of the eastern Himalayan state of Sikkim, and on into the wilderness. From early autumn, last year, he had camped in Yumthang Valley, adrift in the deep snows at the height of bitter winter. Erratically leading a strange life that felt not his own, till he had drifted out of Lachung this spring morning. Yet he was at peace like never before.

The dusk turned the sky a flaming red and purple before dark night claimed the firmament, slowly devouring the thickly-wooded fir forests of North Sikkim. The steep path to Lachen village unwound slowly in the dark; at most points, there was no road at all – just a broken path.

Hammersmith looked at the young monk; Tashi's eyes were drinking in the night and the ride, as though it were his first.

Suddenly, Hammersmith felt himself rudely jolted out of idle contemplation. The jeep was rattling crazily; the driver had lost control. It was making straight for the edge of the precipice and the sharp drop to the swollen waters of a hungry river that glimmered in the twilight several thousand feet below. With screeching tyres, the jeep came to a halt at the precipice. The side door jerked open, flinging out the driver, who managed to hold on to the door, even as he swung wildly over the yawning chasm. Instinctively, Hammersmith found himself moving. The wind rushed past his face like the blade of an icy sword shaving off his skin. Gripping the crazily spinning steering wheel with one hand, Neil seized the driver by the scruff of his neck, breaking the latter's fall with his booted foot and pulling him up from his precarious hold on the door.

Ten minutes of struggle brought the runaway jeep back on track.

'Are you all right, Lama?' Hammersmith enquired as he got back his breath.

'Yes, by the graces, I am still here,' Tashi answered.

'I think I had better drive,' Hammersmith announced to no one in particular.

Hammersmith found himself enjoying the feel of the steering wheel beneath his hands and the shudder of the jeep through his body as it rattled along the mountain road; it felt like a reminder of the real world. Three sharp turns brought him to the outskirts of Lachen and a final turn brought him face-to-face with what looked to be a ghost village shrouded in thick, swirling mist. The village lay in darkness; not a soul moved.

'Where will you stay, driver?' asked a concerned Tashi.

'I have an aunt living here,' the man replied. 'I will have to bang on her front door for a good five minutes, but eventually, she will open up.'

Tashi turned to Hammersmith. 'You are welcome to spend the night at the monastery where I am putting up. The arrangements are not the best, but you will not be cold.'

Hammersmith replied, 'Thank you, Lama. I do not think I have an option and perhaps we will meet your elder lama there as well.'

The jeep turned into the northern spur of the village. A single lamp burned at the gate of the Lachen Monastery; thick mist lay behind it. Hammersmith parked the jeep outside the monastery and soon the mist swallowed up all three figures.

VII

Mist dogged Tashi's footsteps and fear rinsed his insides. The closer he drew to Lama Ozer, the more his fear grew. Hammersmith pulled out a pencil torch from his pocket, its sharp rays penetrating a thick blanket of fog.

'Which way, Lama?' he asked, as a preoccupied Tashi pointed into nothingness.

'Just follow me,' the boy advised the foreigner. 'I shall lead us to the lama's quarters at the rear of the monastery.'

The strange feeling of being in a vacuum seemed to descend on them, as a frowning Tashi opened a door into absolute, inky darkness. The grey-black of the night paled into insignificance as they stared into a seemingly pitch-black tunnel. Tashi shivered with anxiety under his maroon robe and felt the two sides of the narrow opening with his hands; a little way ahead, a torch cast a dull glow of light in the passageway. Small rooms flanked it on both sides and Tashi shook his head, trying to guess in which room Lama Ozer could be resting.

The door to the room at the end was ajar and a small candle burned within. Two maroon-robed figures sat hunched over tumblers of tea. Tashi gestured to Hammersmith, indicating that he should wait outside.

Treading softly, he approached Lama Nyima Ozer and bowed low before him. Silence followed, as Ozer observed the boy with stone-cold eyes. Finally, he enquired, 'Boy, who asked you to follow me? And how do you come to be here at this time?'

Tashi went down on his knees before Lama Ozer. 'Lama, forgive me,' he implored, 'please hear me out.'

'Explain,' said Lama Ozer.

'Lama, it was this very morning that Rimpoche Gyaltsen summoned me and entrusted me with the responsibility of escorting you on your journey and protecting you in life and beyond. Please forgive me if I have offended you,' Tashi beseeched the older man.

Silence followed. Beads of cold sweat appeared on Tashi's brow.

A sigh escaped Lama Ozer. 'Boy, I did not want to take you on a journey as dangerous as the one I have embarked on,' he said, 'but none can free you from the responsibility you have been entrusted with. It is done. Rise and rest.'

'There is one more thing, Lama,' Tashi murmured, looking at both Lama Ozer and his companion. 'With me has come a foreigner. He travelled with me in a jeep and saved my life and the life of the driver. I have taken the liberty of offering him shelter.'

'Then arrangements will have to be made,' said Ozer, looking directly at his companion. Then he turned back to Tashi and introduced him to the other man. 'Meet Lama Topden, boy, Senior Lama at this monastery.' He turned again to the other lama. 'Can you help us, Lama?' he asked.

Two ancient eyes looked out of a wrinkled face. 'The two of you can heat up some soup kept on the stove in my room and you may find some cold rice in the earthen pot. You two can use my room for the night while I share with Lama Ozer.'

Outside in the passageway, Hammersmith pulled out a silver flask from his breast pocket. He took a quick swig of brandy, relishing the burning heat it generated as it travelled down from his throat to the pit of his stomach.

VIII

A golden dawn lit the snow peaks of the surrounding mountains, its glow softly penetrating Lama Ozer's frail flesh and lending his hands a translucent quality as he walked steadily uphill along the banks of the glacial river, Lonak. Just 10 yards away, the shadowy eves of a dense forest of firs stretched into nothingness. They were just five kilometres from Lachen village, but as they walked on, the receding red roof of the village monastery could still be glimpsed from time to time.

Intrigued, Hammersmith watched the lama moving with silent authority in every step. He certainly had found strange travelling companions – an ancient maroon-robed monk, who held on to his rosary in the same manner as he held on to his Browning, and a young acolyte. Even though the lama maintained a rapid pace, the path along the river seemed to stretch interminably ahead of them. The sun was picking up strength and the morning resounded with a mêlée of natural sounds.

Hammersmith lost track of time as early morning gave way to noon. Yet the two monks walked tirelessly and in absolute silence. Hammersmith noted with some surprise that the senior lama seemed to be searching the ground, looking for something.

'As far as I know, the trail goes straight ahead,' Hammersmith said in Nepali.

Lama Ozer continued searching the ground for signs and addressed him in fluent English. 'You do not have to come with us,' he said flatly. 'We journey in haste and will not be following the usual routes. In fact, the shortcut I take will save us two whole days, but involves a much tougher trek. Just carry on down this path; it is the route most mountaineers follow. We are grateful to you for your help, but now that the journey grows dangerous, there is no need for you to accompany us.'

There was an amused glint in Hammersmith's grey eyes as he responded, 'Lama, how else will I get the opportunity to see unusual mountain trails, save with you? Allow me to accompany you a little farther. I am sure I can be of some assistance to you on the road ahead.'

Instinct warned him again – something was very odd here – yet for once, Hammersmith could not put his finger on it. Lama Ozer wasted half an hour hunting for the trail, with Tashi following him around like a puppy. Irritated, Hammersmith stepped aside for a smoke. As the ash drifted down to the pine needle-carpeted forest floor, he saw it – the beginnings of a trail hidden in the undergrowth.

'I think perhaps this is what you are looking for,' he said laconically.

Ozer pushed his glasses back on, looking carefully; and then he too saw the faint signs of a trail. Giving Hammersmith a hard-eyed look, he started off wordlessly down the path into the vastness of the fir-lined forest.

The track spiralled endlessly uphill. Hammersmith found himself enjoying the trek, but it seemed to be telling on the lama. Leaning on his staff, Lama Ozer walked on with steely determination. Tashi tried running to the old man's aid at every point, but Ozer resolutely refused all assistance. As the brief afternoon light made its tremulous presence felt, the terrain started to change; the surroundings became more arid, the firs grew fewer and more stunted and the ground was crowded with low-lying pale yellow scrub. It was only when the last bush vanished and the landscape ahead seemed to stretch into unrelieved snow-covered starkness that Lama Ozer called a halt. As he let go of his staff, his knees buckled and he sat down with a thump on the moss-covered ground.

'Boy, get out the dried plums and rice,' he said, waving away Tashi who rushed to help him.

As Hammersmith left to reconnoitre the area, Tashi got a fire going. Bending over the pot, he threw in the plums to cook with the rice. To the preparation, he added herbs foraged in the forest and let it simmer. In the distance, he could see the foreigner return, his tall form clearly outlined against the horizon.

Lama Ozer said in an undertone, 'Sometime tomorrow, boy, after darkness falls, we will have to give him the slip. By late evening, we will be reaching the vicinity of the Green Lake. Then we cannot allow him to be with us.'

'We are really high up, Lama,' Hammersmith declared, folding himself into a sitting posture. 'This shortcut of yours has taken us a little over Yabuk – a two-day trek managed in one.'

Ozer offered him a plate as Tashi served out three portions. 'I am afraid there are no spoons,' he said. 'We eat with our hands.'

'Do we camp here for the night?' Hammersmith asked, accepting the food gratefully. 'This area is too open and the evening winds will cut through us.'

'No, there is another spot about an hour's walk from here. That should do for the night,' the lama answered.

Silence followed as the afternoon was overtaken by the approaching evening chill.

IX

Silently, the three travellers picked up their packs. Lama Ozer led the way, with Tashi right behind and Hammersmith bringing up the rear. Dusk swiftly gave way to night as high-velocity winds tore through the barren, snow-covered plateau and struck at them from every angle. A ghostly mist, thick as milk, crept up to engulf them.

Where the bare plateau came to an end, the ground started to rise sharply and the luminous, snow-clad shapes of high mountains became discernible.

Hammersmith squinted into the distance. 'Is it wise to travel at night, Lama?' he asked.

'The night camp I have in mind is a good hour's walk away, my friend,' Lama Ozer replied with some asperity. 'There is no shelter on this plateau; we have no option but to move on.'

In the deep silence that ensued, only the sound of boots crunching through snow was audible.

Lama Ozer called a halt at the base of the mountain and began playing his torchlight over the ground again. After a five-minute search, he went on ahead. Snow started falling, gently, at first; then it swirled thickly around them with every step they took. Tashi peered into the night, shivering under his robe; the temperature was plummeting fast. He frowned anxiously as he watched the lama's frail legs struggling up the mountain. Behind him, the foreigner moved with sure, sturdy steps. Tashi somehow felt glad for his presence.

Sharp as a sword, the wind now sliced through them. Snow was piling up high on both sides of the mountain path and progress was torturously slow. Tashi had to throw the bulk of his weight against the wind and wet snow and plough his path ahead, step by laborious step. They carried on walking at this excruciatingly slow pace for an hour until the lama called a short halt in the shadow of the mountain. It took several moments for the three travellers to catch their breath.

Finally, Tashi said, 'This is getting very difficult, Lama. We are crawling at ant's pace. At this rate, we will freeze to death before we reach the shelter.'

Lama Ozer was still winded, but spoke up, nonetheless, his words emerging in gasps. 'It should not have been this difficult,' he panted. 'We do not get such heavy snowfall in late spring. I think this snowfall that impedes our every step is not natural; it is the work of malevolent powers. Be careful, boy.'

'We should retreat and try climbing in the morning,' Hammersmith suggested. 'We can take shelter in whatever little nook or cranny we find on the plateau.'

Lama Ozer shook his head. 'I told you that we travel in haste,' he reminded the other man. 'No matter what, we leave now.'

'If we leave now, we had better use the rope,' Hammersmith replied matter-of-factly.

So saying, he took out a length of rope and fastened it to his waist before passing it to Tashi and the lama. Hammersmith took the lead, stepping out into the snowstorm; Lama Ozer followed, with Tashi bringing up the rear. The snow was blowing hard by now and visibility was zero; taking even a single step forward involved a struggle. Hammersmith threw his weight against the wind and plodded ahead through chest-high snowdrifts. Lama Ozer followed, but the wind buffeted against him, making it almost impossible for him to progress. Tashi literally swam his way forward through the drifting snow.

Another hour of fighting their way through the snow resulted in little progress and Lama Ozer began tiring out fast. Finally, on a scantily sheltered ledge, the lama halted yet again, leaning heavily on his staff.

'I have to go on,' he mumbled, 'but I don't think I can take another step. Tashi, how are we going to manage? This storm is sapping our strength and preventing us from moving forward.'

'Lama, I can carry you,' Tashi offered. 'Please allow me to do so.'

Lama Ozer looked at him, his eyes drooping with exhaustion. 'No, boy, we must go on,' he persisted.

'Have this,' Hammersmith suggested, drawing out his silver flask.

Lama Ozer held up his hands in protest and anger flashed in his eyes, 'Know you that these mountains are holy,' he admonished the other man. 'We crossed the barrier in the evening. Nobody is to touch alcohol or smoke while he travels with me – if he knows what is good for him.'

Hammersmith shrugged. 'I did not mean to hurt your sensibilities,' he said apologetically, 'but you are freezing.'

The snowstorm had taken over the night, a ghostly white-on-black that seemed to smother everything.

Tashi tried moving his stiff legs, only to find himself trapped in chest-deep snow. The light from Hammersmith's torch threw giant shadows in the night and a peculiar paralysis seemed to be taking hold of all three.

'I am afraid, Lama, that if we do not move faster, we will freeze to death here,' Hammersmith cautioned.

Lama Ozer silently held up his hand and stared into the night. 'We have to brave this night,' he said, taking one faltering step after the other. 'The shelter is not far, just two turns away. By the grace of Goddess Tara, the celestial saviour, we will manage.'

Tashi followed, holding Ozer fast on the rope. Suddenly, the snowstorm grew fierce; ice flakes and wet snow, chased by high winds, smacked into the boy's face. A few steps ahead, Lama Ozer stumbled and collapsed in the snow.

Tashi rushed ahead, moving as fast as the snow would allow him. 'Halt, Hammersmith!' he called out, 'the lama has collapsed in the snow. Let me feel his pulse.'

Lama Ozer was lying in a dead faint, his pulse feeble.

'What should we do now?' Tashi asked in consternation. 'He has fainted.'

'I'll carry him,' Hammersmith told him, picking Ozer up in his arms. 'Just follow me. It will be impossible to go ahead with the snowstorm blowing at this furious pace. Your lama said to check the next turn; the cave is there on the leeward side. If we find it, we will take shelter there. Else, we move downhill.'

They moved in single file, pushing their way through the piles of snow, Hammersmith holding his torch aloft in the air, a beacon in the night.

In silence they plodded on – four steps, then a break, four steps, another break. One turn was crossed. The snowflakes whirled around them in a fury as Hammersmith laboriously ploughed his way ahead.

'I am holding him secure,' he reassured the boy lama. 'We have crossed one turn; half a turn should bring us to whatever shelter the lama had in mind.'

Tashi began ploughing his way through the thick snowdrift again. He was exhausted and extremely anxious about Lama Ozer, who lay limply on Hammersmith's shoulder. Tashi touched his hands; they were cold and his pulse was weak.

Hammersmith's eyes scanned the horizon for signs of a shelter. There was none; just the night and the snow. Making his way through the snowdrift at the second turn, Hammersmith spotted an inkier darkness towards the cliffside.

'We seem to be surrounded by nothing but darkness here,' Hammersmith observed, 'but there, in the corner, the darkness is more intense. I will make for it.'

As they neared the spot, the darkness grew and loomed over them. Hammersmith smelt something – dry air. 'There, in there! I think we have hit on something,' he said.

The snow was piled thick near the entrance to an opening in the rock, the drifts rising up to Hammersmith's chest. Virtually swimming through snow, they entered a cave, just large enough for three people. Outside, the wind wailed.

X

Hammersmith's deft hands untied the rope around his waist, as Tashi softly laid Lama Ozer down on the floor of the cave. Hammersmith conducted a quick survey of their shelter by letting his torchlight sweep over it in a wide arc. Unnoticed in one corner and revealed by the dancing beams was dry firewood. He swiftly arranged the wood together in the centre of the cave and lit it with his lighter. Unbelievably, orange flames leapt up. Outside, the blizzard continued to rage in the night.

Tashi looked wonderingly at the fire and slowly dragged Lama Ozer towards it. He rifled through Ozer's jacket, pulling out his packet of herbs. 'This is what I have been wanting to give the lama all evening,' he said, holding aloft a tiny bottle of ruby liquid.

He proceeded to pour two fingers into a cup and held it to the lama's frozen lips, forcing the mixture through them. Having settled the monk by the fire, he wet a corner of his robe with water from the canteen and gently wiped Lama Ozer's forehead, face and hands. He began massaging the old man's hands, hoping to bring him back to consciousness.

After what seemed an eternity, a spluttering cough broke from Ozer; slowly, his eyes blinked open. In a barely audible whisper, he said, 'Boy, you have given me the Rimpoche's herbal medicine. Why did you do it? That is for the worst of times.'

Tashi softly massaged Ozer's hands, his eyes never leaving the latter's beaten face. After some colour had returned to the monk's cheeks, the boy finally gave his attention to getting some supper ready.

'Lama, I am going to heat up some broth for you. I think that will do you good,' Tashi told him.

He quickly melted some snow in a pan over the fire, immersed dried vegetables and potatoes in it and added the fresh herbs he had picked up on the road for seasoning. In no time, the broth was simmering on the fire. Tashi finally sat back to unwind, his skin thawing and his muscles relaxing in the heat generated by the flames.

With at least some of his strength restored, Lama Ozer was now reclining against the cave walls. Tashi poured some broth into a bowl and handed it to Ozer.

The lama took a few sips and, as he regained his energy, murmured in a low voice, 'I fear, boy, that was no ordinary storm. This is but the beginning. Worse could follow. The path I walk leads to the mysterious realm of Shambala. It is a desperate journey, boy, and not one you should make. Will nothing convince you to go back?'

Tashi answered, 'Lama, I will never go back without you. I have been charged with your care and, furthermore, you should not proceed alone. So do not talk of my leaving.'

Ozer smiled. 'Then so be it, but remember, boy, there are malevolent powers that will know of my quest and will oppose it. That snowstorm was merely one sign; others will follow. The way ahead is not an easy one.'

So saying, he gave his attention to the broth, and having eaten, lay down, his eyes shutting almost immediately.

Tashi looked at Hammersmith, who held a pan of stew over the fire. A wholesome aroma rose from it and filled the cave, rousing their flagging spirits.

XI

The earliest dawn light caught Hammersmith's eyes and pried them open. Particles of sunlight seemed to drift in through the cave. A silence so deep as to be almost tangible prevailed. There was also one other thing; the cave was utterly empty but for his light backpack and the previous night's leftovers. The two lamas had vanished. A cold rage – certainly unreasonable, for the two meant nothing to him – possessed Hammersmith. He found himself on his feet, rolling his belongings, packed and ready to move within seconds.

Outside the cave, he found fresh tracks in the snow; the lama and his acolyte were no more than an hour's trek ahead of him. Carefully scanning the horizon and watching the patterns on the snow, Hammersmith started moving at a faster pace. The morning sun was painfully bright, almost blinding in its intensity. The lama seemed to be making for the Green Lake in a hurry. All along, the horizon was empty and wild; one snow-covered peak after another dazzled in the forsaken wilderness. Right before him and towering above stood Mt Kanchendzonga.

Hammersmith's eyes drank in the grandeur of the sight as he scanned the horizon for two moving specks. As the morning gave way to a very fleeting afternoon, a fresh chill crept into the air and the Zema glacier shone in the distance. Hammersmith broke journey for the first time, opening his backpack to pull out a pair of much-used binoculars. His gaze raced across the unrelenting emptiness. Then, just on the outskirts of Zema, he spied them, the two moving specks he had been trying to track down.

Already, Lama Ozer seemed to be slowing down, moving only with Tashi's strong support. A new burst of adrenalin warmed Hammersmith as the thrill of the chase coursed through his veins again. Setting himself an even more killing pace, he started after them. Time and again, he tracked them through his binoculars and as afternoon gave way to evening, he noticed something strange: the two figures had stopped moving. Hammersmith calculated the distance between them and decided the monk and his acolyte were not more than fifteen minutes away.

Rounding the shoulder of the mountain, he suddenly found himself face-to-face with the low-lying valley, the cradle, it was said, for the legendary Green Lake at its centre. A lake only in name, now buried permanently under the refuse of the glacier and the valley plain and no more than a small dirt pond in the summer.

As Hammersmith made to hurry along, the ultimate aberration occurred; his breath caught and the shock riveted his body. It was the twilight hour and as the first chill of the coming night kissed the bowl-shaped valley, he watched it happen, heart pounding, breath suspended.

Lama Ozer was standing erect, hands folded, his face stern in profile, his eyes narrowed in concentration. Unreal though it seemed to Hammersmith, at the base of the rocky crag on which the two sat, a clear emerald lake swelled into view, its sparkling waters gleaming like a million jewels. Hands folded, head bowed, Lama Ozer dived into the emerald waters, with Tashi closely following him. As the two swam into the heart of the lake, it vanished into thin air.

A stunned Hammersmith stumbled to his knees, staring uncomprehendingly at the wild, barren bowl of the valley. There was no sign that a lake had ever existed – just the muddy incline approaching the glacier.

Such was the strange evening of 29 April 2018.

CHAPTER 2

TO THE SACRED REALM

I

Green waves surged all around him as bubbles rose in front of Tashi's mouth. What amazed him was the complete absence of sunlight underwater; nor was a single living creature visible within its translucent depths. Mile upon mile of clear water stretched before Tashi as he swam on tirelessly.

Lama Ozer seemed to be sinking deeper and deeper into the dark labyrinth of water, making no effort to swim. Like a stone, his weight was carrying him into the heart of darkness. Fear possessed Tashi, his eyes keeping desperate track of the Lama, yet, the distance was widening between them. Ozer was sinking with great speed into uncharted depths. Frantically, Tashi tried to keep sight of Lama Ozer, as he himself resisted the will to stay afloat.

Tashi refused to let himself think, his lungs were bursting with the lack of oxygen. Yet, he pushed ahead with his hands, searching for Lama Ozer's elusive dark form. Desperately, he looked around giving up all effort to stay afloat or in command of the situation, sinking further. Only emptiness and thick veils of deep green water filled his eyes, Lama Ozer had become a very dim dot, far away. Tashi felt panic uncurl from the base of his stomach; the Lama was nowhere. Empty liquid greenness filled his sight irretrievably numbing his mind. From another life he remembered 'Demazong' and hauntingly, Rimpoche Gyaltsen's smiling demeanour grew in his mind's eye. 'Through life and beyond, the charge is laid, protect and escort Lama Ozer...do not fail me, boy.' Disjointed images built in Tashi's memory as he struggled afresh.

He felt himself weakening, drowning, yet a peaceful light filled his mind. From far away he beheld a form fairer than light – with cascading raven hair and tilting almond-shaped black eyes filled with light – and this vision of the Goddess flooded his being. In her right hand, she held a shaded lotus suffused with the hues of evening and her mocking eyes smiled serenely, calling to Tashi.

Suddenly, his body slammed into hard rock and reality manifested itself in a fresh burst of pain. Driven by desperation, Tashi, in a final burst of strength, fought for survival and thrashed against the rock face. The rock was very slippery and he had to struggle for a foothold. Without warning, a great wave engulfed him, sending him spinning against the rock and into a crevice. He found himself swept into a niche cut into the rocks, then felt the remains of his resistance crumble as sharp talons gripped him. Excruciating pain shot through his body and his lungs seemed to collapse as the talons dug deep into his forearm, dragging him out of the water.

Hurled to the ground, Tashi lay unmoving, trying to catch his breath. Then he noticed Lama Ozer's maroon robes lying on the floor of the tunnel. Relief overwhelmed him and a familiar feeling of warmth surged through his being. Then sleep took over.

II

Tashi awoke, filled with a sense of well-being. Soft white sand pillowed his head and dim light peeped in through the tunnel. Lama Ozer sat nearby, scrutinizing their environs.

'So you are awake, boy,' said the lama. 'Now hurry up.'

Tashi scrambled to his feet and took in his surroundings. 'Where are we, Lama?' he asked, bewildered. 'How did we get out of the water?'

'Boy, you ask me something I do not know,' Lama Ozer replied, 'but where we are, I can guess. For long have we heard of it and much speculation has there been about it. I suspect this is one of those very tunnels that, according to legend, run the length and breadth of the Himalayas. We have no knowledge of who built them. I can only wonder at the power that had the audacity to criss-cross the Himalayas with such passageways. However, this phenomenon has been well documented in the scriptures. The masters of old knew of it and now, so do we.'

'But what power saved us, Lama?' Tashi persisted.

'So many questions and no answers! I am as much at a loss as you are, boy, except that I allowed myself to drown with the confidence of being rescued, whereas you drowned for me,' smiled the lama. 'All I knew was the mantra needed to summon the waters, nothing more. Well, now we will wait.'

Lama Ozer's restless gaze scanned the tunnel. Ahead, the tunnel ran straight on, without branching off in another direction, till it was out of sight.

Tashi examined the ground, a little laugh bursting from him when he caught sight of his bundle lying neatly behind him. In seconds, he had pulled out some soggy bread and dried fruit and handed Lama Ozer his share.

'Lama,' he ventured, 'whom do you wait for?'

'We wait, boy, for a sign, for our guardian. You did realize, did you not, that someone had pulled us to safety? Well, we await such a one.'

Having offered that patient explanation, Lama Ozer settled back against the dry wall of the tunnel and concentrated on eating his bread.

Tashi eyed the white sandy floor. From the light filtering in through chinks in the rock, he would have imagined it was high noon in the world outside. But where was he? In a tunnel that probably lay under the Siniolchu peak. Wonder filled Tashi's mind. In the distance he saw something red glowing in the dim light of the tunnel. Tashi was attracted to the auburn light. Making fast work of his modest meal, he stealthily inched forward; what was the red glow? Having taken seven steps forward, he finally made out what it was – a long, blood-red feather with a burnished golden streak that ran through its middle. It was like no feather Tashi had ever seen. Gently, he picked it up and cradled it in the hollow of his palm, his heart aching with an all-encompassing love.

'Boy, come back here,' came Lama Ozer's plaintive voice. 'Do not wander, not till our protector arrives. What do you have there?'

The monk's eyes were intent on Tashi's hands. A blood-red glow emanated from the boy's fingers and reflected off his skin.

Ozer approached him. 'What mischief have you got up to now?' he asked sternly.

'No mischief, Lama,' Tashi said. 'I just found this brilliantly coloured feather.'

Ozer examined the feather and an expression of shock spread over his benign features.

'Can this be . . .?' he murmured, stunned. 'Yet, a feather that glows with the rich hue of blood and is streaked with pure gold . . . only the Garuda possesses such brilliant plumage and is found here in this subterranean world! Where else can a gift as ancient as this reside, forgotten?

His hands clasped together in a gesture of age-old reverence, Lama Ozer slowly prostrated himself three times before the feather, while Tashi stood by, uncomprehending, gripped by emotions that made his hands tremble.

The lama turned to him. 'That, boy, is the sign, the legendary feather of our guardian, the Garuda,' he explained in a voice that shook with feeling. 'Bird of myth, lonely sentinel of the mystic realm, messenger between the worlds. This means that our guardian is with us and has sent us this feather as a sign of his favour. The Garuda's feather! none in the world has seen such a treasure, such a sighting has not happened in a millennia, indeed, not since the inception of the fourth age has this feather has been seen. Now you, boy, are the feather's appointed keeper and, according to legend, the sacred bird will answer your summons in times of dire need. It is time to move, boy. Collect your belongings.'

A shocked Tashi stared at the red glow surrounding the feather; it was as if a brilliant white flame had ignited his heart. In silence, he wrapped the feather in a loose cloth and placed it in a pocket of his robe.

A warm glow, like that from a fire at twilight, now illuminated the tunnel as the two monks made their way through it, their maroon robes vanishing into its radiance as they moved out of sight and into the depths of the eastern Himalayas.

III

Time seemed to lose all significance in the tunnel, especially at night, when the gloom darkened further into an opaque charcoal, unrelieved by starshine or moonlight. By day, they had at least some inkling of the passing hours, as the dim light in the tunnel waned.

Tashi's feet, rough and calloused though they were, had swollen during the long journey; each step he took seemed an ordeal. Yet his spirits were high as never before, for resting in his breast pocket was a red fire that had a peculiar effect on him. In the dark caverns beneath the Himalayas, he found himself overwhelmed by an intense joy that he had never experienced in his life.

Leaning heavily on his staff, Lama Ozer walked in silence, fingering his beads with his other hand. The two of them seemed to cover a great distance; yet the scene unfolding before them remained the same. As the day drew to a close, Tashi's tongue was so dry, he felt it was glued to the roof of his mouth. He had been strangely unaware of his discomfort, so taken was he by the inexplicable joy that suffused his spirit. He halted abruptly and turned to Ozer.

'Lama, I think something is not quite right here,' he said, pointing to his mouth.

The senior monk approached the boy and held a small canteen to his lips. 'There's very little water left,' Ozer told him gravely. 'From this point onwards, we cannot allow our pace to flag. It will be a long, arduous walk, for neither do we have the time to tarry here nor the means to subsist, if we do.'

Tashi carefully took no more than two sips of water, handed the canteen back to the lama and resumed walking in silence. Time seemed to lose meaning again and Tashi felt his spirit suspended in what increasingly felt like a warm, dark womb. Lama Ozer pulled out his torch. Guided by the sharp beam it cast on the ground, they walked through the night, the senior monk's frail legs maintaining a surprisingly brisk pace.

Hours passed. As dawn approached, Tashi sensed a subtle change in the quality of the air, but could not define it. With a sharp turn, the tunnel suddenly widened. A few more turns later, it opened out into a small cave; at its far edge lay a pool with an utterly still surface. The water gleamed as Lama Ozer shone his torch on it. Beyond the pool, the tunnel led nowhere; it seemed to have died a premature death. Tashi's spirits plummeted.

'We halt,' Ozer announced abruptly. Without uttering another word, he threw down his staff and lay down on the ground.

'Lama, is all well?' Tashi asked, his brows furrowing with concern.

Ozer remained silent, his eyes drooping with exhaustion, his hands lying limp on the ground. 'Boy,' he said weakly, 'I need some tea.'

An anxious Tashi swiftly pulled out his kettle and rushed to the pool to fill it with water. Lama Ozer had not moved.

'Lama, how do I light a fire?' Tashi mumbled. 'There is no wood, no kindling, nothing ...'

Ozer remained silent. Then suddenly, like a miracle, there was light emanating from the far corner of the cave, golden light that danced over tattered cream robes and a salt and pepper beard. Tashi looked helplessly into cold dark-brown eyes and thin, cruel lips.

'Perhaps this is what you search for?' asked the stranger.

Tashi wasted no time in wondering at the man's appearance. He rushed to the fire the other indicated and set the kettle to heat. Then he ran back and drew out restorative herbs from the pocket of Lama Ozer's robe. As Tashi stirred them into the tea that was simmering by now, the fresh aroma of medicinal herbs pervaded the cave.

Tashi helped the lama sit up. Then he handed him his tea in a tin mug that the old man accepted with trembling hands. With every sip, the monk's stiff muscles seemed to thaw and relax. His eyes fluttered open. Slowly, strength seeped back into his body. For the first time since the stranger had appeared, Lama Ozer raised his eyes and gazed at him. The man sat silently at the edge of the fire, looking malevolently at them. Never had Ozer beheld in human form such an air of command and cruelty. He met the stranger's gaze, only to avert his eyes.

'I greet the keeper and his master,' began the stranger in a deep voice. 'I greet drifters of destiny who travel the hidden road ...'

Tashi felt a chill seize his heart. The firelight reflected off the stranger's dull robes and the orange flames acquired a sinister hue. The man's face was ageless; he could have been anywhere between thirty and eighty. Slowly, he rose to his feet, towering above Tashi and Lama Ozer.

Eyeing the boy, he said, 'So, boy, the keeper has been found at long last! But where do your feet wander? Into ancient paths that none walk now… Perhaps I have neglected the mystic roads too long. A keeper is born and now travels the hidden road!'

The man's tone was mocking. He kept his voice low, almost as if he were speaking to himself.

A great reluctance to answer held Tashi's words in check and it was Ozer who spoke up instead.

'Who are you?' he asked. 'I find your tone rather insolent. What are your intentions here? Will you share camp with us or depart?'

A chilling smile played on the stranger's face. 'Old man, how you found this road, I know, and where your journey leads, I know that too, as I do about your call.' The stranger smiled. 'Harken to one who knows, monk. The call you heard in the winter of your lifetime was a conjurer's trick. None can find the secret realm you search for, divorced as it is from human affairs. The aid you seek, none will give. Abandon this quest, old man, and return to the hills from where you came. This road is not for you. I am here to give you warning. Do not proceed farther; do not try to find the road to Shambala. Go back. Otherwise, certain death awaits you.'

The stranger's gaze moved to Tashi.

'You are a keeper, boy,' he told him, 'born to a dying creed. Puny man, return to your nameless hills, lest even their shadow be denied to your kind.'

The man smiled, then raising his hand, chanted an incantation. Lama Ozer froze in shock. A beam of energy streamed out from the stranger and arced towards Ozer. The lama shook himself free of his numb state, threw his hand up in the air and intoned a protective mantra. The air crackled as the two energies exploded in midair, resulting in a deafening noise that shook the entire cavern. Tashi was flung off his feet and righted himself just in time. The stranger remained unaffected, unmoved. He raised his hand a second time and yet another incantation spewed from his lips and filled the air. Lama Ozer countered it with another word of protection, but to no avail; the energy generated by the stranger's incantation caught Ozer and lifted him off the ground, holding him suspended in weaves of air.

'Now I have you trapped like a fly in a web,' the stranger declared with a bloodcurdling laugh, 'and here you will remain for all eternity!'

With that, he turned his attention to Tashi. 'And what do I do with the keeper born after a millennium, not knowing what he is?' he asked. He seemed to hesitate for a moment before beckoning to Tashi. 'A blessing has been bestowed on you in an age when the gods themselves fear to bless,' he said. 'Show me the feather, boy!'

As if in a trance, Tashi found one of his hands moving of its own volition. Fear clutched his heart, as his hand touched the Garuda's feather in his breast pocket. What followed next was beyond his wildest imagination.

All Tashi later remembered was that he drew out the feather, bathing the room in burning fire. The colours of autumn seemed to leap out of the walls throwing wild shadows about it. A blaze lit Tashi's hand as fear receded and a terrible courage took hold, the cave started fogging up as flames streaked from Tashi's hands towards the stranger.

The man flung his arm over his eyes in self-defence, then smiled, his gaze boring deep into Tashi's eyes. 'Boy, we will meet again,' he warned. 'The keeper will not be allowed to go free; there is a price to be paid for such terrible gifts as yours. Ha, boy!'

With that, the stranger cast himself into the depths of the pool and vanished, even as the blazing red fire tore after him.

IV

Tashi awoke the next day to find Lama Ozer preparing the morning meal. A dim, soft light filtered in through the tunnel.

'Are you all right, boy?' the lama asked. 'You have slept away fourteen hours!'

An embarrassed Tashi sprang to his feet. 'Lama, my apologies,' he murmured, contrite, 'you should have woken me.'

Ozer cut him short. 'No, boy, I dared not disturb your slumber,' he said, 'not after what happened yesterday. It is something I do not understand, for knowledge of the mystery behind these tunnels and the secret of the Garuda's powers have long been lost to mankind.' The lama looked at the boy speculatively. 'I did wrong to let you get involved in such a dangerous quest.'

'You had no choice,' Tashi reminded him. 'The quest sought me out. But what kind of a man was that, Lama?' His voice brimmed with excitement and curiosity.

'There is much that exists beyond our sphere of knowledge and experience,' Ozer's voice was sombre. 'But I suppose I do owe you some explanation. So we will speak of yesterday's incident just this once and never again. The person we saw, boy, was an adept, the kind we have only heard about. He was the most powerful adept I have come across. In fact, there is a possibility that he belongs to the esoteric brotherhood of the black shamans with whom I have an old history of trouble. Why he reacted the way he did, I cannot explain, save that a cruel wind blows over the planet right now, pushing the nations to the brink of war and turmoil. Hatred spills red across a world racked by monumental strife and growing tensions threaten to explode. There are as many questions as there are answers and that is why I have set out on this journey.'

Tashi's expression was intent as he listened to Lama Ozer.

'I had always sensed that this journey would be highly perilous,' the old monk went on. 'And while it remains a mystery as to who that adept was and why he fought us, his very appearance makes it eminently clear that we have to exercise great caution. Now rise fast; we must be on our way.'

Tashi moved cautiously to the edge of the pool to refill the canteen and wash his face. Lama Ozer was now on his feet, closely observing the walls of the tunnel. Beyond the pool, smooth mud-brown walls barred the tunnel's path; nor was any opening visible to either left or right. The dark mountainside seemed to have eaten up the tunnel.

Ozer paced the tunnel floor, lost in contemplation, as Tashi peered into the pool's hidden depths. 'Perhaps the opening lies in this very pool, Lama,' he suggested. 'After all, that man disappeared into it, didn't he?'

An angry Ozer held up his hand. 'Do not open your mouth, boy, to offer your views on things whose nature lies beyond your ken,' he said sternly. 'Now I want silence from you, while I try and find the path ahead.'

The lama seated himself in the middle of the cavern, crossed his legs and closed his eyes. In silence, he brought his palms together and chanted a mantra. Nothing happened. Ozer tried changing mantras, changing postures, sometimes chanting as he sat, sometimes standing, sometimes on one leg. He exhausted half the day chanting relentlessly to no avail. An anxious Tashi watched silently even as hope diminished; he was getting worried about the Lama's frail condition and the fact that he had eaten nothing since last evening.

Finally, as the dim light of the tunnel died away, heralding the onset of evening, an exhausted Ozer sat down and gestured to Tashi for some water. The boy carried the canteen across and held it out to him. Absentmindedly, Ozer took it from him and drank deeply from it. Then he partook of a frugal meal of dry fruit. But he looked preoccupied as he ate and finally, giving in to his frustration, pulled out an ancient-looking manuscript from the back of Tashi's backpack and began poring over it.

'I think I have it, boy,' he murmured after a while. 'The opening to the path has to lie in a mandala. So far, I have been relying on invoking the mantra – to no avail. It is clear to me now that much more is required. It has to be a device, a mandala built in an age long forgotten by this world. What can it be? What could the master initiates have created to access the hidden paths?'

'Why do you not rest, Lama?' a concerned Tashi suggested. 'We can always make another attempt tomorrow.'

'No, boy, there is no time for rest. I fear we must now move with great speed and stealth. Now silence, boy!' The last words were a command.

Tashi sat back quietly while Lama Ozer examined the tunnel's rock walls, touching them with his hands, feeling his way and shaking his head from time to time. After completing a circuit, he sat down again. Soon, he rose to his feet once more to peer into the pool.

'Can it be, perhaps… ?' the monk muttered to himself, his calm face betraying the first signs of excitement.

Taking out a sachet of red powder from his pack, he set to work, drawing an outer ring along the perimeter of the small cavern in which the tunnel had ended. Then he used some saffron powder from the same pack to draw an inner ring around the pool's circumference. Next, he pulled out a paintbrush and gently swept the floor space between the two rings. He toiled tirelessly through the night and finally uncovered by torchlight the faintest markings on the ground. It was more like the dimmest memory of a painting – scraped, faint, forgotten, almost indecipherable shapes, brought to a semblance of life by Lama Ozer's unceasing brushstrokes. Nebulous forms – trees, bushes, animals and sprites – mushroomed on the soil like a dream in the sand.

When all had been readied, Lama Ozer looked at Tashi, his face eloquent with emotion. He gestured for the boy to wait by the pool, while he himself stood at the opposite end. In a raised voice, he invoked the Buddha and the four guardian deities, the holy Bodhisattvas and the priest kings of the hidden realm. Lastly, he paid obeisance to the Goddess Tara. His voice rose as he chanted a potent mantra. Nothing happened. Without a word, the lama sank to his knees and lay on the ground, his attitude one of near despair.

Then suddenly, he rose again and cried, 'The feather, boy! That is it – we have not consulted our guardian!'

With trembling hands, Tashi took out the feather. A soft orange glow spread through the cave. As if of its own volition, the Garuda's feather flew out of the boy's hands, landing pat in the centre of the pool.

'Of course!' murmured the lama 'That has to be the mystic centre.'

As the two of them watched, a glimmering spark broke through the water and tiny flames burst from it, giving birth to bigger ones. Then a volcanic flame soared up from the pool's very depths and kissed the cave's roof, generating intense heat and thick fumes. The mud-brown roof melted away, as a single, razor-sharp flame sliced a passage through the rocks, as though boring a hole in the heart of the mountain. Tashi and Lama Ozer gazed up through the crack and saw sunlight far, far away. Tashi made to retrieve the feather and held out his hand, only to find it lying softly on his palm.

'Move fast, boy!' the lama urged. 'I don't know how long this will hold.'

Bathed in a saffron glow, the two monks began the rigorous climb into the heart of the mountain. Several hours of toil through a sharp, rocky channel as narrow as a drainpipe rewarded a panting Tashi with his first glimpse of blue sky that spread like a vast canopy over a dazzling expanse of turquoise water in eastern Tibet. Soft zephyrs drew ripples across the surface of Mansarovar Lake and gently caressed the boy's face as he scrambled out of the mountain tunnel. Lama Ozer staggered out after him and looked on in awe. Not far away, Mt Kailash rose into the sky, magnificent in its snow-clad glory.

CHAPTER 3

QIANG LA: THE SILVER FORTRESS

I

Despite his laboured breathing, Lama Ozer walked swiftly towards the sacred Mansarovar Lake. He hurried down the gentle slope, bowed to the lake in reverence and proceeded to immerse himself in its freezing waters. An anxious Tashi ran after him, concern for the monk and awe at the magnificent spectacle before him growing with every breath he drew.

Standing on the shore, he felt a strange reluctance seize him. The sight of the icy waters, shining under a bright sun, was daunting. Experiencing a deep resistance to the idea of taking a dip, he found himself in a state of great indecision. Then he saw Lama Ozer surfacing after his dip and beckoning him. Tashi stood frozen on the shore, unwilling to move.

'Boy, what has got into you?' the lama called out in exasperation. 'Bow before the lake and take a dip. The holy Mansarovar lies before you. Hurry! We must plan our next step without delay.'

Taking a deep breath and bowing to the lake, Tashi ran towards the water and dived in. Shivering mightily, he resurfaced and felt Lama Ozer's palm on his head, his angry brown eyes glaring at him.

'This was not the time, boy, to feel shy of the cold,' the monk said disapprovingly. His eyes wandered around the lake. 'If only I could complete a single circumambulation around the holy lake.' His tone was wistful.

Not far away, following the shoreline, the cone-shaped Mt Kailash stood resplendently silhouetted against the bright blue sky. In the distance, snow peaks stretched out in all directions; range after range glimmering in the distance around the Mansarovar this included the Kang-ti-ssu Shan range, the Gurla Mandhata in the south and the Zanskar a faint presence in the west.

Minutes later, Tashi was back on the shore, shivering uncontrollably from the chill. Without wasting a moment, he changed into a dry robe, then helped Lama Ozer to fold and pack away their wet garments. Time was running short. The morning had advanced into an afternoon that wouldn't linger for long. A fierce wind that seemed to cut through their robes was gathering momentum on the arid plateau and churning the surface of the lake. The rumbling in his stomach reminded Tashi that he was hungry.

His eyes scanned the horizon and came to rest on the stark contours of the Chiu Gompa or 'bird-like monastery', standing out against the barren landscape.

'Lama, may we sleep under a roof tonight?' Tashi asked hopefully

His eyes on his master, the boy soldiered on, struggling through every step as the wind picked up gravel and tossed it around wildly. In the distance, he could see straggling knots of Tibetan pilgrims, bundled up against the cold, trudging along the shore as they circumambulated the holy lake. His spirits lifted as he thought of the Chiu Monastery and contemplated the possibility of them staying there for the night.

Lama Ozer finally answered Tashi's query. 'Yes, boy, yes,' he said. 'Tonight, you will get both a meal and a bed at the monastery. As for tomorrow, I cannot tell what course of action we will take. I can only promise you that the path we follow next will be far tougher than the one we have left behind.'

Tashi could not help smiling at the monk's reply. Nothing could possibly go wrong today, he reassured himself. Not a shadow cast itself on the divine waves of Lake Mansarovar. In the distance, small herds of sheep and yaks grazed on new shoots springing up through the hard ground. Pale pink rushes gently raised their heads on the banks of the lake in celebration of spring. Tashi's heart soared and touched heaven. He thought he even detected a spring in Lama Ozer's step. He fingered the feather in his robe pocket and calculated the remaining distance to the monastery, dreaming of hot butter tea and *thukpa*, a flat-noodle soup garnished with chunks of meat.

A careful four-hour trek along the lake's barren shore finally brought the two monks to the gates of Chiu Monastery, which stood on a slight incline. Tashi felt warmth flooding through him as he crossed its threshold. Familiar smells assailed him, triggering a powerful wave of nostalgia for Demazong. Curious lamas and young monks gawked at the visitors. Tashi could not help smiling at them as he folded his hands in salutation. Lama Ozer, however, did not pause, striding on purposefully till he had reached the quarters of the Head Lama, Sangye Rechen.

In a sparsely furnished room, a middle-aged man, short of stature and wiry in build, sat by the window; a rosary lay forgotten on his lap. At the sound of approaching footsteps, Sangye brought his attention back to the room and almost jumped as Ozer entered. Springing to his feet, he rushed towards his visitor, hands outstretched in welcome.

'Tashi-delek, Lama! What stroke of good fortune brings you here today?' he cried excitedly. 'Had you informed us about your visit, I would have personally come to the barrier and escorted you in. Just to have you grace us with your presence is a great honour for us.'

His eyes curiously took in Tashi.

Lama Ozer held up his hand, requesting silence, so he could speak. 'I do not come on a visit, Lama Sangye, but on a most important mission,' he announced. 'I also bring with me young Tashi Thendup from Demazong.'

Sangye smiled at both Tashi and Ozer, eager to please. 'Anything, Lama, anything!' he said. 'Just let me know how I can assist you and what arrangements I can make for you.'

'I do not need much,' said Ozer, 'just one night's shelter for myself and for young Tashi here. We will not impose further on your hospitality. Tomorrow, we leave at the crack of dawn.'

'Just one night, Lama?' Sangye said, 'and after so many years? Can I not prevail upon you to extend your visit by at least a day?'

Lama Ozer smiled tiredly. 'Alas! Time is not a luxury I can afford,' he replied.

'In that case, it will be as you wish, Lama,' Sangye responded. 'At least you will bless the monastery with your presence tonight.'

'Perhaps you remember, Sangye, that I had an old friend here whom I used to consult on my journeys. I trust all is well with her?' Lama Ozer enquired.

'Of course I remember her, Lama!' Sangye answered. 'I will summon Tshering La immediately. She has quarters within the monastery, but is somewhat incapacitated by arthritis and old age.'

'In that case, I will meet her right now, unless she has already retired for the night. May I ask you to lead the way and also make arrangements for this boy? He is rather tired and hungry, I fear.'

Lama Sangye Rechen nodded his acquiescence. He signalled to a pair of boy monks loitering outside his door and asked them to take Tashi to the kitchen, then bowing before Ozer, he indicated with a sweep of his hand that the monk should follow him.

II

As they turned a corner of the wind-swept corridor, Lama Ozer beheld from his vantage point one of the most beautiful spectacles in the world – dusk unfolding in soft waves over Lake Mansarovar. The turquoise lake took on the hue of the darkening evening, ripening into a scarlet-shot, midnight blue. Ozer let his eyes dwell on the wonder and for a few moments felt young again. Feeling the healing qualities of the lake, he felt the weight slip off his shoulders.

The two lamas moved on and reached the far end of the corridor which was obscured in darkness but for a single flickering light. Lama Ozer paused at the door to the room from which the light emanated, lifted the curtain hanging in front of it, then gestured to Sangye to leave him. Entering the room he looked into gentle brown eyes peering out of a pale face rendered almost unrecognizable by an intricate network of wrinkles.

Her white hair tied neatly in a bun, Tshering La sat waiting by the stove. As Ozer approached, she unclasped her hands and held them out to him in welcome. Her frail form swayed slightly as she rose unsteadily to her feet and greeted her twin. Lama Nyima Ozer smiled shyly and bowed low before his only kin, his sister, Tshering.

'For the past two weeks, brother, I have sensed you coming,' she told him. 'Deep inside, I knew you were travelling impelled by dire need. So has the time come? Is this your last journey?' Her voice broke.

'I am afraid it is so, Tshering La,' Lama Ozer sighed. 'What was prophesied in my infancy has come to make its demands in the winter of my life.'

'Then so it is, brother. This is, indeed, your last journey,' Tshering said sadly. 'Remember how I used to say I would accompany you when the time came? And look at me now; my legs refuse to carry me. What is, is. What will be, will be. Our wishes are just that – wishes. However, I will be with you in spirit. But before you resume your journey, I have something to give you.'

Supporting herself on a staff, she moved to the wall of her ancient cell and opened a hidden compartment from which she withdrew a package wrapped in faded brocade.

'This, brother, contains the map of the initiates which used to be kept by the custodians of the central monastery in the heart of Mt Kailash,' she explained. 'It is the only surviving relic of its kind and I have spent a lifetime in its quest. The true worth of this map cannot be measured, brother; drawn on it is the design of the hidden road to the mystic realm, the lost city of Olmo-Lungring – what some know as Shambala. Although it is three thousand years old, it will serve your purpose. However, only in worthy hands will the map unfold and divulge its secret. Should the undeserving seize it, it will simply disintegrate and turn to dust. Mind, unfold it only by the light of morning and away from the monastery. I also bestow on you my blessings; may they protect you.'

'Sister,' said Lama Ozer, 'a more precious gift you could not have given me. I will take great care of it.'

Smiling tiredly, Tshering said, 'Mind the map, brother. Hunt not for the monastery of the initiates in the heart of Mt Kailash; it has been extinct for several thousand years. Perhaps this last relic will serve as your guide. Now leave, brother, tarry not. Your task is mine. But there is one more small thing I ask of you.' Tshering smiled again and her black eyes suddenly looked haunted. 'Accept, brother, spirit to spirit, life that is no more, life that is ever. I am asking for freedom from a form which is no longer of any use to me. Remember, even when I am not there, I will always be with you. Now accept my last breath, take it and fling it over the holy Lake Mansarovar.'

Lama Ozer raised his hands and Tshering's lifeless form sank to the floor and lay still. The waning light of dusk played across her face, more beautiful in death than it had ever been in life.

'I absolve you, sister, of all sin,' Ozer declared, raising his hands in farewell. 'I myself shall carry its burden. May you soar free in the heavens.'

Lama Ozer stood silently by his sister's chair as a single burnished ray of the setting sun suffused Tshering's lifeless form with singular glory. Then he worked in silence through the descending night, performing the last rites and preparing his sister's body with loving care before arranging it on the solitary bed in that austere, isolated room.

III

The same tentative light of daybreak had sent out feelers and nudged Tashi awake. As his eyes adjusted to the early-morning glow, he noticed Lama Ozer at the door, summoning him with a gesture. Tashi sprang to his feet, all drowsiness gone, and dressed quickly. Then he raced outside to take his place by a rather sombre Lama Ozer who was bidding Lama Sangye a gracious farewell.

'Much as we would have liked you to spend a few more days with us, it is time for you to leave, Lama, given your commitment to your mission,' Sangye said. 'However, we would like to be of some help. So we are providing you with a few packets of paddy and tea, some dried *churpi* and a pair of sturdy staffs from our stores.'

Lama Ozer and Tashi folded their hands in gratitude and bowed. Then invoking the divine Buddha and the Goddess Tara, the lama and his keeper set out again on their journey.

For a while, the two walked in silence, enchanted by the serenity of their beautiful surroundings, but as time went by, the journey became arduous. After a long, gruelling trek, Lama Ozer called a halt on a rocky crag some distance from the lake. Sighing deeply, he turned to Tashi.

'Sit down, boy, sit down,' he urged. 'I don't mind confessing that I am well and truly stuck now. I cannot decide which course to take and will need all your help. When we started out, I was confident about obtaining clear directions to the location of the legendary Shambala at the monastery of the initiates in the heart of Mt Kailash. However, I discovered that the monastery had been long abandoned. Where, then, boy, will I find the answers?'

Cool zephyrs blew in from the lake, but Lama Ozer and Tashi were too caught up in their troubles to notice them.

'Lama, you know I will do anything you ask of me,' the boy said earnestly. 'You have only to say the word. Should I pull out the feather? Perhaps it will show us the way?'

Lama Ozer held out his hands. 'Take it out, boy,' he urged, 'but unless I am mistaken, the feather is not going to be enough to help resolve our dilemma. Something more is required, the knowledge of the ancients, perhaps, which has been dead and buried for several centuries. But pull out the mark of the Garuda, by all means, and let us see where it takes us.'

Tashi gently drew the red-tinted feather from his pocket and held it in his cupped hands, where it glowed warmly. Eyeing the feather wearily, Lama Ozer untied the string around the brocade-wrapped package containing the map of the initiates. As the string came loose, the monk's hands began to tremble uncontrollably.

'Lama, should I?' Tashi volunteered.

Ozer held up his hand, dismissing the offer, and stared at the parcel with ferocious concentration. As the last string fell open, Ozer unveiled flap after flap only to find emptiness – the package seemed to contain nothing. In terror, Lama Ozer shook out the brocade willing the map to appear. The folds fell open, yet again revealing nothing.

'Boy, this is it,' Lama Ozer said grimly. 'If we do not get our answers here, nothing will work. It will be the end of the road for us.'

Tashi looked at his master, dumbfounded. In silence, Ozer held out a trembling hand to the boy, who, on an impulse, placed the feather in it. Moving his hand with infinite caution, the monk gently placed the feather in the centre of the crumpled folds of brocade fabric. Minutes passed without any developments. Several minutes followed and then a misty picture started forming on the cloth, a picture from a time before human memory.

What formed at first sight was a counter-clockwise swastika formation. From the heart of the swastika came a silver-hued, fast falling river flowing through some of the wildest country Tashi had ever seen. The river sliced its path through steep canyons and terrible gorges. Deep caverns, ravines and black tunnels lined its crystal clear course. The countryside consisted of stark rock formations cut by the fissured course of the river and was surrounded by a distant circle of snow clad mountains. As the river misted, the wild, lonely country of gorges, canyons and fissures narrowed, getting caught in a circle of lunar rocky crags. A thin path revealed itself, cutting through the mountainside into an amazing bowl-shaped valley. In this nest in the wilderness, rose an awe-inspiring structure surpassing human beauty. Hammered out of diamond-edged starlight, the remnants of an ancient fortress came into view glimmering above the valley. On the ramparts of the fortress, an image swam into view. Barely visible, the picture formed of a tall youth, clothed in a white robe, adorned with a crown made of fiery feathers. Pale as starlight, with red hair spilling down to his shoulders, he carried a golden mace in his hand and on his brow sat a fiery crown of writhing feathers.

Silver turrets on silver turrets, halls of light shone through the lost ages – tapestry edged with glittering stones, fair people of a race that seemed to have died – floated through creating a bizarre picture. Last, hauntingly, appeared a face of terrible beauty, the warm hue of ivory lingering on her skin and her raven tresses running wild, black haunting eyes smiled mockingly, a golden lotus sat in her palm. Suddenly, a single flame sparked from the already fading lotus setting the brocade alight.

Lama Ozer sat glued to the ground, his gaze unmoving, his hands stilled. 'Prostrate yourself, boy!' he exclaimed. 'We are blessed! We are blessed many times over, for that was none other than the Goddess Tara, the divine saviour!'

Both monks performed the ritual prostrations. When the two were finally seated again, the senior lama said, his voice brimming with emotion,

'That map, boy, unless I am much mistaken, showed us the ancient kingdom of Qiang La. And the diamond-edged fortress was none other than the silver fortress, a seat of great mystical power in an era long gone by. We have been summoned to the heart of the mystic kingdom, boy, to what was once the seat of the holders of Bon, a religion that held sway in pre-Buddhist Tibet. But that is still not our ultimate destination. We have merely been shown the way.'

There was a long silence. Neither of them uttered a word.

Lama Ozer's eyes had a faraway look as he began speaking again. 'Boy, I speak of times whose faintest echoes have passed out of human memory,' he said. 'The Bon religion of Tibet originated in divine Olmo-Lungring or Shambala, the abode of the gods – call it what you will. Today, few traces survive of what was a deeply mystical religion. Listen carefully, boy. Qiang La or the silver valley, as depicted in the map, seems to be the gateway to the mystic realm. According to an ancient legend, this connection between Qiang La and Shambala does exist. The silver fortress was rumoured to contain the hidden gateway. Many have tried to find it in these degenerate times, but none have succeeded so far.'

Tashi looked at the lama in amazement. 'Then, Lama, we should make for Qiang La, should we not?' he suggested. 'Does such a place really exist?'

Ozer smiled. 'Exist it does, boy, in an obscure corner of western Tibet. Geographically speaking, it is there, but there is little else at Qiang La. I spent my youth exploring that valley and its mystery, boy, but to no avail. It is not a simple matter of chance that points us that way today.'

Tashi's expression was serious. 'Then it is to Qiang La that we journey today, Lama?' he asked.

Lama Ozer smiled at him benevolently. 'Yes, boy,' he replied, 'but first we must make haste and reach Chu Gumba town. From there, we must arrange transport for our journey. Hurry, boy, we need to move fast.'

IV

Lama Ozer walked swiftly, with Tashi following right behind. In less than an hour, they could see bright sunlight glancing off the sloping roofs of Chu Gumba. Tashi made a serious effort to ignore the familiar hunger pangs as he walked into the shanty town sheltering in the shadow of the towering, snowbound Mt Kailash. He looked longingly at the Tibetan tea stalls lining the streets, but Lama Ozer seemed to be in no mood for a tea break.

'Lama, where are we headed?' began a hopeful Tashi.

'Silence, boy!' the lama said sternly, 'discipline your urges. Today, we move forward on the wings of the swallow.'

The lama made straight for the tourism office, a makeshift structure at the centre of town. Rows of trucks and taxis were parked near it. Ozer approached a battered Chinese four-ton truck which had seen such rough use that all the paint had peeled off its body. A heavily built middle-aged driver stood leaning against the vehicle, sipping a cup of tea. Ozer silently walked up to him. With a shock of recognition, the man bowed low before the lama, oblivious to the tilting cup in his hand and the hot tea he had slopped over his shirt.

'Lama!' he exclaimed, 'am I really seeing you or is this an apparition? It has been years since we last met!'

'Pema, I come to you in urgent need,' Lama Ozer began swiftly. 'As always my friend, I will impose on you greatly.'

'It has always been an honour to serve you, Lama,' Pema responded.

'Today, I will make many demands, my friend,' the lama said. 'We journey to the west and are in a tearing hurry. We must reach Tirthapuri at the earliest and, from there, make our way to Qiang La.'

'When do you leave, Lama?' Pema enquired.

'As soon as I have bought a few provisions,' Ozer replied.

Pema remarked, 'I just refuelled my vehicle to take some foreigners back to Lhasa, but now they will have to wait. I will drive you wherever you wish to go.'

'Just give me half an hour to purchase whatever we need for the journey and then we can leave,' the lama told him. Then Ozer turned to Tashi. 'Boy, you can accompany me to the market nearby,' he said, before turning back to the driver. 'Pema, I trust you will wait for us here?'

Tashi followed Lama Ozer down the narrow street and a quick turn led them to the sprawling shanty market. Ozer immediately turned left and walked down the narrow path between the fruit- sellers' stalls to a rundown general store that stood in the corner.

Before entering the crowded shop, Ozer turned to Tashi and said, 'Boy, wait outside. I shall call you when we are ready to leave.'

As the lama went in, Tashi took up position by the shop's entrance and surveyed the bustling market-place. An unpleasant odour assailed his nostrils and his gaze was drawn to the fish-seller who was haggling loudly with a number of women customers. Some urchins played marbles in a corner of the market. Tashi's attention was diverted from the boys by the sight of two tall, well-built men, dressed in dark robes, making their way rather purposefully across the market. They carried stout sticks in their hands.

His curiosity aroused, Tashi continued to observe them. When they had covered a quarter of the distance into the market, they separated, one going to the right and the other to the left. By the way their eyes scanned the crowd, it was clear they were searching for something or someone.

Suddenly, one of the urchins approached Tashi. 'If you give me ten yuan, I may tell you something that is of interest to you,' the boy said.

Tashi smiled. 'I will give you five yuan boy. What do you have to tell me?'

The boy smiled back, then whispered, 'You see those men dressed in dark robes? They are looking for two lamas; one is supposedly old and the other, young. The description fits you and your companion, does it not?'

Of the two men, the one who had veered to the right was caught in the midst of a throng of women. Tashi could see him surveying the crowd and talking to bystanders. He suddenly felt fear in the pit of his stomach. There was something brutal about those men and one of them was now very close to the shop outside which Tashi stood.

Tashi darted inside and caught sight of Lama Ozer paying at the counter, a basket loaded with provisions in front of him. He hurriedly approached the monk and said in an undertone, 'Something strange is happening outside; there are two men hunting for us. We should leave immediately.'

Lama Ozer looked up, startled. 'Men looking for us?' he mused. 'Stand right here, boy. I will have a look.'

'They are outside, Lama,' Tashi warned.

Lama Ozer stepped out and scanned the crowd. 'Boy, I see them,' he said. 'Those are no ordinary men. They are acolytes of the master of the black shamans. They are neither Buddhist nor Bon, but practitioners of the dark arts, spirit wielders. Pick up that basket and drape this cloth over your head. Then follow me. We have no time to waste.'

Lama Ozer walked swiftly through the market, Tashi at his heels and the crowd swarming all around them. Suddenly, the boy looked up and saw one of the dark-robed men making his way towards them. They had been spotted.

'Run, boy!' Lama Ozer urged. 'Make for the truck near the tourism office.' With that, the Lama set off, sprinting through the market-place as fast as his frail legs could carry him, with Tashi following close on his heels. Glancing over his shoulder as he ran, Tashi was alarmed to see their pursuers just ten paces behind. He and his master raced towards the exit and through it. Lama Ozer ran down the narrow lane and took a swift right turn. Tashi followed. The two men in hot pursuit were desperately trying to catch up with them. Then one of the men caught up with Tashi and lashed out with his stick. The boy struck the the man in the face with the vegetable basket he was carrying.

Just then, the man flung his hands up in the air and muttered a mantra. Tashi felt a force hit him in the centre of his chest. The impact sent him sprawling. The man brought his stick down on the boy, hitting him hard. Tashi raised his arms in self-defence, trying to ward off the blows.

'Run to safety, Lama!' Tashi yelled.

But aware of the boy's distress by now, Lama Ozer had already come to a halt. He held out his hand and chanted a protective mantra. Energy streaked across space towards Tashi's pursuer, throwing the man back with superhuman force. His companion had almost caught up with them by now.

'Run, boy!' Ozer yelled. 'Make for the truck!'

Seizing the advantage the lama's incantation had given him, Tashi was up and sprinting through the street in seconds. He followed Ozer's example and took the turning which would lead to Pema's truck, parked not far away.

Lama Ozer spotted the driver standing next to the truck. 'Start the engine, Pema!' he yelled from a distance. 'Hurry! We're in danger!'

A startled Pema leapt into the driver's seat and started up the engine. The truck roared into life. Lama Ozer flung himself into the front passenger seat and Tashi jumped into the back.

'Move, move – and fast!' Lama Ozer urged.

Tashi looked out of the moving truck to see the two men rounding the bend and rushing towards them. But the truck was much too fast for them. It roared down the road and made for the highway, leaving the men far behind.

The mid-morning sun burnt brilliantly in the sky throwing jewelled reflections off the lake. In no time Tashi felt the cold breeze rising off the plateau rucking up his hair. Already, Chu Gumba was disappearing from sight to be replaced by brilliant emptiness. An anxious Tashi continued to scan the road, looking out for signs of their pursuers, but there were none.

Pema looked at Lama Ozer. 'Lama, what was that?' he asked. 'Who was pursuing the two of you?'

Leaning back, an exhausted Ozer looked at the driver, his face pale. 'Those men, Pema, were dark shamans and they will continue to shadow us on our journey,' he explained. 'You can be sure that we haven't shaken them off. They're still on our trail and may reappear sooner than we expect.'

'We'd better get off the main highway, then, and use side lanes as far as possible,' Pema decided.

V

Swift moving hours were eaten up by the smooth rolling truck as it roared on into the barren countryside. There was no sign of their pursuers; for the time being, Pema seemed to have succeeded in throwing them off their trail. By late afternoon, the four-tonner had crossed into the watershed of the upper Indus and was making its way into western Tibet. An icy nip came into the air as the truck meandered towards Bogo-La pass, where a bleak landscape of mountain, snow and fast moving winds greeted them. The most stunning sight was that of the ribbon-like River Sutlej, as it separated from the River Indus taking on a wild beauty in utter loneliness.

Afternoon melted into a fleeting evening as dusk descended on the infant river following its swift, westward course. Tashi's stomach growled with hunger, diverting his attention from the constantly changing panorama. Suddenly, in the distance, he spotted blinking lights and a plume of smoke rising in the air.

Excitedly, the boy burst out, 'Look, Lama! It seems we're approaching a village!'

'Yes,' Pema confirmed, 'that is the small hamlet of Nudrul. We can get some refreshments there and I have relatives who will gladly take us in for the night.'

'I think not, Pema,' Lama Ozer said sternly. 'You forget that we are on an urgent mission. Moreover, we are being pursued by the dark shamans. Even if we cannot see them, you can be sure they are on our trail. The danger we face will simply increase as we move ahead and we need to take great precautions to protect ourselves. There is no time to waste, I fear. Pema, I mean to work you very hard and make you drive through the night.'

'Why do you say the danger will increase, Lama?' Pema asked.

Lama Ozer sighed. 'The black shamans have their stronghold in Qiang La, where their master resides. They are not to be trifled with; they have great magical and spirit powers and their master is an adept of the first order. I am afraid we will see more of them as we go along. Somehow, they have come to know of our journey and the purpose behind it. They will be aware of our plan to enter Qiang La and will certainly oppose us.'

'Then we had better take all necessary precautions,' said Pema, whose exhaustion was beginning to show, 'but we will still need some refreshment to sustain ourselves on the journey.'

'I suggest we drive through Nudrul at top speed,' said Lama Ozer. 'Once we have left it far behind us and night has fallen, we can heat some tea on the stove you keep in the truck and share the bread which the monks at Chiu were kind enough to provide us with.' The lama paused for breath, then added, 'Pema, I am no stranger to you; we have travelled together in the past and you know how I travel. I am sorry, old friend, but our present journey together promises to be a trial for you.'

'It is always a pleasure to serve the lama,' Pema responded sincerely.

The deep hues of dusk spread across the sky and the village disappeared as though it had been no more than a mirage in the surrounding wilderness. The lay of the land changed and the occasional patch of cultivation started appearing on either side of the road.

As the first few stars began twinkling in the sky, Lama Ozer called for a halt beside a fallow field lined with stunted, thorny trees whose silver blossoms exuded a surprisingly fresh fragrance and looked like trailing nocturnal mist trapped between the thorns. Pema parked the truck under the shadow of one such tree. A relieved Tashi stepped out of the truck to stretch his limbs and loosen his cramped muscles.

'Mind now,' Lama Ozer cautioned. 'Do not even dream of lighting a fire. And please switch off the truck's lights. We have not made a full hour's journey from Nudrul simply to announce to the entire countryside that we are camping here. However, there is one thing that you can do, boy,' the monk suggested, looking at Tashi. 'There is an abandoned well over the mound there, to your right. Its water used to be sweet and fresh. See if you can refill our canteens from it, but hurry.'

'Certainly, Lama,' Tashi said, diving into the dark interiors of the truck for their three canteens and a staff.

Slinging the canteens around his shoulder, the boy made for the mound, using the staff to feel his way in the dark. Having been confined to the truck for the better part of the day, he enjoyed the familiar crunch of soil under his feet. He smiled with pleasure, as the fragrance of the blossoms on the thorny trees wafted across, and climbed with long, loping strides over the mound looming in the darkness. Just ten steps ahead, an abandoned brick well stood out clearly in the moonlight; the rope used for drawing water from it lay in a tangle on the metal rod overhead.

As Tashi tied the first of the three canteens to the rope and sent it swishing down into the well, he felt a prickle – no, an itch – at the nape of his neck. Then he decided it was neither. He contained an almost overwhelming urge to turn back and swiftly untied the brimming canteen he had drawn up from the depths of the well. He tied the other two canteens to the rope and lowered them, hearing the 'thunk' as they hit the water.

An eerie sensation of being watched overtook Tashi. Pulling the rope up in a hurry, he untied the canteens and quickly slung them over his shoulder. Gripping his staff, he turned to go, but stopped short, when he noticed something glimmering in the moonlight just fifteen paces away.

A tall, dark-robed stranger stood on the mound, towering over him, his gaze locked on to Tashi's. As the boy took a tentative step forward, the stranger held out his palm. Almost spontaneously, Tashi's hand went to his pocket, reaching for the security of the feather. He heard the stranger's magic intonation and felt its force lift him clear off his feet and fling him hard against the well, his shoulder painfully striking its brick wall. Throwing off his confusion, Tashi stumbled to his feet and broke into a run, but the man appeared directly in front of him, barring his way. Tashi gripped his staff firmly and lashed out with it. The man side-stepped the blow fluidly and then spoke a word of power. Tashi found himself lifted clear off the ground and suspended in midair, his arms frozen immobile behind him.

Eyeing the boy stonily for a few seconds, the stranger declared, 'You are in no position to resist my commands and will do as I say. I will set you down, but you must hand me the feather when I do.' The stranger held out his palm.

Tashi crashed to the ground as his body was released from the state of paralysis induced by the stranger's spell. A force like a hammer blow struck his injured shoulder, causing him to cry out in pain.

'Hurry, boy! Pass me the feather!' the stranger snapped.

Tashi pulled out the feather and held it in his palm. A soft red light danced out from it, moving towards the shaman.

'No tricks now! Hand it to me,' the man commanded.

Tashi held aloft the feather and red light swirled out greedily, making for the shaman. It enveloped him in a red haze till the man was lost in its swirling glow and flames broke out around him. The flames picked up speed, engulfing the man. The shaman shrieked violently as the flames consumed him and in no time nothing was left – not even ashes. The man simply disappeared, empty moonlight glimmered on the dewdrops in the grass.

Not wasting another moment at that spot, Tashi rushed back to the camp. Relief swept over him as he saw Lama Ozer preparing tea on the stove at the back of the truck.

'Boy, do you have to rush in like the north wind caught in a blizzard?' the lama began, then stopped short when he observed the expression on Tashi's face and the damp patches where water had spilled on his robe 'Did you run all the way here, boy?' he now enquired. 'Your face is white as chalk! Did something happen out there? Sit down, boy, and let your breathing return to normal before you speak.'

Tashi sat down in front of the monk. Quietly accepting the proffered mug of tea, he said, 'It was nothing serious, Lama. Just some trouble with a stranger.'

'Since when have you started keeping things from me, boy? Tell me everything – from the very beginning,' Ozer demanded.

'I was filling the canteens with water, Lama, when I felt a terrible itch on the nape of my neck, as though somebody or something were watching me,' Tashi told him.

'Go on,' the lama urged, his dark eyes gleaming in the moonlight.

When Tashi finished recounting his story to the Lama he said, 'We must leave this place right now and exercise utmost caution during the rest of the journey. They must have been supremely confident of their success to send just one man after us. The next time, they may send several and the feather may not be enough to save us.' The monk turned to the driver. 'Pema, prepare to leave immediately.'

'I'm ready, Lama,' said a shaken Pema. 'I fear the black shamans, but with you around, I know there is nothing to be afraid of.'

'Be very careful. More of them will follow,' the lama warned.

Having uttered those words, the monk handed out sliced bread with red chilli pickle. The meagre snack, hastily devoured, would serve as their meal for the night.

The truck roared into life. The road stretched endlessly before them like a thin ribbon unspooling itself under a dark firmament teeming with stars.

VI

As dawn broke out across the skies, Tirthapuri approached. The grey mist of dawn was heightened by a damp fog that hung over the town like a shroud. In the greyness pale prayer flags floated like reminders of the spirit world. Tashi saluted the approaching town from the distance, it looked formidable, the hallowed site of pilgrimage since ancient times. The city served as a centre for both Hindu and Buddhist pilgrimage. Pema brought the truck to a halt to follow suit, even before the boy could voice the multitude of questions forming in his mind. Softly, the driver began chanting the prayer to the dead.

'I salute bygone spirits,' he intoned, 'I salute our long-departed forefathers. I salute the family deity visible here in all his glory.'

The incantations went on as Pema paid obeisance to the site famous for its ties with death and the other world. A scattering of Buddhist and Hindu pilgrims could be seen moving around, performing their rituals.

Lama Ozer sat alone, unmoved, his hands calmly fingering his beads.

'Lama, may I have your permission to complete the ceremony at Tirthapuri and to take the auspicious bath in the hot springs here before we move on?' an eager Pema enquired.

'Yours is a request I cannot turn down, Pema,' the lama replied. 'But after yesterday's incident, I think you are well aware of the kind of danger that hounds us. Do what you need to, but remember, the sooner we're on our way, the better for us all. And while you are at it, you may also show this boy how to perform the rituals. Something tells me that in the days to come, he will need all the blessings he can muster.' There was a twinkle in Ozer's eye.

'I do not like the idea of leaving you alone here, Lama,' Tashi began.

'I deem such sacrifice pointless, boy,' Ozer told him. 'I sense in you a desire to participate in the ceremony and have the ritual bath. Go ahead and do what you need to, but do not tarry. It is not for nothing that we have halted here. I wait for someone. Perhaps he will come.'

Pema and Tashi bowed to Lama Ozer, stepped off the truck and hurried to the hot springs, the grey light of dawn gave way to a hazy morning, as Tashi completed the ritual dip at the hot springs. He felt clean and fresh and safe, with no sign of dark-clothed shamans anywhere to spoil his mood.

'So this is your first visit to Tirthapuri, is it?' a smiling Pema asked him.

'Yes, it is. I had never imagined I would visit such a sacred site one day,' Tashi answered. 'Perhaps, I should refill the canteens with water from these hot springs. It will come in handy for the lama.'

Pema gave him a wide smile as he splashed around in the gushing spring water.

'Will Lama Ozer not be coming out to the springs?' Tashi wondered.

'Young Lama, this is not Lama Ozer's first trip here,' Pema explained. 'He was here thirty-five years ago; in fact, this area used to be his haunt. I was but a youth at the time. The lama would pass through this corner of Tibet, ever wandering, making his way towards Qiang La, seeking paths that most had forgotten. But now that I am meeting him after more than a decade, it warms my heart to be given yet another chance for such an encounter, though it revives sad memories of dark days – the Chinese storm over Tibet. You cannot imagine how many young people the lama had escorted at the time across the border to Nepal, to Sikkim. We revere him as a living legend among us.'

When Tashi and Pema hurried back to the truck, they found Lama Ozer busy preparing the morning meal of rice gruel. As Tashi sank back on his seat with a piping-hot bowl of gruel, the strangest sight met his eyes: a half-naked old man with a dark visage was hobbling towards their truck; the orange *tilak* on his forehead identified him as a wandering Hindu mendicant. For the first time since they had arrived in Tirthapuri, Lama Ozer stirred from his self-imposed vigil by the truck's window. He thrust his hand out of the window and held it high to attract the mendicant's attention.

The holy man staggered up to the window and exclaimed, 'You come at last, Lama! At last! I had news that you had taken to the road again.'

Ozer offered the mendicant some rice gruel and touched his hair in a gesture of affection.

'I knew I would meet you here, old friend,' the lama said. 'What news do you bring?'

'The road you take is watched and guarded,' the old mendicant warned. 'Beware of the master of the black shamans, currently residing in his monastery in Qiang. I fear he knows you are on the move and awaits you. There is talk among the shamans of your quest and of having you shadowed. Beware! The path to Qiang, the fortress and the old city is sealed off by powerful mantras,' the old man continued. 'There will be obstacles along the way. And lastly, old friend, I have a small gift for you.' The mendicant opened his fist and offered the lama a small, crumpled piece of newspaper tied with a saffron string. 'Guard this well,' he urged. 'It will help you see what the mortal eye cannot. Now I will ask of you one favour: let me behold the sign, the mark of the Garuda.'

Lama Ozer gestured to Tashi, who found himself spontaneously pulling out the feather from its resting place in his breast pocket. A dull red glow spread through the truck. The mendicant folded his hands at the sight. The next minute, he was gone. Dust devils whirled in the cool, misty air.

VII

The truck moved sluggishly through a sunny mid-afternoon. Tashi glanced at Lama Ozer furtively. The latter seemed to be fast asleep, his breathing even. Unbidden, the boy's eyes met Pema's. The driver put a finger to his lips, requesting silence. Soon, the truck was climbing. Dark mountains loomed ahead, casting long shadows around them.

With a jerk, Lama Ozer woke up and signalled to Pema to halt. The driver braked suddenly, throwing Tashi off-balance.

'You asked me to stop, Lama?' enquired a bemused Pema.

'Yes, my son,' Ozer smiled, 'your part in our journey ends here and you have played it well. We will part company here.'

'But I can take you at least a little way into Qiang La and set you down where you choose,' Pema offered.

'No, son, this is it,' Lama Ozer told him. 'You have served an old man to the best of your ability; may the graces guard you well.'

With that, the lama held up his hand and brushed it over Pema's forehead in the time-honoured gesture of blessing.

The afternoon was waning as the truck dropped Tashi and Ozer and headed down the road towards civilization. Tashi's eyes followed its course wistfully before it disappeared into the distance.

'Now, boy,' Lama Ozer said, 'you had better be prepared for what is to come. We stand outside the gates of what was once the kingdom of Qiang. Nestled within the folds of these towering mountains lies the long-forgotten silver valley. And somewhere in the wilderness of that valley stands Qiang La, the silver fortress, a fortress so ancient and so mystic that today, it is lost even in fables, all but the faintest hint buried deep in crumbling manuscripts.' Lama Ozer's penetrating eyes bored into Tashi. 'Think hard, boy, before you decide to continue on this journey with me. I should warn you that you will not come out of it alive. And if you wish to return to Demazong, I shall arrange a pardon for you from the Rimpoche. Now it is up to you.'

'Lama,' said a resolute Tashi, 'there is no way that I will desert you. Whatever lies ahead, we shall face it together.'

Lama Ozer shook his head sadly. 'So be it, boy,' he sighed. 'And now we will eat. I fear there will be no rest for us tonight, once we have crossed that pass ahead, beyond which lies the silver valley. Somewhere in that valley stand the hidden portals of Qiang, none have found it, boy. I tried for eighteen long years but to no avail; perhaps you will bring me luck. Do remember, however, that the black shamans have their stronghold in that valley and we will have to act with great speed and stealth.'

Longing for a steaming cup of tea, Tashi quickly took out strips of *churpi* from his bag and mixed them with cold rice. A cold breeze swept over them, chilling them to the bone.

Lama Ozer set out on the next leg of the journey, with Tashi close behind. The winding road seemed to stretch out endlessly before them, but their ascent was swift and smooth, for Ozer had set a killing pace. As dusk approached, Tashi surmounted the pass. What followed was a yawning valley of magical, lush green paddy fields lay yawning forming a perfect bowl ringed in by purple cliffs. It could not have been more than 40 kms long. In stark relief, lit up by the last ray of the sun, stood a marble white 'chorten' a holy Buddhist relic, and on an incline highlighted against the approaching night, the white-washed walls of the ancient monastery of Qiang that had been taken over by the black shamans. In minutes, dark night descended, the only light being starlight and the blinking lamplight from the monastery.

VIII

Lama Ozer's frail legs seemed to fly down the road into the heart of the valley, with an anxious Tashi trying to keep up. Tashi looked longingly at the monastery and the warm lights that lit it up like a beacon in the dark. The surrounding land seemed serenity itself and the air felt honey cool against his skin – the towering crags seemed to have blocked out the severe cold of the Tibetan plateau. Under the bright star-shine, Tashi could see Yaks resting under shelters provided probably by the monastery, the occasional rabbit could also be spotted scurrying between the paddy fields.

A strange lassitude gripped hold of Tashi, he had a great yearning to stretch out under the starlit sky. However, Lama Ozer was rushing forward at a killing pace, abandoning the road for small paths running between the fields and keeping well away from the houses or the lights of the gleaming monastery. He seemed to be cutting a path directly towards the mountains at the back of the monastery.

Hurrying to match Ozer's pace, Tashi suddenly felt his arm gripped by hard fingers. He spun around to face the person who held him and discovered it was a young shaman in a dark robe. As Tashi turned, equally abruptly Lama Ozer stood arrested in his flight looking directly at the stranger.

'So, Nyima, as ever, you return in a great rush and in characteristic stealth,' declared the shaman, an insolent smile playing on his lips.

Exhaustion lined Lama Ozer's face as he retorted, 'And, as ever, you get to know of my arrival the moment I cross yonder cliffs. Now, as you can see, I am in a great hurry. So let me through.' Ozer grasped his staff more firmly as he stood his ground.

'Ever in a hurry!' the shaman mocked. 'You know you trespass through Qiang, without even paying obeisance to the custodians of the ancient land.'

He stepped forward barring their way. The starlight threw his sharp profile into prominent relief.

'Thirty summers ago,' he went on, 'you were warned against entering Qiang. However, again you come searching what cannot be found by one like you. Now Nyima suffer, I must take you to the Master, he awaits you, trespasser of the silence'

The last few words were spat out with venom. The next moment the shaman was muttering a mantra holding aloft his 'Nga chung', a leather-thonged rattle drum, the incantation of the mantra reverberated eerily to its erratic resonance.

Tashi found himself desperately looking for some means, any means, to prevent the man from completing his mantra. Under the brilliant starlight, he saw a flat white stone gleaming in the night. Without thinking twice he crouched low and grabbed the stone and launched it, hissing, in the purple night. As, Lama Ozer gripped his staff and chanted the counter mantra, Tashi's stone found its mark hitting the stranger bang in the centre of his forehead. His hand raised, Lama Ozer serenely completed his own mantra. A gentle wind swept over them, as the shaman's head sank back on the ground in the deepest slumber, his rattle drum abandoned to an uneasy silence.

'We must move fast, boy,' Ozer urged Tashi, breaking into a measured run to continue their journey. 'That one was dangerous,' he went on, 'far beyond the range of my own powers. He has learnt his tricks well from the Black Master. As for the Garuda's feather, guard it well, boy.'

Tashi promptly accelerated his pace.

'If only we could make it out of this valley and into the hills, boy,' the lama said, panting as he ran, 'we would be safe.'

Reaching a few straggly bushes that cast a long shadow over the ground, Ozer stopped short.

'Boy,' he said breathlessly, 'we are in the valley of the Garuda and not once have we consulted the feather! Bring it out – fast!'

Tashi quickly groped under his robe and pulled out the feather. It gleamed dully in his hands. Then a soft red light began spreading from it. Instinctively, the boy found himself making a fist to hide the feather. The red tendrils of light escaped into the night, nonetheless, dancing between the paddy fields. Then, almost 20 paces away, Tashi sighted the same shaman who had intercepted them not moments ago. He was on his feet now and flanked by two other men. Within minutes, they were joined by a tall, powerfully built, yet majestic-looking man of indeterminate age in regal brown robes that blew about in the breeze. Tashi's gaze was drawn to the stranger by the hypnotic pull of his snake-black eyes and he was mesmerized by the man's aura which suggested immense power, even as it generated intense fear. He felt Lama Ozer tremble next to him.

'Flee, boy, flee!' the monk cried out. 'That is the master of the black shamans!'

Tashi felt the wind rushing past his face as Lama Ozer and he began a wild run towards the mountains. As they rounded the bend parting the paddy fields upfront they felt themselves running into a thin barrier of air; the very air writhed pinioning their arms. In desperation, Ozer tried to flail the air as he mouthed a counter mantra. Right in front, Tashi beheld the coldest face he had ever seen, hands aloft, dark robes flapping in the wind, the Master of the black shamans stood effectively barring their path.

'So you come again, Nyima!' said the man. 'This time, there is no escape for you, for I will take you prisoner.' Turning to his acolytes, he commanded, 'Tie them up and bring them to the monastery.'

At that very moment, Lama Ozer broke free of the spell's constraining hold and chanted a mantra. Immediately, a force streaked across towards the master, but collapsed against him, vanquished by his greater power.

'It is not that easy to trap me, Nyima,' the master said with a disdainful smile. 'It seems you have learnt nothing from the past.'

With that, the man held out his palm. A wind rose from it and rushed towards them, catching Lama Ozer and Tashi in the centre of its turbulence and freezing them in its volatile centre. Tashi felt as though he were standing in the eye of a blizzard and that any minute, his legs would collapse under him. He saw that Lama Ozer had already fallen to the ground. The relentless wind held them both captive. In moments, however, it had subsided and the master spoke.

'Tie them up and bring them to the monastery,' he ordered his acolytes.

Lama Ozer swayed weakly on unsteady feet as a shaman swiftly tied his arms behind his back. Another shaman approached Tashi.

His mouth dry with fear, the boy groped for the feather as a last resort. And then it happened. There was a rush of wind past Tashi's face; then sharp talons grazed his skin and he was lifted high in the air. He felt, rather than saw Ozer being lifted in the same way. Then deep sleep overtook him. Under the light of the stars, the massive Garuda's coat gleamed a burnished red; this mythical bird had not been sighted in the silver valley for more than a millennium.

IX

The dawn wind blew freezing cold. The sun had barely started painting the sky in delicate hues, when Lama Ozer looked up from his prayer beads and glanced fondly at the sleeping boy. In his right hand Tashi clutched the red feather, which glinted madly in the cold morning. It was clear to the monk that destiny had charted an extraordinary course for the boy, but even Ozer could merely divine its strength, not its direction.

As the light of the new day grew in intensity, it roused the sleeping Tashi who blinked at its brightness. Stretching himself awake and a little embarrassed that he had overslept, he enquired, 'Lama, where are we?' Then hazily remembering recent events, he asked, 'How did we escape?'

Lama Ozer smiled at him benevolently. 'It is clear, boy, that some power watches over us,' he explained. 'It warms my heart to know that we are protected.'

Tashi stretched lazily. 'So it was real, Lama,' he mused. 'We have, indeed, reached Qiang and the events of last evening did occur. It was not a phantom from my dreams that I saw.'

'Have your wits dulled with the rest of you, boy?' the lama said with some asperity. 'Now hurry up and get dressed. We have a lot of work laid out for us. We will be looking for the fortress today. This promises to be the most difficult quest of all, for long have I searched for the old city and the silver fortress – in vain. I wonder if we can do in a day what I could not manage in eighteen years?'

Tashi quickly walked across to a nearby rivulet to complete his ablutions. He could not help but admire the freshness of the morning and the flawless beauty of the valley that stretched out at his feet. A short distance away the monastery flashed white in the morning light. Tashi could not shake off the feeling that he was being observed but allowed to go unscathed. He turned around to see Lama Ozer readying some cold rice gruel for breakfast, a left-over from yesterday. Smiling, Lama Ozer handed out Tashi's portion on tender leaves picked from the apricot tree. In the distance rice fields could be seen merging peacefully with delicate apricot trees replete with orange coloured fruit. Tashi turned to scrutinize the dark caverns glinting from the face of each hillock, in the surrounding mountains.

Following the direction of the boy's gaze, Lama Ozer smiled ruefully. 'So you're finally looking at them, boy,' he observed. 'These mountains were regular havens for Qiang's mendicants in the old days. For many moons was this valley fair and just, known for its deep-rooted asceticism. The old ways of the Bon were followed without hindrance and the valley was regarded as the gateway to the Bon paradise of Olmo-Lungring or what would later come to be known as Shambala. Long did I search and little have I learnt, save that a great secret lay lost in this valley and the key was to be found in the old city and the silver fortress.'

Tashi looked at Ozer, mesmerized. 'But, Lama,' he said in consternation, 'the valley is so small and no fortress is in sight, not even the ruins of an ancient city. Could they, perhaps, lie buried under the paddy fields?'

Ozer dismissed the suggestion with an impatient wave of his hand. 'Boy,' he exclaimed with exasperation, 'your wits seem to have gone wandering again! Where do you think a fortress would have been built in the old days? Obviously at a height, with a clear view of the surrounding terrain so that invaders could be spotted from a distance and intercepted in time. It is more than likely that the silver fortress too was constructed on a high ridge of these purple mountains. According to ancient manuscripts and legend, it stood to the north of the old walled city which was compact in size and painstakingly carved out of a single, colossal chunk of rock on a ridge overlooking the valley'

'Then our task is not so difficult, Lama,' a cheerful Tashi piped up. 'All we need to do is wander around the hills examining its ridges and rock faces.'

'I truly believe the yak butter you have been fed since infancy has clogged your brains!' Ozer snapped. 'Allow me to remind you, yet again, that I have been exploring these mountains for eighteen long years; not a single rock, gully or cave have I left unexamined. Many centuries have passed since Qiang was known to the world; many more have followed its demise. Nothing survives the ravages of time and tide. Yet Qiang La was a fortress of such exceptional mystic power that I firmly believe its shrine room and the artefacts contained therein are intact.'

Tashi felt his body relax in the warmth of the summer sun, now at its zenith. 'Where, then, will we begin our search, Lama?' he asked, before adding, 'something has been playing on my mind for the past few hours: if our guardian delivered us last night from the clutches of the degenerate shamans, only to leave us on this gentle slope overlooking the valley, could there, perhaps, be a reason for it? Could this very place hold a clue to the object of our quest?'

Lama Ozer looked pensive. 'The morning sun seems to have melted the lard from your brain at last, boy!' he quipped. Then his expression turned grave. 'The issue you have raised is one I too have been pondering on. Consider our strange location, Tashi. We were left blissfully asleep on the slope right behind the monastery, screened by this grove of apricot trees. We are too close for the master of the black shamans not to have sensed our presence. Yet it is clear that he remains unaware of it, for had it been otherwise, would he not have been upon us by now?

'Then again, this spot is just fifteen minutes by foot from the cave at the back of the monastery where the great Bon master, Tonpa Shenrab, used to meditate,' the lama went on. 'Somehow, instinct tells me there is something in that cave. Many a time have I wanted to visit it, but the shamans succeeded in frustrating my every attempt. Everything points to the cave. The dangerous location in which our guardian chose to deposit us is but two turns away from the cave. Let us rise and make for the cave before the shamans are upon us.'

Tashi sprang to his feet, swiftly gathered up their few belongings and joined Lama Ozer in a quick, quiet prayer to the Lord Buddha and the Goddess Tara. He felt naked and exposed as they walked out of the grove; he had felt safe in its shelter, believing, somehow, that the Garuda had cast a spell on it, protecting it from the shamans' evil influence. And now they were vulnerable once more. He cast a furtive glance at the monastery, not more than a couple of miles away, its white walls gleaming in the distance.

Lama Ozer moved at a very fast pace, his dull maroon robes contrasting with the lime green fields and the silvery trees. Tashi followed, matching the old monk's pace. As they drew closer to the monastery, he found himself glancing back every few minutes. There seemed to be no sign of life at the monastery, the surrounding fields rustled in emptiness. Yet, Tashi could not help turning every few minutes expecting a hand to stop him.

Another turn brought them face to face with a moss covered cavern, like a hole in the fair morning. Cold water dripped from the green growth on the cave. Lama Ozer stood rooted like a stone in front of the cave.

Finally, he spoke. 'Boy,' he said, 'although I do not know exactly what I am searching for, we will have no more than four or five minutes to explore the cave. For even as I enter, the magic spell that guards the cave will warn the dark master of our presence. Then we will have nothing to save us but our luck. So may the Goddess Tara protect us, boy, as, hand in hand, we enter.'

X

The interior of the cave was damp. There was barely any light inside the cave and everything seemed bathed in a greenish glow. The walls were bare but for a beautiful mural of the Bon sage, Tonpa Shenrab, seated in the lotus position. Against a backdrop faded with time, Shenrab was depicted in midnight blue, his gaze direct and serene, his right hand touching the ground in the oft-portrayed posture of the Sakyamuni Buddha.

Before the painting stood a well-worn stone seat, covered in frayed brocade; it was undoubtedly the seat on which the sage had meditated. Next to it stood a small flagon of ritual water topped with peacock feathers. Other than these few objects, the cave was bare. A precious minute had already passed and Tashi felt time hanging by a thread. Oblivious to everything, Lama Ozer had prostrated himself before the seat of the ancient master.

Mesmerized by the sage's blue-clad, seated form, Tashi approached the painting gingerly and examined it. He was especially intrigued by the way Shenrab's fingers seemed to point to the earth.

Lama Ozer came to stand by Tashi's side. 'Yes, boy, you have found it,' he said. 'Look carefully at the ground where the finger of the sage points.'

The surface was indistinct, but when Tashi touched it, he felt the presence of a cavity.

'This is the spot from where we descend,' Ozer announced, lowering his slim body into the ground. The next moment, he was gone, swallowed by the darkness.

As Tashi prepared to follow the lama and lower himself into the cavity his eyes went to the entrance and he saw a pair of malevolent black snake eyes boring into him. The Black Master held aloft his palm, blocking Tashi's way as he entered the cave, dark robes flapping in the wind. The boy felt his heart quail before the intensity of that gaze. Instinctively reaching into the pocket of his robe, Tashi held out the Garuda's brilliant feather. Red light curled out from it in tendrils and spread across the room, emitting little sparks.

The dark master's eyes narrowed. 'So it is true! The moment prophesied has arrived. The bearer is among us,' he said, his words booming within the confines of the cave. 'Come, boy, there is much you can learn at Qiang.' The shaman's reptilian eyes glinted with a hypnotic power, arresting Tashi's movements and his desperate attempt to flee.

Then a strange courage took hold of the boy. Holding firmly on to the bright feather, Tashi flung himself with all his might into the depths of the cavity. All thought and feeling were suspended as he hurtled down into darkness. Then Lama Ozer's familiar hands reached out with their reassuring touch. With the helplessness of a tiny infant, Tashi hid his face in the folds of Ozer's robe. The lama held his head gently and poured some of Rimpoche Gyaltsen's ruby brew down his throat.

A bitter, burning sensation spread through Tashi's throat, bringing him alive to the nature of his current situation. He looked around and realized they were in some kind of subterranean chamber; it had obviously been carved out of the rock by human hands. Ahead of them lay a yawning black chute, just wide enough for a boy to squeeze through. Fear rose unbidden from the pit of Tashi's stomach as he raised his head and looked up into the cavity through which he had just descended. Again his eyes met a pair of malignant snake-black ones.

Tashi felt Ozer's arms go around him protectively and he heard the monk whisper in his ear, 'We are safe here for the time being. Unless I am greatly mistaken, the shamans cannot follow us here. These passages were hewn out of the rock by followers of the ancient Bon religion, who set up safeguards against evil and impure beings, regardless of the creed they belonged to. However, those safeguards risk being breached at dusk, for their power will wane as the light of day starts dying and night falls.'

Tashi looked on, bemused, as Ozer went down on his hands and knees and then lay flat on his belly before laboriously crawling into the dark depths of the narrow chute. The boy followed by placing his bundle in front of him, tucking the feather into his pocket and pushing his lean body through the small aperture. In a few seconds, they were swallowed up by absolute, unrelenting darkness. The roof of the tunnel seemed to gradually descend as they progressed till Tashi could feel damp mud slicking on to the back of his neck and head. His arms hurt with the effort of crawling forward and an icy wetness seeped through his belly from the damp tunnel floor. In the distance, he saw Ozer's torch winking in the dark like a ray of hope.

As the lama's torchlight became an increasingly tinier speck in the distance, the memory of the Black Master's snake-like gaze haunted Tashi and fear rinsed his soul. The walls of the tunnel seemed to close in on him till every movement was agonizing. His stomach was beginning to cramp painfully from the damp beneath. Soon, even the faint glimmer of Lama

Ozer's torchlight had disappeared. Panic clutched Tashi's heart. In acute pain now, he stopped crawling and let his tired head sink on to his arms. and forced himself to think of Demazong.

Something stirred within him. Once again, he felt the gentle touch of the spring breeze in Yumsamedong, saw the swollen lips of the violet rhododendron petals and smelt the fragrance of incense oil. Keeping his mind firmly focused on these images, Tashi began crawling forward again. After what seemed like an eternity in that dark, subterranean chute, he sensed a change. Inch by inch, the space within the tunnel increased until Tashi found he could sit up without banging his head on its roof. With a pang, he remembered Ozer and began crawling forward once more with renewed vigour. Soon, light filtered through and the warm rays of the waning afternoon sun greeted him. With a shock, he realized that evening was fast approaching. Rounding one last bend, he finally caught up with Lama Ozer.

'Boy, whatever happened to you?' the monk asked, a worried frown puckering his forehead. 'I have been waiting for you for the past one hour! I was even considering going back into the chute to look for you. Hurry, boy, please hurry! The evening is almost upon us. We must reach the portals of Qiang La before sundown. Night will bring out the degenerate shamans and then there will be no hope of escape. Time is a sharp-edged knife, boy. You have to flee before it or risk being grievously wounded.'

Tashi realized that they were standing on some kind of a ledge high in the mountains. Far below, the valley stretched out eerily. An icy blast of mountain air slapped Tashi's face and he was stung into mobility. Right ahead, he beheld Lama Ozer striding forward, softly disappearing into the mist.

He heard the monk's strident tones exhorting him to follow. 'Hurry, boy, hurry,' Ozer called back, 'and keep close behind. We can't afford to lose sight of each other.'

Tashi ran to join his master, walking single file behind him. The cleft in the mountain soon gave way to towering walls of rock that flanked them on either side as they hurried along the narrow path which seemed ancient, but was well maintained and clear of major rock falls and overgrown bushes. It wound on endlessly, climbing higher and higher. From a gap between the rocks, Tashi beheld the flawless purple mountains splashed red in sunset and the valley below took on a dazzling golden hue

'Boy, we must hasten!' Lama Ozer urged. 'This trail is well known to the shamans; I see their signs everywhere. Already, the safeguards grow weak; they could be upon us at any moment.'

Silently, the last rays of the sun burnt through a wild dusk, across the wilderness of the silver valley, as yet another turn brought them face to face with the night. Blackness cloaked the valley, and brilliant stars arose in the heavens. Softly, the lantern moon floated into place in the sky. The air thinned and fearsome cold gripped Ozer, as he ran up the path.

'I can sense their presence, boy!' the lama gasped as he ran. 'They are coming and Qiang La is still not within our reach!'

Snow crunched under their feet as the path thinned, moon-light turning to silver brilliance in the night. The severe cold grew as the summit neared another turn, bringing them to a massive break in the rock wall. The moonlight shone blindingly silver against the overhanging rock-face. 'Boy, I can see nothing!' the lama exclaimed. 'My eyes are blinded by the night and this maddening moonlight.'

A sudden thought crossed Tashi's mind. 'Lama, do you remember the mendicant at Tirthapuri giving you something?' he asked with some urgency.

'So he did, boy,' Ozer replied, 'so he did! Bring it out.'

Tashi groped in his backpack and pulled out the small newspaper packet tied in saffron thread. Ozer untied the thread and soft, scented white powder spilled on to his hands like tiny flakes of snow.

'Let me see,' the lama mused. 'The mendicant had promised that this would help us to perceive what mortal eyes could not.'

He held his hands up in front of him and blew the powder off. He blew out the powder in front of his eyes and on the overhanging rockface the silver moonlight grew even more brilliant, revealing silver towers atop silver towers. The silver fortress stood tall on the rockface in slim moonlit brilliance, softly caressing the night. The gateway to Qiang La glowed not more than ten paces away. But menacingly, the great silver gateway stood shut and flanking it, burning snake-anger in his eyes, stood the Master of the Black shamans, his *nga-chung* in hand, surrounded by his disciples.

As he spoke, his deep, booming voice seemed to emerge from the very heart of the mountain. 'You, Lama Nyima Ozer, and your disciple, one Tashi Thendup, the dark shamans condemn you to eternal slavery and a less-than-mortal existence, for no mortal of this era is allowed to behold Qiang La,' he spat out, standing with his feet apart, his robes fluttering in the nocturnal wind. 'From this day onwards, your very souls will be enslaved to the order. Here!' His *nga-chung* held aloft, the master prepared his curse, even as he spat forth the lethal mantra.

Tashi felt a great chill seize his soul, as though it were being bound in heavy chains. Lama Ozer raised his palms in a protective mantra. The next moment, a bloodcurdling shriek escaped his lips. Brilliant moonlight caught the movement of Ozer's flailing arms before he crumpled to the ground. Less than ten paces away, the hidden fortress beckoned. Terror struck Tashi's heart as black snake eyes turned their glare on him. Robes blowing wildly in the mountain breeze, snow crunching under his feet, the Black Master advanced on the boy. Tashi instinctively clutched the feather in his sweat-slicked palm.

With the shaman standing two paces away now, he felt paralysed, defenceless. *Nga-chung* rattling, the mantra drifted out of his mouth in an endless stream, as ice on his soul, Tashi trembled. Yet, something reared; he would not let himself collapse; not when the Lama needed him. In a desperate moment, calling to reserve all that was human in him, he forced himself to move towards Ozer, thinking: 'Anything, anything to break the flow of the mantra.' From somewhere red courage throbbed, Tashi hurtled towards Ozer's immobile form, grabbing Ozer, he threw him across his shoulder and rushed towards the gate. Behind him he heard the rattling sound of the *nga-chung* raised in rage. Willing the last flush of strength in him, Tashi stormed the gate, moonlight played wildly across the forms of the shamans as they stood barring his path.

The forms of the dark master's disciples cast dancing shadows on the moonlit ground as they stood barring his way. Tashi looked up to find snake eyes glinting coldly at him. The master stood before the door, hand held out. Something died within the boy as he heard the last lines of the mantra being uttered. He had lost. The very air writhed with evil; he had been caught in the act of flying and was now trapped. The dark master approached, his palm held out for what he wanted from the boy. Tashi felt his own hand open. Silently, he handed the Garuda's feather to the shaman. It looked like a splash of fresh blood in the master's palm. As hope died, Tashi felt himself uttering a final prayer under the moonlit skies.

The shamans crowded around their master who held the feather aloft. A stray moonbeam struck it. Instantly, the all-too-familiar red tendrils began unwinding from it and moving towards Tashi. As each strand strayed in the moonlight, lending its silver glow a bronze overtone, the boy felt the stirrings of something positive, a dead hope shimmered. A pale whiteness grew on the frozen air before the moonlit gate, as though spirits were dancing in the night. Then it emerged, the legend: Blood hued gigantic wings streaked with the gold of ambrosia, arose from the shoulders of an immortal golden-hued youth, blazing red was his hair and a wild fire raged in his eyes. The glory of the very sun burnt in his form. The 'Garuda' stood yet again after a millennia on the outskirts of Qiang La, the silver fortress of legend.

Molten fire raged from the palm of his hand causing the thunder-struck shamans to flee like fishing boats in the face of a sea storm. Gently he stooped before Ozer touching his forehead with light-filled palms. Soon a wonder-struck Tashi watched Ozer come to life, then stagger to his feet, palms folded in obeisance.

The golden youth smiled at Tashi. 'Your journey is almost done, son of man,' he declared. 'Yonder, the gates of Qiang await your entry. Cross them and make your way to the shrine room. There you will find the lost road, the hidden path to Olmo-Lungring, the abode of the gods.'

Tashi looked on in wonder.

'After a millennium do I serve the son of man again, but so it was willed. My duty by you is done for now,' the Garuda went on. 'The rest will follow as ordained. When you cross yonder gates, you will be on the threshold of the mystic kingdom. Farewell.'

The Garuda raised its brilliant wings in the moonlit night, then disappeared in a white mist. Tashi stared at the red feather shining on his palm, ahead the moonlight played brilliantly on the now open gates of Qiang. The two lamas from the mortal world crossed them swiftly. Then the gates closed and vanished into thin air.

Chapter 4

SHAMBALA

I

The pink blaze of dawn spread across the skies over Qiang La, the silver fortress, its light making Tashi's pale cheeks glow with the sheen of pearls. For the first time since they had been on the road, the boy found himself waking up before Lama Ozer. The monk was still in deep slumber, oblivious to the growing light of a new day.

Awestruck, Tashi looked around him at the old city strangely revealed in the morning light. Ruins of ancient structures emerged through the thick, swirling veils of morning mist. Rising out of the debris of old rubble, the silver citadel towered above the fortress, glowing with an unearthly aura of power. Tashi felt drawn to it like a magnet. Reluctantly, he tore his gaze away and glanced at the lama, who was beginning to stir.

Lama Ozer's eyes fluttered open weakly, resting on Tashi, before shutting again. 'Boy, I am sorely depleted,' he confessed in a bleak, tired voice. 'The confrontation with the black shamans has taken a great deal out of me. Get me Rimpoche Gyaltsen's ruby brew. Somehow, I must get this withered body of mine to move. Time is of the essence, boy. Hurry!'

Tashi rose swiftly, rifling through his backpack for the potion. He pulled out a slim bottle, then set out in search of water to mix the potion before offering it to the lama. In the distance, he heard the light, tinkling of a mountain spring.

Tashi made his way to the spring, guided by the rippling melody of the bubbling water. The ground inclined sharply as he walked on, making for the base of the citadel. The ruins giving way to a city built of a clear white stone that shone with the glimmer of the far stars. Like a vision from another world, the citadel filled his sight. Intricately worked silver gates barred entry to what must at one time have been the very heart of Qiang. Ten paces behind the gate flowed a bubbling brook brimming with clear mountain water. Beyond it appeared the palace, preserved in all its elusive beauty. Next to it stood a pillared hall. Silver pagodas gleamed in the light of dawn. And standing aloof on a hillock towards the east was the most arresting sight of all – a monastery with a golden dragon crowning its pagodas – ablaze with the glory of the rising sun. It was like no monastery that Tashi had ever seen. To his mesmerized eyes, it seemed more than anything like a temple to the immortal spirit.

Tashi stepped past the gates, walking swiftly towards the brook. As he bowed over the brilliant white waters to refill his flask, silken black hair tumbling loose over a flawless ivory face, filled his vision. Royal black eyes smiled mockingly like the first blush of dawn over Mt Kanchendzonga. Tashi found himself falling headlong into the water till he was neck-deep in it, the icy contact bringing him back to the reality of a desolate place where there was nothing but cold hard stone and freezing water. Shrugging, he climbed out, hastily refilled his flask and rushed back to Lama Ozer.

The old man lay on the ground, moaning softly, in a fitful sleep. Tashi woke him and helped him up. Mixing the ruby potion into the cold, clear water, he helped Lama Ozer drink it. Gently laying him back on the ground, the boy began preparing the morning meal. It had been many days since he had lighted a fire, but within the fortress, Tashi felt secure and emboldened enough to risk it. All he had left from their supplies was rice, some jaggery, dry fruit and a few strips of *churpi*. Getting to work swiftly, he began preparing a simple gruel of rice, mixed with dry fruits and sweetened with jaggery. As a fragrant aroma rose from the pot, Tashi's mouth watered; he had not eaten anything since their hasty breakfast the previous morning. He risked a quick look at the lama who was now seated in the lotus posture, meditating. Tashi smiled in relief; the lama seemed to have recovered somewhat and this breakfast would restore him further. As the steam gently wafted up from the rice pot, Tashi felt himself relax. Unbidden, an image appeared in his mind of commanding black eyes smiling serenely at him and loose tumbling silken hair framing a face that was not human.

Tashi shook himself free of the image, only to see Lama Ozer coming out of his meditation.

The lama gestured to him now. 'Boy,' he called out, 'already the chill afternoon wind begins to blow. We must make haste.'

'Certainly, Lama,' Tashi replied, 'but first, I shall bring some refreshment for you. It is ready to be served.'

Pouring the gruel out into the lama's wooden bowl, he placed the food respectfully before him and returned to the fire to spoon out some gruel for himself. In minutes, their breakfast was over. Tashi quickly cleaned the utensils they had used and returned them to his backpack.

In no time, he was ready; he had brushed his robe out, tied an orange sash around his waist and secured the backpack to his shoulders. The Garuda's red feather was wrapped in a piece of paper and placed in his breast pocket. Lama Ozer was also ready for the next leg of the journey, having changed into a deep maroon habit. Staff in hand, he stood waiting. Tashi sensed the day would be a special one; the lama had changed his habit; that in itself was a sign.

'Boy, are you ready?' the lama enquired. 'We should be moving now. But first, let me take a look at you. Come here.'

Tashi walked up to Ozer.

'Show me your hands, boy,' the monk ordered in a stern voice.

Tashi held out his strong, well-formed hands for Ozer's scrutiny. After the vigorous scrub he had subjected them to in the morning, they shone a light brown.

The lama inspected his hands, then eyed him critically. 'All right, boy,' he finally said, 'your robe will have to do, as you have brought no other. Your hands are clean, your face is oiled and you have cleaned your boots as well. I guess this will have to do. We must now travel at great speed, boy. I don't have to tell you that this day marks the most critical point in our journey.'

'Where do we go now, Lama?' Tashi enquired, puzzled, 'we are already within the silver fortress, are we not?'

'It *has* to be the yak lard,' Ozer muttered sarcastically. 'What else could have frozen such young brains? Were we not directed yesterday to make for the shrine room, boy? That is where we head now. We must reach the citadel.'

'This way, Lama,' Tashi urged, taking the lead, 'I went there this very morning.'

Already the morning light was waning and thick mist rolled down from the frozen peaks. Tashi strode purposefully ahead, making straight for the citadel. Soon, they had crossed the silver gates and reached the little brook, not far from the square that faced the pillared hall. To its right stood the palace. The nameless golden monastery glowed on a hillock to the left, overlooking the citadel's eastern face.

'We have reached the citadel, Lama,' the boy announced. 'All we need to do now is find the shrine room. Where do you suppose that is?'

'If only you talked less and thought more, it would have helped!' Ozer snapped. 'Follow me. We will head for the monastery. There it stands, gleaming softly through the mist under the afternoon sun.'

Tashi found himself falling behind the lama as they hurried along what must once have been a thoroughfare. Ozer reached the base of the small hill on which the monastery stood and began climbing it swiftly, all traces of his extreme weakness of that morning having disappeared. His renewed vigour reassured Tashi, but the boy still could not shake the feeling that they were being watched. He felt, at times, that black silken tresses were caressing his face, only to find it was the wind. Climbing higher and higher, the narrow trail wound its way up to the monastery, now shrouded in mist. Soon, Tashi could see very little, apart from Lama Ozer's flapping maroon robes a few paces ahead of him.

All at once colossal bronze gates appeared before his eyes; the metal had retained its sheen and gleamed as though it was regularly polished. Embossed on the gates was an ancient carving of the Garuda in flight, hurling maces of lightning at demon-infested grounds. Lama Ozer touched the gate of the monastery lightly with his staff and the huge doors swung open, revealing pitch-dark interiors. The lightest breath of wind seemed to follow the lama and Tashi felt, yet again, as though ivory feet were pattering into the monastery along with his own. Tendrils of silken black hair seemed to brush his face as he stepped into the portal, pitch-blackness encompassed Tashi, more complete, more dark, than anything he had ever encountered.

His mind went blank as he stepped into the monastery, for the gates automatically shut behind him, plunging him into a darkness more intense, more absolute than anything he had ever experienced.

II

It felt like the interior of a womb. Tashi sensed pre-natal memories and sensations that had long died, awaken once again. Then Lama Ozer switched on his torch, illuminating their surroundings with false light. Tashi heard the monk stumble, then the clatter of the torch as it fell from his hand and rolled around on the floor, its light bouncing around the room and bringing alive giant shadows before it came to a halt, focusing its beam on an old brass candlestand that still retained its lustre. Unbelievably, the wick in the candle was intact. Lama Ozer walked up to it and took out matches from his robe pocket. In no time, the wick was alight and a warm glow enveloped the place.

'Lama, how can there be a wick here, all ready to be lit?' Tashi asked, his voice full of awe.

'Some questions are better not asked, boy,' the lama whispered. 'This is not the time for questions.'

Tashi looked around him for the first time and observed what the flickering candlelight had revealed – a vast hall.

'Look, boy, there are more wicks in this place; start lighting them all,' Ozer told him. 'First, we must be able to see our way through. Only then will we find what we are looking for. The lost road lies somewhere here.'

With the lama's words spurring him on to action, Tashi moved quickly. He pulled out a box of matches and lit the nearest candle. Primeval painted figures of gods and goddesses stood out prominently on the walls of the shrine room. Remarkable were the scenes depicted: on verdant green pastures frolicked translucent forms; golden pagodas, crowned by a solitary gold dragon, then twins of the same mythical creature, followed by hydra-headed versions, rose into the sky; in one clear representation, the lustrous, rainbow-hued form of the ancient Bodhisattva of compassion,

Avalokiteshwara, the very picture of serenity, stood on a brilliant white lotus, bearing a staff in one hand and a lotus in another.

As Tashi prostrated himself before the icon, Lama Ozer's voice floated down to him. 'That, boy, is Avalokiteshwara, the Bodhisattva of compassion, as you know him.'

'Lama, that is a rather unusual portrait, is it not?' Tashi remarked. 'I have never seen him represented thus.'

'Truly, boy, that is a rather unusual rendering of the Bodhisattva,' the lama agreed, 'but then, it is not surprising that we should find it here, in its current location, for by entering the silver fortress, you have crossed the familiar boundaries of human existence and the universe and stepped into the unknown. Here, you must open your mind to all that you have never experienced before.' Then Lama Ozer held up his palm, demanding silence.

Golden candlelight danced across the shrine room as he bowed before the chief deity. Treading as silently as a cat, Tashi approached the monk, only to be thunderstruck by the sight that met his eyes. Instead of the usual representation of a male deity seated in the lotus position, he saw a portrait in gold of the primeval essence of womankind. Dread, fed by superstition, filled the boy as he walked, unbidden, towards that golden form. He felt something stir deep within as he looked at it closely, the ivory face, the tumbling black hair, the majestic black eyes and the serene smile that was nature itself; it was the face he had seen in the brook.

'Don't gawk, boy,' the lama admonished him. 'Prostrate yourself before the deity.'

'But Lama,' Tashi said in consternation, 'who is this? This is no Bodhisattva or known deity. This is no god or goddess that I recognize. Could this beautiful woman be an unknown primeval goddess of the Bon?'

'Prostrate yourself before her, boy!' Ozer commanded sternly. 'That is Yum Chenmo, the great goddess of light, mysterious beyond compare, beauteous beyond human imagination, ancient mother, precursor to the saviouress, Goddess Tara, wielder of the swastika, destroyer of evil, goddess of the moon; Prostrate yourself before her, boy, lest we are made to pay for your ignorance.'

Shaken and abashed, Tashi looked at the stone figure now grinning with the gaiety of a girl of sixteen.

'Lama, this cannot be the great goddess, Yum Chenmo, mother of the Buddhas,' the boy remarked. 'The image bears no resemblance at all to the goddess, but seems to be that of a young girl. Perhaps this is a shrine to the royal princess and the one we are to go to lies elsewhere?'

'Prostrate yourself at once, boy!' Lama Ozer's voiced boomed, causing more shadows to emerge from the walls. 'How much knowledge do you profess to have gained in your fifteen years? Prostrate yourself before I lose all patience!'

Reluctantly, Tashi went down on his knees and prostrated himself before the image. At that moment, his eyes darted to something unusual: to the left of the goddess was a holy painting, a *thangka*, except that it was like no *thangka* he had ever seen. A dull light softly filtered out of the cloth, as burnished blankness gave way to living, glimmering images. The images changed with an amazing frequency, showing shifting scenes, birds frozen in flight flew far away and then disappeared into white light. The trees shook with a far divine breeze, a frolicking band of 'Dakinis' or female 'sky dancers' formed patterns in the skies. Suddenly catching Tashi's eye, one fairy form drifted towards the room as, light-filled hair afloat on the air of another world, she opened her arms to Tashi.

Like a bewitched man in a dream, Tashi felt a massive jolt pass through his body, as though a thick cord had hooked into his soul and was pulling him inexorably off his feet and into the very centre of the glowing *thangka*. He felt himself being swept towards the painting on a gigantic wave of blazing golden light that seemed to eclipse the glory of the sun itself. As if from a distance, he saw Lama Ozer take up position on the right of the golden-hued damsel, the creature of light. A tremendous roaring grew in his ears as he came face-to-face with the painting's blazing golden surface and the smiling visage of the dakini beckoning to him, her graceful arms extended in welcome.

Yet he held back, reluctant to let go.

Then, softly, twilight speech blossomed in his mind. 'You have to let go,' it whispered, 'let the carcass fall ...'

'Why? How?' Tashi shrieked, his soul atremble with fear.

'We know,' said the words, 'that unlike the other, you are neither ready nor deserving. Mortal, we cannot stand eternally on the bridge connecting the worlds. Let go. Listen carefully and try to feel the unknown aura of a world beyond your comprehension. Here, I offer you the gift of experiencing sensations alien to mortal man. The gold of my lips trembles for a mortal embrace; fail me not, feeble monk!'

Thrilled and mesmerized by the twilight speech, Tashi felt himself letting go, melting in the divine embrace of a creature of light, his soul merging into hers and acquiring its own aura of divinity. The boy felt himself soaring in the golden light of a lost world, heedless of his mortal form that crumpled, then collapsed lifeless on the dark floor of the shrine room.

III

A great sense of freedom filled Tashi as he flew across strange, golden skies and between billowing clouds, lunging out at the naked rays of an unknown sun. It was then that he noticed the azure waters stretching out endlessly in what looked to be an oceanic world. He smelled the surf and silver dolphins, gleaming in the light, caught his eye, but still he flew on, seemingly unaware of it all.

A bell-like voice tinkled through the lukewarm air. 'Where do you wander wildly, son of man?' it asked. 'We fly to the north. Come hither.'

Tashi felt a golden hand upon his arm, the colours of the sky forming a circlet around it. The dakini glowed with the warmth of the sun, her light-filled hair streaking out behind her. On her head flamed a fiery coronet, a brilliant emerald stone ablaze in its midst. Her form was slim, like a young woman's. Her upper body was bare; in the daylight, it gleamed an immaculate, polished gold, displaying to advantage a tiny, perfectly shaped waist and small breasts. Between her golden breasts nestled a necklace of deep green emeralds. A diaphanous pale yellow stole drifted casually around her shoulders and just below her navel, she wore a loosely tied pale yellow skirt, held in place by a saffron girdle. In her right hand was an intricately carved, elongated *vajra*, a mythological weapon of great power;

in her left hand, she held an auburn-tinted mirror. Light shone through her indescribably beautiful form and her golden eyes smiled at Tashi, as she beckoned to him.

The boy looked on, wonderstruck.

It was then that the oft-repeated words took shape in his mind: 'Don't gawk like a sheep-herder, boy! Has the yak butter so completely frozen your brain that you have forgotten me and the mission we are on?'

It was Lama Ozer's stern voice.

Consumed by guilt, Tashi spun around to face the monk. Ozer wore his earthly, dull maroon robes, but looked washed out and ghostly, as did the boy himself, beside the unearthly beauty of the dakini.

Suddenly, the twilight speech blossomed in Tashi's mind again.

'Lama Ozer and the boy, Tashi,' said the dakini, 'you are in the realm of light – fair Shambala. Your mortal souls have been granted an indefinite stay in the blessed land till your work is completed here. Meanwhile, your mortal forms will be preserved at Qiang La. We will now make all haste to reach Mt Meru, the axis mundi that runs from the navel of your Earth to the subtle worlds. It is there, in the holy city of Kalapa, that the sacred court of the Rigden king, the Buddha lords and the Great Secret Queen, Yum Chenmo, awaits you. I will pilot you there.'

In a fluid motion, she held aloft her arms and six companion celestials materialized out of the ether within moments. Tashi looked on, mesmerized. These were undoubtedly lesser sprites in service to the golden-hued dakini. All six had dark hair held in place by simple bands of gold and wore identical sky-blue shaded skirts with snow-white girdles. Their bodies were translucent, undistinguishable from the sky; Tashi could just about make them out by the faint light that played on them.

Suddenly, Lama Ozer stepped forward and bowed before the golden-hued dakini.

'Lady of great mysteries,' he said solemnly, 'bearer of the magic mirror, wielder of the mighty *vajra*, messenger of the great mother, I bow to you.'

The dakini floated in the air, unmoving, as she inclined her head slightly, gesturing at the monk to continue.

'Lady,' Ozer went on, 'I beg your forgiveness, for the era of degradation in which I have had to spend my life has left me sadly unenlightened. Fortunate as I am to have beheld a true dakini, protector of the sacred teaching, I am ashamed to confess that I am ignorant of your name, lineage and history.'

The dakini smiled. 'Despair not, venerable one,' she consoled him. 'Such knowledge has not been sanctioned for the denizens of the Fourth Age. However, an exception has been made for you, Lama, and for the one that accompanies you. I am Dakini Yeshe Nam Lha, daughter of the Goddess Tara and belonging to the Lha lineage of the higher gods of light. I am a wielder of high wisdom and a protector of the sacred doctrine. I am in service from time immemorial to the primordial queen, the great mother, Yum Chenmo.'

Lama Ozer bowed, yet again. 'I am honoured and overjoyed, Dakini, to meet a daughter of the Goddess Tara. You are undoubtedly a goddess in your own right. '

The dakini now introduced her entourage. 'These are the Dpa-Mo, female warrior sprites of the Werma lineage,' she said. 'They are sworn into my service and will serve as your escort for this journey. Now, venerable one, you must make ready to travel, for we must hasten to the city of Kalapa. You are awaited.'

Swiftly, the Dpa-Mo arranged themselves in arrow formation, veiling their faces in a single synchronized movement in softly glowing amber light. They manoeuvred Lama Ozer and Tashi into the centre of their formation and, like a bolt of lightning, hurtled across the skies. Tashi surrendered to the only sensations he could feel – roaring winds, brilliant light and vast waves of emptiness. For miles, there was nothing but tranquil blue water. Tashi found himself being lulled to sleep by the soft rays of the sun. As his form drifted, one of the sprites created a net of luminosity, laying out his astral body on it. Contemplating the boy's form, Lama Ozer could not help smiling.

IV

This world seemed to exist outside of time, somehow eluding its all-pervasive presence. Lama Ozer felt as though he were coming apart, the core of his being disintegrating in this limitless dimension. He shut his eyes, capturing the elusive subtlety of this realm, where he felt like a husk afloat in the breeze. He smiled as he noticed that time was not the only concept that had fled; there was no thought either, he felt incredibly rooted in the endless moment.

On a roller coaster of bliss, Ozer felt Shambala stretching away to eternity. Suddenly, the oceanic world opened up to reveal an incredible land-mass, glimmering with the molten shades of a pink-hued world, an eight-petalled lotus that seemed to kiss the heavens. In tandem, four continents, shaped like dusk-hued lotus petals reclined on the waters and, in perfect synchrony, another four petal-shaped continents rose lightly into the skies, bearing a steeply inclined mountainous land mass. From their unifying midst, the navel of the world, rose the axis mundi – all-sovereign Mt Meru, symbol of power from time immemorial, a power that had remained forgotten in the Fourth Age of the universe, the Kalyug. Rising to immeasurable snowy heights, Meru disappeared from view.

Lama Ozer sighed, then plunged into the waters and prostrated himself. The host of sprites arrested their flight in midair as they waited for the lama to complete his prostrations.

'Arise,' said Dakini Yeshe Nam Lha. 'Learned one, blessed are you, indeed, for having beheld today immortal Meru. However, venerable one, we must make haste. The celestial city of Kalapa is still many leagues away and you are awaited.'

The host rose effortlessly into the skies and travelled with speed.

A rested Tashi awoke as the sprites neared the land mass. They seemed to be hurtling from the skies towards this land. The speed at which they travelled made him dizzy. As they neared land, a strikingly beautiful landscape came into view. In the shadow of Mt Meru, a vast city stretched out – undoubtedly, Kalapa. The terrain to its north was hilly and thickly wooded; just leagues away glimmered Mt Meru, wearing a crown of fresh snow and flanked by a glowing range of crystalline peaks that fanned out in a wide arc. Towards the south, on undulating ground, were lustrous groves of sandalwood trees; beyond, as far as the eye could see, lay open fields. A beautiful white-water lake spread all the way to the east of the city, surrounded by cultivated fields and small villages. To the west, the country seemed speckled with smaller lakes and fields abundant with wild flowers. At its peripheries lay a dense, mist-shrouded forest. Tashi discerned the location of the villages from the wood smoke drifting up from various settlements.

The sprites slowly started circling the city in a wide arc as they began their descent. As they lost altitude, Tashi curiously looked about him; they were heading directly for Kalapa and he could clearly see the great walls of the city coming closer and closer as they approached, shimmering with an unreal glow in the afternoon light. He had never seen anything like this in his young life.

The young sprite flying nearest Tashi smiled at him. 'You are surprised, mortal. Before you stands the immortal, celestial city of Kalapa, headquarters of the Rigden kings of Shambala, containing the sacred-heart presence of the Great Secret Dakini Queen, Yum Chenmo, mother of all creation, the highest and most secret dakini.' The sprite added, 'The shining outer wall that surrounds the sacred city protects it from unwanted denizens from different astral and gross worlds. Unbreachable, it was created through powerful magic in the days when the Rigden kings battled with the Asur, elemental sorcerous demons of great power. Within lies the sacred city. Soon, mortal, you will behold it.'

Tashi gazed below him and saw a fragrant grove of sandalwood trees, their foliage shining with a rare lustre. It was bound on all sides by gently rising fields. Flowing through the grove was a small rivulet.

'Can you tell me something about these demons that posed such a threat to Shambala in the past?' he asked the sprite.

Sighing, she replied, 'We have a long history of strife with the demons. Since the beginning of time, they have been trying to capture Shambala and, at least three times, they almost destroyed it. This strife is not merely a thing of the past; the war continues to rage, though for the past century, we have managed a truce of sorts. But they are always sending spies to infiltrate Shambala and we have to stay alert. There are eight classes of demons in all, but the worst are the Asur, the royal élite among demon kind, who rule over millions of cold worlds in the far eastern corner of the universe. The higher gods and the Asur have been at war for aeons and the jewelled trophy in this war is the world of Shambala and of course immortal divine Amravati, the abode of the Higher Gods.

'Then there are the lesser categories of demons, who are deployed in the service of the Asur in their war against us. However, they serve both factions; sometimes, they cooperate with us and, sometimes, with the Asur.'

The young sprite took Tashi by the arm and began gently steering him towards land. 'Come on, young mortal, we are almost there,' she urged. 'The dakini, Yeshe Nam Lha, means to land near the sacred grove, as she always does.'

The greater part of the company had already landed. The dakini, Yeshe Nam Lha, stood to one side with Lama Ozer; four other sprites had taken up position around them. In seconds, Tashi felt soft grass scrunch under his feet as he landed. Tashi looked about him, the air was warm and fragrant, trees were softly sighing in the afternoon light, their leaves glittering, he could hear the music of the rivulet that ran in the heart of the grove. It was perfect, flawless; perhaps human life was a dull reflection of this perfection?

Tashi saw Lama Ozer disappear into the grove with the dakini. He made to follow, but the young sprite restrained him.

'No, no, mortal,' she said, 'none can visit that grove unless especially summoned. It is sacred. It is a sign of the regard in which your lama is held that he has been permitted to visit it. The dakini, Yeshe Nam Lha, will pay obeisance to the sacred mandala that lies within before entering the city.'

Tashi looked dismayed. 'But I am not allowed to leave my master alone, good sprite,' he protested. 'I am to follow him everywhere.'

The sprite smiled. 'Not *everywhere*, mortal,' she corrected. 'In this realm, there is no cause for you to worry on his behalf. We will wait here; they will come out soon.'

Meanwhile, the other sprites had spread out around the grove and were almost invisible. Sighing tiredly, Tashi flopped down on the grass, delighting in its feel and texture. Then he looked up at the sprite again. She stood erect and aloof, staring into the distance. She appeared to be rather young, her pale body merging with the environment, her skirt fluttering in the wind as though it were a turbulent piece of sky.

Then she turned to glare at Tashi. 'Were you taught no manners, monk?' she reprimanded him. 'Do you always stare so?'

Tashi stood up, agitated. 'Forgive me, Dakini, but I have never seen anyone who looks quite like you. If it bothers you, I shall not stare.'

The sprite shook her head. 'And where would you see one like me in your world, monk?' she enquired. 'You have not even made a proper study of your scriptures. I am not a dakini. I am of Werma lineage, a female warrior sprite, sworn to the service of the dakini, Yeshe Nam Lha.'

'We are aware of the Werma sprites, lady,' Tashi protested. 'We of the mortal world are not as ignorant as all that.'

The sprite glared at him again. 'Now he calls me a lady! Mortal, if you must call me anything at all, then address me by my name, Byung Mo.'

Tashi smiled nervously. 'As you wish, gracious sprite, Byung Mo.'

Byung shaded her eyes with her hand and looked into the distance. A frown of anxiety passed over her transparent features.

'I see a party of celestials of high lineage, the Lha, coming this way. Sit still, mortal. Try to be inconspicuous. They will not be expecting to see you here and I do not want you to attract their attention.'

Byung signalled to the sprite nearest her and within moments, the sprite was up and flying towards the edges of the grove. She paused silently in the shade of the trees and peered within, then sped towards Byung on light feet. Tashi had to concentrate hard on her movements to catch them, for her build was slighter than Byung's and her form still more intransient; at times as transparent and ephemeral as a snatch of breeze.

She came to a stop before Byung and began, 'The dakini is not finished yet and there is no time to hide the mortal. A seven-member company of the higher gods, the Lha, is making its way towards us. They would have sensed the mortal's presence in the air by now; we will come under scrutiny for sure.'

'Immediately round up the others and ask them to come here!' Byung commanded. 'Hurry!'

As the sprite sped away, Byung drew a circle on the ground around them and chanted a mantra; instantly, a flaming orange shield sprang up around them. The five other Dpa-Mo sprites gathered near them and took up positions of defence; in their hands were long, sharp-tipped rods, from which emanated a bronze luminescence.

The Lha were almost upon them and looked formidable, even from a distance. They were incredibly beautiful to behold. Taller than most humans, their bodies were slender, like that of an athlete's, well muscled and glowing with vitality. Garbed in simple, dark blue flowing robes with matching pants, they wore shining black armour beneath that merged with their forms. Astride black steeds, they were well armed, with a *vajra* in their right hand and a sword strapped to their backs. Their bodies radiated a silver light which enfolded them in its aura. All the Lha, but for their leader, had thick, blue-black hair which hung down limply to their shoulders. Their faces were fair, with sharp features emphasized by a hooked nose, and their eyes were deep black, glittering like obsidian gems against the pallor of their skin. On their forehead was the mark of the sun, tattooed in fiery gold; underneath it was a single golden line.

The leader of the Lha company stood out in contrast; Tashi's eyes were riveted on him. He was but a youth; yet he had silken silver hair that fell to his waist. His eyes were the colour of the darkest night and on his head he wore a crystal helm. He was dressed in a mantle of the most pristine white and beneath it, his body was sheathed in crystal armour, ablaze in the light. He stood a head taller than the rest of his company and sat astride a stunning white stallion. On his forehead blazed the very glory of the sun and in his hands, he held a golden *vajra*.

Byung Mo moaned under her breath, 'Mortal, this has to be our bad day. The dakini is not here and the fiery one is almost upon us. Do not stare like a fool, mortal. Ah, but you don't know who he is, do you?'

Tashi looked at Byung. 'But he is glorious, Byung!' he declared. 'Who is he?'

Byung now moaned aloud, 'You are so ignorant, mortal! That is none other than Prince A-KarO, the heir-apparent of the high gods and I have no power in his presence. I have no authority to go against his word. Yet if I obey him, I will be disobeying my liege, the dakini, Yeshe Nam Lha.

If only she would come now! Otherwise, I will fail to keep my word, one way or the other.'

Tashi looked around him in amazement, rubbing his eyes to make sure he was not dreaming. Only then did he become aware, yet again, of his dim astral form.

There was a dream-like quality to their movements as the Lha company rode up to them. The Dpa-Mo sprites stood disheartened, their heads hanging, their hands by their sides. The Lha surrounded them and ringed them in, walking their horses in a circle around them. A-KarO dismounted in one fluid motion, tossing aside the reins of his horse. His silver hair blew in the wind and a faint smile played on his lips as he approached Byung Mo.

In ringing tones, he addressed her. 'What is this I see?' his voice boomed, 'an unworthy mortal in Shambala, one who brings the taint of his impure "mind" to the sacred land. On the air is the stain of yet another, but this other is a mantric adept. Hmm … what is this mystery?' A-KarO stepped forward, smiling nonchalantly. 'And what is more, a band of the Dpa-Mo encircle and protect the mortal. They have even raised the shield of fire against me! Aha! I address you, those responsible for bringing the taint of mortality here, just leagues from the sacred city and in the environs of the sacred mandala! Answer me!'

Byung stepped out of the golden circle, causing the shield of orange flames to vanish with a gesture of her hand. 'High Lord, heir to the throne of the celestial Lha,' she began, 'I beg forgiveness for raising the shield in your presence. I am Byung Mo and these are my companions in service to the dakini, Yeshe Nam Lha. The dakini assigned us the duty of bringing two mortals from Qiang to Kalapa. Such was the will of the High Council. The mortals are the young monk, Tashi Thendup, and his senior lama, Nyima Ozer, who hail from the Demazong Monastery in Sikkim. The dakini and the lama have entered the sacred grove to pay their respects to the sacred mandala. On their return, we are to escort them into Kalapa.'

The High Prince A-KarO listened to Byung in silence, then shading his eyes with his hand, peered in the direction of the grove.

'We will await your dakini, sprite,' he announced, 'and then decide on the next step. Unworthy mortals are not allowed into the sacred lands. The secret of Shambala has been breached and in this dark age, this cannot be allowed. As guardians of the sacred land, we cannot permit this.'

A-KarO signalled for the Lha to dismount and as their feet touched the soil, their horses rode off and repositioned themselves to the left of the grove, a short distance away from the sprites.

Byung snapped her fingers, indicating that the sprites should return to their positions. Then she flopped down on the grass and sighed softly, letting the tension slowly drain out of her body.

'Oh! That was close, mortal!' she said. 'The fiery one took pity on us and understood my conflict of duties. However, the dakini will have a hard time explaining herself. The Lha are celestial gods of light. They are creators of the cosmos, warriors par excellence and the guardians of the sacred lands. They do not cede ground so easily. In the three worlds, there are none to best a Lha.'

V

Evening was softly stealing over the sandalwood grove and the fragrant plains, when the dakini, Yeshe Nam Lha, and the lama emerged. Yeshe took in the scene in a glance, and flew towards the Lha, the Dpa-Mo sprites following her. Tashi and Lama Ozer were left standing by as the two parties met. Neither the boy nor the lama had seen them move; yet the dakini, Yeshe, now stood right in front of A-KarO. Nor could the two mortals hear a single word as the two groups stood in confrontation. They seemed to be communicating through direct thought transmission.

Lama Ozer sighed deeply. 'Boy,' he said, 'now we have seen everything. Even I did not ever imagine that I would get to see the celestial Lha here.'

'But Lama,' Tashi reminded him, 'we on Earth are barely aware of the Lha! The sprite told me that the silver-haired one, A-KarO, is the crown prince of the Lha.'

Lama Ozer frowned in disapproval. 'Do not compare yourself with everybody, boy!' he admonished Tashi. 'Some enlightened lamas are well aware of the Lha and the mysteries they guard. In almost every culture on Earth, there is a mention of the celestial beings, though the names and the legends associated with them differ from one culture to another, but the diligent searcher knows that the crux is the same.'

Tashi stared at the band of immortals who seemed to have frozen into immobility. In an undertone, he said, 'Lama, I am ashamed of how little I know. I wish I had applied myself to my texts with greater perseverance.'

Lama Ozer smiled. 'Boy, do not berate yourself,' he told him in a gentler voice. 'You were doing fine, even though your progress was a trifle slow. I would have prepared you better, had I known what the future held in store for you.'

'But how do they understand each other, Lama?' Tashi asked, intrigued, watching the two groups engaged in dialogue. 'No words are audible and yet they seem to be communicating.'

'Boy, they are conversing in Namig, the tongue of heavenly beings that is beyond our comprehension,' Ozer replied.

Suddenly, Yeshe wheeled around, signalling for her sprites to be prepared to move. Byung raced up to Tashi and the lama on light feet.

'Gracious Lama and young Tashi,' she said, 'we are preparing to enter the city. Please ready yourselves.' Then she addressed Ozer alone. 'Lama, the dakini bids you both to ride with the Lha,' she told him. 'Prince A-KarO has conjured up winged chargers for the two of you and it is his desire that he escort you both into Kalapa. The dakini will be riding by your side and we will follow you.'

Dusk was descending gently over the plains when Tashi saw a tall Lha warrior approaching them with two black steeds. His eyes widened in awe as he beheld the horses – gigantic in size (over 20 hands in height) and coal black, with velvety eyes and emerald green wings on their hooves.

The warrior approached and bowed slightly. 'Here are your steeds, mortals,' he announced. 'This one is Chetak and that is Vajrashakti. Now mount them; the prince wills that you ride by his side.'

Lama Ozer and Tashi bowed three times and were magically transported on to the animals' backs. The warrior took the reins of the two steeds and led them towards the prince's entourage.

'Mortals, do not fear the chargers,' the warrior reassured them. 'Remember that you are not riding them; they are bearing you on their backs. Just sit back; the steeds will do the rest. You are luckier than you know, mortals, for these immortal steeds are celestial wind horses, desired by many, but given only to a very few, even in the astral worlds.'

A-KarO and the dakini were waiting for them. Lama Ozer and Tashi folded their hands before the prince. A-KarO inclined his head in acknowledgement and gave the signal to move.

The great horses sprang forward. Tashi, astride Chetak, felt a tremendously powerful wind rushing past his face. His mount threw back his great head and grinned at him wickedly. In no time, the world was reduced to a blur. Tashi hung on to his saddle with both hands and rejoiced in the motion. He could see Lama Ozer streaking ahead like a bullet astride Vajrashakti. In the distance, the silvery walls of Kalapa glowed in the dark.

'We are almost there,' said a disembodied voice.

Tashi looked around, confused. Had someone addressed him?

Again, the voice announced, 'We are there,' and Chetak came to a standstill.

Tashi looked around, bewildered.

The great steed threw back his head and laughed. 'Ha, ha, ha!' he snorted, 'it is a long time since one of you rode me. Now get off. It is discourteous to linger on my back longer than you need to.'

Had the horse really talked or had he imagined it? Tashi looked down before dismounting; it was a sharp drop to the ground and he could break his leg if he landed awkwardly. He found himself hesitating.

The horse neighed, moving friskily. 'Now, now, don't be foolish,' he went on, 'you won't break your leg. There is no leg to break here – you do realize that, don't you?'

Tashi blushed in embarrassment. Of course! He had left his body in Qiang; only his subtle form had reached this place. He swung his leg off the horse and found himself wafting down.

The rest of the company had already dismounted and was moving towards the great wall of Kalapa. It flowed smoothly without a break. Light reflected off it in waves and no gate was in evidence. The dakini and the prince moved towards the wall together and vanished. Lama Ozer followed them and was soon invisible. The Lha company and the gentle sprites too disappeared. Tashi was left out in the cold. He shivered in apprehension, looking around him in the darkness, but there was no one in sight. Suddenly scared, he moved towards the walls and was amazed; they had no substance but shone with rainbow shaded light. The colours of life seemed to break off them disappearing into the sapphire blue night skies, leaving their resonance shimmering behind, with the cutting-edged beauty of flawless diamonds, sapphires, and emeralds.

Mesmerized, Tashi floated towards the light, his pale arms playing with the luminous waves, as though participating in their immortal dance. As he floated through the brilliance, marvelling at the shield of light that banded Kalapa, his attention was distracted by a glimmer of something. Then, magically, in the midst of the multi-hued shafts of light, a bright yellow lotus of unparalleled beauty took shape. In the heart of the lotus appeared an inverted triangle with a flame in the middle. It was the very essence of being. Drawn to it, Tashi felt his heartless heart miss a beat as he was sucked into the fiery vortex at its core.

VI

Tashi's first thought on crossing over was that there had, indeed, been a gate; and what a gate it was! He seemed to be in a small chamber made of a dim, golden, metallic substance; it was bare of all adornment and light shone through it from all sides. The world outside was a blur; it was somewhat like standing within a prism. Before him stood Lama Ozer and the rest of the company; their steeds were nowhere to be seen.

Lama Ozer had a smile on his face as he observed, 'You took your time, youngling!'

Tashi felt his cheeks flush as he saw an amused look flicker across Prince A-KarO's face. He noticed Byung and the sprites and moved towards them.

'You certainly took your time, mortal,' Byung remarked. 'The light is attractive, is it not? You should consider yourself lucky; none who have not mastered the higher wisdom have ever been allowed to view what you just saw. Now prepare to walk into Kalapa. Look, already the prince is intoning the sacred mantra.'

Tashi looked in A-KarO's direction and felt the vibration of an unknown mantra stir the air as the world dissolved around him.

As the air cleared, he beheld Kalapa; unimaginable, sacred Kalapa. Tashi's eyes misted over and his breath caught as he gazed at the celestial city. He set foot on grass that was the very essence of grass and beheld foliage that was the inspiration for all vegetation on Earth. A small parkland stretched before his eyes, its cherry blossom-laden trees bowing before the surreal purple of the night. An ethereal sickle moon glowed in the heavens. Ahead were structures like none he had ever seen; in sheer geometric shapes and crowned by strange spires, they were the colour of moonlight. Clearly discernible though they were, they did not stand out against the night sky, but melded into its purple ether and the soft glow of heavenly bodies – a hint, as it were, of a perfect daydream. Before Tashi stretched a never-ending thoroughfare, like a slick river of coal black with bright green-glow lights.

Yet nothing he had witnessed before could prepare him for the vehicles he saw on the roads criss-crossing the city: mythic silver and golden chariots, drawn by sleek, lithe trios of identical unicorns bearing unusual signs. Here and there an occasional winged horse, with its master astride its back. The skies too were teeming with life; millions of airborne beings and diamond-shaped, mauve-hued crafts that moved at unimaginable speed across the skies.

Suddenly coming back to himself, Tashi turned to look at the rest of the group. Lama Ozer stood engrossed in a discussion with the dakini. The Lha were lined up behind their prince, while the sprites were clustered in a small band to their right. Only Byung stood silently by Tashi's side, looking at him with some amusement in her eyes.

'Is this really a place, Byung, or am I dreaming?' he asked. 'You are part of my dream, aren't you?'

Byung smiled and tossed back her dark hair. 'Ah, mortal, it is always so!' she replied. 'The first experience of Kalapa for a denizen from another plane defies all description. You do realize one thing, mortal, don't you? That Kalapa can't be seen; it can only be sensed, not analysed or explained. The high astral world of heavenly Shambala can only be experienced; it is known to one who is blessed to know. Your dilemma arises from the fact that you are trying to "see" it. Just feel it, mortal. Undeserving as you are, even *you* cannot miss it.'

Tashi looked perplexed. 'But Byung,' he countered, 'I do see it. There is colour here and a city there, flowers and foliage and buildings like none I have ever seen. There are mythical beings too. I see it all, Byung, but what am I missing?'

A light, tinkling laugh escaped the sprite's lips. 'Foolish mortal,' she said, 'who "sees" Kalapa? Where are your eyes, mortal? Your physical body, devoid of heartbeats, lies in Qiang. What are you, son of man? A clod? Look at yourself the way I see you, clothed in your dark astral form. Impure spirit creature, with which "eye" do you see Kalapa? To see it, you need the third eye. Let me say it again, child of man: it has to be perceived, not seen.'

Tashi looked at Byung. 'Gentle sprite, I am trying to understand you,' he said, 'but I see the most wondrous colours here. I smell the celestial fragrance of beauteous blossoms. I see the city yonder, incomparable in its splendour. How can you say it can't be seen?'

The sprite laughed. 'Spirit child, stop seeing,' she exhorted him. 'Then you shall know the truth of Kalapa.'

Baffled, Tashi looked about him; he felt like a fool. Byung doubled over with laughter and the other sprites were staring at him, their expressions mischievous.

Suddenly, Byung turned serious. 'Tashi, I think it is time to move,' she told him. 'The High Council has sent a lama to receive you. Look there.'

Tashi followed her gaze. A tall monk had appeared, dressed simply in a deep yellow robe. Yet he looked insubstantial, like a figure out of a dream. Once again, words formed in Tashi's mind and he thrilled to the twilight speech, the unique lingua franca of the universe.

'Son of man, fortunate are you to enter the nameless realm, fortunate beyond compare,' were the words Tashi read in his mind, 'and awaited is your master, the venerable one, Lama Nyima Ozer. The Great Secret Queen herself, Yum Chenmo, queen of the dakinis, lady of light, mother of the Buddhas, the purest essence of the universe, the hand that holds, the power that is, the secret one, awaits the venerable one and his follower.'

The monk stopped short, holding his hand out in welcome. From the air, he pulled out *khadas*, the sacred raiment of welcome, placing one around Lama Ozer's neck and the other around Tashi's.

The lama continued in ringing tones, 'Welcome, venerable one, the reigning Rigden king, Rigden Aniruddha Magakpa, scion of the Maitreya lineage, upholder of the cosmic dharma, bearer of the sacred Kalachakra tantra, sovereign of the three worlds, awaits you. The Buddha Lords of the five sacred families also await you. The august assembly of celestial beings and sages awaits you. Wondrous will be the meeting of minds, bringing prophecy to fulfilment, ringing in another age. Called are you today by vows ancient, bound are you by rites primeval to the mission that unfolds. Come, refresh, feel the resonance of reality!'

With his head bowed low and palms held together in salutation, Lama Ozer stepped forward, clearly overwhelmed by the lama's welcome. The lama smiled graciously at Ozer and enfolded him in a deep embrace.

Then he turned to Prince A-KarO. 'Mighty Being, lord of light, heir-apparent of the celestial Lha, I welcome you on behalf of the secret one and the Rigden king,' he declared. 'The sovereign himself awaits you in his private audience chamber. Please travel to the palace, where your usual quarters have been prepared for you.'

A-KarO inclined his head and, with the flick of his wrist, conjured up glistening sable-hued wind horses. Then he bowed gracefully before the lama.

'Gracious one,' he said, 'the Rigden's desire is mine to fulfil. I depart with my retinue, leaving these mortals in your care.' Then he turned and bowed mockingly before Dakini, Yeshe Nam Lha. 'Undoubtedly, beauteous one, we will meet again and discuss this mystery at length,' he said, addressing her. 'I leave you to your mortal concerns.' Finally, he faced Ozer and Tashi. 'Perhaps we will meet again – soon,' he told them. 'To both of you, I offer a small gift. To you, venerable Lama, I present this ancient text of higher wisdom teachings and tantras; it may be of use in the days ahead.'

With that, he plucked from the air a slim papyrus manual which he handed to Lama Ozer, who fell to his knees in gratitude as he received it.

'And to you, boy, I present Chetak, a wisdom horse blessed by my father,' said the prince. 'May he aid you in your journeys and bring you to the singular unity.'

Then the prince signalled to his retinue. Astride on their swift steeds, they soon disappeared from view.

Tashi sighed deeply as he saw A-KarO and the band of Lha melt into the city. Yeshe, the dakini, and the unknown lama were in conversation. Lama Ozer stood to one side, lost in thought. Magically, a sleek golden chariot had appeared, drawn by three identical unicorns limned by an ethereal glow. They stopped right in front of the party. In minutes, they were aboard and the world was reduced to a whirl of motion.

Yeshe turned to Ozer and remarked, 'We are making for the guest apartments to the north of the city. They have been prepared for your comfort and there you can rest and revitalize yourselves till you are summoned. In terms of Earth time, you have one night's rest ahead of you before you are called to the Council tomorrow.'

'You are very gracious, Dakini,' Ozer murmured.

Tashi stared out of the chariot, fascinated by the rather surreal sight of the city rushing by. Beautiful buildings appeared here and there in open parkland which seemed to flow on endlessly. Groves of crimson trees glowed in the night; sparkling water bodies shimmered in the moonlight; pale, glassy structures kissed the heavens and gleaming, ornate chariots sped down the thoroughfare. The boy could only gaze at everything around him in wonder. In the distance, he saw a silver-hued wind horse racing across the road and then galloping up into the heavens. On his back sat a golden youth with red cheeks and a mass of bright gold hair. Tashi shook himself. Where was Chetak, he wondered? Even as the thought crossed his mind, Chetak materialized before him and began trotting beside the chariot, a decidedly naughty look in his eyes.

Suddenly, the chariot took a turn and entered a narrow, cobbled lane flanked on both sides by high walls. Ahead of them loomed a crystal gate, bathed in a phantom glow. As they neared it, it swung open of its own accord. Beyond it stretched grassy meadows, dotted by silver-barked trees with fluorescent lime-green leaves that shone in the night. A rising wind gently caressed Tashi's face as he looked around him in wonder. A gentle turn in the lane brought a small, circular lake into view. Its silvery waters lapped against the grassy shore. In its eastern corner, a tiny cottage stood out against the night sky. As they neared it, the scent of jasmine greeted them. The cottage was a small, compact structure, with white walls and a sloping roof. Its façade, made of a translucent material like glazed glass, looked out over the lake.

The chariot came to a stop near the cottage and, in moments, the party had alighted. Despite the absence of his physical body, Tashi felt strangely tired. The dakini, Yeshe, was in conversation with Lama Ozer and the sprites stood together nearby. Tashi looked around and saw Chetak grazing peacefully by the lake. Their eyes met and the horse smiled at him benignly, flicking his tail gently in the dark.

Suddenly, Yeshe beckoned to Tashi.

'Young monk,' she said, as he drew near, 'as I have informed your lama, so will I tell you. We take your leave now. In the morning, I shall send an escort for taking you to the palace. In the cottage yonder, arrangements have been made for your stay tonight. Do not wander out of the lodge at night and under no condition should you leave the compound of the Wish-Fulfilling Gardens, where you are right now. I am leaving my young captain, Byung Mo, and two attendant sprites to watch over you. Rest well, sleep contented and let the holy energy of Shambala wash over you.'

Tashi and Lama Ozer bowed low as the dakini took leave of them. Then they entered the cottage.

Inside was a vast room, comfortably furnished. It contained two simple cots and armchairs; a thick white rug lay on the floor. A window on the eastern side opened out into the starry night sky. Fruits, a flagon of golden liquid, rice and a steaming broth were laid out.

Byung broke the silence. 'Listen, mortals, eat well and let your soul rest. What you consume here is not a repast for the body, but for the soul. Rest, and in the morning, the holy assembly will be awaiting you.'

With that, Byung stepped out through the door and joined the sprites outside.

Lama Ozer seated himself on the chair and shut his eyes as Tashi handed him a tumbler filled with the golden brew. The monk's eyes were already drooping with fatigue. Tashi helped him eat a little, then led him to the cot and made him lie down.

The silence of the night closed in on him at last, embracing him with its magical quality. Tashi felt strangely restless and wandered up to the third window. The night sky, ablaze with a million stars, lay open to him; in the distance, a beacon of light greeted him. It was the same face, the same wafting raven tresses – the ivory-faced damsel with the mocking eyes. Lotus in palm, a serpent wound around her wrist, a bow strung in her right hand, she smiled at Tashi.

The twilight speech formed in his mind. 'Welcome, fledgling,' it began, 'does Shambala please you? Favoured are you, son of mortal man! Come now, the heavens open to you. Feel the pulse of the universe, feel me ... do you not know me? Innocent, how many are sacrificed in the games of destiny? How many die not knowing? Till tomorrow.'

Like a mighty huntress, she sped through the heavens, bow in hand, lady of the night, the unknown one... Tashi felt as if his soul were being returned to him after a tigress had mauled it.

Chapter 5

IN THE HEART OF SHAMBALA

I

The grey light of dawn was filtering into the room, when Tashi felt light hands on his shoulders gently shaking him awake. Blearily, he opened his eyes. Before him stood Lama Ozer, an expression of displeasure on his face.

'Boy, it is time,' the monk announced impatiently. 'Get dressed fast. Soon, our carriage will arrive to convey us to the palace.'

Embarrassed, Tashi jumped out of bed, hoping that the sprites had not seen him in this state. 'Lama, my apologies,' he murmured, 'I should have risen before you did.'

By then, Ozer had retreated to his chair by the window and was reading the manuscript gifted to him by Prince A-KarO. Tashi rushed about completing his ablutions, discovering that in this realm, there was precious little to be done by way of cleaning himself. The astral form, unlike the physical body, did not require the kind of cleansing he was familiar with; by willing himself to be clean, he became clean. When he willed warm water to flow down his body, he felt it run down in rivulets, energizing him in a way earthly water could not.

Tashi imagined he was garbed in a beautiful dark blue habit with a bright orange girdle and an orange inner shirt, then added a pair of sturdy walking shoes and something resembling his earthly backpack. To his amazement, he saw that he was clad in the selfsame habit. Its fabric had the sheen of the purest, starched cotton and his boots felt as soft and comfortable as a well-worn pair. He was busy admiring his clothes when

Lama Ozer looked up from the manuscript. 'What is this, boy? Since when has a monk started wearing a royal blue habit of the finest cotton? Boy, this is no time for finery.'

At that very moment, Byung entered. 'Lama, the chariot is here, as is your escort,' she announced. 'It is time to depart for the palace.'

'We are ready, Captain,' Ozer responded in clipped tones, gesturing to Tashi to follow him.

Lime-green trees glittered, jewel-like, in the distance against the backdrop of the emerald velvet of the parkland that stretched away as far as the eye could see. At its heart, the tiny circular lake sparkled like an enormous diamond, the gentle breeze playing with its shining waves. Tashi took in the fresh, heady air.

'Ah, Tashi, I see you have dressed up for the palace,' Byung observed in mocking tones.

Tashi found himself tongue-tied and turned a bright red.

'A dark blue,' the sprite went on. 'Now when did a monk ever wear that hue?'

Tashi bowed his head. 'I got a bit carried away, gentle sprite,' he admitted, 'and I don't know what to do now. The lama is angry with me.'

Byung's tinkling laugh floated in the air. 'You have to be careful here, boy, careful with what you think. Next, you'll be growing horns if you don't watch out.'

A miserable Tashi turned at the familiar clicking sound of hooves approaching. It was Chetak. The horse had a gentle look on his face.

'Let the sprites say what they will, Tashi,' the horse reassured him. 'You look fine today, just right for an audience at the palace. I will be carrying you there now.'

'But I have to accompany the lama,' Tashi reminded him.

'We will both accompany the lama,' neighed Chetak. 'I will keep pace with the chariot. Come now, mount me.'

In moments, Tashi was sitting astride the steed and waiting patiently for Lama Ozer to join them. Chetak moved forward in silence, till he was next to the chariot and had positioned himself on its right.

Climbing aboard the chariot, Lama Ozer cast a glance at Tashi that bristled with disapproval. 'What foolishness is this now, boy?' he snapped. 'Get off this moment and come here.'

'Lama,' began Tashi in hesitant tones, when Chetak intervened with an assertive neigh.

'Lama,' said the steed, 'as you well know, I have been tasked by Prince A-KarO to carry the boy on his journeys. I am aware that he is accompanying you and will ride alongside your chariot as you are driven to the palace. Let him be, Lama. Whether he is seated in the chariot beside you or on my back is irrelevant. He will always be by your side.'

Lama Ozer inclined his head in agreement and the party took off.

II

In the day the city was even more surreal. Flowing parkland with distinctive, silver-barked trees that bore crimson leaves and were dotted with snow-white blossoms, covered most of the city. The streets were uniform, their layout orderly. In the residential section that they seemed to be traversing, the modest-sized homes had a cosy, wholesome air about them; all were painted a pale lemon yellow, had thatched roofs and looked on to small, identical gardens. Floating in the heart of a lake to their right was a vision of transparent loveliness – a glass edifice shaped like a pyramid. A little farther down the road stood a white marble structure, spherical in shape, with huge crystal windows that shone brilliantly in the daylight. Stranger still were others made of unknown materials. It was apparent to Tashi that important activities were carried out within these buildings, but he could merely wonder at their nature.

As they approached the heart of the city, a shining river following a circular course came into view; on its far bank, rich green lawns stretched away and tendrils of mist curled up from the water, casting a fine veil around the park. Tashi could vaguely discern the shapes of tall, oak-like trees.

'There, Tashi! We are in the centre now and will be crossing the Bridge of Innocence,' Chetak announced.

'Then we must be near the palace!' Tashi said excitedly.

'Forever talking in terms of near or far, here or there, past or future,' Chetak neighed. 'Mortal, the flow of time ever is; the subtle ground of all being ever is; this purity cannot be explained, this intrinsic oneness of being and its divine flow, ever is. It cannot be explained it can merely be known – a perception gifted to the knower. Shambala is timeless. Do not pollute its pure air with concepts nurtured by your earthly mind.'

Tashi hung his head in embarrassment; this was his second reprimand of the morning.

The soft tinkling of a dozen bells diverted Tashi's attention. As he looked up, a delicately filigreed bridge, bathed in an opalescent glow, came into view. It spanned the waters of the narrow river and tiny silver bells hung it. An awestruck Tashi realized that the bridge was made of moonstone.

'Now, boy, you are on the Bridge of Innocence,' Chetak announced. 'Look at it carefully. It will revive in you the wonder of the newborn as he beholds the world.'

Tendrils of mist were rising from the park and floating onto the bridge, vanishing with a moist touch as they made contact with the skin.

Ahead of them, the mist lifted, here and there, to reveal jade-green lawns. In moments, Chetak had trotted across to the greenway. The chariot followed.

Through the thick veils of mist, Tashi made out a forest of immensely tall trees that seemed to stretch endlessly. A well-maintained path ran from the park into the forest.

'There boy, lies the Forest of Everness, where bloom the hue-less Flowers of Eternity and in its heart, you will see, boy, what lies in the heart of the forest. But, mark well, it is seen only by the deserving,' said Chetak.

In no time they were engulfed by thick, unknown trees, Tashi had never seen their kind. They looked like huge oaks but weren't, they were tall, with glistening light green leaves and with a strange flower that had no colour. It simply glowed on the trees like a firefly.

A strange, deep peace descended on Tashi as they went into the forest, his heart sang as the road twisted snake-like, fountains of joy gushed forth from within, simply out of being here. Tashi folded his palms and hung his head in reverence; he knew he had entered a sacred space. His head felt light, his palms ablaze, currents of energy flowed through his body, thoughts died, visions burst asunder and then descended the peace of the sacred, overwhelming, silent, empty, just like that, known to the knower, the chalice drunk by the seeker. Something died within Tashi, as another dimension was born.

Chetak tossed his head back and neighed, 'Boy, it has happened; you have passed, surrendered. None can enter and survive the Forest of Everness without surrendering to the will of the Eternal Being. However, do not imagine that you are liberated; you have merely gone through and survived the first level of purification. You have surrendered. That is a cosmic step in your evolution. Had you not taken it, your astral self would have been evicted from here and taken rebirth on Earth.'

Tashi smiled and then, just as suddenly, frowned. 'But my lama?' he enquired anxiously, casting a hasty backward glance at the chariot following them.

Lama Ozer's face was ablaze with a quiet joy as he clapped his hands and beamed his approval to Tashi.

'Silly boy!' neighed Chetak. 'Your lama is an adept, with many lifetimes of austerity behind him. Worry not for him. It is not for nothing that the prince, in his magnanimity, gifted me to you. Do you know what I am, boy?'

'What?' Tashi asked, his bewilderment apparent.

'Ha, ha, ha! We'll let you figure that one out!' Chetak neighed.

Through a break in the trees, Tashi glimpsed a vast water body gleaming in the sunlight. And then they took yet another turn that brought the lake closer into view. On the scintillating brilliance of its surface, blue lotuses bloomed.

Chetak let out a ringing laugh. 'What do you think that is, boy?' he asked.

'A wondrously bright lake with lovely lotuses,' Tashi answered.

Chetak threw his head back again in mirth. 'Look sharp, boy,' he said, 'not everything is what it appears to be, especially not here.'

Tashi looked about him curiously. The vast expanse of forest came right up to the shores of the shining waters. Then it happened. First, a few droplets of light rain seemed to fall on his face. Only, these were bright blue, filled with light, like tiny blue diamonds that clung to his body. Tashi shook them off and watched them fall harmlessly to the forest floor, where they were absorbed. One last droplet, however, shone on the back of his hand. Curious, he touched it and realized that it was made of light, not liquid.

'Yes, boy,' said Chetak, 'that droplet is pure energy, which you understand as light. That is your first discovery. Now look carefully at what you called the lake.'

The steed trotted right up to the shining expanse of water and Tashi gazed deep into it. Then he realized what it was.

'So you see it now, boy,' Chetak observed. 'That is a lake of light, of pure *shakti*, the primeval ether of the universe, the substratum. This is the heart of Shambala; would you dare to tread within?'

Astounded, Tashi gazed at the lake, which seemed to be vibrating with energy. He could sense an intense build-up of heat energy within it.

'But Chetak, what, then, are those blue lotus-like shapes?' he asked.

'Those, boy, are intense channels of energy and more; their mystery cannot be fathomed.'

The chariot too had stopped by the shores of the lake and Lama Ozer and the rest of the group had already dismounted. Tashi watched in amazement as they stepped into the light-filled lake and were consumed by it.

As he made to dismount and follow them, Chetak stopped him. 'No, boy, do not even think of it,' he cautioned. 'You cannot go in there without me; you would be burnt to cinders. Your astral body is not yet ready to venture into the core of Shambala.'

'But Chetak, I cannot stay here,' Tashi protested. 'I have been tasked to follow my lama, no matter what.'

'Boy, I shall carry you in,' the horse promised, 'but remember, while we are in there, you must stay with me.'

'But Chetak, how can I enter the palace of the Rigden kings and present myself before the sacred court while mounted on your back?' Tashi asked worriedly. 'That would be sacrilege.'

'Worry not, youngling,' Chetak reassured him. 'Get off now, fast!'

Tashi floated down and gently came to rest on the grass growing by the lake. Then he beheld Chetak's transformation. Before his very eyes, the steed's fine, dark frame began to disappear, only to be replaced by an intense flame. Blinding white light radiated from Chetak and within moments, his form had contracted into a small ball of light. Tashi looked on, mesmerized.

'This is how we will travel now, boy,' Chetak told him. 'For only those who have unveiled the mystery of melting their gross form into a body of flame can venture into the lake.'

'But Chetak, how, then, will I . . .' Tashi began.

'At least, let me finish, boy,' Chetak interrupted. 'You will have to hold out your hand, palm up, and hold me. Then you must take my essence to your heart and let it settle there. Hurry now!'

Tashi held out his hand and the ball of light floated into it. Gently cradling it, the boy carried it to his heart centre. Then the oddest sensation took hold of him. For a moment, he experienced excruciating pain; his astral body shook with it. Then the ball of light disappeared into his body, leaving it with an unusual feeling of lightness. In moments, a sharp tingling had spread over his form, as if ants were crawling over it. With a shock, he saw himself being transformed. Joy awoke within him and coursed through him in currents. His awareness expanded and the universe opened up before him.

Chetak's disembodied voice reached him now. 'Hurry! Step in,' it commanded.

III

Tashi stepped into the light-filled lake and then stopped short. In front of him eternity stretched. He felt an incredible beauty surrounding him; it was a world beyond description, the boundary beyond which words fail, the reality that cannot be understood but is intuitively felt. The essence of matter condensed around him, intense light forms blazed in the void. Tashi felt himself buffeted on clouds of joy, lost to all, he felt his grip on life as he knew it, disappearing in the face of this emptiness. Lama Ozer and his group were nowhere to be seen, Tashi sighed as he felt himself vanishing into the void.

'Don't drift, Tashi,' Chetak's voice told him. 'Now is not the time for that. Remember why we are here.'

The boy stirred.

'Come on, Tashi,' Chetak urged, 'we have to take the channel that will convey us to the royal palace.'

Tashi shook himself slightly. 'Which channel? Where?'

'Just do as I say, boy,' Chetak told him. 'Will yourself to turn to your right. When you do, you will see an enormous lotus radiating scintillating blue light. The rays will be so intense, they will hurt your senses; yet they will draw and hold your attention the way a magnet does. Just face them, bow deeply and will yourself into the royal palace of the Rigden kings.'

'That sounds easy!' Tashi said jubilantly.

'Nothing here is easy for an untrained mind, boy,' the steed cautioned. 'Be very careful to keep to what I have specified; otherwise, we may end up just anywhere in Shambala and wander around for an eternity.'

Slightly apprehensive now, Tashi turned to his right. Directly in front of him floated an enormous fluorescent blue lotus, emanating beams of azure light, like a brilliant jewel in the heart of the firmament.

'Come on, boy, stop gaping!' Chetak's words resounded like a gong.

Swiftly, Tashi folded his hands and bowed low, willing himself into the palace. A single ray of fluorescent blue light streaked towards him and absorbed him. The sound that rose around him seemed to his ears like that of the ocean in high tide and Tashi felt himself sucked into it. In moments, he became aware of a gentle breeze blowing over the tops of elegantly swaying palms. He had landed on a patio paved with shining slabs of bright turquoise. In the centre stood a transparent crystal fountain from which spouted a spray of azure water. Overhead, a perfect, cloudless sky stretched as far as the eye could see. Creepers bearing bright orange flowers grew over white walls that soared up on all four sides. Tashi felt completely at peace and in tune with his environs.

Seemingly out of nowhere, Chetak's voice reached him. 'Yes, Tashi, you are feeling the harmony of your surroundings, but we have to move on,' he reminded him. 'Right now, you have entered the palace and are standing in the Turquoise Courtyard fronting the reception hall. We have to make for the hall. Please move towards the exit that will take us out of here.'

A bemused Tashi looked around. A single arched exit was built into the wall on his right.

'Tashi,' Chetak continued, 'head for the arched entry there. Beyond it lies the great hall. I expect that is where we will find Lama Ozer and the rest of the party.'

Tashi moved out of the Turquoise Courtyard and crossed into a vast pillared hall which was unlike anything he had ever seen. It had an airy feel and light reflected off it in ripples. The floor was transparent like glass, but obviously made of a far superior material with a brilliant sheen to it. The pillars were of pale, glowing moonstone and the vaulted roof, rising, apparently, with no end in sight, was lost in a mist through which light rays shone, refracting into rainbow shades. Groups of beings, their forms beautiful beyond compare, stood individually or in small clusters around the hall. They blazed with light, as if it were their very essence. In one corner, clad in silver garments, stood a group of violet-hued dakinis, their bodies reflecting subdued violet light, their lustrous purple hair shimmering down to their waists.

'Those are dakinis from the Northern Paradise, boy,' Chetak explained. 'Keep an eye out for your lama and his group.'

Tashi turned a corner and almost bumped into a fiery Heruka and his consort, lost in each other's embrace. Four-armed and impossibly tall, his powerfully built body dressed in saffron robes and rippling with passion, the Heruka had deep blue skin and fiery orange hair. In one hand, he wielded his weapon – a *vajra*. Clad in snowy garments, his silver-haired consort stood passively by his side, a white lotus in one hand, her pale face blazing with light. She smiled right into Tashi's eyes.

Chetak's disembodied voice resounded within Tashi. 'Bow, boy!' it commanded. 'That is none other then the heroic Heruka, Vajrakilaya, with his consort. The lady has already blessed you with her grace.'

Tashi fell to his knees in reverence and when he looked up, the pair had vanished, leaving only a single glowing white lotus for him.

'Boy, you have been bestowed a mighty gift by the goddess, consort to the Heruka!' Chetak exclaimed. 'A white lotus! You are lucky beyond compare!'

As Tashi picked up the flower, it melted into his palm.

Looking up, he saw before him Lama Ozer, with the dakini, Yeshe Nam Lha. Standing by his side and smiling at him were Byung Mo and her group of sprites. Tashi moved towards them.

'There you are, boy! We've been waiting for you a while now,' began a harried-looking Lama Ozer. 'What took you so long?'

'Lama, I came as quickly as I could,' Tashi answered in a flustered voice.

Yeshe inclined her head in understanding. 'It was bound to take the boy more time, gracious one,' she explained gently. 'We must make for the Inner Council chambers now. We must reach before the members of the Transcendental Council arrive. Protocol has to be maintained.'

Lama Ozer straightened up, casting Tashi a glance of deep disapproval from beneath his brows.

Yeshe turned to Byung. 'Lead the way to the Inner Council chambers, Byung,' she commanded.

Byung led the way, cutting across the vast reception hall with speed. And yet the hall seemed to run on interminably. Finally, with a turn to the right, they stepped out of the hall and into bright sunlight. Before them lay a little walled garden with a carpet of jade-green grass that sparkled in the light and a small lily pond in the centre, where deep blue lotuses floated in carefree clusters. Overlooking the scene were filigreed, sunset-yellow balconies. Byung carefully stepped on to a path laid through the garden, making for an arched entrance that led back into the palace. Following her, they entered a cool, dimly lit corridor. Flanked by pale yellow walls and paved with fine white marble, it was decorated at every 10 paces with an urn bearing exotic, multi-coloured blooms. Within moments, they had filed out of the corridor into yet another vast hall.

'We have entered the Hall of Dynamic Space,' announced Byung, as they stepped through.

Tashi's eyes widened in awe at his surroundings. Floors of the deepest ocean blue stretched away, glowing with unimaginable lustre. The pillars were of sapphires and amethysts. Sunbeams, shining down from great heights, refracted into violet and blue light. Both Lama Ozer and the boy stopped in their tracks, carried away by the wonder of the place.

Yeshe smiled benignly at them. 'Yes, mortals,' she said, 'it is always so. A first glimpse of the palace leaves you bereft of thought and speech. However, we must move on.'

They followed Byung as she headed for a black marble staircase that ascended grandly from the middle of the hall. A few denizens moved about, glowing like fireflies. As the group approached the staircase, Tashi saw two female sprites taking up position on either side. Their forms, clad simply in silvery skirts, glowed surreally in the blue light. Their upper bodies were naked, but for the jewels that gleamed on them. Their riotous black hair cascaded down their backs and was held in place by a gold circlet. Inclining their heads to acknowledge the dakini, they gestured for the group to proceed up the stairs.

Yeshe turned to Lama Ozer and said, 'In the Rigden's palace, the sprites form his guard of honour, although the royal guard comprises other beings as well.'

'Indeed, dakini, the truth of the Rigden's palace defies every expectation,' Ozer smiled.

Byung led them solemnly up the grand staircase. On the first floor, a ringed corridor ran circling the hall that lay below. Directly above, an enormous glass atrium let in the light. Along intervals, arched entrances stood out leading into different chambers. White light shone here as huge windows lined the vast corridor looking out into the many worlds. Interestingly, some of the windows opened into azure skies that stretched endlessly, yet others, into the deep night of dark space and still others, opened into a panorama of verdant greenery – sunset over choppy seas, barren hot worlds with a red sun, or into a stark landscape of rock, cold dark gravel and a pale horizon.

Yeshe smiled. 'Lama, you are the first mortal in many years to behold the "eyes of Shambala",' she said softly. 'Right now, this area is empty. But normally, this space is occupied by some of our most revered astronomers, astrologers and analysts who have dedicated their existence to the study of the worlds and the four directions of space. It is here that work is done on the Doctrine of Great Time and prophecies are made after carefully charting trends apparent in the four corners of manifestation.'

'Dakini, my existence has been blessed and made worthwhile beyond what it deserves by the many sights I have seen here,' Lama Ozer sighed.

Yeshe smiled and indicated to Byung that she should lead on. They turned into a vast, arched entranceway that opened in the middle of the corridor. Beyond lay a small antechamber to which a colossal gold door stood closed.

'That is the door leading into the chambers of the Inner Council,' Yeshe announced. 'Now follow me.'

With those words, she stepped forward. Immediately, the huge door swung open. The space beyond it lay in deep shadow. The dakini and Lama Ozer stepped in. Byung and the sprites fell back, taking up position near the door. Tashi stopped short at the door, looking wistfully at Byung whose face was turned away from him.

'Boy, don't tarry,' Chetak's voice reverberated in his mind, 'walk in fast, lest the door closes in our face.'

IV

As Tashi stepped in, the door swung shut behind him. Ahead, emptiness loomed, an infinite stretch of darkness, unrelieved by starlight or moonshine; there was neither earth nor sky, nor form, nor mist, nor even shadow. It was then that Tashi became aware of the strange luminosity that welled up from the heart of that darkness, like a spring in the middle of sand dunes, until every inch of space was shot through with subtle radiance. He felt his very core come apart as he gazed upon purity itself, the mother essence, the substratum of the universe. Like the radiance that permeated space, Tashi felt himself infused with utter joy, till he was like a bubble in the sky, alight with a subtle happiness. The deepest love filled his being and it was then that he became aware of the love-ecstasy that permeated space, uniting it, forming the incredible harmony.

'Welcome, mortals, to the Inner Council chambers of the Rigden,' said Yeshe. 'This is where truth dwells; feel its resonance.'

The dakini stood suspended in the dark, surrounded by a nimbus of golden light. Lama Ozer stood next to her, giving off a faint radiance.

'I am glad, Lama, that we have reached this place before the assembly and are the first to arrive,' she went on. 'Now please move towards the chamber's southern side and visualize whatever seat you are used to placing yourself on; it will appear.'

The dakini guided them towards the space she had indicated. Then she caused a beautiful white swan to materialize before her and seated herself on its back.

Lama Ozer bowed before her and murmured, 'Dakini, it is not my place to be seated on this hallowed ground. Tashi and I will remain standing, with our hands folded in reverence.'

The dakini inclined her head in agreement and settled back into silence.

Tashi felt Chetak stir within him. 'Well, this could take a while, you know,' said the horse. 'I am glad the lama chose to stand, though, personally, I'm never comfortable sitting.'

'When will the gathering turn up?' Tashi asked him.

'That depends, Tashi. There is no time here, you know. Look, the dakini has already drifted into silence.'

'But Chetak, at least tell me who all will come? Will I get to see the Rigden?' the boy persisted.

'I should think so, boy. Yes, you will. As for the rest, the core Inner Council members who govern the four directions of space hold sway over the three worlds and the six realms. They are twelve in number. And yes, you will see them today. Be alert.'

Looking about him curiously, Tashi sensed a change in the ether, a kind of tremulous movement near the door. Then it swung open magically to allow two figures to enter. Tashi started forward as he saw the familiar figure of the Lha prince, A-KarO. Glowing with white light, he was dressed even more austerely today in plain white trousers; his chest was bare and a white stole lay draped on his shoulders; on his brow, a single bright diamond glowed. The prince was in conversation with a tall, rather noble-looking figure standing by his side.

'That, boy, is the crown prince, Narsimha Miyi Senge, heir-apparent to the Rigden's throne,' said Chetak's voice. 'Be sure to bow before him in the approved manner.'

Tashi turned to gaze at the approaching figures with awe. The crown prince had a dark brown complexion and a rather mature, though regal face, with sharp cheekbones, thin, but artistic brows, dark brown eyes, a straight Roman nose and dark brown hair which fell to his waist in a straight shower of strands. His body was well contoured, muscled, yet lithe, and there was a lightness about him as he literally flowed through the ether, his keen gaze taking in both the lama and his acolyte.

As the duo approached, Yeshe Nam Lha, reclining languidly on her swan, stirred and opened her third eye, which glowed eerily in the dark. The two princes bowed slightly to her, as she inclined her head and swung off the swan.

'We see, Dakini, that you have completed your task and delivered the lama and his protégé here,' said Narsimha in deep tones.

The dakini smiled. 'It has been a pleasure, Lord, to escort them here. May I present them to you?' She gestured towards Lama Ozer. 'This is the honoured Lama Ozer, one who has kept his *samaya* and the trust bestowed on him. And that is his young disciple, Tashi Thendup, a flower of innocence.'

The lama and Tashi bowed deeply before the two princes.

'It is a pleasure to meet the two of you; you have been long awaited,' Narsimha declared. 'Over many moons have we studied the prophecies that foretold this moment.'

A-KarO smiled at Tashi. 'So we meet again, youngling,' he said. 'Today, you will see much and very fortunate are you to witness the Council of Twelve together.'

Then the two princes floated away to the eastern side of the space where A-KarO conjured up a simple wooden seat for himself, marked with the motif of a lethal black panther in motion. The crown prince produced a tiger hide and seated himself on it, assuming the lotus posture.

'The crown prince looks formidable, does he not, Chetak?' said an awestruck Tashi.

'That he does, Tashi,' the steed affirmed. 'In time, he will sit on the Lion throne and it is prophesied that he will be a stern upholder of universal law and will spare none but the meritorious. However, there are some who say that his reign will be short-lived, as the road clears for the advent of his successor, Rudra-Chakrin or Maitreya, the ringer messenger of the Golden Age.'

A smiling Tashi said enthusiastically, 'Even we have heard about the great hero to come! At the monastery, Lama Ozer himself had explained to me the key prophecy about him. Is he already born? Chetak, will I see him here today?'

'Easy, easy, Tashi! What do you take me for – a walking information directory? And what a dumb question! The great one is yet to be born; he rests in the perfect Buddha realm.'

Tashi looked around him. Seated on her swan again, the dakini was lost in silence; Lama Ozer stood quietly by her side. On the other side, the two princes seemed to be engaged in a discussion.

'Chetak, I have seen two of the members. When will the rest arrive?' Tashi asked.

'Tashi! Did nobody teach you patience?' Chetak said sternly. 'What are the monasteries coming to these days, nurturing such impatient young monks? Learn to wait in silence. Just be. And what gave you the idea that you have seen two of the members?'

'But …'

Chetak cut him short. 'The Lha prince is here on invitation,' he explained. 'He is not a member and must have been summoned for a purpose. As for the crown prince, he is the juniormost member of the council. He is under training and is expected to reach early. Even the dakini, Yeshe Nam Lha, is not a member, but is here on summons, like the Lha prince. Now, if your curiosity is satisfied, just relax and let me be.'

Tashi hung his head and stood in silence, quietly observing nothingness. He risked a sideways glance at Lama Ozer. The latter seemed lost in deep reflection; his features were relaxed and his eyes wore a faraway look. Suddenly, a faint red glow began to emanate. The radiance intensified in degrees until the entire western quarter of space was bathed in an incandescent golden-red light. Tashi experienced a curious blend of the most extreme forms of fear and joy as he gazed at the light and sensed what was happening. From the core of the red radiance, a single form stepped forth; his body was of rainbow shades, yet strangely transparent, like a reflection in the clearest water. Golden-red hair was pulled into a topknot on his head; his face was that of dazzling youth itself and his smile, one of compassion. In one hand, he held a lotus; in the other, the celestial gem, *mani*. The being smiled benignly as he conjured up a white lotus and took his seat on it.

Looking to his right and then, to his left, Tashi noticed that Lama Ozer, the dakini and the two princes had fallen to their knees. The being smiled at Tashi as the latter swiftly went down on his knees as well.

'Remain in that position, Tashi,' whispered Lama Ozer. 'The rest of the Council will arrive any minute.'

Tashi could not resist asking, 'But Lama, who is that?'

Lama Ozer gestured for silence. 'Boy, I see the yak lard still holds sway over your brain,' he observed tartly. 'That is none other than the Bodhisattva, Avalokiteshwara, and he always heralds the advent of the Buddha Amitabha and his consort, the goddess, Pandaravasini. Now remain silent. They will appear any moment.'

As Tashi looked on, a couple materialized from the etheric core of the red luminescence. Clad in pale yellow garments, the Buddha Amitabha's tall and fiery form blazed with deep red light. Perfect of feature and mature of look, he had magnetic black eyes. By his side stood a lithe goddess clad in a simple white skirt that flowed down to her feet. Draped around her shoulders was a diaphanous white stole that set off her beautiful, glowing form to perfection. Serene dark eyes gazed out of her radiant face and rich black hair fell to her waist. The Buddha Amitabha caused a wondrous peacock seat to materialize and the couple settled themselves on it. Then he looked about with energy and gestured to the dakini, Yeshe, to approach. The dakini immediately rose from her swan and rushed towards the western quarter of space where the dynamic trio had taken their seats.

Tashi looked on, mesmerized. Lama Ozer stood silently by his side, his hands folded in reverence, his expression ecstatic. Yeshe was now engaged in conversation with the trio. At that moment, the great golden door swung open and a goddess walked in. Perfection itself, her form was the hue of diamanté-edged starlight. Her glossy dark hair was arranged in an elaborate topknot. Her features were serene, a sculpted nose, high cheekbones and fine brows arching over eyes that held the infinite quality of nocturnal skies. She was clad in a pale green skirt, leaving her slender upper body glowing and bare but for the sparkling emerald necklaces that adorned it. She wafted past Tashi and paused before Lama Ozer, looking at him intently.

'Finally, you have come, heart of my heart! Long have we awaited this day.'

The monk looked overcome and fell to his knees before her. The goddess smiled and gently put her hands on his shoulders.

'No, no, my dearest!' she protested. Come, you will sit by my side and witness the proceedings from there.'

Smiling gently at the lama, she led him away to a brilliant white lotus that she had conjured up. Then seating herself upon it, she invited Ozer to do the same.

Is that who I think it is, Tashi wondered.

'Yes, Tashi,' Chetak's voice replied, 'that is none other than the blessed White Tara; your master's heart practice rested in her. That is why she has carried him with her.'

Tashi smiled. 'This is unbelievable! Am I really here, Chetak? Or asleep in my room in the monastery, dreaming about it all?'

Chetak snorted, 'You may wonder, boy. But look sharp. The Rigden himself is about to enter.'

There was a small commotion by the portals. Then the door swung open and the Rigden king, Aniruddha Magakpa, entered, accompanied by a guard of sprites that escorted him in before disappearing. The Rigden was tall and spare of form, the very embodiment of divinity and royalty. Well-defined features stood out prominently on his pale, unlined face and his almond-shaped black eyes were of unfathomable depth. His silver hair was held in a silken knot on top of his head and he was garbed in a deep wine-coloured robe. As he walked towards the Goddess Tara and Lama Ozer, the monk prostrated himself. The Rigden gently helped him up and engaged him in conversation. Tashi looked on curiously.

Suddenly, a sharp green light emanated from the northern aspect of space and a figure wreathed in green light stepped forth. His stern face was painful to behold in its implacability and his eyes were the substance of the void itself. Although his features were even, they radiated immense power. His dark hair was held in place by a topknot. Though of medium height, he was powerfully built and wore garments of the deepest sage green, edged with black. In one hand, he held a sword; in the other, a crossed *vajra*. Silently, he conjured up a seat secured by two enormous black Garudas. On that massive throne, a goddess appeared, her very presence projecting the quality of lightning ready to strike. Her stark naked body glowed with the hue of polished emeralds and her thick black hair tumbled down to her slender waist. Numerous shiny gold ornaments were her only adornment. Her face was fearsome in its beauty, her deep green eyes sparkling with a ruthless lustre. Her posture was arresting – back arched, one leg flung down and the other positioned sideways; her expression was bold as she looked around her. In each hand, she held a deep blue lotus.

'That, boy, is the goddess, Samaya Tara, consort to the Buddha Amoghasiddhi, who appeared just before her,' murmured Chetak. 'Together, they hold sway over the northern direction of space and govern from the pure northern realm of accumulated action.'

Tashi looked at the green-hued goddess and felt powerfully drawn to her. With a shock, he realized that she was staring back at him.

'Avert your eyes quickly, boy!' Chetak murmured. 'It is not proper to stare at the fiery one. You never know what she might decide to do.'

Reluctantly, Tashi tore his gaze away, but in a trice, the sensation of liquid fire swept through him as he felt himself lifted and then conveyed by an invisible force towards the green goddess.

'Now we are in for it, boy!' There was desperation in Chetak's voice. 'Listen carefully. No matter what she says, just keep your head bowed and your eyes averted. Do not answer her. If you speak, we will be done for. Hold your tongue and prostrate yourself.'

In moments, Tashi was set down in front of the huge Garuda throne. He felt himself trembling and looked up, only to be lost in a whirlpool of green light. The goddess languorously uncurled her legs and straightened. She leaned forward and placed her hands on Tashi's shoulders, guiding him to an upright position. Then she gently tapped his chin with her green-tipped nails. Tashi felt currents of fire race through him and found himself staring back at her boldly.

'Interesting,' said the goddess. 'Clean, pure, so innocent! Yes, I approve.'

Captivated by the wonder of her sparkling eyes, Tashi stood there, unable to keep himself from smiling, unmindful of Chetak's advice which had long fled his consciousness.

'So you are the lama's young protector and escort?' asked the goddess, Samaya Tara.

'Yes, Lady,' Tashi found himself answering.

A tinkling laugh resonated in the air. '"Lady", "Lord" – it has been many millennia since someone addressed me as "Lady",' the goddess remarked, addressing Lord Amoghasiddhi, who reclined on the throne.

'Indeed, beauteous one, he is pure,' Amoghasiddhi responded in a deep voice, his smile cutting through the boy like a crystal knife, twisting his guts and setting afire his very being.

The goddess too smiled at Tashi. Then, without warning, her right hand flashed out, a pointed knife in its grip. In one smooth gesture, she brought it down and plunged it into the boy's breast.

The goddess smiled again as searing pain engulfed Tashi. He heard her voice boom into the depths of his soul: 'With this knife, I claim you as mine. I initiate you into my sacred teaching. With the sacred alphabet, Hri, I anoint you.'

Tashi fell quivering before the great birds and darkness claimed him.

When he came to, he found himself back where he had been earlier. His etheric body felt strange, filled with an exquisite pain and yearning. He saw the green goddess glowing fierily in the northern sphere.

He felt Chetak stir within him. 'Did no one teach you to obey, boy?' the steed said. 'You are very lucky to be around, you know. However, a dagger hangs over your head now; the fiery one will not rest till she has claimed you.'

'Claimed me? How?' Tashi asked.

'Did they not teach you anything in that monastery, boy?' Chetak said in exasperation. 'She has initiated you into her heart practice. Now you have no option but to surrender to her guidance and she is the toughest taskmistress there is in the universe.'

'What!' Tashi exclaimed.

'You will see, Tashi, you will,' Chetak went on, 'she is a deity who brooks no resistance. She will trample it out of you. However, there is a positive aspect to the situation as well: her practice is the swiftest there is; it is complete annihilation or surrender; one way or the other, she will take you across.'

Slightly dazed, Tashi looked around and realized with some surprise that the gathering was more or less complete; some more Council members had arrived. Seated on an immense blue lotus at the very centre and emanating blue light was a phantom being. His intransient form, covered in a white robe, was pale and misty, almost merging into space. His face was so nebulous that his features could barely be discerned, but here and there, where the mist lifted, the very brilliance of the sun shone through. His silver eyes reflected lightning. Perhaps the only clearly discernible object was a single eight-spoked wheel that he held in his right hand. Throbbing with light, the being emanated from the dark blue of space and, phantom-like, evaporated into it.

'Chetak, who is that there?' Tashi asked.

'That,' explained the horse, 'is the Buddha Vairocana. Lord of the *dharmadhatu,* he represents the wisdom of limitless space. He has come forth today from the pure realm in the centre of the mandala.'

With difficulty, Tashi tore his gaze away from the misty figure and looked to his left. Just a few leagues away, a soft golden light was filtering through. A golden being of incredible beauty was seated on a golden lotus. His silken saffron garments were set off by a multitude of shining jewels and held in place by a belt of amber set in gold. On his head sat a circlet of shining rubies and around his neck was an array of rubies and topaz. In his right hand, he held a nugget of the dark *chintamani* stone. Perfection itself, his face blazed with transcendental beauty. His eyes were the colour of honey and his unbound hair, the hue of ripe corn, fell past his shoulders and down to his waist in a shower of rich golden strands. His features were well defined, but soft, seemingly sculpted with loving tenderness, his eyes a clear amber. He sat at ease, smiling benevolently.

An utterly bedazzled Tashi could not take his eyes off him.

But before he could ask Chetak about this being, the steed spoke up. 'Before you parade your ignorance, Tashi,' he said, 'that is the Buddha of the Ratna family, Ratnasambhava. He is the lord of the southern realm and represents the wisdom of equanimity. He is the possessor of the *chintamani*, the wish-fulfilling jewel. Today, he has come without his fair consort, the golden Mamaki.'

Tashi sighed deeply.

'Now let me finish this commentary. Look to the eastern firmament; there, boy, is seated the Lord Vajrasattva, Buddha of the Vajra family.'

Tashi looked to the east and saw him. Short in stature and firm of build, the Lord Vajrasattva was, nonetheless, extremely slender. His complexion radiated a pale blue light and his dark, penetrating eyes gazed out of a serene face. His deep blue hair was tied in a topknot. The Buddha Vajrasattva wore austere white garments and sat on a wooden seat carved with elephants. In his right hand, he held a five-pointed *vajra*.

'He is a Vajra being,' Chetak continued, 'and possesses mirror-like wisdom which reflects the manifest and the unmanifest. Now, boy, almost everybody is here. Only the great queen of primordial wisdom is awaited. As usual, she will be the last to arrive.'

Tashi looked about him restlessly. And then from the north she came. Fierce Mamo dakinis and Yidams without number filled the void for an instant before flickering out, as though vanishing into nothingness. Like a bolt of lightning, the primordial dakini queen, Yum Chenmo, floated into position. With a flick of her wrist, a throne of brilliant blue sapphires rose up from the inky blackness and she casually took her seat. Night-black hair tumbled over ivory shoulders. Great equanimity shone forth from a face that was beyond beauty, beyond life, beyond death itself. A black cobra circled her wrist, softly caressing her taut arm. Her scarlet skirt was held in place by a gold belt and her bare upper body glowed with a pale light. On her abundant hair she wore a crown of skulls studded with blood-red rubies and around her neck were several necklaces of multi-coloured gems. Tashi felt himself drowning in her fathomless eyes. A mind that was nature itself. He sighed as he felt his last grip on existence, as he knew it, loosen and drift away.

The dakini queen seated herself on the right of the Rigden king, Aniruddha Magakpa, who was ensconced on a massive golden throne carved with the likeness of lions. On either side of Yum, a token guard of two fierce-looking dakinis stood in position. Their ruddy forms were completely naked but for the ornaments they wore: circlets of human skulls and necklaces fashioned from the bones of myriad beings of the gross worlds.

Tashi looked about him in awe. Alive with the radiance emanating from the Councillors, the void seemed to shimmer with intense energy. In a practised gesture, the Rigden king inclined his head and raised his hand. As he did so, fiery letters formed in the darkness at the centre; an ancient mantra emanated from the void in a script created by fire. The mantra writhed and winked before disappearing in the void.

Tashi felt Chetak stir. 'Thus, by manifesting the primordial word, the Rigden king has given the signal for the deliberations to begin,' the horse explained. 'Pay attention now.'

From the western dimension of space, the Bodhisattva Avalokiteshwara slowly rose to take centre stage. His vibrant face glowed with a gentle light as his twilight speech reverberated in the air. 'Primordial Mother, Devi, Queen of existence and the void, Yum Chenmo, Great Monarch of the paradise world of Shambala, the Rigden, Aniruddha Magakpa,

Transcendent Buddha Lords of the Five Families that hold sway over space and time, Revered Goddesses and Buddha Lords! We are gathered here today in accordance with the manifest common will. Ancient promises have been fulfilled, the hour of prophecy has ripened and the wheel of the worlds has come full circle. Destiny sits awaiting your command, Primeval Ones.'

The Rigden smiled and, with a casual flick of his wrist, indicated that the Bodhisattva should proceed.

Avalokiteshwara pressed his palms together in respect before the assembly and began his actual address. 'The prophecy has come to pass, the sacred gathering has been called today and two mortal souls are now in Shambala; souls whose karma has yet to be fulfilled in the world of light, souls that have not yet attained the liberation necessary for them to enter Shambala. Yet summoned they were, guided they were, by the workings of prophecy and the manifest divine will. I think you will agree with me today that the sacred hour of prophecy is here. Give me leave to utter the ancient syllables of prophecy.'

The Bodhisattva looked to the Rigden and the gathering. The Rigden gave his ascent with a turn of his head.

The twilight speech shivered across the air as Avalokiteshwara voiced the prophecy of old. 'So it was told to the great sage, many aeons ago, by the innate power that is the universe:

Two shall come by the path of the arrow,
From the world of men in the Fourth Age,
When truth lies raped and the word be forgotten.
Two shall come by ancient paths,
Led by forgotten gods to the centre,
To the axis mundi,
To the holy isle,
Thus reversing the age.

By fire and storm,
By battle and sacked lives,

By divine rage and terrible unrest,
Let the men of the Fourth Age learn the ancient lesson.
Let the first stone be laid for the churning of the ages,
Let the terrible conch be blown for the new age that is come.

So shall the teachings of fire pass again into the world of men;
So shall the word be made manifest again;
So shall a new age be born on the blood and debris of the old.

The twilight speech shivered in space and the lords of light smiled serenely as Avalokiteshwara gave voice to the prophecy.

The Bodhisattva held aloft his hand. 'Their presence here merely rings in a fresh period of churning, yet another age of strife, agony, turmoil. The worlds will have to be disturbed again, shaken out of their lethargy, out of the numbed dominion of the mind. I gather the assembly knows what this means? Devi, ancient beyond compare, Great Queen, Shambala will have to come out of its self-imposed silence. No longer will we play mere monitors to destiny, graphing the course of the worlds. After millennia will we let loose a race of men whose very memory has been wiped out, whose songs lie forgotten, whose word has been abandoned and whose last records are buried in oblivion. We shall step out of silence to shake the worlds in divine rage. Devi, today the churning has begun; we will again rouse destiny.'

Even as the Bodhisattva fell silent and retreated, Samaya Tara stepped forth in a fluid movement from her perch atop the Garuda throne. Glowing a vivid green, she strutted into the midst of the gathering and, facing both the Rigden and Yum, held forth in a voice that rolled out like thunder raging from dark monsoon clouds.

'For ages, countless aeons gone by, have I waited for this day,' she declared. 'Let the churning begin, O Great Monarch and Most Primordial Queen, even as I monitor the graph of the worlds, from the realm of mortal denizens under the baleful yellow sun to the realms of subtle denizens under the red sun and the denizens that dwell in the black marshes of space. It is all amiss and the dharma lies forgotten. It is agreed that the sacred moment has come. Let us monitor no longer, but intervene. My hosts of valiant Yidams stand ready. You have but to command. Great Monarch, you have but to command and righteous thunder will roll out from the clouds, fire will rain, the worlds will quaver and the lamps will be lit again, as the cry for mercy rings out.'

The dakini queen, Yum, raised her brow as she looked towards her silent counsellor, the Lord Amitabha. With the flick of her graceful wrist, she communicated her words: 'And what do you have to say, Compassionate One?'

With heavenly grace, the lord of the western spaces rose from his seat in the void. His face glowed and his voice was seduction itself, as he proclaimed, 'Devi Most Graceful, Most Beneficent, unfortunate by far and yet fortunate by many counts are the innumerable souls that will witness the great churning scheduled to begin. Yet it has been our policy for the aeon which is ended to meddle as little as possible in the destiny of the worlds, merely assisting them in evolving on their own and intervening only in cases of dire catastrophe. However, Primordial One, a new aeon is now in its infancy and the teachings of fire are ready to be sent out into the four corners of manifestation. Now, as ever, the greatest battles of destiny will be waged in the world of the yellow sun, the world of men being foremost, as there lies a unique opportunity for the true seeker. So, Devi, let us make a great beginning. Already, the wheel has spun out a new course and Destiny is about to take her great new step. For whether we shake the worlds or offer them minimal assistance, nothing can stop the churning that is beginning and the new age that glimmers on the far horizon.'

With feline grace, the great dakini queen, Yum Chenmo, gestured for silence. Then slowly, she rose to her full height, towering above the assemblage. Great power and an aura of austerity radiated from her.

'It is true that the churning has begun,' she affirmed. 'Let the sages begin their propitiatory prayers for the period.'

In the silence that followed her declaration, the void reverberated with her words. The dakini queen held her hand out to the Rigden, who silently stood up, holding aloft his *vajra*.

In a ringing voice, he declared, 'We honour the great Wisdom Queen's words; the very essence of the void has proclaimed the sacred decree. As of this moment, the new age is rung in. Buddha Lords that govern space, I request you to let the vibrations of the new fire be released from the countless stars that shine in the universe. I urge you to let their powerful waves carry the transformative energies of the new fire that will rend the worlds, cleanse them and bind them afresh. Sacred Dakinis, I ask that you lift the veil and offer glimmers of the cutting wisdom of perception to the deserving in the myriad glens of manifestation. To the high gods, the Lha and other celestial deities, I advise preparation to travel and serve as messengers. To celestial agents in all four directions of space, to the teeming worlds bearing the new word and, most of all, to the great brethren of Bodhisattvas – I request, O Compassionate Ones, that you prepare to embark into manifestation in order to grind the wheel of the new age. To the forces of Mamo Dakini and wrathful Herukas, I advise that you prepare to descend in fury and carry away evil beings who refuse to yield.'

The dakini queen smiled and her scarlet skirts fluttered, as though lifted by a high wind. 'Let the churning begin in the three worlds and let the battles be fought in the world of men,' she declared. 'By decree of the law, the One, Shambala lends its offices to the process that is about to begin. With one hand, we will nurture; with the other, destroy. No quarter is to be given. Long have we waited for this hour and it has come. We will let loose the forces that will beget events, but as always, the choice will remain with the mortals. And now, Yeshe Nam Lha, Dakini of the Yellow Order, please bring forward our guest from the world of men, the venerable Lama Ozer. Let us hear him out on this day, when his presence marks the passing of an age and the beginning of the great churning.'

In the centre of the void, a soft saffron light grew as the celestial sages appeared and began the chanting that commemorated the onslaught of the churning. Soft yellow flames from the *yagna* flew into the air as the mantra picked up pace. The dakini, Yeshe Nam Lha, wafted through space, leading a dazed Lama Ozer before the assembly. His hands folded in supplication, the lama prostrated himself three times before the dakini queen, the Rigden and the august gathering. Then he began in earnest.

'Mighty Rigden, Primordial Queen and Sacred Mother, Transcendent Buddha Lords and Dakinis! Never in my life did I imagine that a day would come to pass when a mere mortal like myself would be addressing an assembly such as this one,' he declared. 'Alas, today, in the world of men, few know that such a place as Shambala exists. Fewer still believe in such a court as this one. Today, the sway of Kalyug, the Fourth Age, is complete. Greed, rage and frustration rule the world of men. There is strife everywhere; creed is pitted against creed, religion against religion, nations against nations; races war with each other. The Fourth Age rules mightily and is manifest today in its completeness. The news from the world of men is fraught with nothing but tragedy and can only get worse.'

The dakini queen raised her hand and leaned forward. 'What else, Lama?' she asked. 'We have had a steady flow of reports from different parts of the world of mortals and the trends are interesting.'

Lama Ozer continued, 'Great Mother, my understanding is limited, but I am sure you have mighty hosts at your disposal who have given you sounder insights on the current status of the world. But briefly, the nations to the extreme west have done well since the wars that afflicted the first half of the twentieth century. A mighty nation has grown to the west; untold riches have they accumulated, along with unimaginable military and economic power. They hold sway over the world. The nations of the cold continent, Europe, have also prospered, but strife ravages their eastern cousins. I hear, Great Mistress, that nations war in the ring around Russ. The Slavic people suffer, with fear and hunger dogging their footsteps. The military might of the giant Russ of old is no more; in the cold, they walk, their hearts numb, searching, searching ... However, Devi, it is from the east that strife grows. There is great anger among the people of the Crescent. From the cold shores of eastern Europe, through the countries that blaze under the hot sun and right up to the desert sands around the Gulf, the brethren of the Crescent are suffused with rage. In the wild land bordering the blue jewel, Indus, the river of ancient Hind, they have raised their weapons in anger, tied the green cloth of martyrdom to their heads and fired the Buddhas. A new breed has been born in the wild lands and its reverberations have been felt in the world. Devi, you must have noted the grave portents of September 2001.'

The dakini queen smiled enigmatically and addressed the Buddha Vajrasattva. 'What does the good lama talk of, Lord?' she asked. 'We have heard tell of the winds of distress and agony that wail over the worlds. What does the monitor have to say?'

The Buddha Vajrasattva rose to respond, 'Devi and Rigden, we have noted and discussed the new trend that grows in the land of men, the rage that builds in the sons of the Prophet. During nights of despair in the wild countries of the east, reduced to starvation, beggary and desperation, the sons of the Prophet exist in the shadows. Among them, Devi, destiny has crafted a strange breed as ancient as time, proud, angry and endowed with great power. A trace that we engineered has taken root and the time has come for chaos, rebirth and anger.'

The Rigden addressed the Buddha Amitabha. 'And what do you say, Compassionate One? At what point does the world of men stand today?'

The lord of light rose to answer, 'Righteous King, Upholder of the dharma, the world of men is arcing towards a great turn in its evolution. This strife and battle have become necessary today; three decades of peace and stability had brought its growth in spirit to a halt. The mortals grew in riches, they constructed beautiful cities, their culture evolved, but much they also forgot … Half the world thrived; the other half thirsted. Then we sent the trace, threw the dice. Chaos will spread, a great war for dominance will take over, blood will splatter the earth with vermilion, but they will grow in spirit now.'

Yum threw back her head and laughed. 'So the great lords of light have prepared for the churning even before it starts!' she observed. 'Now, about our intervention in the world of men which is imminent, is all in readiness for us to send down our people to begin the churning?'

Amitabha looked up. 'Yes, my Queen,' he replied, 'in accordance with your wish, a group of people from Shambala is ready to follow Lama Ozer back into the world of men. They will initiate our work there, Great Mother. Three from Shambala have willingly offered their names for descent into the mortal world. The first is the dakini, Yeshe Nam Lha, currently present at the Council. Her name was mentioned in past prophecy as part of the group of five that will begin Shambala's intervention on Earth. The second is Crown Prince Narasimha Miyi Senge, skilled in many arts and sciences, including medicine. He has offered to accompany the lama. The third and last name may come as a surprise for one and all; the panel has chosen the Lha prince, A-KarO, as an escort for Lama Ozer and Tashi. The prince is a being of great power, profoundly learned in the wisdom lore and a skilled warrior, adept at using many weapons. All three have offered to descend to Earth with Lama Ozer and his acolyte, Tashi Thendup.'

Yum held up her hand. 'Then all is in readiness,' she concluded. 'Now I would like the two princes, the dakini, Lama Ozer and young Tashi to present themselves before me.'

Immediately, Tashi found himself standing in front of the dakini queen, with Lama Ozer next to him. Alongside were the two princes and the dakini, Yeshe Nam Lha.

The great queen, Yum Chenmo, said, 'Get my bow, Lord Amitabha.'

Amitabha strung the bow with an arrow and handed it to Yum. She stood tall, her arms taut. Then she lifted them and let loose an arrow, which disappeared fast into the far skies.

'The first is the sign of the churning,' she announced. A second arrow flew. 'This is the sign of the new fire that streams into the worlds.' A third arrow flew. 'The last, the hope of the age of men and of their necessary evolution. Either they will evolve to spiritual ascendancy and Shambala again will be or, my Lord, we will wipe the slate clean and begin afresh.' Yum's thoughts flew far, her eyes lost in the glow of the ages. 'Ah, yes, my good Lama,' she said, 'humans are allowed free will and it is something we do not tamper with. It is given and the choice is theirs to make: evolution or annihilation. The Golden Age or the dark night of *pralaya*. Either way, they will know unity of consciousness.'

Suddenly, the great dakini queen looked frail. Her head drooped as she took her seat on her sapphire throne.

A moment of intense silence followed and then the Rigden spoke up, his voice even. 'Lama Nyima Ozer, Prince Narasimha Miyi Senge, Prince

A-KarO, the Golden One, Yeshe Nam Lha and last, but not least, young Tashi Thendup! You have all been called today before the sacred court and from now, in every breath, in every heartbeat, in the shadow of every moment, in the intensity of the thoughtless state, in life, and in not-life, in physical or subtle form, we declare you our emissaries, our sacred envoys to the world of men. Shambala has a task for you. For you will be Shambala's hand in the age that is now upon men.'

As the Rigden fell silent, the dakini queen held up her hand. 'All five of you are assigned a mission on Earth to prepare the ground for the birth of the Immortal One, the long-prophesied saviour of the three worlds, the avatar of the one transcendental being of great perfection, who is the beginning and the end of all that is, the almighty creator, destroyer and preserver. You are assigned to prepare the ground and the conditions for the birth of the saviour, Maitreya. First, you will give protection to the mother of the saviour; she will become apparent to you. Second, you will create a favourable environment for the birth of the holy child. Let me warn you that you will face a direct threat from the Asur demons, for even as I speak, they are preparing to launch their battle against you to sabotage the birth. Protection is the direct responsibility of the Lha prince, A-KarO, general of many cosmic battles against the Asur. The mother and the child will need special nurturing and healing and that will be made available. This is the direct responsibility of Crown Prince Narasimha Miyi Senge who is renowned as a healer. The Golden Dakini, Yeshe Nam Lha, your role will become both imminent and apparent while all of you are on Earth. I will not spell out what it will be.'

Yum continued with a smile, 'After the birth, you will protect the child all through his vulnerable growing years, till he comes into manhood. Lama Ozer, I will expect you to provide the wisdom and guidance that the child will need. Young Tashi Thendup, you will train under the Lha prince, A-KarO; he will guide you. It is possible, fledgling, that you will surprise us all; is it not so? Now, your final orders – the details of your mission, its nature and your own great task in it – will be given to you later at the second Council meeting held before the High Council of Sages at Aggartha.'

Then the primordial queen, Yum, turned to the Buddha Vajrasattva. 'Lord of the eastern span of the universe, we come now to more dangerous matters,' she said. 'I would have you report before the assemblage today the latest developments among the Asur demons and the threat the mission faces from them.'

The Buddha Vajrasattva rose to speak, his pale blue form glowing in the void. 'Primordial Queen,' he began, 'developments among the Asur demons are very disturbing of late. On the surface, the status quo is maintained; the truce seems to be holding even after two centuries, but inside, there is a strong stirring. Leading the Asur demons today is a very dynamic Asur king, Nyamat ti Nazer Basher. He is not only highly intelligent, but shrewd and calculating in the extreme. A bold and ambitious monarch, he is bent on changing the balance of power between the gods and the Asur.' The Buddha Vajrasattva held aloft his hand. 'Nyamat has strengthened and infused new life into the Asur armed forces; their spy networks have been revived. We have confidential information that Asur spies have infiltrated the paradise worlds; they have cut a swath through the Lha empire and I believe they even have a presence here in Shambala and in Amravati.'

The Buddha Vajrasattva inclined his head, his dark eyes glinting. 'What is, perhaps, much more dangerous is the strong Asur presence on Earth. We have reason to believe that the Asur have established their encampments in the mortal world and their evil influence – albeit disguised – on mankind is growing. Moreover, there is evidence confirming that the Asur have intelligence on our proposed mission on Earth. They are well aware that the time is ripe for the birth of Maitreya, the next messiah, and the dawn of the new age. Our mission on Earth will be in great and constant danger from the Asur. Our emissaries will have to struggle hard to survive and our own hands are tied; there are conditions to be met and we cannot give them more aid than is allowed. So I urge the group of five to remain vigilant. Once they reach Earth, their very existence will be a threat for the Asur and they will strike hard. Prince A-KarO, I recommended your name for the mission and am confident that you will rise to this challenge and give the Asur the fight of their lives. Our hopes rest with you.'

The dakini queen smiled. 'Lord Vajrasattva, your deep insight is welcomed,' she declared. 'The threat from the Asur is dire and our mission will be in peril, but all possible support will be extended to our emissaries by Shambala and the Buddha lords. Now, before we deliberate further, all five of the mission members may retire to the city. Remember, our hopes rest with you. In a few days, we will arrange for your second briefing, which will be with the sages at Aggartha, who will bless you before sending you to Earth.'

As soon as Lama Ozer and Tashi made to rise, they found themselves on their way out of the chamber.

Meanwhile, the Council chamber was bathed in light as the councillors blazed in the void. Their forms reverting into the ether, into nothingness, where their discourse continued in emptiness.

CHAPTER 6

THE AZURE PALACE

I

A burnished sunset reflected in the clear waters off the Pool of Tranquillity at the Dakini, Yeshe Nam Lha's, estate in far Shambala. Manicured emerald lawns flanked the half-moon shaped pool and glowing, well-maintained groves laden with flowering trees dotted the vast parkland. The dakini's gaze wandered across its tranquil expanse and over to the right, lingering over the ivory-hued, finely arched and filigreed summer gazebo where she loved to sit, before moving on to contemplate the hues of the evening as it descended over the gardens, the waning light blending into the growing shadows. Then her eyes came to rest on the central grove, where heavily scented red flowers bloomed.

From the heart of the grove rose the graceful spires of the silver temple to her mother, the White Tara. Already, her maidens were lighting up the grove with lanterns, preparing for the evening prayer, and the unmistakable fragrance of sandalwood wafted in the air. The dakini sighed, letting her head fall back as she settled herself on her favourite seat on the edge of the Pool of Tranquillity. Instantly, two maidens stepped forth and fell on their knees before her, their heads in a deep bow. With a gesture, Yeshe indicated they should rise.

'Dakini, may we begin?' the maidens asked.

At a nod from Yeshe, they gently unclasped the clips fastening her thick dark hair and let it fall to her waist in cloudy waves. One of the maidens produced a brush and began vigorously running it through its length. With each stroke, it seemed as though starlight itself were caught in the glowing raven strands and reflecting off their darkness.

'Dakini,' one of the maidens began tentatively, 'the water has been readied in your chamber for your ritual bath. Also, the turquoise robe has been set aside for you tonight. I hope that is to your liking.'

Yeshe smiled gently at them. 'Whatever you do is always to my liking, dear ones,' she murmured. 'Now run along. I'll follow in a moment.'

'Dakini,' the maiden said, 'your mother, the White Tara, the protectoress and wisdom goddess, is coming for the prayer service tonight.'

Yeshe inclined her head.'I am aware of it. I trust all is ready for her visit?'

'Yes, Dakini. Also, there is one more matter ... Tonight, we have guests for dinner invited by the goddess.'

'Guests?' said Yeshe. 'This is a surprise. We have not entertained for many months ... I trust you have made preparations as the goddess desired?'

At this point, the older maiden intervened. 'There is one small issue, Dakini; the goddess has invited Prince A-KarO, the heir-apparent to the throne of the higher gods in the celestial realm, and Crown Prince Narsimha Miyi Senge for dinner.'

Yeshe's calm expression gave way to agitation. 'What! My divine mother has invited the Lha prince and the crown prince to my abode? She knows well that I allow no male to enter my premises; this is a maiden's home. Yet if that is her will, so be it!'

'It was the goddess's express wish that you entertain them for dinner, Dakini,' the maiden went on.

Yeshe stood up. 'Then it will be done. Have the outer dining hall and the sitting room in the temple premises prepared for them and have the priest attend to them.'

The maiden smiled. 'Dakini, the goddess has given specific instructions that the Rose Chamber in the Azure Palace be prepared for their visit. Moreover, you are to personally attend to them and should be present with your maidens. None of the priests should be there. She even gave specific instructions about the banquet to be laid out for the two princes.'

Yeshe massaged her head wearily. 'It's been a tiring day and now this ... But my divine mother's wish has to be obeyed. So prepare the Rose Chamber for the evening.'

Slowly, she rose and stepped into the shimmering waters of the pool. Within moments, she had disappeared into its azure depths at the heart of which lay her glowing sapphire-hued underwater abode, lit up with dazzling gold rays. Soon, she was standing on the canopied porch, the warm air from the magical Azure Palace drying her body instantly. She could not help but smile as she gazed at the pure, glowing sapphire waters that surrounded her palace and the surreal sight of brilliant underwater flora and fauna floating past. Silver-coated fish swam serenely by and multi-coloured underwater snakes dived in and out. For moments, she stood quietly, becoming one with the water, the dying rays of the sun and the glowing crimson flowers that bloomed in abundance around her aquatic abode.

Then silently, she stepped through the indigo arches into the corridor that opened into a modest-sized ivory-hued hall lit up with the diffused blue glow from lamps. Screens of blue lotuses stood here and there and dull gold settees and divans were placed artistically along the walls. The dakini contemplated her home with contentment before moving through the hall into a corridor that branched off from the side and opened into her apartment. The floor of her room was inlaid with rainbow-coloured shells and its glass walls showed off to perfection the aquatic paradise that lay beyond. Simple, but elegant, with ivory covers, her bed was made on the floor.

As Yeshe entered, three maidens bowed in deference. At this point, her old nurse, a matronly-looking being endowed with natural grace stepped into the room, folded her palms and bowed deeply before the dakini.

'Yeshe, my golden flower,' she said, 'I have been intimated by the Goddess's staff that she is on her way here. Let me dress you tonight, as is my will.'

'Whatever you say, dear one,' Yeshe sighed. 'I will not tarry, then.'

The nurse stepped forward and started gently massaging Yeshe's neck. 'Then, child, we will forgo the bath tonight,' she said. 'I myself have prepared steaming hot towels to refresh you.'

Yeshe stood still as the three maidens removed her stole and skirts, took off all her jewellery and pinned up her hair. The aroma of steam filled the room as they rinsed off her shining body with the hot towels and applied an unguent that gave off the scent of pine needles and forest herbs.

The nurse brought forth a transparent turquoise skirt edged with silver, along with a matching turquoise stole.

At this point, Yeshe intervened. 'Bring only my pink coral necklace and its accompaniments. Nothing more,' she declared.

The nurse frowned. 'The occasion demands more,' she protested.

Yeshe looked at her directly. 'No, it does not,' she countered. 'Also, remove this stole and bring the white one I wear to the temple. That is all.'

The maidens immediately brought forth a simple white stole of fine material that Yeshe herself arranged around her shoulders, discreetly covering her breasts. Then she placed a single strand of corals around her neck, adding matching armbands of coral and a bracelet on her right wrist.

'This is it,' she said with finality. 'Now, no elaborate coiffure, please. I will wear my hair loose and unadorned. It is time for the temple service. My mother, the Goddess, will be there in a moment. I must leave.'

The nurse looked up at her imploringly. 'One moment, Yeshe, my child, hear me out,' she urged. 'This evening is not an ordinary one. I entreat you to be wary. The Goddess bears a message for you and also comes to prepare you. Yeshe, be wary of the Lha prince. I cannot understand why the Goddess has invited him, but her intentions are mysterious. The prophecies speak much of the prince. His is an unfathomable personality. Do not be charmed, do not trust and do not give offence. His legacy is beyond compare. Not only is he heir to the celestial Lha throne and an adept in all the higher tantras, he is also a master of creative forces. His is the union of day and night. Do not forget that his mother is the Nag queen, Nilamani, she who possesses the *nil mani*, the sapphire. It is through her that he has access to forbidden knowledge entrusted to the Nag, knowledge that their kind jealously guard. Yeshe, surely you know Prince A-KarO is the offspring from a secret union between Nilamani, the Nag queen, and the Lha king, Ragen SakarO, when she was a maiden visiting the Lha court? The prince was born before her marriage to her betrothed, the Nag king. As such, Prince A-KarO is a rare combination of Lha strength and Nag fire. Beware of him.'

Yeshe inclined her head and smiled. 'Do not worry,' she said. 'We will see what this evening brings.'

II

Diffused light glowed from the lanterns as Yeshe made her leisurely way into the sacred grove, taking in the familiar sights and smells. The night was restive and a gentle breeze played with the leaves. Yeshe sighed softly. Then casting off her stole, she raised her bare arms to accept the night's caress, welcoming the moment utterly. Her eyes lit up with inner bliss as she saw the temple emerge in the clearing, and she stood still, bowing quietly as she let the sacred wash over her. Waves of intense ecstasy twined themselves around her and silence brimmed over, swaying with the breeze, Yeshe entered the portal.

The Priestesses within washed her hands and showered her with jasmine leaves and a spray of perfumed water. Yeshe walked through the narrow but well lit corridor and then into the sanctum. The wisdom Goddess, the White Tara, sat glowing on a vivid white lotus, her hair held up in a complicated chignon as loose curls blew astray on her fair shoulders. The Goddess's chiselled features shone to perfection as a beatific smile lit her face. Yeshe folded her hands, then prostrated full length on the floor, her forehead resting in emptiness at the Goddess's feet. Slowly she stood up and then seating the Goddess by the side of the naked flame lit to the glory of the White Tara, Yeshe began the ritual.

Yeshe offered red and white flowers to the Goddess, adorning her with garlands, then placed bowls of clear water before her. She anointed the Goddess's forehead with sandalwood paste, offered her trays of fruits and nuts and lit the lamps and the sandalwood sticks. The Goddess smiled as Yeshe slowly removed her white stole and let the priestesses invoke the sacred letters on her body. After the invocation, as the mantra arose from within her, Yeshe danced each letter; the syllable, the movement and spirit uniting in perfection. Her body shone with incredible lustre as she brought the rite to a conclusion, gracefully bowing then prostrating herself at the Goddess's feet; being melting into emptiness.

'Beloved flower, child of my heart, golden Yeshe, maiden of infinite bliss, vehicle of perfection of the twenty-one Taras! Come, child of my heart,' invited the Goddess, holding out her arms.

Yeshe effortlessly floated into them, melting into the Goddess's body and silence. The priestesses prostrated themselves on the floor, participating in the moment of intense perfection. A brilliant white light flashed from the Goddess's form and merged with Yeshe's. Her eyes glowed with a rare brilliance as she gazed into infinite space, smiling slightly. Balance in her right hand, she sat rooted.

'Beloved daughter, heed me well tonight,' began the Goddess. 'I come bearing a message for you from the Council.'

Yeshe pressed her palms together in reverence and looked up at her divine mother.

'Innocent one, you have been selected to accompany Lama Ozer and the boy, Tashi, to Earth and see to the successful fulfilment of their mission,' declared the Goddess. 'This week will be your last here for a long time to come. You will leave your divine manifestation and your essence will be transferred to a mortal form.'

Yeshe listened to the Goddess in silence.

'Daughter, your essence will be transferred into a mortal body, you cannot come back here till your mission is fulfilled, which means one earthly lifetime – or more if required. You will lose all your divine powers, but you will carry with you your vast knowledge, your infinitely perfect nature, your intense innocence, your compassion and the nakedness that is "Yeshe" – my inner wisdom.'

Yeshe bowed her head, acknowledging her divine mother's words.

'Beloved one, such is the will,' the White Tara continued. 'My child, you are the *homa ahuti*. In the great *yagna* of Mahakundalini, which is being undertaken to purify the age, you are our sacrifice. Only when your body and your secret nature are consigned to the flames will the age be renewed and the channel be provided for the teachings of fire.'

Yeshe raised her head and gazed at the Goddess with rapt attention.

'My child, this sacrifice is possible only when eighteen mortals unite in heart and mind and become one. Mark my words well: from different nations, from various walks of life will they come, but they will come. Your challenge is to look for these people, bring them together and mould them into the arrow that will find its mark and help you accomplish your task. Your given role is to expose these eighteen souls to the ancient teachings and impart the knowledge of Shambala. More than anything, imperative is the creation of this body through which Mahakundalini can be channelled and the teachings of fire spread.'

As she listened to the divine mother's words, Yeshe's face was calm, her eyes aglow with magnetism.

'All this must be accomplished, Yeshe, in the shadow of war and under threat from the Asur demons. Not everyone will survive. Stay alert, daughter. Beware of the cunning of the Asur. Prince A-KarO and Crown Prince Narasimha will protect you, but you must see to your own defence, daughter. You must use the inner shields that are your gift. I know you cannot engage in combat, but you can defend yourself as the shield maiden, a hidden knowledge you possess and which will remain with you.'

The Goddess smiled and went on: 'Once all is in readiness, you, my daughter, will undertake a journey with this band into ancient territory, where the Hindu Kush and the Himalaya meet. Mark my words well, daughter: this is a turbulent region; at the time of passage, it will be struck by famine and ravaged by war; the first snows of winter will have fallen and with this group and an escort of warriors, you will make the passage into high mountains and from thence to the abode of Mt Meru itself. The sacred mountain's earthly manifestation is shrouded in mystery and its exact location is lost, even to us. At a marked place on Mt Meru, you will hold a great fire ritual, the details of which are known to Prince A-KarO. And then, my beloved, you will offer yourself to the flames. Even Shambala will watch what emerges from the flames, as your untarnished divine essence unites in sacrifice with the sacred word. What will emerge from this fire is the child of perfection, the holy child, the saviour of the three worlds. Yeshe, the holy child will be conceived in the flames and you will be its mother. It is through your essence that a great blessing will pass on to the mortal world. However, remember, daughter, that the fire may make some unusual demands at this time and those demands will have to be fulfilled.'

Yeshe's expression remained unruffled, her dark eyes calm.

'This is easier said than done,' the Goddess continued. 'The war being waged on Earth, the calamity and chaos that prevail will, however, come to your aid. Remember, it is the circumstances that will produce the people; from negative and destructive events will the auspicious hour for this deed be born. Lastly, Yeshe, you have two divine protectors on this mission: the Lha prince and heir, A-KarO, and Crown Prince Narasimha Miyi Senge.'

Yeshe's eyes glittered as she asked, 'Why the two princes, Goddess?'

The divine mother smiled. 'It is the will of the Council. The Lha prince has extensive powers and is skilled in warfare and statecraft. The other, Narasimha, is a skilled healer; few can rival him in this sphere and his compassion is infinite. He will be a great asset to you in your work, my daughter.'

Yeshe shook her head. 'Why the Lha prince, Divine Mother?' she persisted. 'He will be more a nuisance than anything else on this journey!'

The Goddess smiled benignly. 'Yeshe,' she said, 'A-KarO is guided by his own will and compassion. His evolutionary journey is beyond compare. Trained by a mysterious Mahasiddha, he is a cosmic creative force in his own right. Other than being the heir to the throne of the higher gods, he is an adept in various fields of knowledge and manifold skills rest in him. You do not need to know why he is chosen, simply that he is; and his role, as of others, will be crucial on Earth.' The Goddess raised her hand. 'Daughter, you will be ordained for the mission and provided its details at the Council meeting in Aggartha.

'Now, I want to share more with you. You, Yeshe, are the hidden card in this game. You are the foundation on which the coming age will unfold. You have two divine lords accompanying you; pay heed, daughter, for they are your suitors. You are destined to accept one of them as your lord; the other will be your friend. Then you have Lama Ozer and Tashi. These are the basics you are provided with, my child. Other than that, the Council and their messengers will contact you from time to time. Daughter, be prepared; in two days' time, you will depart.'

Yeshe looked at the Goddess, a frown marring her features. 'What is the need for suitors, Mother?' she asked. 'Is it not enough that I am to birth a child? Why a lord? What is the need?'

The Goddess's eyes twinkled with humour as she looked at Yeshe. 'The divine child will need a father,' she explained. 'It is the will of the Council. It is true that the child will be born of a *yagna*. Yet there is a mystery here that none know of. The conditions laid down for the birth specify that you will be mated and this is likely to happen during the *yagna*. Remember, the fire will make demands; so choose well, Yeshe. It is time to surrender your maidenhood, daughter. It has lasted for centuries and I never was in favour of it. Now it is the manifest will.'

Yeshe sighed, her eyes welling up with unshed tears.

'There is more, my child,' the Goddess continued. 'As each one of you is manifested in a mortal form, you will lose the powers you possessed in this dimension, though some semblance of them will remain. Much of your occult power will also cease to exist. What will remain, along with your wisdom nature and your vast knowledge, is your deep compassion; these attributes can help you overcome many hurdles. Narasimha and A-KarO too will retain certain central aspects of their divinity. However, the crafty one, that is, A-KarO, will, I suspect, retain much of his knowledge, power and wisdom. He is trained by the Siddhas and rest assured, he will find a way for himself, as also for Narasimha.'

'Mother, when will I see you again?' Yeshe asked. For the first time, her eyes expressed emotion.

'Beloved, only when your mission is fulfilled. However, I will always be with you in essence.'

Yeshe's legs gave way and she crumpled to the floor. Kissing the hem of the Goddess's skirts, she asked, 'Goddess, beloved! In the end, will you take me back into your arms?'

'My arms will always await you, my own essence, my heart! Even parted, we are together,' the Goddess replied.

'So be it, Mother. I will abide by the manifest will,' whispered Yeshe.

'Your mortal body shall resemble your immortal form, my dearest,' said the Goddess. 'Your face shall remain the same. Although your complexion cannot compare with the one you had here, it will be similar. And yes, daughter, your hair will be the same. However, the vessel will be a little weak; so be careful. Means will be provided to all of you,' she concluded. 'Now it is time. Soon, your guests will be here for dinner. Be attentive to both.'

'As you wish, Goddess,' Yeshe murmured.

Quietly, they floated out of the prayer-room and into the fragrant grove.

III

The lights in the Rose Chamber were suitably dimmed as Yeshe walked in. She observed that everything had been laid out to perfection. Subtle pink and lilac hues predominated. The vaulted roof was inlaid with mauve crystals tracing a pattern of flowers arranged in clusters; suspended from its centre was a majestic purple chandelier composed of pieces shaped like teardrops frozen in motion. The delicate pink walls were lined with *thangkas* and huge mirrors. Crystal lamps cast diffused light over the low couches, upholstered in burnished pink, dull gold and mauve silk, that stood about the room, along with matching low tables. Bowls of water, in which floated scarlet rose petals, sat on the tables; laid out alongside were dishes of candied fruit, dry fruits and nuts. All was in readiness.

Yeshe then ushered the Goddess into the Rose Chamber, where the latter seated herself on a rose-coloured divan in the centre and surveyed the room with pleasure. She gestured for her daughter to sit by her side.

'This evening is more important then you imagine, my child,' the Goddess began. 'I want you to be at your best. You will need to work very closely with both Narasimha and A-KarO; the fate of your mission will rest on your successful collaboration, your solidarity. Lama Ozer is skilled, no doubt, but your task in the mortal world requires careful handling; otherwise, the entire enterprise will fail. That will mean delay, repeated efforts … Ah! You know what all that leads to.'

Yeshe sighed softly and inclined her head in acknowledgement.

'Mutual trust is vital to the mission. The group must not fracture in the face of delusion. Time is short and you will all be sent out together. Each of you will be assigned tasks that are clearly laid out. The lama will remain the leader of the group, but you, my child, and your partners, have to keep it together and ensure that the vast energy we are sending forth from here does not get dissipated.'

Suddenly alert, Yeshe looked up at the Goddess. 'The princes have entered the compound, Mother,' she informed her. 'They will be with us soon.'

Unruffled, the Goddess settled back into the divan. Yeshe gracefully rose from her habitual seat.

'You could change that stole for the royal visitation,' the Goddess suggested.

'Now, Mother …' Yeshe remonstrated.

The Goddess's eyes lit up with laughter and, in a trice, the plain white stole had disappeared, only to be replaced by a diaphanous turquoise and smoky pink one that Yeshe carelessly threw about her shoulders.

'Your hairstyle looks a little too plain,' the Goddess began. 'I know you like it so, but a little adornment …'

Pale pink jewelled flowers dropped twinkling into the dark depths of Yeshe's hair and a single strand of deep blue sapphires fell into place around her pale throat. Matching sapphire earrings, intricately designed and set in gold, dangled from her ears. Yeshe carefully arranged a sapphire and gold double-link jewelled belt around her waist, while delicate sapphire ornaments shone with cerulean lights around her ankles.

A slender sprite stepped into the room, prostrating herself before the Goddess and bowing to Yeshe. 'Prince A-KarO and the royal heir, Prince Narasimha Senge, are here,' she announced. 'May I bring them in?'

Yeshe inclined her head in consent and the sprite stepped out.

Dressed simply in cream silk pants, with a matching silk stole around his shoulders, Prince Narasimha entered first, his tanned body radiating a golden aura of deep serenity and well-being. His rich, dark brown hair was tied back and his dark eyes gleamed with intelligence and compassion. Around his neck hung strands of pearls and a thick gold piece of intricate design. From his earlobes swung gold *kundals* and on his hair sat a circlet of woven gold from the centre of which glowed a single piece of uncut amber.

Narasimha paid his respects to the Goddess, bowing low before her. Lines of humour appeared on his face as he took Yeshe's hands in his own.

'This is the first time, golden flower, that I have crossed the threshold of your home,' he murmured. 'Its magnificence defies description. It is an honour being here tonight.'

Yeshe inclined her head and responded, 'The honour is all mine. The Goddess's wish is my command. It is by her will that you are here tonight.'

Smiling slightly, she stepped forward and led the prince to a low seat to her right.

Moments later the celestial Prince A-KarO, stepped into the room and it felt as though lightning crackled in the firmament. A-KarO's silver hair fell serpent-like in a straight shower on his bare back. His navy silk trousers fit him perfectly and his upper body was bare, save for a silken length of white cloth that hung carelessly over one shoulder. His sole adornment was a dark oval stone strung on a red thread around his neck. He glided, rather then walked forward, and stooped low to kiss the hem of the Goddess's robe.

The Goddess smiled benignly at him. 'My son appears well,' she observed.

A-KarO smiled. 'Mother, you remembered me. That is enough for me.'

Her eyes beaming, the Goddess leaned forward and caressed the prince's cheek.

With feline grace, the prince glided up to Yeshe, acknowledging her folded hands and bowed languidly. Lightly brushing her hair aside, he said, 'Blessings, daughter of the Goddess ...'

Yeshe stepped back involuntarily, her eyes meeting her mother's which sparkled with wicked mirth.

Meanwhile, A-KarO's gaze roved around the room at leisure. 'Hmm ...' he murmured, 'pink and gold, like the boudoir of a virgin. Plush too! I would have thought you lived like a nun in a cloister, Yeshe. This is a surprise, but a bit extreme, nonetheless, isn't it? Perhaps the owner had some other in mind while decorating this home, hmm?'

Yeshe glanced at him sharply. 'Ah! So this surprises you?' she remarked tartly. 'These shades are pleasing to the eye – and warm. My divine mother prefers warm colours in the evening. So naturally, this was how my abode was done up.'

A-KarO seated himself next to the goddess and, in an instant, was rapt in a silent conversation with her. No words were uttered, as Namig, the heavenly tongue known only to a few in the hierarchy of the universe, flowed between them, the only hint of communication apparent in the alert stillness of their eyes. Their interaction over in moments, A-KarO stepped down off his seat, still holding the Goddess's gaze, and touched his forehead to her feet. As he sat up again, the goddess blessed him. Then she drew out a magnificent sword, its hilt studded with rubies, and, then blade first, sheathed it in his body. For a moment, a great, fiery, auburn-hued ring blazed around A-KarO. Then it disappeared. Only then did the Goddess look up and Yeshe signal for an attendant sprite to step forth with goblets of a misty golden liquid.

The Goddess beckoned to Narasimha, who came and sat by her side in one graceful move.

The Goddess smiled. 'You know what is expected of you, noble one?'

'Gracious Mother,' he replied, 'I was informed about it this morning during an audience with my father, the Rigden king. I am aware and ready.'

'Strange winds blow in the mortal world and the mind breeds corruption there,' the Goddess observed. 'Its stink reaches even the outskirts of the holy kingdom. As you are aware, a decision has been taken to arrest this tide and rechannelize human evolution. The infusion of pure cosmic energy is imperative. For that purpose, we are sending our architects from here. Narasimha, you have been selected to go to Earth, along with Prince A-KarO. Both the Buddha Avalokiteshwara and I seconded your name; your talents are sorely needed there. Your healing wisdom, innate compassion and infinite gentleness pair well with the vigour, dynamism and sheer energy of the dark prince, A-KarO. I think the two of you will make a good team.'

Narasimha bowed. 'I am honoured, Mother, to have been so chosen; it speaks of your trust in me.'

The Goddess held up her hand. 'I have something for you that will come in useful.' She opened her hand. A milky white opalescent stone with a pale thread strung through it lay shining on her palm. 'Here,' she offered, 'let me tie this on you.'

As Narasimha leaned forward, the Goddess tied the talisman around his neck.

'Keep this on you at all times,' she urged. 'With time, its multiple uses will become apparent to you.'

Narasimha bowed low again.

In one graceful movement, the Goddess was on her feet. She looked first at A-KarO and then at Narasimha. 'There's one more thing,' she said. 'Golden flower, Yeshe, ... goes with you.'

A stunned silence followed.

Narasimha was the first to address the Goddess. 'This is unprecedented, Mother,' he said. 'Of course, we had heard at the Council that the golden dakini, Yeshe, would be part of Lama Ozer's group on the mission to Earth, but we had assumed that you were transferring some of her energy to a mortal female form, as is the set norm for Devi emanations. Surely you are not sending Yeshe herself?'

There was a strange electric alertness in A-KarO's eyes as he looked up at the Goddess. 'A pure Goddess emanation has not stepped forth for aeons, Mother,' he said. 'And when that last happened, there was chaos. Battles broke out between the gods and the Asur. The cosmos was young, the need dire and Mahashakti herself answered it. Since then, she has rarely stepped forth herself, preferring to send her *shakti* into a human female primed for the task.'

The Goddess's eyes were mysterious as she answered, 'Perhaps now, more then ever before, is the need dire enough for her to step forth. Yes, my sons, the Council has decided to send Yeshe herself. The hour has come for the tide to be reversed and the universe to develop along untested evolutionary lines. I am sending forth my daughter; for aeons have I trained her for this day. Now it is come. Also, she does not go unaccompanied now; I entrust her to your care ...'

The Goddess rose and indicated that both princes should step forward. 'You will both protect her, aid her at every step and stand by her,' she declared. 'It is destined that while one of you will be friend and counsellor to her, the other will be her mate, joined with her in ancient rites to bring forth a new age. One will be the foundation, the other the releaser of unrivalled force; one the grounding essence of Earth, the other, *agni* itself. She is my daughter, mistress to none. Her essence is lightning; she walks in freedom. Mind, treat her accordingly. I charge you with the task of standing by her, never abandoning her. And now I will bond you.' The Goddess looked at Yeshe. 'Daughter, come!'

Yeshe stepped forth slowly, her face pale, her eyes inscrutable. She came over and stood in the centre. Narasimha stood to her right and A-KarO silently took up position to her left. The Goddess took Yeshe's right palm in her own. Then she took Narasimha's hand, placing her palm on his. 'Yeshe,' she said, 'hold Narasimha's hand.' The Goddess took A-KarO's left hand and placed it, palm down, on Yeshe's hand. 'A-KarO,' said the Goddess, 'hold Yeshe's hand.'

Silently, she let a spray of red light melt into Yeshe's left palm and a clear spray of white light into her right palm, until her left hand had merged into A-KarO's left, forming a vortex of red light and her right hand merged into Narasimha's right, forming a vortex of white light.

'*Om*,' said the Goddess. 'The bond is formed; it will answer to its holders. The holders will answer to the bond.' She smiled as she brought the rite to a conclusion. 'Now, do any of you have any questions?' she asked.

A-KarO stood in silence, looking at her from beneath hooded eyes. Then he spoke. 'No, Mother, your words are binding and there is immense clarity.'

The Goddess then looked at Narasimha. 'And you, my son, is it clear?' she asked.

Narasimha smiled, his gentleness enfolding all in an embrace. 'Mother, can one question you or the manifest will that you represent?' he said.

The Goddess smiled at him. 'Ever artful, hmm, Narasimha?'

At last, she addressed Yeshe. 'I shall take leave now, my daughter. I leave you to attend to your guests. Look after them well.'

So saying, she disappeared, leaving a silent vacuum behind.

Without a word, Yeshe walked back to the centre of the room and sat down on the divan the Goddess had vacated. For a space, utter silence reigned. Narasimha gazed reflectively out through the vast windows. A-KarO leaned back in his seat, a half-smile playing on his face. And Yeshe sat leaning forward, watching the lamplight filter through her fingers.

At last she looked up. 'Forgive me,' she said, 'I forget myself ...'

At a signal from her, the sprites in attendance brought forth refreshments. Yeshe handed out goblets of a frothing golden brew to the princes. Both accepted the drinks, but declined everything else.

Narasimha looked at Yeshe and said, 'Change comes. What I had sensed was impending for some time has occurred.'

'Yes,' Yeshe smiled. 'I wonder what this will mean. Time is intruding upon us now. I can almost sense its beat even here in our midst.'

A-KarO remarked, 'Back into time, hmm, and into the mortal world? Good sport out there.'

Yeshe looked at him sharply. 'Much preparation has to be made ...'

A-KarO butted in with, 'Travel light, my dear, take little. Anyhow, I don't think you will be allowed much, if anything, from here.' He looked at Narasimha. 'You too. Just what you wear and what you will have dire need of. That too the Council will consider and decide on. It is very doubtful if they will allow anything at all, but preparation of another kind can be made.' Prince A-KarO turned back to Yeshe. 'One hint I'll give you, daughter of the Goddess: ask your divine mother to arrange an audience with the Nag queen, Nilamani; request her to arrange for it now, before we leave, for there is something that the queen, my mother, would like to give you. You may need to make a short journey to acquire this gift, but I would advise you to carry it on you once it is in your hands.'

Yeshe looked up at him. 'All right,' she agreed, 'I shall ask her.'

The light shone golden on her face and, for a moment, it looked intensely fragile. Silence descended on the room again, an uninterrupted stillness. A heady feeling of exhilaration arose from the three and danced in the fragrant air, spinning gossamer-fine patterns across it. At a gesture from Yeshe, a *tanpura* was brought in. As her fingers delicately danced across the strings, divine melody rose from them and wafted in the air. Outside, raindrops fell softly and moonlight caressed the leaves and ferns that grew wild. Finally, as the strains of music died into the night, Narasimha and

A-KarO rose to take their leave. Yeshe held out her hands to both and, silently, they held her hand for a moment then took their leave off her. Swiftly leaving the opulent room and accompanied by attendants they made their way to the corridor outside. Yeshe stood alone with a bemused expression on her face.

IV

Lama Nyima Ozer and his endearing young disciple, Tashi Thendup, sat near the crescent-moon-shaped crystal pool, enjoying the indescribable beauty of the scene that unfolded before them. Tashi held a bag of peanuts in his hand; from time to time, he offered generous helpings from it to an indolent Chetak, the midnight-blue wind horse who stood by his side.

'Ahh! Lovely clean open air, at last, and real fresh grass to feed upon,' Chetak neighed merrily. 'This is a delight for any horse, even us wind horses. Being in the palace is always an intense business, my boy.'

Tashi nodded his assent, looking at Chetak with wide eyes. 'Yes, Your Horse Lordship,' he said, 'it is a relief being out of the palace. This vista is stunning. Now only if one could get a bowl of *thukpa* and butter tea – ah!'

Chetak turned his long, dark muzzle towards Tashi and his bright green eyes sparkled with mirth. 'It is ages, my beloved boy, since anyone called me his "Horse Lordship". This is a sore point and you have scored high. We wind horses are celestial creatures, lords in our own right, but most denizens who acquire us forget this very conveniently. For this alone, I shall grant your wish.'

In a flash, a steaming hot bowl of *thukpa* – Tibetan noodle soup – appeared out of nowhere, along with a cup of butter tea.

'Now, boy, eat swiftly,' Chetak urged. 'I am screening us with a spell, but it won't last long.'

Lama Ozer looked up abstractedly from his meditation on the still pool. 'Even here, boy, you and that horse of yours can only think of eating,' he remarked with asperity. 'Now kindly move towards that knot of trees and leave me alone with the silence.'

'As you wish, Lama,' Tashi hurriedly responded, gesturing to Chetak to follow him.

The boy walked at a leisurely pace, with the steed following him.

'Lamas are strange creatures, my boy,' Chetak observed. 'It is wisest to keep away from them. The stronger they are, the more prickly they get and your priceless lama is a perfect example of this. Take my case, for example. For aeons, I have kept well away from the priestly set. Oh, I've served the gods all right. By choice, you know. I've run errands for them, fought in cosmic battles, carried messages. You cannot imagine the life I've lived. But a priest, a sage or an adept? I've kept well away from them. Now thanks to you, I'm in the hands of the worst category – an evolved lama, a mysterious adept, whose depths even many of the gods know not. Mark my words well: that lama of yours will surprise many – perhaps himself as well – with what lies within him. All I know is that life for the two of us – you and me – is not going to be easy at all, nor even comfortable. But anyhow, it is what it is.'

Tashi made his way into a small cluster of golden-hued oak trees with auburn leaves and sunny flowers that grew along the edge of the pool. He settled himself there, his back resting against a huge tree stump, and dug into the steaming noodle soup. In minutes, his meal was over. Tashi closed his eyes as he savoured the familiar taste and warmth of the salted butter tea. Beautiful as Shambala was, he was suddenly overcome by nostalgia for home and the hidden Demazong Monastery. Chetak grazed languorously, the afternoon sun picking out velvety glints in his perfect coat. It was so peaceful. Butterflies with red-tipped wings fluttered about in the slightly humid air. A profusion of violet and purple wild flowers dotted the foliage. Tashi let his head fall back. Sated, he contemplated the perfect crescent-moon shape of the silvery pool as it stretched before him. Shining wavelets glowed in the afternoon light, throwing off bright reflections into the fragrant air. Overhead, an immaculate blue sky, streaked with feathery white clouds, stretched away endlessly. Tashi tossed off his slippers and let his bare feet feel the grass and the earth. His being shone forth, unblemished, and his soul soared, untrammelled in its purity ...

Tashi refocused on the grove and found Chetak nudging him out of his somnolence.

'Boy, don't doze by the poolside. Else, it will take you days to recover and we have but a few left in this dimension. Now I have some good news for you. As was revealed in the Council meeting, it is our good fortune that the prince, A-KarO, and the heir, Prince Narasimha Senge, are both accompanying us on our journey to Earth. This is unexpected good news. I already feel much better about this excursion into the human dimension.'

Tashi jumped up in delight. 'The great Prince A-KarO is coming! I know this is unbelievable! And the Crown Prince too! This was announced at the Council assembly. I was stunned to hear it then. Also, Chetak, the dakini, Yeshe, is accompanying us.'

'Shh ... Relax, boy! Most of Shambala knows this,' Chetak said.

Tashi smiled broadly. 'Thanks to the presence of the princes, we are sure to succeed in this mission. At least, we have a fair chance of it.'

A few paces away, Lama Ozer had completed his meditation by the poolside and had risen to his feet. He beckoned for Tashi and Chetak to join him. In minutes, the boy was standing by his side.

'It is time, my boy, to return to Kalapa,' the lama announced. 'The Buddha Avalokiteshwara will be expecting us soon. Do not forget we have an audience with him later this evening.'

Tashi nodded.

'Also, boy, the Council at divine Aggartha meets soon. We have to be prepared for that. Many decisions will be taken there, along with the day and time of our departure.' Lama Ozer smiled at Tashi. 'Rest while you can, boy. The days ahead will be tough. Now we head back into the city.'

Lama Ozer stepped into a golden chariot parked unobtrusively by the side of the pool. Tashi mounted Chetak and the steed trotted alongside the chariot as it moved ahead.

CHAPTER 7

NILAMANI

I

Standing alone in the temple sanctum at the heart of divine Shambala, Yeshe sighed deeply; it was almost time for her journey into the depths of the ocean, to the subterranean shores of the Nag kingdom. On Prince A-KarO's advice, Yeshe had immediately urged her mother, the White Tara, to seek an audience with the Nag queen, Nilamani, on her behalf. And the latter had asked the dakini to pay her a swift visit before she departed on her divine mission to the mortal world, as the Nag queen had something of great import to convey to her.

Yeshe slowly began performing the rites for her journey. A brilliant sphere blazed in the heart of emptiness as she formed the subtle mandala and let the mantra reverberate through it. Dark red energy floated through the void and the dakini released herself into its vortex, as it carried her away. In moments, the temple had disappeared. Encased within the bubble of ruby light, she hurtled through the skies towards the vast water body that glistened off the shores of Shambala. The silver ocean shone in the morning light and teeming waves rose and subsided with a gentle rhythm. Yeshe watched the play of the silver waters, her being becoming one with the rise and fall of the waves. Where did the waters end and the sky begin? There were no boundaries, as one melted into the other in silence, nothingness merging blissfully into nothingness.

Yeshe smiled as she submerged herself in the waters; ribbon-like, her essence rippled through their depths. The silvery waves on the ocean's surface gave way to a clear aquamarine centre that ripened into a pure emerald as the depth increased. The dakini could hear the song of the fish and the silent communion of the fragile plant life that mushroomed everywhere. Onwards she travelled, moving swiftly through the waters. Past hillocks, teeming flora and shoals of fish she went, till she had come upon a vast mountain that rose up from somewhere close to the centre of the ocean. Music reverberated off this mountain, as did iridescent light patterns. Three shining figures detached themselves from its base and floated towards her. The central figure was a Mer maiden, with a pale, silvery green tail that gleamed in the waters. Her upper body was bare but for the rare precious jewels – coral and pearl necklaces – that adorned it. Her long, lustrous silver hair floated around her, reflecting a myriad lights and, on her head, she wore an amethyst set in gold that flashed deep purple sparks. The two Mer maidens accompanying her were much younger. They had flashing green eyes and wore bright coral clips in their long, dark hair. Their only other adornment, strings of rich, crimson-hued flowers, cascaded colorfully over their silvery bodies.

All three Mer maidens pressed their palms together and bowed low before Yeshe. Then the older one stepped forward.

'Dakini,' she began, 'we were intimated of your passage and have been waiting here in readiness to guide you to the shores of the Nag kingdom. I am Ngi Wo-Tsen, younger sister of Queen Ngaki Rhi Tsen, regent of the Mer people, and these are my twin daughters, Chen-Ma and Chen-Chu. We have prepared an arbour for you to rest in and some entertainment for you. We hope it will be to your liking.'

Yeshe inclined her head in acknowledgement and held up her palm in blessing. 'Dear ones,' she responded, 'there is no time for rest. I must travel in haste. So let us put the entertainment aside and move with all speed towards Nagpuri. I thank you, however, for making this effort on my behalf.'

Ngi Wo-Tsen sank to her. Her two daughters followed suit. In a moment, they were up, with Ngi taking the lead and the twins flanking Yeshe on either side. Swiftly, they streaked through the waters in an arc, making for a tunnel at the base of the mountain.

'Dakini, the Nag country is located exactly in the centre of this mountain, Nagdhenu,' Ngi told Yeshe. 'That vast tunnel opening just ahead leads straight to their cities which are located under the ocean floor. We will lead you directly to their capital, the Kalrajya Soma Nagpuri.'

With that, Ngi picked up speed, lithely cutting through the ocean waters, her slim body a blur of light-filled motion.

Yeshe inclined her head, letting her arms drift in the waters and gently pick at the sunbeams that filtered through. Soon, the small group had become just a shimmer in the rich emerald waters, indistinguishable from one another. Yeshe's mind was suspended in the light particles as they hummed and created myriad vibrations. She listened with delight to the silent communion of the subterranean creatures and gently diffused peace into their core as she passed them by, like the unknown whisper of a pleasant breeze from a magical shore that had somehow wandered through.

The ocean stretched out in serene quietude, the silence intense; all that could be heard was the occasional tinkling of the silver bells in Ngi's hair. The twins maintained a stoic silence, with Ngi checking on their progress from time to time. The Nagdhenu Mountain loomed ahead, growing larger and larger. Without a speck of soil on it, it seemed to be made of a shining black stone, its surface polished and gleaming with subterranean lights. No foliage grew on it and subterranean creatures seemed to avoid the mountain, leaving its environs free of all marine life, except for the occasional dark, smooth, glistening Nag or long, winding sea serpents that swam past, unconcerned. Once in a rare while, one of the Mer people drifted by, bowing to Ngi in passing.

As Yeshe and her escort of Mer maidens neared the towering Nagdhenu, the water became darker and heavier, like oil. While crossing into the shadow of the glistening stone that jutted out, the dakini let her fingers lightly skim the polished mountainside. The mountain felt alive, throbbing and pulsing under her touch, enticing, inviting. Yet an involuntary shudder ran down her spine. They had entered the Nag kingdom's heated and deeply sensual energy field.

Ngi shook her head, indicating that they should stop. 'Dakini, we have crossed into Nag territory,' she explained, 'and I have made contact with the Nag authorities; they have an escort waiting for you a league or two into the tunnel. I will accompany you till that spot, but do excuse the twins; we do not permit our Mer maidens contact with the Nag energy.'

Yeshe inclined her head in acknowledgement. 'Whatever you deem best, Ngi,' she said, 'though I think all three of you should take leave now. I'll make my way to the place where the Nag escort awaits me. I really do not want to impose on you further.'

Ngi bowed her head and murmured, 'Dakini, your journey into our lands is a rare honour. Do allow me the pleasure of accompanying you into the tunnel.'

Yeshe nodded her assent. The twins bowed low before Yeshe, hands folded, and touched her feet. The dakini smiled softly, running her fingers through their hair and handing each sister a fistful of glistening turquoise stones.

II

In moments, Yeshe and Ngi had crossed into the tunnel. In an instant, the dakini felt the change, the heightened vibration, the wild turbulence of the Nag *kundalini* and, underlying it, the perfect control. Yeshe let her etheric body dip into the oil-smooth waters and felt their current run through her. Slowly, she lay back, letting the current carry her. Released by the very touch of the waters, bliss arose within her and as she looked at the roof of the dark cavern, she heard the laughter of the mother essence all around her. Ahead, Ngi swam lithely through the waves, but her body was tense, surrounded by vibrations of nervous energy. Yeshe sent forth a tendril of bliss to melt Ngi's tension. And then, a blush of rose suffusing her etheric cheeks, her gaze intoxicated, she drifted silently towards the Nagmandali, where Nilamani waited.

Ngi turned to look back at her companion and halted in consternation. 'Dakini, look!' she called out. 'Some kind of transformation has overtaken you. Arrest it, goddess! These waters are infamous for accomplishing just such a mutation.'

Yeshe looked down at herself and laughed uproariously. Her body, now shorn of all clothing, had lost its faint ivory hue and floated on the waters, a bright emerald green. Wound around her neck was a gold necklace. A weighted chain of emeralds set in gold was linked around her waist, the gems sparkling down till her thighs. She wore armbands of obsidian, with a black cobra twisted around them, and on her head sat a coronet of gold and emeralds, again with an obsidian cobra resting in the centre. Her dark raven hair spilled wildly down to her waist, shielding her breasts from the kiss of the oceanic waves.

Looking down at her lush emerald body, the dakini laughed wildly, 'Ah, Ngi!' she said, 'do not take fright. This is not the effect of the waters, my dear. Are you not learned in my lore? This is my central aspect, the Green Tara, which has unveiled itself in bliss here. In the Nagmandali, I shall be green, shorn of everything, naked as the skies, and so shall I meet Queen Nilamani who has summoned me there.'

Ahead of them, the tunnel narrowed and, a few leagues down, branched off into two smaller tunnels. Awaiting them to the left of the smaller, darker tunnel was the Nag escort – a Nag lord and, flanking him, two Nagins. Yeshe and Ngi halted for a timeless moment, watching the company glide up to them. The Nag was well over seven feet tall. His upper torso was bare and of a pale yellow hue; the lower portion of sandy golden skin that shone even in the dim light of the tunnel was pure serpent. His dark hair was tied back in a severe style. His dark, well-defined eyes glowed with a reddish glint and around his neck hung several gold necklaces studded with precious gems. As he neared Yeshe, the Nag lord went through an instant transformation; his reptilian lower body disappeared, giving way to a man's form, clad in a light gold silk dhoti and sandals. The Nag folded his hands and bowed low.

The Nagins were a different matter. They stood by the Nag's side as pure black cobras, hoods flared, dark eyes alert. As the Nag completed his bows, however, they uncoiled their bodies and stretched, transforming themselves into two similar-looking Nag maidens of exquisite beauty, their forms glowing with a strange, indefinable radiance. Identical in height, they were clad in scarlet and gold dhotis and scarlet blouses. Their night-black hair was tied back in elaborate chignons. Their complexion was dark, their features well defined. Their light brown eyes shone a burnished gold in the dark tunnel and their gold nose-rings enhanced the feature they adorned, making it distinctive.

The Nag maidens now stepped forward and embraced Yeshe wholeheartedly. For a few moments, laughter filled the air and the tunnel sparkled with an electric current.

'Dakini, it has been long since we met,' said Lopala, one of the twins. 'Yet there has never been a day when we did not remember you or the period you spent among us at the Nagmandali.'

Her sister, Tripala, smiled archly at Yeshe and said, 'How could you, Dakini, take such an age to pay us another visit and that too such a hurried one. Hmm, Yeshe, you have almost forgotten us. How could you do this?'

Yeshe laughed, the sound trilling like a million chimes ringing in the distance. 'Ah! You all complain so! All you had to do was send word that you were missing me and I would have had you lifted and taken to the Azure Palace. Now let the lord get a word in; he looks most uncomfortable with the way you are carrying on.'

Gracefully, the Nag lord, Sa Nagen Vardhmana, bowed low before Yeshe, then rose and folded his hands together. 'I, Sa Nagen Vardhmana,' he declared, 'am here to welcome you, O Devi, on behalf of the reigning Nag monarch, Neelkantha Dharmapala, and our gracious queen, the Nagrani Nilamani Devi, and escort you to our capital city, the Kalrajya Soma Nagpuri, the Nagmandali that shines bright in the heart of the Nagdhenu.' The Nag touched his hand to his breast

Yeshe offered her divine smile and inclined her head. 'I am ready, Lord Sa Nagen Vardhmana,' she said. 'We can leave at any moment.'

'Then we must depart immediately, Devi, for the Nagrani awaits you most eagerly. We also welcome Ngi Wo-Tsen of the Mer people, should she wish to serve as your companion during your journey to the Nagmandali and your sojourn there.'

Yeshe looked at Ngi and said, 'My dear, you have travelled long and must be tired. Would you like to accompany me into the Nagmandali and rest there for a while? And if you are not too busy, why not spend a few days with me there?'

Ngi bowed before Yeshe. 'It is an honour, Dakini, to serve you,' she murmured. 'I was hoping you would allow me to accompany you into the Nagmandali.'

Yeshe looked at the Nag lord and declared, 'That is decided then, Lord. Ngi accompanies me. Lead on.'

Nagen bowed before Yeshe and moved ahead. Pulling out a slender black rod, he ignited it; a pulsing beam of red light shot out from it and into the dark, narrow tunnel. In moments, a smooth, streamlined black and silver craft had glided out of the tunnel. Shaped like a black diamond, the craft was a magical vehicle powered by the turbulent Nag *kundalini* – a massive energy source for the Nag kingdom. Compact in size, it glowed with sparkling red lights. Nagen pointed the rod at the craft and lights shimmered brightly as one part of it slid open, revealing the interior. From the portals, a sharp blue beam of light fell on the company and sucked them in.

From within, the craft was spherical in shape. The interiors were made of a smooth, glowing transparent material devoid of all colour. Comfortable plush seating lined the walls and transparent low tables were laid here and there. At the centre of the craft was a black stone engraving depicting two intersecting triangles suspended in a glistening sphere that hung in midair. Other than for this, the craft was devoid of all decoration. Yet in no way was it lacking in comfort. Subdued music played; the lighting was unusual but muted and the entire ambience had an incredible electric charge.

Lopala and Tripala attended on Yeshe, while Ngi settled back in her seat which, amazingly enough, moulded itself around her body. The Nag lord positioned himself in the centre of the craft, facing the floating sphere.

'Dakini, we are ready to leave now,' he announced. 'We will head towards the city and, in fifteen minutes, if we go by Nag time, we will have reached the capital in the heart of Nagmandali.'

For a moment, his eyes shimmered with a strange intensity as his focused thought waves impacted on the intersecting triangles, setting the craft in motion. Yet there was no sense of movement whatsoever. Only the scenery outside the window kept changing as the craft moved at incredible speed through a maze of tunnels that cut directly into the heart of the Nagdhenu Mountain. As they shot through its centre, they came upon a vast, perfectly spherical cavern, a kind of hangar for crafts in transit. Some were parked there, while others moved at high speed, navigating their way through the tunnels. The cavern was brightly illuminated with blue light, though its source was not apparent; it simply welled up uniformly and filled the vast space.

In the space of an instant, their craft had shot through the cavern into a huge underground chute that led into the Earth. The vessel went into a freefall and descended a few leagues below the cavern. Then turning right, it emerged on emerald grounds under an endless purple sky. They had finally reached the Nagmandali. Yeshe smiled in delight, as fresh currents of air danced around and nipped at her, invigorating her system. Black basalt rocks crunched under their feet as they stepped on to Nag soil. Ahead of them, huge unbroken pieces of black rock, glowing with golden lights, soared into the sky. This felt so familiar. Yeshe remembered how, an aeon ago, she had spent her tender years here under the tutelage of Queen Nilamani. With the Nag lord leading, Yeshe followed, flanked by the two Nagins. Ngi brought up the rear, her head drooping from the onslaught of Nag energy and its after-effects. Awaiting them on the tarmac ahead was a welcoming delegation: six Nag maidens, led by a silver-haired noble. Yeshe recognized Tsatsum Jejun Tsela, the royal priestess and elder sister of Queen Nilamani.

The priestess presented a regal, if formidable sight. Her light-filled deep blue eyes shone through silver lashes and her silver hair, veiled in a filmy grey wrap that fell to her waist, was tied back in a bun. Although her features were regal and her golden skin unlined, there was nothing youthful about her; authority and penance had left their undeniable stamp on her. Beneath the simple, light grey robe that fell to her ankles, her body was lean and spare. Her only adornment was a simple silver belt around her waist.

As the dakini approached them, Tsatsum sank to her knees, as did her six maidens.

'At last, Golden Flower, at last you come and at what a time!' she murmured. 'The very sight of you is bliss, O Eternal One.'

Yeshe smiled and went down on her knees before Tsatsum. 'When was I ever parted from you, my dearest?" she responded.

Silently, she extended her arms and enfolded Tsatsum in an embrace. Warm tears rolled down the priestess's cheeks. The six maidens formed a circle around them, screening the pair from curious eyes.

III

A recovered Tsatsum turned to the Nag lord. 'We will take over now, Lord Sa Nagen Vardhmana,' she declared. 'You have done well and may retire for the day.' She turned to the two younger Nagins. 'As for the two of you, you may return to the royal palace and to your duties there. That will be all.' Finally, Tsatsum addressed the Mer maiden, Ngi, gently welcoming her. 'We have not met before,' she said, 'but it is an honour to meet you, Ngi Wo-Tsen of the Mer people. You are blessed, indeed, to have been selected as a companion by the wisdom dakini, Yeshe.'

Ngi folded her hands and bowed before Tsatsum. 'It is an honour to meet you, Royal Priestess and Ancient One, O Tsatsum Jejun Tsela,' she said. 'I am sure this visit is going to prove most delightful; I have long wanted to visit the Nagmandali.'

'You are most welcome here and can stay as long as your heart desires,' said Tsatsum.

The royal priestess gestured towards a waiting vehicle, a sleek, streamlined black craft that was angular in shape. As they neared it the doors opened soundlessly. Stepping inside, Yeshe found that the interior was comfortable, with adequate seating arrangements. An arched transparent bubble covered the top.

'Dakini, please take a seat,' Tsatsum urged, ushering Yeshe into a comfortable position in front and taking a seat to her right.

Ngi and two of the maidens sat at the back, the rest being accommodated in another craft that was waiting inconspicuously by the side.

'We head for the temple grounds just outside the city, Dakini,' Tsatsum told Yeshe. 'I have made arrangements for your stay at our temple guest-house, instead of at the palace, though the queen would rather have had you stay there. But I insisted. I hope the guest-house meets with your approval. Along with my maidens, I will personally wait on you there.'

'As ever, you know my mind well, Mother Tsatsum,' Yeshe smiled. 'While in the Nagmandali, I have always stayed on the temple premises. And that is where I would like to be. Now when do we meet with the Queen Mother? As you know, time is short and this visit of mine is a hurried one.'

'This very night, after you have refreshed yourself, I will take you to the queen's apartments. You will have an informal audience with her followed by dinner. She is very keen to meet you at the earliest. That is the programme. I was rather hoping you would have your meeting tomorrow, but this is the royal commandment.'

'That is as it should be, Tsatsum,' Yeshe said. 'As I said earlier, this visit is a hurried one. I will, most likely, leave the Nagmandali in the morning and head back to Shambala.'

As the black craft gracefully moved ahead, they saw the Nagmandali stretched out below them. Dark, writhing buildings, their surfaces gleaming, rose into the air. Wide thoroughfares spiralled in an elliptical design and vast water bodies dotted the city, as did expanses of forest. Dense forest lined the city's outskirts, where the craft stopped for several minutes, waiting for the massive traffic that came in from the hinterland to clear. Then it shot forward again. The skies were stained a deep, blushing pink as evening descended. Suddenly, the craft moved at speed into a vast forest reserve, dense with trees that had white barks and thick, fleshy leaves which gave off a wonderfully heady aroma.

Yeshe looked around her with delight. A fragrance here, the rustle of a leaf there, awakened memories of moments from her younger days. In the heart of this glade and on the edge of the Nag Kund, a circular, pitch-dark lake, whose waters shone the same velvety black by night and by day, stood the Nag temple. On either side of it were well-laid-out lawns and small glowing white monasteries to house the priestesses and acolytes. Towards the southern end sat the temple guest-house with its distinctive sloping silver roof and plain white walls overrun with creepers.

The craft came to rest on the driveway and Yeshe stepped out. Evening was about to overtake dusk, the crimson glow from the skies creating a strange fire within the heart of the Nag Kund. Laughing softly, the dakini walked to the edge of the black waters. Throwing off her slippers, she let her bare feet rest in their coolness. The waters frothed around her feet in greeting, the bubbles surprisingly white against the black lake.

Tsatsum silently came up to stand by her side. 'Always you do this, Yeshe,' she observed. 'Next, you will immerse yourself in the lake if I am not there to remind you that we are time bound here, unlike in fair Shambala.'

Yeshe looked up at the priestess. 'Ah, yes,' she agreed. Then let's get ready for the audience with the queen. That's what I am here for and there is no time to waste.'

Tsatsum and her maidens ushered Yeshe and Ngi into the temple guest-house with its pastel interiors and subdued lighting. The dakini had barely taken a seat when a priestess entered and bowed low before her and Tsatsum.

'Mother, the palace has already sent a winged chariot for the dakini,' she announced, addressing Tsatsum. 'They have also sent a suitable escort for her and the official representative is waiting outside.'

Tsatsum looked up at the priestess. 'But this is unprecedented,' she protested. 'The dakini has barely landed. It was agreed they would come after an hour. Well, tell the official representative to wait and have refreshments served to him.' Tsatsum turned to Yeshe apologetically. 'I am sorry, dearest,' she said. 'The Queen Mother must be really anxious to see you. More so than I imagined.'

Yeshe looked unperturbed. 'Then it is time for me to leave for the palace,' she decided. 'Ngi waits here.'

'Dakini,' Tsatsum interrupted, 'the maidens are about to bring refreshments. Also, I have had a formal robe prepared for you to wear for your audience with the Queen Mother. Surely you do not intend travelling there unadorned as you are? And as usual, you are carrying no baggage with you.'

'You know, Tsatsum, that I require no refreshment,' Yeshe smiled. 'The waters from the lake were enough to do the needful, as was the fragrance of yonder trees. As for the garment, you know me; I will neither dress in anything elaborate nor adorn myself with finery!'

A pair of maidens brought in trays laden with sweetmeats and a vast array of delicacies. Another poured tea into a silver bowl and placed it before Yeshe, bowing low as she did so.

'Ha! Now look what you have done, Tsatsum,' Yeshe said tartly. 'You've had half your kitchen turn up here.'

Unruffled, Tsatsum handed the dakini her tea. Yeshe accepted it with a sniff, but shook her head at the lavish spread of delicacies that had been placed before her.

'Dakini, I know you like these; so take one, for my sake,' Tsatsum suggested, holding out a silver salver with small brown sweetmeats.

Yeshe grudgingly took one, gently biting into it and then closing her eyes as the familiar flavour burst in her mouth, the sweetness and spice delighting her.

In silence, she finished her tea. Then she stood up quickly and addressed Ngi. 'My dear, relax here,' she told her. 'Be at ease. I will return once my obligations at the palace have been duly fulfilled.' Then she turned to Tsatsum, 'Well, let us be off, then,' she declared.

Tsatsum shook her head. 'Not till you have worn something, Dakini,' she reminded her. 'The Queen Mother will not like you landing in nothing but your gorgeous emerald hide.'

Yeshe looked at her and said patiently, 'Then produce whatever you want me to be clad in, Tsatsum.'

At a gesture from the priestess, one of the maidens stepped forward with a stark white robe of soft material.

'I know well your taste, Devi,' Tsatsum said. 'The white robe you like is ready.'

She helped Yeshe into the garment herself, then tied the ribbons that held the back in place. The fabric, fine and gossamer-thin, fell like a cloud around her body and clung to it softly. The robe was gathered together at the waist by a thick black belt that encircled it three times. The simple, V-shaped neckline showed off to perfection the glowing emerald form underneath. Tsatsum brushed out Yeshe's hair, letting it flow naturally down to her waist. Then she fastened the dakini's thick gold-and-emerald belt around her waist, adjusted the coronet of emeralds on her hair and arranged her numerous necklaces to her satisfaction.

'I think this is enough,' Yeshe said decisively. 'We should leave now.'

Tsatsum fussed over the dakini for a few moments more, then escorted her into the winged golden chariot which was harnessed to a pair of golden winged chargers. Soon, they were flying over the temple grounds and into the hills that lay beyond.

IV

The palace lay in the heart of the purple mountains that shadowed the city and embraced it from three sides. Wrought from a material that glowed in the moonlight, the sprawling structure nestled like a diamond in a deeply forested belt and was surrounded by carefully nurtured gardens. The chariot landed on the extensive lawns facing the central palace with its shining, filigreed columns that soared up into the dark night.

As Yeshe stepped out with Tsatsum, a royal delegation was waiting to welcome them. Her body laden with sparkling jewels of rare value, a tall, stern-faced Nagin dressed in a gold blouse and a green flared skirt with a gold border and elaborate pleats stood facing them. Accompanying her were two noble Nagins of lower rank. Both were dressed to the hilt as well, but did not match the grandeur of their senior.

The older Nagin put her palms together and bent low to touch Yeshe's feet. 'Dakini, it is such an honour to have you here, to be in your presence,' she murmured.

Yeshe stepped forward and raised her hand in blessing towards all three.

'Dakini, I am Utpalini Senge and this is Niral Streepalini and Nandini Dharmapalini,' said the older Nagin. 'The Queen Mother awaits you. I shall escort you to her.'

Tsatstum looked at Utpalini pointedly. 'We need to hurry,' she reminded her. 'This is no time for formal welcomes and speeches, Utpalini. Now let's get started.'

Utpalini bowed low before Tsastum and murmured, 'As you wish, Mother Tsatsum.'

Soon, Yeshe was walking through midnight-blue corridors, done up in turquoise and gold, that opened into vast halls glistening with amber light and rich furnishings. Nag lords and Nagins could be seen moving about with ease and guards in royal regalia were stationed at the gates. Utpalini led them up a winding flight of stairs which opened on to a sprawling garden on the roof of the palace, lit up with blue and pink lanterns that hung suspended from artistically trimmed tree branches. Groves of Ashoka trees cast deep shadows on the emerald carpet of manicured grass that stretched out in every direction. In the centre of the garden, a circular pool lay under the shadow of a huge banyan tree. Queen Nilamani and her entourage stood waiting there.

The Nag queen stepped forward and embraced Yeshe as the dakini moved into the tree's shadow. 'At last, Golden Flower!' the queen exclaimed. 'It has been an aeon since I beheld you! At last, Celestial Maiden, O Mistress of the Word! Long has my heart thirsted for this very moment! And into what beauty you have come now, when you were but a girl here under my care!'

Yeshe lightly floated out of Nilamani's embrace and tinkling laughter wafted away in the heady breeze, suddenly redolent with the perfume of rose blossoms.

'Ah, dearest Queen Mother, for you, I shall ever be a maiden,' she said. 'And in my timeless world, ever am I a maiden. For me, neither dawn comes nor dusk. Just one exists, just one beat – that of eternity.'

Nilamani and Yeshe looked at each other, the deepest love welling up and pouring from their eyes to light up the environs. It seemed as though a thousand bees were buzzing over an immortal blossom.

A soft breeze blew past Nilamani's auburn tresses as they spilled on to her sapphire blouse and played with her skirts that hid her lithe and vital form. Sapphire light emanated from her dark eyes and a coronet of sapphires sat on her head. The sapphire and gold jewellery she wore threw cerulean lights across her form that swayed lightly with the breeze.

The colour of her skin was a perfect, untarnished gold, as it shone with vitality in the night air.

From a gold salver, Nilamani picked up rose petals and showered them on Yeshe's head. She garlanded the dakini with orange blossoms and then looked directly at her.

'Are you ready, Peerless One? It is time. I will now begin the ritual for which you have come.'

Yeshe looked back at her, standing erect, the breeze playing with her thick, tangled hair.

At a signal from the Nag queen, two Nagins stepped forward instantly and bowed to Yeshe before beginning to undress her. Silence fell over the gathering as the light, gossamer-thin gown was pulled over the dakini's head and set aside. In the yellow light of the lanterns swaying in the breeze, Yeshe's skin shone a deep, golden-hued emerald. With practised hands, the attendants removed her jewellery, till she was shorn of everything except her glowing hide.

Queen Nilamani gestured towards the still pool. 'Begin with the ritual bath, Yeshe,' she directed. 'Take care to swim to the centre of the pool before immersing yourself in the water.'

On cue, Yeshe floated towards the pool and gently stepped into the black waters which felt distinctly warm to the touch. Then she was swimming towards the centre. Reaching it, she immersed herself. The pool linked the Nagmandali to the nether region and an orange glow permeated the semi-heated waters. Yeshe felt her being empty there as bliss waves reached out from the heated rocks and the gravelly sand at the bottom of the pool. Her ethereal skin glowed as she let herself sink deep into the waters and softly settle on the sandy floor. Heat waves from the earth poured light into her being, till she felt herself burn with vitality and energy.

Then with a swish he came, the giant Nag, the colossal black cobra that rested in the dark pit below the earth. He flowed out of a hole in the earth, his massive serpentine girth filling the pool, till nothing else was visible. Coil upon coil of serpent skin settled around Yeshe, till she was ringed by the serpent in a neat but precise circle. The heat in the pool was unbearable now, but the dakini floated in the waters peacefully, her skin smooth, fragrant and cool to the touch, her mind still, calm as a spring day in the highlands and empty of thought, carefree as the breeze that blew between the clouds. She watched the serpent as he moved lethally through the waters, the ancient Nag, emperor of the cosmic ocean, a being unparalleled. Finally, his gigantic head swung around and his burnished copper eyes came to rest on Yeshe. The dakini looked deep into those eyes, absorbing the massive cosmic *shakti* that radiated from the celestial serpent. There was a distinct, supranormal hum in the waters that frothed with energy as the serpent sent wave after wave of heat energy into her. Yeshe felt herself filling up like a dynamo and then the serpent established telepathic communion with her.

'You are ready, little one,' he said. 'And now, I shall inject my essence into you. Henceforth, you are empowered to channel Mahakundalini and bring in the new age of sacred fire, of sacrifice and rejuvenation. For aeons, Dakini, have you been readied and prepared, purely for this great celestial task of ringing in the age of fire, of Mahashakti, the Golden Age in the mortal world. The time has come. The moment of sacrifice is at hand. You will incarnate in female form in the mortal world.'

Yeshe looked straight at the celestial serpent. 'O Shesh Nag, Monarch of the Cosmic Ocean, I am in readiness,' she announced. 'The trust will be fulfilled.'

The Nag's dark eyes looked directly into Yeshe's, the mirror of emptiness. His forked tongue shot out and wrapped itself around her neck, stinging her ethereal body sharply. The dakini's head jerked back, as currents of pain and fire were unleashed into her body. Her green skin grew transparent and copper fire roiled wildly within her, moving with hurricane fury. Her form wilted as she fainted under the waves of pain that hit her being. The Nag swayed rhythmically, patiently, waiting for her to revive. The pain seemed to magnify a thousandfold as Yeshe let it consume her completely. Then, as she surrendered to it, it reached its climax. A massive spatial light grew within the firmament of her being and assumed the form of a fiery circle. Yeshe's awareness coalesced into this circle and, suddenly, she opened her eyes to the rhythmic swaying of the Nag. She felt the fire within her contracting and expanding, felt currents of cosmic space expanding and contracting. And then the pain was subsiding, giving way to an incredible expansiveness. Yeshe sat up slowly.

'Awaken, Cosmic Mother, awaken!' said the Nag.

Yeshe looked at him, bemused.

'It is time to go back up. The queen awaits you,' said the Nag. 'Give her this.'

With that, he handed the dakini a smooth, night-blue gem from which emanated a deep oceanic glow. Yeshe gazed at it in wonder. She had beheld many gems, but few had caught her attention the way this one did.

The Nag looked at her with a glint in his beautiful eyes. 'Yes, Yeshe, that is the primal *mani*,' he declared. 'It will be embedded in you, my dear one. In the age that is unfolding, your body and being will become one with this most precious of *mani*s. Dakini, you will, by this act, become a *yantra* to fulfil the will of the cosmic mother. This *mani* adorns her being and now that you will embody it, the most amazing alchemy will happen in the universe. Even the Devas are waiting to see this unfold. The sapphire is a harbinger of cosmic peace, equanimity and equilibrium. It has another aspect to it as well, Devi; it will accelerate the end of an age and begin the process of renewal. All nature will answer to you; the elements will play on your fingers; you will be the emissary of peace, as also the harbinger of destruction.'

Yeshe accepted the *mani* from the Nag.

'Dakini,' he went on, 'moments after it is embedded, the *mani* will be absorbed into your being and dissolve, becoming one with you. Dear one, embodying it is a great sacrifice; you will lose everything that you once were. These are your last moments as Yeshe. Henceforth, you will be nothing but the representation of divine will. Even I cannot predict what you will flower into. But you will never be what you were, Yeshe. Gone is the eternal maiden; left is only the will of the One. Are you ready, dear one? The road ahead is uncharted.'

Yeshe looked at the great Nag and said, 'Divine One, I am ready.'

The great Nag looked on, smiling, 'Ah, child! You are the sacrifice, for you will burn to make the waters flow forth.'

The dakini looked on with equanimity. 'So be it, 'she declared. 'I shall be aflame to the heartbeat of the cosmic mother.'

The Nag nodded and then disappeared. Without his presence, the pool suddenly looked much larger. Yeshe began floating up towards the surface. Cool air touched her forehead as she broke the surface of the water and began making her way back to the gathering under the banyan tree.

The dakini's attendants were soon towelling her dry. Nilamani looked on silently.

'You took far longer then we expected, Dakini,' she observed.

Yeshe unclasped her closed fist; the *mani* nestled in her palm, lighting it up with a sapphire glow. 'Nagrani Nilamani,' she said, 'I was given this by the great Nag that slumbers below. He asked me to hand it to you.'

Nilamani looked at the *mani*, an expression of awe on her face. 'The primal *mani*!' she murmured. 'The Nag has parted with the primal *mani*, the very heartbeat of the cosmic mother! This is far more then I expected.' She took the *mani* from Yeshe and gazed at it in silence. 'This has to be embedded in your essence, Yeshe,' she said. 'Let us begin.'

As the Nag queen intoned a mantra over the *mani*, the gem started vibrating, slowly, at first, and then, as the mantra picked up pace, at a faster rhythm.

'Ha! It is time now,' said Nilamani.

She picked up the *mani* and ran it across Yeshe's naked body, finally holding it over her navel till it was slowly absorbed into the dakini's flesh. For several minutes, the Nag queen held her palm over Yeshe's stomach. Then slowly, rotated her hand, first in a clockwise direction, then in an anti-clockwise one.

'It is done, Yeshe! The deed is done!' Nilamani announced. 'You will birth the new age that dawns. You will also give birth to the one symbol of utter perfection, the new evolutionary design of the universe.'

For the first time, Yeshe looked up, an amused smile on her face. 'Give birth?' she asked.

The Nagrani threw back her head and let out peals of laughter. 'Yes, Eternal One,' she said. 'You shall give birth to a child, a child born of the flame and the word. The universe awaits what Mahashakti will gift it and the new path that this energy will forge.'

Yeshe looked up at the Nag queen. 'A birth of an age, I understand,' she said, 'but must I birth a child? A child ... even my mother, the Goddess Tara had mentioned this. She also said that I am to be mated and now have two suitors!'

The Nagrani looked at the dakini, amusement dancing in her eyes. 'Yes, Dakini,' she affirmed, 'and one of those suitors is my son. Yet I have always known this would happen. Let's see what the future brings. And yes, you will bear a child, a child born of flame from the great *yagna* that you will perform alongside your companions. The child will be a gift to the universe; long has his advent been prophesied. Even the Devas and the Rishis await his coming, for an incredible alchemy will birth him. In Kalyug will you conduct a *yagna* never performed before. While it is Prince A-KarO who will actually perform the rites, it is you who will step into the fire, offering body and being for immolation. What emerges will be unprecedented.'

Yeshe sat back in shock. 'Not only must I leave the Silver Lode and the Azure Palace, lose all the grace and freedom of my divine manifestation, I must also birth an age and a child!' she exclaimed. 'Ah, Mother, who is behind this creativity?'

The Nagrani smiled. 'It is the manifest cosmic will. You have been a stubborn celestial maiden for millions of aeons. It is time, my dear.'

Yeshe laughed, her long, dark hair flowing across her emerald body. 'Ah! So be it, then, Nagrani,' she declared. 'Let this unfold.'

The Nagrani smiled. 'Now there is a message for you from Shambala,' she announced. 'Your mother, the Goddess, requires your return after the ritual is complete. I have prepared a magical mandala that will make your journey instantaneous.'

Yeshe slowly rose to her feet, light currents of bliss enervating her body.

'Now please partake of a small feast that I have had prepared specially for you, Dakini,' said the Nag queen.

Yeshe nodded. As a heady breeze swept past, together they walked under the light of the swaying lamps to the low table on which the feast had been laid. Garden lamps had been set up and backrests provided around the table. Yeshe inhaled the aroma of the dishes prepared for her. This was really enough for her, but etiquette demanded that she sample every item. The Nagrani personally served her the delicacies. In the skies above floated the crescent moon. Yeshe blissfully contemplated the splendour of the heavens as it unfolded little by little. A breeze blew in from between the clouds and Yeshe felt a sense of completion.

As if in a dream, the meal was over and the gathering rose. Tsatsum's face wore a wan expression, as Yeshe gently enfolded her in an embrace.

'Yes, my dearest, it is over even before it is begun,' said the dakini. 'Again, I have to answer to the heartbeat of time, now that so much passes away. Yet so much shall flow in.'

Tsatsum clung to her. 'We part so soon,' she murmured. 'This meeting wears the appearance of a mirage, Yeshe. My heart is full of pain.'

Yeshe held Tsatsum's hands. 'This is required, dearest,' she consoled her. 'And consider, are we ever parted? Is there a separation? Is there a moment when I'm not with you? When there is no separation, there is no parting. Only ever is there this flow from heartbeat to heartbeat, from pulse to pulse, from existence to existence, to endlessness.'

Tsatsum looked up, her expression stoic. Yeshe faced the rest of the gathering and blessed them. Lastly, she enfolded the Nagrani in her embrace. Then silently, she walked towards the mandala laid out in one corner of the garden and, with one hand raised, merged into the vast light energy that emanated from it, disappearing instantaneously.

Chapter 8
WITH THE PRINCE

I

The lilac and purple hues of evening invaded the horizon and its shadows slowly lengthened across Kalapa, casting their veil over the eternal city. Tashi rushed through his evening preparations; it was almost time for their audience with the Bodhisattva Avalokiteshwara. Without wasting a moment, he tidied his ochre robe and fastened his maroon sash. His hair was already neatly combed and slicked back with oil. With a last critical look at his appearance, Tashi nodded and stepped out of the guest-house, only to be met with a glare from Lama Ozer.

'What took you so long, boy?' he snapped. 'Do you want us to be late for our audience with the Bodhisattva? Now listen to my instructions carefully. Do not talk, unless asked. At all times, be polite and keep your eyes on the floor. Also, boy, stay alert and in a state of mindfulness, as I have taught you, time and again. Under no condition, offer a response, unless invited to do so. Leave the talking to me and listen to the Bodhisattva carefully.'

Tashi smiled. 'I will be very careful, Lama,' he promised.

Lama Ozer grimaced. 'Do not shame me, boy, or the monastery that reared you. Remember, you represent the young of Demazong Gumpa, the hidden monastery. I repeat, be mindful and careful.'

'It will be as you say, Lama,' Tashi smiled. 'I will take care. Now, we should depart. I see that the good sprite, Byung Mo, has readied the chariot for you, Lama. And Chetak, of course, is right next to it, just waiting to be off.'

Lama Ozer smiled grudgingly. 'Then let's be off, boy. You, as usual, will be astride that impossible horse of yours. Please instruct him to keep pace with us and not to tarry. But I specifically do not want him riding ahead of the chariot, blowing dust devils at me.'

Tashi smiled. 'Let me assist you into the chariot, Lama,' he offered.

He held out his hand and took Lama Ozer by the arm, helping him into the chariot to which a trio of matched white mares had been harnessed. In no time, Tashi was astride Chetak and they were soon moving out of the guest-house compound in the gardens and on their way into the city.

As Chetak maintained a brisk pace, Tashi took in the various sights of the city. The thoroughfare teemed with plying chariots. The occasional rider sped by on a wind horse. In the skies above Kalapa, winged chariots harnessed to pairs of wind horses flew at high speed – there, one moment, gone the next.

Chetak neighed, bringing Tashi out of his musings. 'I notice you are observing the skies, Tashi,' he said. 'Those fast-moving chariots you see are the *subaru*, constructed here in Shambala and harnessed to select wind horses especially bred for the purpose. They are famous for travelling at great speed.'

Tashi nodded. 'So the wind horses are reared in Shambala?' he asked.

Chetak tossed his head. 'Wind horses are native to many paradise worlds spread across the Lha empire and Shambala. Also, Shambala has a very select breed of winged horses highly valued in the celestial market,' the steed neighed. 'Tashi, I am not sure which aspects of Shambala you have taken note of, but I would like to emphasize that while its culture is steeped in tradition, it is very advanced technologically. Briefly, our technology is built on precious and semi-precious gems, which constitute a vast reservoir of both fuel and energy that serves Shambala. In fact, the illumination for most of the buildings here is provided by the precious and semi-precious stones embedded in their walls or hung from chandeliers within.'

'Tell me more about the horses, Chetak,' the boy urged.

'Ah, the horses! I can understand your fascination for them. In Shambala, the horses are magical creatures. They are very expensive and revered by the people here. Of course, at the top of the horse pyramid is the wind horse. It will take you a long time to understand what I am, Tashi, and I will not lecture you about my nature, but leave you to discover it by and by. Rare is the being who possesses a thoroughbred wind horse of the Suba breed native to Shambala. And you, Tashi, have been gifted one by none other than the celestial prince. This is not a small matter; it will have repercussions on your future. I sense that your destiny is aligned to the prince and this will become clear to you in the days to come.'

Tashi looked around him in awe. Chetak had moved into the heart of the city and was passing through gates that led to a colossal, pyramid-shaped glass building.

'Ah! So this is our destination today!' the boy observed.

'Indeed,' the horse snorted. 'It is here in Shambala's Inner Treasure Library that you have your audience with the Bodhisattva.'

Tashi scrambled off Chetak's back and saw Lama Ozer's chariot turning into the driveway. He assisted the lama to alight before giving his wholehearted attention to the building. The library was housed in an enormous triangular glass structure which floated over a huge lily pond and had a glass doorway that shone in the sunlight. As they neared it, a guard opened the door from inside and ushered them in.

The library's interior had diffused lighting and Tashi looked around a white hall that branched off into other rooms. A sprite, her head bent low over a *khada*, approached them.

'You are Lama Ozer and this is your disciple, Tashi, right?' she said, addressing the lama. 'I have been waiting for you. I will now lead you to the Bodhisattva's sacred presence.'

'I hope we are on time and have not kept you waiting?' the lama said softly.

'You are well on time,' the sprite assured him. 'Silence has to be maintained here in the library, until we reach the audience chamber where I am taking you now. The Bodhisattva is there now and expecting you.'

Tashi and Lama Ozer followed the sprite into a long, narrow corridor that ran on for a while before branching off sharply to the left. She led them into a medium-sized room, dimly lit up by the glow from a chandelier made of pearls. The room was bare, save for a single divan in one corner and many large grey cushions on the floor.

'Please be seated. His Eminence will be with you shortly,' said the sprite before withdrawing from the room.

Tashi and Lama Ozer had barely taken their seats when the Bodhisattva Avalokiteshwara manifested in a swirl of rainbow-hued light. He was clad in a robe and his hair was tied back in a topknot. His face was serene. Lama Ozer and Tashi immediately prostrated themselves before him and the Bodhisattva raised his hand in blessing.

Namig, the silent speech of heaven, blossomed in Tashi's mind.

'I bid you welcome,' began the Avalokiteshwara. 'Be at peace here. I am especially pleased to meet with you, Tashi, and the venerable Lama Ozer.'

The Bodhisattva smiled and more words in Namig bloomed in Tashi's mind.

'First of all, I would like to inform you both that your stay in Shambala has been fixed for three weeks, a period covering two months in the mortal world. Of course, your bodies will remain perfectly preserved at Qiang, awaiting your return to Earth. During your stay in Shambala, you will be trained in certain disciplines that will aid your mission on Earth.'

Lama Ozer inclined his head and folded his hands. 'We are blessed, Lord, that you have chosen us for your good work,' he said.

The Bodhisattva smiled. 'Briefly then, Lama Ozer,' he went on, 'you will be trained in both the inner and higher tantras at the temple of the great Goddess Yum by her priestesses. From tomorrow morning, you are to report at the temple at six o'clock sharp. Your training will go on till midday. We have noticed that you are weak in the offensive and defensive tantras used in battle. This was clearly apparent in your interaction with the black shamans based in Qiang. The Goddess felt, therefore, that it was imperative for you to be drilled in those tantras for the mission. In addition, the priestesses will impart to you knowledge of various healing mantras. These should come in handy for the mission.'

Hands folded, Lama Ozer murmured, 'Your word is my command, Lord.'

The Bodhisattva smiled. 'The sprite, Byung Mo, your escort, will convey you to your destination and wherever else you go. We also expect you to have meetings with your companions on the mission: the dakini, Yeshe Nam Lha, the celestial prince, A-KarO, and the crown prince, Narasimha Miyi Senge. They will be getting in touch with you. Lama and young Tashi, you will also get a private audience with the Rigden before your departure for Earth.'

Lama Ozer bowed low in acknowledgement.

The Bodhisattva added, 'Now, young Tashi, we have not forgotten you. You will also undergo intensive training while at Shambala. First, you will be trained in the martial arts of the celestial Lha by Prince A-KarO himself. The Goddess Yum herself has decreed that you receive in-depth martial training from the celestial prince. You will begin your training here under his tutelage, but it will continue in the mortal world. Prince A-KarO will also train you in the use of various mantras, an art we deem absolutely essential to your preparedness. This training too will continue on Earth. Starting from tomorrow, you will report to the prince's quarters at dawn.'

Tashi folded his hands and bowed.

The golden speech blossomed in his mind again. 'It is our wish that you serve Shambala's cause as a celibate warrior adept, Tashi. You will take the vow of celibacy when the time is right.'

'You must be wondering about the stress on battle preparedness,' the Bodhisattva smiled. 'Well, I would like to warn you that you face a direct demon threat the moment you leave Shambala. In fact, even while you are here, you will have to be cautious. The Asur are aware of your mission and will do everything to foil it. Hence the necessity of preparing you for battle.

'Also, Lama, young Tashi is the keeper of the Garuda's feather. Such a mark of divine favour is always extended to one who has the soul of a warrior. Tashi's innate potential will not be wasted. The celestial prince is already looking forward to beginning the boy's training from tomorrow.'

Tashi said excitedly, 'I will do my best to please you, Lord!'

The Bodhisattva smiled benignly. 'You must first please your teacher, Prince A-KarO. You must serve him as you have served your lama. Both of you are aware that after the full moon, all five of you will travel to Aggartha and receive your final orders for the mission from the sages there. They will also bless your endeavour.

'Now, in your free time, Lama Ozer and Tashi, you may roam Kalapa without hindrance, but please do not go beyond the city limits without an escort provided by the Rigden. My blessings are with you and I shall meet you again before you depart.'

Tashi looked on in wonder as the Bodhisattva vanished in a spray of rainbow-hued light.

Moments later, he was stepping out of the library excitedly. 'Lama, this is a dream come true!' he exclaimed. 'I am to train under the prince to become a warrior. I could never have imagined that such a thing was possible.'

Lama Ozer's eyebrow shot up. 'You must work very hard and serve your new teacher diligently, boy,' he reminded his acolyte. 'It is a great honour that you have been chosen to receive training in the Lha martial arts from the celestial prince himself. I think I will try and meet Prince A-KarO tomorrow to discuss your training. You should also be prepared to stay with the prince in his living quarters and serve him as you have served me. However, this is a very fortuitous development for you.'

A fresh night wind blew gently through the trees, making their leaves dance. Tashi smiled; life could not get better. Lama Ozer's chariot had already set off and soon they were heading out of the library grounds and into the city. Evening had turned to night and the first bright stars had appeared on the firmament.

'You look very pleased with yourself,' Chetak observed. 'So, what happened?'

Tashi laughed. 'Chetak, it was great!' he exclaimed. 'The Bodhisattva has decreed that I am to be a warrior and train under Prince A-KarO.'

Chetak threw up his head. 'That is good news, boy!' he said. 'When does your training begin?'

'I am to report to the prince's residence tomorrow at dawn. I wonder where he stays and how I will reach the place.'

Chetak neighed, 'The prince has his suite at the royal palace. I suppose that is where you will have to report at dawn and, of course, it is I who will convey you there. However, I am sure that at least on your first day, the prince will send you an escort. Now, let me warn you that the prince is reputed to be a hard taskmaster. He will really push you. Also, since you are to be trained in the martial arts, he will, most likely, require you to stay with him. The celestial martial arts of the Lha represent a high art, a deeply spiritual discipline that in itself serves as the path for the warrior of light. Did the Bodhisattva mention celibacy?'

'Now that you mention it, Chetak, yes, he did. He said I was to be a celibate warrior adept and would take my vows in a ceremony presided over by the prince at a time he deemed ripe.'

'That is most interesting,' Chetak snorted. 'The Lha warriors consist of two types: the high adepts, the Ningran, and the warriors of essence, the Chungran. The Chungran warriors are celestial warriors of light; they are celibate and adept in the warrior arts. I will not divulge more about them, as it is the prince's right to reveal the details to you.'

'But what about the high adepts, the Ningran?' Tashi enquired.

'Well, to put it briefly, the high adept is a Chungran warrior who has excelled for centuries in the warrior arts and then mastered the high warrior discipline of Ningran. This is the battle of spirit. Such a warrior is invincible. He can manifest in any form he desires and he battles not with his given body, but with the unity of the soul. This is the high art of perfection and such a warrior is a master. The Ningran warrior is not bound by the vow of celibacy and may take as many wives as he pleases or none at all. Prince A-KarO is a Ningran warrior, one of the very few around.'

Chetak rounded the corner and, suddenly, they were outside the gates of the Garden of Bliss, where the guest-house was situated.

'Oh! We are already here?' Tashi remarked 'I did not even see the city pass by.'

As soon as they had dismounted in front of the guest-house, Lama Ozer went inside, but Tashi walked Chetak to the stables located just behind it. He removed the horse's saddle and spent the next half an hour brushing his midnight coat to a fine lustre. Then he carried in a bucket of water and filled the feed bin with oats. While Chetak munched happily, Tashi was lost in his own thoughts.

'A warrior! I am to be a celestial warrior of light!' he exclaimed. 'It is so great an honour that I almost feel unworthy of it. Chetak, do you think I can do justice to the role bestowed on me? Or will I turn out to be a disappointment for the celestial prince?'

Chetak threw up his head and neighed, 'Worrying needlessly will not help, Tashi. You must simply gird your loins, work hard and give your best. You have what it takes. You are the Garuda's choice and he has always been one to back the winning horse.'

'I hope you are right, friend,' Tashi sighed. 'I am just a simple boy from the highlands of Sikkim. At times, all this seems so unreal, like a dream I may wake up from any moment.'

Chetak snorted softly, his voice husky. 'Now Tashi, leave your fears be,' he urged. 'It is time to rest. Tomorrow will bring its own destiny. Now retire and leave me in peace with my meal.'

Throwing a last, lingering look at the horse, Tashi began walking to the guest-house. A million bright stars splashed their cold light, filling the gardens of bliss with a blinding beauty.

II

Tashi felt a bony hand shaking him out of the depths of sleep. Lama Ozer was bending over him.

'Boy, it is time to wake up!' the lama said urgently. 'The good sprite, Byung Mo, has already called for you. Prince A-KarO has sent an escort to conduct you to the palace. Quick, boy, get ready! It won't do to be late on the very first day of your training with the prince.'

Tashi immediately scrambled out of bed, panic throwing his thoughts into disarray. He swiftly made his way to a pitcher sitting on a side table, poured water from it and splashed it on his face. He hurried through his ablutions and donned a maroon tunic tied in place with a bright yellow sash. He slicked his hair back with oil and tied it back. He was about to wear his slippers, when Lama Ozer handed him a pair of tough, shining brown leather boots.

'I think you should wear these from now on,' the lama suggested. 'They will come in handy for you. Slippers won't do. You will be required to ride horses, engage in combat and practise different forms of martial skills. Even when we reach the mortal world, I will have to consider getting you new gear and boots.'

Wearing his new boots, Tashi raced through breakfast and stepped out of the guest-house and he sighed with pleasure as clean fresh bracing air touched him with the tang of ocean salt on the breeze. Then almost immediately, he sighted Byung Mo.

'Tashi, I see that you are ready to depart,' the sprite observed. 'Your escort has been waiting to convey you to the royal palace.'

Tashi noticed two strapping Lha warriors in dark robes observing him. One of them walked right up to him and asked, 'Are you ready? We leave for the palace now.'

'I am ready,' Tashi told him, 'but I must fetch Chetak first.'

'The horse is ready and saddled for you,' said the Lha. 'Come this way. Dawn is already breaking. We had better be off. If you are late, the prince will be displeased.'

Tashi nodded and was soon astride Chetak.

'Now, boy, remember,' the Lha warrior cautioned, 'we will be moving at wind speed. You may not have experienced this before. So grip the saddle hard, hold tightly on to the reins and don't let go.' The Lha now turned to address the steeds. 'Chetak, Salem, Khwab, wind speed it is!' he commanded.

Tashi watched in amazement as all the horses sprang forward as one. Then a massive jolt ran through his body. He gripped the saddle hard with his thighs and held on to the horses' reins desperately as they streaked like a bullet through the city. Tashi's head spun as the surrounding city was reduced to a blur. In moments, it seemed, they had left the city behind. Chetak flew over the silver Bridge of Innocence and into the tranquillity of the Forest of Everness. The horses did not check their pace even once, as they raced through the thick trees and on into the heart of the forest.

Nor did they seem to tire. They flew on, right up to the vast lake that lay at the heart of the forest, the lake of light that frothed with bubbles of scintillating light as forms coalesced and came apart in it. Tashi and his escort halted on the shores and Chetak prepared the boy for the journey that lay ahead.

'You know the drill, boy,' the horse reminded him. 'You cannot head into the lake, for you are not yet ready for that. You will have to accept my essence willingly into yourself. I will lead you through the lake till the royal palace. There, we will be back to normal and become our separate selves. This is yet another benefit of having a wind horse; the prince knew what he was about, when he gifted me to you. Now take me into your heart and, as you head into the lake, remember to correctly visualize the blue lotus that bears the palace.'

Tashi stepped off Chetak's back and, before he knew it, the great horse had condensed into a pulsing beam of light. The boy held it to his heart and soon, it was absorbed within.

Chetak's disembodied voice now came forth. 'Now swiftly, Tashi, step into the lake.'

Tashi looked around and found that his escort had already disappeared into the lake. Then he stepped into the lake and Chetak took over.

'Bow before that huge blue lotus, the seat of the Rigden's palace,' his voice directed.

Tashi swiftly complied and, guided by Chetak's essence, streaked like a beam of light through the lake which was pulsing with primeval *shakti*. Almost instantly, they were alighting at the huge royal stables that were filled with horses. Tashi looked around him with wonder. At this early hour, young grooms could be seen working at the stables, filling the troughs with water, brushing the horses down or leading them out for their morning exercise.

'We are finally here, Tashi,' said the young Lha warrior, 'but we must make haste. The prince is expecting you.'

Chetak manifested beside Tashi, just as two grooms came forward to take the horses out.

'Please rub them down and water them,' the warrior instructed the grooms. 'Also, give them feed. We started early. So they have missed out on their morning meal.' The Lha turned to Tashi. 'Now, Tashi, I shall lead you to the northern field,' he said. 'It is there that the prince will meet you.'

The Lha warrior led the boy monk through the royal gardens which stretched away as far as the eye could see. A profusion of rhododendron flowers bloomed. They appeared on shrubs the size of small tea bushes and entire forests of them grew wild across the gardens. There were also bunches of narcissus, clumps of bluebells, their heavy heads drooping, and yellow daisies growing wild. Tashi feasted his eyes on the gardens, where the wilderness of rhododendrons presented a beautiful contrast to the manicured carpet of emerald green lawns. Soon, they had left the gardens and moved on. Along the horizon, Tashi made out the graceful arches and minarets of the royal palace.

Stretching away for miles near the northern quarter of the royal gardens was a vast field.

'This, Tashi, is the northern field the prince favours for combat practice for himself and his warriors, while in Shambala,' the Lha warrior pointed out.

In the centre of the field lay a clay court, ringed on all sides by a seating area.

'The clay court is used for wrestling and hand-to-hand combat as well as for sword-fighting practice and duels,' the Lha went on. 'Archery lessons, on the other hand, take place on the green. Well, we are here right on time. The prince will join us shortly.'

Many Lha warriors could be seen riding out on the field, leaping over obstacles and galloping at speed, while bending low to slash dummies with their swords.

'As you can see, it is at dawn that warriors warm up with a horse-riding drill. You will soon find out that the life of a Lha warrior is exceptionally hard and held together with great discipline.'

'I am honoured that you choose to share this information with me,' Tashi told him.

'Well, we have all heard that you are to be trained as a Chungran warrior, the celestial warrior of light,' said the Lha. 'I welcome you to the brotherhood. You are surely the first mortal in many aeons, if ever, to train to be a Chungran warrior.'

The gentle blush of dawn was staining the skies when Prince A-KarO stepped out on to the field, flanked by his honour escort of six Lha warriors. As the prince raised his hand, the warriors ceased their horse drill, dismounting quickly and running forward to fall into three columns before him.

The prince addressed them in a loud, confident voice. 'My brothers,' he began, 'we are gathered today to welcome a new brother in our midst. Also, unlike ever before, he is a young mortal, the boy, Tashi Thendup – till now, Lama Ozer's assistant. From this moment onwards, he becomes my apprentice. I will be undertaking his training personally. I also ask that all of you assist him to the best of your capacity, as and when desired. Now take up your positions and let the Chungran sky drill commence.'

Tashi stepped forward and bowed low before the prince.

The prince inclined his head and said, 'Observe, Tashi. Let this be your first lesson in the high art of the sky drill.'

Tashi now turned to watch the warriors who spread out across the field, then halted abruptly to take up their positions. The warrior directing the drill blew the conch and, at the signal, his fellow warriors ever so slowly, launched into their practice session. It was like the movement of the wind over the plains, like a leaf wafting down a tree, like moon beams spreading out over a lake. Tashi watched mesmerized as the warriors began their drill moving first slowly and then magically from one position flowing perfectly into the next. They moved in perfect coordination, each movement a seemingly impossible one, but executed in perfect synchronization with the others. Taking an incredible leap, for example, a warrior would suddenly be airborne. The rest would follow. Their torsos went through unbelievable contortions, a testament to the extraordinary agility and flexibility of their bodies. And thus the drill continued in the skies, as the warriors performed, united in thought, imagination and action.

Tashi watched in awe. 'My Prince,' he remarked, 'each movement of theirs seems an utterly impossible one. And they actually become airborne! How is that possible and how will I be able to replicate it?'

'The Lha sky drill makes the impossible possible,' Prince A-KarO smiled, 'and you will be able to do it, Tashi. The warriors flow, move and fight with the one eternal life force that flows in all beings and all things. The Lha warrior fights immersed in the one essence; this makes the seemingly unattainable possible. You are lucky that in Shambala, it is your spirit body that is present. I will first train your spirit body. This will make it easier for your gross body to perform the drill. But of course, the real challenge will come when your gross body is called upon to perform it. Now observe the warriors with care.'

Tashi's attention turned back to the warriors, who moved in perfect synchrony high above them. Their positions flew from one pose to the other, they kicked, twisted, spun from one position to the next in the skies and then suddenly, they landed on the ground yet again. The Lha warriors then positioned a hand by their navel and disappeared, their essence scattering to the winds. In minutes, they had taken form in the skies again, only to gently waft down to the ground. Then their bodies stilled into immobility and stood to attention, the posture held with a high degree of alertness.

Prince A-KarO turned to Tashi. 'Now you have seen the Lha's sky drill, few have viewed it though it is a legend among the Gods. The Lha drill symbolizes an unusual mastery over the mind and body. The Chungran warrior performs the drill seated in the centre of the heart lotus chakra but the adept the Ningran warrior performs it seated deep in the embrace of the thousand-fold petal, the sahasrara chakra. Perhaps, one day you will have the fortune of seeing that too.' Then the prince faced his assembled warriors. 'Be at ease,' he commanded. 'Commence the hand-to-hand combat drill on the clay court. Drill-masters, please take over now.' The prince turned back to Tashi. 'Now, Tashi,' he said, 'a few details. How old are you?'

Tashi smiled. 'Lord, I am fourteen. I will be fifteen in six months.'

'Any illnesses?'

'None that I know of, Prince.'

'Your lineage?'

'I am an orphan, Prince.'

'From today, you are an orphan no longer,' Prince A-KarO smiled. 'I am your teacher. You will obey me.'

'Your word is my command,' said Tashi.

'So let it be noted,' Prince A-KarO declared. 'Now, young Tashi, I will initiate you into the brotherhood of the Lha warriors.'

The prince inclined his head and a man stepped forward with a blindfold and swiftly proceeded to tie it over Tashi's eyes.

'Now listen carefully, Tashi,' said the prince, 'what follows will be crucial to your career as a Chungran warrior. I am lining up four warriors. Each bears a weapon. You have to feel your way around all four of them and then select one weapon.'

Tashi nodded, nervously feeling the air around him. His vision completely obscured by the blindfold, he was overcome by apprehension. 'How am I going to manage this?' he murmured uncertainly. 'I could easily mess this up.'

Prince A-KarO's confident voice came through. 'You can do this, boy. Just let your inner senses lead you. I will be doing the rest. Now lay down your burden of worries before me and proceed with a free spirit.'

Tashi felt his apprehension ease.

'Now begin, Tashi,' the prince commanded.

Tashi stepped forward and approached the first warrior, feeling the weapon in the latter's hand. To his touch, it felt like a long spear, razor-sharp at the tip. Tashi fingered it tentatively, but somehow, it did not feel right. He moved away from the warrior and moved towards the next, feeling his weapon with care. It seemed to be a knife, but it did not appeal to him. Tashi did not tarry, allowing his curiosity to lead him to the third warrior. Feeling the Lha's weapon, the boy concluded it was a perfectly balanced sword with a sharp edge. He caught the hilt in his hand and felt drawn to it as though to a lodestone. It was almost as though he were being sucked into the weapon. He allowed his inner senses to guide him and decided that something did not feel right. The weapon was too overpowering by far. Tashi now stepped up to the fourth warrior; immediately, he felt a sense of connection, of wholeness. His heart sang out and his hand itched to touch the warrior's weapon. Tashi went ahead and did so. It was a bow and, lying next to it, a quiver of arrows. He picked up the bow. It was light to the touch and he strung an arrow and let it fly.

'Ah, so that is it!' said Prince A-KarO. 'Remove the blindfold.'

The warrior complied.

'The path of the archer – what some call the path of the arrow – that is your initiation,' the prince explained to Tashi. 'The high path of archery is your path, hmm, Tashi? The high art of archery is a path of unique mastery. When learnt effectively, one arrow can flatten a city; such is its power. At the first level, you will master marksmanship. At the next level, you will align your essence with the arrow and learn effectiveness. At the third level, you will align mantra, essence and arrow; and then you will have the power of the gods. There is yet much for you to learn.'

Tashi was trembling by the time the prince had finished speaking. 'My Lord, what is this essence?' he asked.

Prince A-KarO smiled. 'Essence can neither be divined nor explained. It is a knowing that comes from deep within. Essence is the divine energy that permeates everything. You are a child of essence, of divine light; and until you learn to know, worship and work with it, you are not alive, Tashi. To be alive is to know essence; and to be a warrior, you have to battle with the power of essence behind you and the power of divinity within you. The true Chungran warrior is steeped in the unity of essence or eternal being. This is a high art, the essential mastery of the warrior; and it is indispensable for the true archer. To learn this, know this, feel this and worship this is your destiny, Tashi. Above all, the Chungran warrior is a worshipper of the divine being, the almighty, universal, ever-present divine being that some call God. This is a path to unity and unity is achieved in the inner mastery of the Ningran adept. Also, the warrior of light only fights the righteous war; he battles nothing but evil. Since time immemorial, Chungran warriors have been the arm of the gods in their battle against demonkind, against the Asur.'

Tashi looked at Prince A-KarO with awe. 'My Prince,' he finally said, 'I am a mere boy from a very humble background. How will I achieve this?'

Prince A-KarO lifted his hand and said, 'Enough! Harbour no doubts, Tashi. I will teach you the path of knowing, the inner fire, the battle of ecstasy. You, a mortal, will follow the Swan's path to unity. The martial arts practice will train you in outer discipline, but perfection will be attained through the inner transformation of your consciousness and the blessing of the being of light. Tomorrow, I will begin your training. Since you are my apprentice, you will, of course, move in with me and take up residence in my apartments at the palace. Now report to the drill-master for your apprentice kit and then report at my apartments.' Prince A-KarO gestured at a Lha soldier and commanded, 'Convey the boy to the Lha drill-master and then escort him to my apartments at the palace. Also, see to it that he gets his lunch.'

A bemused Tashi stepped away and followed the Lha soldier. Soon, they were making for the clay court, where a number of Lha warriors were engaged in combat drill. Tashi looked around him, wide-eyed.

'This is the first time, I think, that a mortal has been chosen to be trained as the favoured warrior of the gods,' the Lha soldier accompanying him remarked. 'Today, you have become an apprentice in the high warrior discipline of the Chungran. I hope, boy, that you realize what an unprecedented favour has been bestowed on you.'

'Believe me, I am aware,' Tashi assured him, 'but I wonder how I will achieve the goal set before me.'

'You should consider yourself blessed to have been chosen as the prince's personal apprentice,' the warrior snorted. 'and you should know that he has not taken one for five centuries of earth time. The prince is a hard taskmaster and will keep after you, till perfection is attained. Ah! Now we are almost there. There is the drill-master.'

The Lha warrior led Tashi towards a stocky, bare-chested Lha, built powerfully like a bull, a fact that more than made up for his lack of height. Heavily muscled, his body shone with oil and sweat. He wore loose navy pants that ended at his ankles and his dark hair was tied back in the queue favoured by the Lha.

The Lha warrior accompanying Tashi bowed low before the drill-master. 'Master Topen, I present to you our new mortal brother, Tashi Thendup,' he announced. 'He is the prince's apprentice. The prince has asked that he be presented to you and provided with his kit and the practice schedule.'

Feeling tongue-tied, Tashi bowed low before the drill-master.

'Tashi ... so that is your name, youngling! How old are you?' asked the drill-master.

'I am fourteen years old, Sir.'

'Hmm ... that's the correct age to come to the Lha,' Topen observed. 'You have to report here every day at dawn, boy. Drill continues till eleven in the morning, after which you may retire for lunch. The meals are served at the warriors' mess in the eastern wing of the palace.' He turned to the warrior who had accompanied Tashi. 'Ti Shan, you will take him there for his meals today.' Topen turned back to the boy. 'You are very fortunate to be the prince's personal apprentice, Tashi. You must know that he has taken an apprentice after a long break. To be trained by the prince, a Ningran adept, is a great honour indeed.' Studying Tashi's expression, Topen smiled. 'Don't look so worried, boy. You will do just fine; the prince will see to it that you do. Now here is your kit; keep it in good condition.

'Your duties are as follows. Report for drill in the morning and serve the prince to the best of your capacity after the practice session is over. It is the apprentice's duty to oversee the upkeep of the prince's wardrobe – no need for panic, for his sartorial tastes are simple and Ti Shan here will guide you – and to fetch his meals from the royal kitchens. You will also be responsible for keeping his weapons in superlative condition and grooming and exercising his steed and keeping him ready for use as and when the prince requires it. You will also groom and look after your own horse; you will be trained in the particular care a wind horse needs as soon as the prince decrees it. Of course, you will stay in the prince's apartments; a pallet will be assigned to you. It goes without saying that in all matters, you must obey the prince. Your kit consists of two sets of clothes; take good care of it. I have also added a sturdy pair of shoes that should serve you well. Maintain them with care. Also, once you travel to the mortal world, this kit will manifest there as well.' He turned again to the warrior. 'Now, Ti Shan, you may take Tashi for his afternoon meal and, after it is over, convey him to the prince's apartments.'

Tashi bowed low before the drill-master and left with Ti Shan. 'How may I address you, good Lha?' he asked the warrior.

Ti Shan smiled. He had fine, dark eyes that twinkled merrily and a mop of light brown hair, casually groomed. Of a tall and slender build, Ti was dressed simply in loose, light blue pants and a white tunic.

'I am Ti Shan,' he replied. 'You may call me Ti. I belong to a team of seven warriors whose duty it is to guard the prince at all times, with each of us taking his turn to do so. I have much to show you, young Tashi.'

Ti set a swift pace and soon Tashi was heading out of the northern field into the royal gardens, where he threw one last, lingering glance at the prince and his escort before carrying on.

'I will guide you through your daily round of duties for the prince, as I have been performing them so far,' said Ti. 'Now we will make for the warriors' canteen first. It is nearby.'

Tashi looked around him with curiosity as they crossed the royal gardens at a spanking pace and sighed with nostalgia; the gardens brought back memories of the hidden monastery.

III

Soon, they had left the gardens behind and entered a narrow corridor leading to the main building of the royal palace. The corridor opened into a medium-sized hall, the Hall of the Sacred Flame. At its centre was a huge hearth, where rested the dancing, sparkling sacred fire, nurtured by priests standing in attendance around it. Many warriors could be seen mingling with each other in the hall and conversations hummed across the room.

'This is the Hall of the Sacred Flame,' Ti told Tashi. 'Located in the palace's eastern wing, it serves as a congregation area for warriors and, as you can see, the priests who attend to the sacred flame. It is used mainly by warriors whose apartments are nearby. The warriors' mess is also located not far from this place.'

Tashi looked around him with great interest. The place had a cosy feel to it and looked warm and inviting, unlike some of the formal halls Tashi had seen in the palace. The walls here were lined with large quartz crystals, the pillars carved out of amber and cat's eye. The floor was of a clear polished marble of high quality and low divans and tables stood at strategic points across the room. Holding pride of place above the hearth was a huge chandelier of polished yellow sapphires that reflected the light of the sacred flame in scintillating shards of light.

'We'll make for the mess now, Tashi,' said Ti. 'You must be hungry. Did you have any breakfast?'

'Ti, I left in a great hurry,' Tashi smiled, 'and did not have time for a morning meal. In fact, I could not even say a proper good-bye to Lama Ozer.' Looking disconsolate, he murmured, 'I wonder when I will get to meet the lama next and how he will manage without me. He is used to me doing everything for him.'

Ti shrugged. 'Change is a constant, Tashi. That is the law of life. I am sure your lama will manage on his own. As for you, you are going to have your hands full with the prince. Now pay close heed to what I say, boy. So far, you have led the sheltered life of the monastery, but life with the prince will be very different. He lies beyond your sphere of experience. So pay attention, observe and learn. Now, Tashi, there are certain dont's you must heed under the tutelage of the prince: never enter his rooms in the evening without his permission or unless you are summoned; and under no condition must you disturb him at night, unless he asks for you. The reason behind this you will learn soon enough. As a Ningran warrior, our prince is not bound by the vow of celibacy. Moreover, he does like the ladies. In fact, they flock to him, with many a beautiful *apsara* or divine maiden throwing herself at him in vain. The prince has no consort, but he does have many concubines; they come and go at his sweet will. So this is going to be a very different situation for you.'

Tashi blushed. 'The prince has concubines,' he murmured. 'This possibility would never have occurred to me.'

Ti shook his head. 'Boy, you are so innocent!' he remarked. 'How will you manage in the prince's household? As his apprentice, the sole responsibility for his personal care is yours. Pay attention, boy. The prince maintains a harem of concubines and some of them have travelled with him here. Do not be shocked, Tashi. For a god and a Lha, the prince is young, his age the equivalent of a mere millennia and a half in human years, which is nothing for a Lha. However, he acquired mastery in the Ningran and other high arts at a very young age. Come now, we are almost near the mess. It is time to eat.'

His stomach rumbling with hunger, Tashi entered the mess, a long, rectangular room lined with tables that had low stools set around them. Washing his hands, he sat down next to Ti. A server walked up to their table and set silver platters, glasses and bowls before them. Another server approached and placed a large helping of rice on Tashi's platter. This was followed by a serving of fragrant vegetable stew, salad and a big bowl of potatoes served in cream.

'We do not talk in the mess hall while eating. So dig in, Tashi, and concentrate on your food,' Ti urged him.

The boy nodded and began to eat with gusto.

When the meal was over, Tashi followed Ti out of the mess and into the hall, from where they turned into a corridor with serpentine twists and turns. Prince A-KarO's suite of rooms was located at the end of the corridor. Tashi followed Ti in through the door and into a palatial sitting room with a chandelier of sparkling cut rubies. A silk carpet lay on the floor in the middle and silken divans and low tables were placed artistically around the room. Tashi looked at everything with avid interest.

'This is the prince's formal sitting room,' Ti announced. 'And in there is his bedroom, which leads into a smaller, more informal sitting room to the right. That will undoubtedly serve as your room at night. There is a kitchen and pantry to the right there, if the prince desires home-cooked food.'

Tashi looked panic-stricken. 'Will I be required to cook?' he asked apprehensively. 'My skills are very basic.'

Ti smiled. 'Don't worry, Tashi. We always have our own cook accompany us wherever we go. However, when you are travelling with the prince in the mortal world, you will need to prepare his meals for him.

So I suggest you meet with the cook and learn to prepare a few of the prince's favourite dishes.'

Passing through two arched doorways, Tashi followed Ti out of the room and into one of the connecting rooms. Situated on the right, this was undoubtedly the prince's bedroom. The low double bed on the floor was piled high with silken cushions. There was a wine cooler on a table near the bed. A silken couch sat near the window, with a low table before it. On display at one end of the room was an enormous armoire.

'You do not need to clean the room or make the beds,' Ti reassured Tashi. 'Those chores are taken care of by palace staff. But before evening falls, you need to check that there is always wine in the cooler. You must also go over the dinner menu with the cook; the prince tends to enquire about it. I might as well familiarize you with the prince's wardrobe. Its upkeep is part of your duties, after all.'

Tashi listened on, bemused.

'Now here is the prince's wardrobe,' Ti declared.

Tashi observed with care, as the warrior opened the vast armoire.

'Right on top is his ceremonial dress kit – two of them,' Ti went on. 'Here, at the second level, is his formal evening wear; there are eight pairs of trousers and *fluten*. The *fluten* is the prince's formal dress robe; open down the front, it is held together with silk ties. You will have to help the prince don it, when he goes somewhere in the evening.'

Tashi nodded. 'I am amazed at the variety,' he remarked. 'How will I manage all this?'

Ti smiled. 'Not to worry,' he said reassuringly, before going on. 'Here, at the second level, are his day trousers and short tunics. There are several of these and right here at the bottom of the armoire is his nightwear, but that is never used. It is superfluous, for the prince sleeps naked.'

Having gone through the prince's wardrobe, Ti had just lapsed into silence, while Tashi was still trying to absorb all the information he had been imparted, when there was a subdued murmur of conversation and Prince A-KarO walked in. The sound of feminine laughter filled the air and Tashi looked around, amazed. The prince was accompanied by three beautiful *apsaras*; two held on to his arms, while the third trailed behind, carrying a *veena*.

'Ah, Tashi, you have had your lunch, hmm?' the prince observed. 'So you have been familiarizing yourself with my apartments. Now just pour me a glass of wine, will you? Then you may retire to your room.' He turned to the soldier. 'Ti, keep the boy company today.'

Tashi bowed low before the prince and averted his gaze from the beautiful *apsaras*, who were eyeing him curiously.

'So, my Lord Prince, this is your young apprentice!' said one of the *apsaras*. 'He looks so shy!'

Tashi ignored the comment and poured wine for the prince, holding the goblet out to him and never raising his eyes.

'Revati, do be kind,' said Yamini, one of the other *apsaras*. 'The boy is blushing. Look, even his ears are staining red!'

The third *apsara* was obviously a performer. She seated herself on the couch, positioned the *veena* carefully and began tuning it. A string of musical notes floated up into the air.

Prince A-KarO inclined his head towards Tashi and said, 'You may now withdraw.'

Tashi hurriedly scrambled out of the room.

'So now you get what I mean, boy,' Ti remarked, smiling broadly at Tashi's confusion. 'Don't go in there till the prince calls for you.'

Tashi followed Ti into a smaller room, which was comfortably furnished with a pallet on the floor, two couches and a low table.

'This will serve as your room,' the soldier explained. 'There, your pallet has already been arranged for the night.'

The muted but beautiful strains of the *veena* rose into the air, the sound filtering in from the prince's room.

'So those were the prince's concubines?' Tashi ventured to ask.

'No, boy, they were the royal *apsaras*,' Ti explained. 'They will entertain the prince.'

'*Apsaras*, the beauteous *apsaras*,' Tashi murmured in wonder.

'One and the same,' Ti answered. 'Such a shame that you kept your face averted the whole time! You did not even get to see them, Tashi.'

'I was scared,' the boy confessed. 'I have seen very few women and interacted with fewer still; just old nuns at the monastery.'

Ti laughed. 'That was quite apparent, boy! And *apsaras* are not women; they are divine nymphs, born to entertain the gods. The prince is a favourite with them and, along with his concubines, they vie for his attention.'

'All this is quite new and amazing for me,' Tashi admitted.

'Why don't you rest, boy,' a smiling Ti suggested, 'and let me get some sleep as well? We all rose before dawn. In the evening, I will take you to the kitchens and we can fetch some wine to replenish the supply in the prince's room. We are running short.'

Tashi settled back on one of the couches and gazed out of the window. The afternoon sun blazed outside. Ti lay back on the floor, slumped against the couch. Within minutes, he was fast asleep. With growing bewilderment, Tashi mulled over the events he had lived through in the past month. Reflecting on them, he felt his life had become utterly strange. Then he settled back against the couch and allowed sleep to embrace him.

Chapter 9
MIMAKI AND THE DARK MIRROR

I

Prince Narasimha Miyi Senge, the heir-apparent to the Rigden's throne, suspended all stray thoughts as he attended to his patient, his hands moving with the lightness and grace of a symphony being performed. The prince held out his palm for the healing salve the nurse handed him, smearing it liberally on his patient's leg, before applying a binding poultice and breathing the healing mantra over the injured area. In very little time, bone and muscle had knit back together and the patient's leg had healed to a great extent. Narasimha signalled for the stretcher-bearers to enter.

'He is still unconscious and will be out for another half an hour, at least,' he told the nurse. 'After that, his injury will have healed, but he will still need rest for a minimum of two weeks. You may keep him at the infirmary for the rest period and release him after it is over. Now is there anyone else out there who needs attention or are we done for now?'

'My Prince, we are done for the day,' the nurse told him. 'No other patient waits outside. Besides, you must be exhausted. Also, your concubine, Mimaki, has been awaiting you for long.'

'Please ensure that the attendants clean up after me,' Narasimha told her. 'I want the operating room spotless for tomorrow. Also, I will be handing over charge of the infirmary to the venerable physician, Kyatba Lirang, tomorrow. Please see to it that all preparations are complete for the handing-over ceremony at dawn. As you are aware, in a few days' time, I leave for Aggartha. And from there, I am bound for the mortal world with my companions. I will be gone for an indefinite period of time and expect all of you to serve Kyatba well in my absence.'

The nurse bowed her head. 'We will miss you greatly, my Prince,' she murmured. 'Your absence will be a sad loss for the infirmary. Do not worry about tomorrow. I will keep everything in readiness for the ceremony at dawn.'

Narasimha inclined his head and held aloft his hand in beneficence. 'Then be at peace, Sylvana,' he said. 'Also, here is a list of the herbs, potions and salves I wish to carry with me on my journey to the mortal world. Please have them ready for me to collect after the ceremony.'

The nurse bowed again. 'It will be done. I must remind you, my Prince, that Mimaki has been waiting for you since early afternoon.'

Prince Narasimha nodded and stepped out of the room. The first thing he noticed was that dusk had already given way to night. And then he saw Mimaki. She sat there, her head in her hands, weeping silent tears.

'Dearest one, why do you wait here so disconsolate?' he asked. 'I would have come to you the moment my work was done.'

Mimaki looked up at him through tear-laden lashes, her dark eyes inexpressibly sad. 'How could I stay away, Narasimha, when a few days are all I have with you now?' she murmured.

Narasimha shook his head at her. 'Mimaki, Mimaki, what am I to do with you?' he said imploringly. With that, he walked up to her and swung her light form into his arms. 'Know this, my beloved,' he went on, 'that wherever I may be, my heart will always be with you. Besides, this is not a permanent state of affairs. I will return and, for all you know, my stay in the mortal world may end sooner then you imagine.'

More tears rolled down her cheeks as Mimaki rested her head on Narasimha's shoulder. 'However will I manage while you are away, Narasimha?' she asked helplessly. 'How will I bear your absence? I had begged the Rigden to allow me to accompany you, dearest, but he will not be swayed from his decision. What he is willing to grant me, instead, is a boon.'

Narasimha smiled as he entered the gardens with Mimaki in his arms, walked up to a bench under a shady arbour, redolent with the fragrance of jasmine, and sat down. 'So, a boon, Mimaki?' he murmured. 'Something is better than nothing. Is that not so, dearest?'

Mimaki smiled through tears. 'I tried to convince the Rigden that the only boon I craved was to follow my lord, but so hard of heart is your father that he would not entertain my plea. In its stead, he has granted me three visits to you in the mortal world, as and when I want them. He made it clear that during each of those visits, I would be allowed to be with you at night, but would have to return to Shambala at the first light of dawn.'

Narasimha held Mimaki close and gently kissed her eyelids. 'So that, my sweet, is better than nothing,' he said.

Mimaki laughed, a light tinkling sound that floated in the air. ''Tis coins to a beggar, but what becomes of me when all three visits come to an end?' she asked. 'Oh, Narasimha, won't you petition the Rigden on my behalf?'

The crown prince lightly kissed Mimaki on the forehead. 'You know better than to ask that of me, my love,' he said gravely. 'I will not petition the king. I am bound by his word. We should be satisfied with what we get. Our lives go on for aeons, beloved. What are a few hundred odd years? Fret not. You know I will return to you.'

Mimaki gently threaded her fingers through Narasimha's hair. 'There is more, my Lord. Your father promised that a child would be born to us from my third and final visit to you in the mortal world and that with this child's birth, he would elevate me from the position of a concubine to that of your wife though only a junior wife and not consort. He gave his word that he would grant me recognition.'

Narasimha laughed. 'That is very well, my sweet, but you are already my wife. If the Rigden sanctions your position by granting it recognition, so be it.'

'Ah, Narasimha, but you won't be there at your child's birth nor enjoy his babyhood,' Mimaki lamented. 'You will neither witness his first steps nor hear him utter his first word. Knowing that, how can the Rigden not let me accompany you?'

'Mimaki, my beloved, we have what we have. And I will, one day, return to you and our child,' said Narasimha.

Having said that, the Rigden king's heir-apparent gathered Mimaki up in his arms and began walking towards his rooms.

'Narasimha, I will beg the virgin daughter of the Goddess for a dark mirror,' said Mimaki. 'Surely she will give me one?'

'A dark mirror?' Narasimha repeated. 'Only Yeshe can give you that. Yes, I think if you ask her, she just might give it to you.'

'Then there is hope, my Lord,' Mimaki smiled. 'At least, I will then get to see you and converse with you every day.'

Narasimha planted a kiss on Mimaki's lips as light as the breath of a swallow. 'My dearest,' he said, 'entreat Yeshe to make you a dark mirror from her lake. That will work best.'

Mimaki smiled. 'That would be best, my Lord,' she agreed, 'but the matter is more complicated than it seems. Is it not true that Yeshe is the most likely mother of the future child of light, the prophesied one? Moreover, I wonder if there is substance to my conjecture that either Prince A-KarO or you will be her consort. If that is, indeed, true, do not forget your Mimaki, my Prince.'

Narasimha shook his head. 'Lay not your trust in hearsay, Mimaki,' he cautioned her. 'Believe in me, in our love; in my heart, there is no one but you. We will not discuss this matter now, but do go and ask Yeshe for a dark mirror tomorrow.'

Mimaki looked solemn. 'So I will, my Prince,' she promised.

Narasimha entered his chambers and set down Mimaki on the chaise longue. Then lighting the lamps, he returned to Mimaki, lay down beside her and took her in his arms.

'Mimaki, this is heaven for me, being with you, this is home for me,,' he murmured. 'Being with you symbolizes the heart of Shambala. When I leave, you must see me off bravely. You will anoint my forehead, arm me with weapons and send me off with blessings for a warrior on your lips. I must exhort you not to pine for me, but to keep yourself busy in my absence with your tasks at the infirmary and with the child that will come. I will communicate with you daily through the dark mirror, beloved. Fear not, even when apart, we will be together.'

Mimaki wound her arms around Narasimha's neck and felt a strange strength enter her soul. 'As you will it, my love,' she sighed.

II

The skies had just welcomed the first light of dawn when Mimaki approached the threshold of Golden Dakini Yeshe Nam Lha's palace. As she stepped out of the waters of the Pool of Tranquillity into Yeshe's underwater abode, straightening her skirts and willing the moisture out of them with a thought, an attendant came out of the palace to meet her.

The latter bowed low before her and asked, 'How may I be of service?'

Mimaki smiled and said, 'I am looking for the dakini. Please let her know that I am awaiting her here. May I also request you to convey my apologies for seeking her presence without sending a message to her earlier.'

The attendant bowed again and led Mimaki into a small chamber off the entrance that was made of glass and lined with shells. It projected into the lake, bringing the subterranean world around it to life.

'Please wait here, gracious sprite. I will convey your message to the dakini,' said the attendant.

Mimaki inclined her head in acknowledgement and took seat on a low silk divan.

Nervous, she dreaded the meeting that was to follow, but the dark mirror was a priority she could not set aside. She gazed out of the window and her sadness settled around her like a pall. Mere moments had passed, when Yeshe entered the room. Mimaki rose and bowed low before the dakini, folding her hands in time-honoured salutation.

'Dakini, I am honoured that you have chosen to answer my call,' she said.

Yeshe smiled. 'Be at peace here, Mimaki,' she said. 'My home is open to all feminine beings irrespective of race and regardless of age or circumstance. Now please be seated.'

Mimaki and Yeshe settled down on the divan.

'Would you care for some pomegranate juice?' the dakini offered. 'I have some fresh from my orchard.'

Mimaki inclined her head in acceptance. 'As you please, dakini.'

Yeshe ordered the refreshments and then settled back for their talk. 'I trust all is well with you, Mimaki?' she enquired.

Mimaki's smile was sad. 'How can it be normal for me, Dakini?' she said. 'As you are aware, Narasimha is to depart for the mortal world and will be away for an indefinite period.'

Yeshe held out her hand to Mimaki. 'I fully empathize with your sorrow,' she murmured. 'Our impending journey to the mortal world has thrown us all into chaos. I myself will be parting from my divine mother, a prospect I dread. But she has reassured me that she will be with me in essence. You too must look for Narasimha in your heart during his absence from Shambala and find strength there.'

Mimaki shook her head. 'It is not so easy for me, Dakini. Narasimha could be gone for well over a hundred years. I despair over our separation and am overwhelmed by the thought of what lies ahead. I also understand, Dakini, that you are to accompany the two princes on their mortal quest. I have a small request for you. In my absence, please take care of Narasimha. He is always so preoccupied that he tends to be careless about his meals and his clothes. What is still more worrying is his habit of concealing his ailments when he is ill and ignoring them for the most part. Will you watch over him, Dakini?'

'That is something I will do for you gladly,' Yeshe smiled. 'I am well aware of Narasimha's abstraction and his single-minded devotion to medicine, to the exclusion of all else. Do not fret. I will take good care of him. Narasimha and I have a shared childhood; our early years were spent together. He has always been a dear friend and close confidant. Mimaki, I give you my word that I will look after him.'

Mimaki smiled nervously and said, 'That eases my mind greatly, Dakini. Now I have a greater favour to ask of you and beg your forgiveness for imposing on you so.'

Yeshe smiled. 'You are not imposing on me, Mimaki. It is a joy to have you with me.'

'I come to beg you for a dark mirror, Dakini,' Mimaki began, 'one made from the waters of your own pool. This is the only way I can keep in touch with Narasimha during this long separation that is being thrust upon us.'

'A dark mirror? But of course,' Yeshe smiled. 'I shall create one for you this very instant. Now, Mimaki, first walk out to the pool and fetch just enough water that you can carry cupped in one hand.'

Mimaki did the needful and turned to walk back to Yeshe.

'Hold it carefully, Mimaki,' the dakini cautioned, 'don't let even a drop fall.'

When Mimaki had returned to Yeshe, the dakini bent over the concubine's cupped hand and breathed over it. Instantly, the water cleared, crystallizing into one glassy fragment. Yeshe took the fragment in her hands and let a mantra vibrate over it. The chant ran on for a few minutes. Then Yeshe breathed over it and uttered a word of power. The air in the room began to vibrate. Then, suddenly, all was still.

The polished oval surface of the mirror in Yeshe's hand shone darkly in the morning light, giving off glimmers of light, as though a sliver of moonbeam had been trapped and fashioned into a mirror. Its frame was set with the palest of translucent pearls and rich corals studded the handle.

Yeshe handed the precious object to Mimaki, who gazed at it with wonder in her eyes.

'This is my gift to you,' the dakini said to her. 'Use it well. But remember, it will work only at night and you must never expose it to sunlight. If you need to carry it with you during the day, keep it in a dark box, where the rays of the sun cannot melt it. Also, when you use it, softly whisper the name of the person you wish to see and breathe his name over the mirror. The image of that person will appear in it. You can communicate with the image, for the mirror will carry your voices to each other. As for Narasimha he will need water or a mirror to see you though he will hear your voice the moment you contact him. Any mirror will do for him.'

Mimaki smiled. 'I am eternally grateful to you, Dakini,' she said.

At that moment, the attendant entered, bearing a tray of refreshments: sliced peaches and crimson-hued pomegranate juice on a bed of crushed ice.

'You know, Dakini, that this mirror will be my mainstay; it will help me retain my sanity,' Mimaki told Yeshe.

'You have much to look forward to, Mimaki,' Yeshe smiled. 'You will soon bear your son in your arms and he will be the source of your joy, till Narasimha returns.'

Mimaki laughed, the sound carrying on the wind and tinkling lightly in the air. 'Dakini, I will keep your gift next to my heart,' she promised. 'And now I must take my leave. I have taken up enough of your time.'

She rose to her feet and bowed low before Yeshe, who escorted her to the edge of her pool and said, 'Till we meet again, Mimaki. May you then be in better spirits.'

III

Prince Narasimha was in a hurry; he was already late for his appointment with his father, the Rigden king. Turning into yet another serpentine corridor, the crown prince knocked on Prince A-KarO's door. It was opened at once by the young apprentice, Tashi.

'Tashi, we are already late for our meeting with the Rigden,' said Narasimha. 'Is the prince ready?'

Tashi smiled brightly. 'Prince Narasimha, the celestial prince will join you in a moment.'

The heir-apparent strode up to the inner door of Prince A-KarO's chamber and shouted, 'A-KarO! Hurry! We are late.'

In moments, the door to the celestial prince's inner chamber opened and Prince A-KarO stepped out. 'I have been ready and waiting for you for the past half an hour,' he explained. 'Let us be off. It ill behooves us to be late for our meeting with the Rigden.' He turned to Tashi. 'Wait for me here in my apartments and have my evening kit laid out for my dinner engagement with the queen's court,' he commanded.

The heir-apparent matched the celestial prince's long almost gliding stride and they were soon outside in the corridor, making with haste for the Rigden's audience chamber. They rushed through the snaking corridors and large halls lit with the sparkle of gems and were soon standing outside the royal chamber.

The sentry at the gate stepped forward. 'I will announce you, my Lords,' he declared.

Prince Narasimha inclined his head and followed the sentry into the Rigden's spacious, richly appointed inner audience chamber. The silken rug on the floor and the velvet couches arranged around the room were bathed in a lovely glow of light cast by the enormous chandelier of rubies that hung from the centre of the ceiling. Surrounded by his court of nobles and high priests, the Rigden sat on his magnificent jade throne, dressed simply in royal blue robes. The light caught the silver glints in his snow-white hair that was bound in a topknot and presented a striking contrast to the silver and jade crown he wore, the luminescence of a full-moon night trapped in its intricate workmanship.

Prince Narasimha and Prince A-KarO stepped forward and bowed low before him.

The Rigden looked at them and inclined his head. 'Be seated,' he said. 'I will be with you soon.'

The crown prince led Prince A-KarO into an alcove. 'Relax,' he urged. 'With the court around him, I assume the Rigden won't be joining us for a while.'

Prince A-KarO smiled and said, 'So what has been keeping you busy these past two days? I have barely seen you.'

'I have had my hands full winding up my affairs at the infirmary and handing it over to my successor,' Narasimha explained. 'Also, Mimaki has been taking up my time. She is completely distraught at the thought of my impending departure. Frankly, I don't know how to handle her.'

Prince A KarO looked amused. 'That's what comes of having only one concubine and taking no other. The more attention you give a woman, the greater her demands and the more complications you must face. Thank the Lord, I have no such problems!'

'You are truly incorrigible, A-KarO, and well you know it!' Narasimha smiled. 'I heard you had a meeting with the sage, Amu Revati. What was that about?'

Prince A-KarO hesitated. 'So the palace spies still report to you, do they?' he observed. 'Revati's forecast for our sojourn in the mortal world was a very dark one,' he said. 'He warned me that the Asur demons are already well aware of our plans. It appears that they have a plan in place to disrupt our mission and they have already started acting upon it. Revati stressed, again and again, that the Asur have grown bold and will try to abort our mission, not only on Earth, which is a given, but – what is more troubling – here in Shambala too. He also warned me that the dakini, Yeshe Nam Lha, who is the prophesied mother of the divine child, is under direct threat from the Asur. He predicted that they would attempt to abduct her and bind her and we must be alert to this threat, especially when we reach the mortal world.'

Prince Narasimha looked at A-KarO. 'This is troubling indeed,' he declared. 'We need to intimate the king about this threat and also see to the dakini's security. I think both of us should arrange a meeting with Yeshe to share this piece of intelligence.'

Prince A-KarO nodded. 'I completely agree with you on this matter. In fact, I am supposed to be meeting her at the queen's court this evening. I ask that you join me there so that we can both have a quiet word with her. But merely cautioning her will not be enough. She requires our presence in her vicinity, along with an élite guard behind her. According to me, this arrangement should be put into place immediately.'

'Yes, immediately,' Narasimha agreed. 'But surely there is no threat to her while she is in Shambala? The kingdom is impregnable and its defences unbreachable.'

Prince A-KarO shook his head. 'Even Amravati was impregnable, but it was breached by the Asur, nonetheless,' he reminded the crown prince. 'Let us not be complacent. We cannot allow our level of alertness to slacken at any point and need to be really vigilant about the dakini's security, even in Shambala. As for our sojourn on Earth, we need to implement practical measures for that phase of our mission and this is where the Council comes in. Call it gut instinct or what you will, but I strongly feel that in addition to your presence and mine on this mission, the Council must allow my honour guard of élite Lha soldiers to follow us into the mortal world. An aged lama, an untrained boy and the two of us are simply not enough to ensure the dakini's safety. Failing to recognize this reality is asking for trouble. I have every intention of presenting the case frankly to the Rigden and urging him to do something about it.'

'You could be right,' Narasimha agreed. 'Ah! The crowd of courtiers around the Rigden is dispersing. We had better get into position for our audience with him.'

The two princes now approached the Rigden king and bowed low before him. The room had almost emptied of the royal courtiers, but for the Rigden's First Counsellor, who remained. The Rigden looked at the two princes and indicated that they be seated. Then he held up his hand, requesting silence.

'I have sent for you today,' he began, addressing the two princes, 'because I wish to apprise you of the gravity of your mission and the full extent of its perils. We have received disturbing intelligence from one of the guardians who patrol the borders with the Asur kingdoms; it seems that the Asur are plotting to thwart our mission. Be warned that the moment you touch down on Earth, you face grave danger. According to the guardian, the Asur have already launched their offensive by deploying an Asur demon prince of their first family and his forces to foil your mission. It is evident that they are already on the move. Therefore, I cannot overemphasize the importance of ensuring the security of the dakini, Yeshe Nam Lha, and the divine child she is prophesied to birth. It is your first priority on this mission. Both of you have been tasked to manage her defence and see to her health and well-being. The same goes for your duties towards the divine child, once he is born.'

'My Lord, if I may put in a request,' Prince A-KarO began. 'It is my humble contention that to ensure the dakini's security, we must put in place the best arrangements possible. To this end, I would suggest that we organize unbreachable security for her here in Shambala itself. I ask for your permission to deploy my élite Lha guard at the dakini's residence with immediate effect. They will shadow her every movement and keep her safe. With the Asur already on the offensive, I feel this is imperative.'

The Rigden held up his hand. 'There is no need for panic, Prince A-KarO,' he said. 'The Asur cannot breach the defences of Shambala. The dakini is safe while she is here. My intention was to alert you to the dangers that prevail and urge you to be ready for battle when you landed on Earth. The mortal world is the real danger zone and it is there that you must be ever vigilant about the dakini's security. So I must turn down this request of yours. Now, let us move on to the next issue.'

Prince A-KarO held his hand out in a gesture of appeal. 'My Lord,' he persisted, 'I humbly submit that we face grave dangers even now, here in Shambala. I entreat you, once again, to provide me the means to ensure the dakini's safety. Please give us your permission to have my Lha élite guard and my scouts accompany us to the mortal world. Without our forces to back us on Earth, Prince Narasimha and I will be severely handicapped.'

The Rigden shook his head resolutely. 'No, Prince A-KarO, my decision is final. We cannot provide you more support than is permissible from Shambala or allow the Lha forces to accompany you to Earth. We cannot risk the mortal world becoming a battlefield for the demons and the gods and causing great suffering to humanity as a result. My Prince, you are strength personified. You do not require forces to meet the challenge ahead of you. What you do need to use to your advantage are your knowledge and your inner resources. I fully expect both of you to build a magnificent defence for the dakini on Earth. You will not only manage; you will prevail. This is our conviction.'

'My Lord,' Prince A-KarO implored, 'if not on Earth, at least help me to secure the dakini here in Shambala. The sage, Amu Revati, has warned me, my Lord, that the Asur may move against us very soon, even here in Shambala.'

The Rigden was firm. 'The Asur will never make a move in Shambala,' he declared. 'There is no way they can breach our borders. It is in the mortal world that you need to concentrate your energies. So there is no need to assign a special guard for the dakini here.

'Now, I would like to inform you both that two days hence, I have asked for a huge banquet to be organized in honour of all those of you who are participating in this important mission. I will naturally expect you to attend and carry my invitation to the dakini and Lama Ozer. Also, Prince A-KarO, please bring your apprentice, young Tashi, as well.'

Prince Narasimha began, 'My King, when do we journey to the mortal world? Has a schedule been decided for us?'

'A schedule has, indeed, been worked out for your departure,' the Rigden smiled. 'All of you are to leave Shambala on the morning following the banquet. In other words, three days from now. You will be travelling to Aggartha to receive your blessings from the sages. They will initiate you into the spirit of the mission and also give you your final orders.

'You will each incarnate in a mortal form. With that transformation, all three of you – you, Prince A-KarO and Prince Narasimha, along with the dakini, Yeshe Nam Lha – will, of course, relinquish the affluence you enjoyed in the divine world. Your vast wealth will be held in trust by the Rigden crown, till you have each finished your assigned task in the mortal world. You will also lose your divinity and, along with it, the entire range of your divine powers. However, you will retain such power as is based on your innate talents and the extensive knowledge that you had accumulated in your divine incarnation. We expect this to be an asset for you in your mission. So you will have to rely on mantra *siddhi* or powers based on mantra and a *yantra* – a device fashioned by you. To survive and succeed, you will have to innovate with the help of your vast knowledge base.'

'Why do you choose to make the situation more difficult then it already is, my Lord?' Prince Narasimha asked, perplexed. 'Why hamstring us with all the vulnerabilities of a mortal body? Why not let us go forth in our divine incarnations and use our divine powers to their optimum capacity? Would that not guarantee greater effectiveness and success on the mission?'

The Rigden smiled. 'The conditions imposed on you have to be met for the birth of the divine child,' he explained. 'To operate in the mortal world, you have to assume a mortal form. All we can do for you is enhance it with some of the talents inherent to your divine incarnations. Look to knowledge and to the wisdom of the dakini, Yeshe Nam Lha, to guide you through this trial. Both of you must accept the guidance of Yeshe, who is a wisdom dakini and will be the embodiment of compassion in her mortal incarnation.'

'Whatever the circumstances, whatever the obstacles, we will prevail, my Lord,' Prince Narasimha assured the Rigden. 'Your word is our command.'

The Rigden smiled. 'Let me assure you that you will not be without help in the mortal world. Where circumstances warrant it, we will send you such aid as we can. When you least expect it, help may come.'

The Rigden held up his hand and said, 'There is one last matter we must discuss. The dakini will select one of you as her consort. It is for her to choose. If she fails to do so, he will be chosen by divine decree. A time will come, Prince A-KarO, when you will be required to perform a *yagna* for the birth of the divine child. On this occasion, the dakini must accept the path of the flames, for only when she is seated in the heart of the flames and the demands of the *agni* or sacred fire are met that the conditions for the birth of the divine child will be fulfilled. Pay heed to this, both of you: the demands of the sacred fire must be fulfilled for the impregnation to take place and it is you, my Princes, who will be called upon to answer the demands of the sacred fire and help fulfil the conditions for the birth of the divine child. This is hidden knowledge and its secrecy must be preserved at all costs.

'Prince A-KarO, you will be intimated by a guardian of the sacred fire as to when the time is ripe for performing the *yagna*. The ceremony must take place in the valley of the Alos flower on sacred Mt Meru. The sacred mountain is hidden on Earth and you will have to pierce its veil to locate it. You will receive directions about it from time to time. In fact, your first duty on Earth will be to locate Mt Meru and then travel to it. Once you are there, you are to wait in readiness in the Valley of Alos. Narasimha, you are an excellent tracker. I will expect you to locate Meru, while Prince A-KarO handles the defence of your group against the threat posed by the Asur.

'Now both of you heed my words: you are allowed to collect a troop of eighteen mortals on Earth. Prince A-KarO, you have divine sanction to train them in the high art of the Lha to form your defence. These mortals, both men and women, will come to you while you are travelling. They will feel impelled to join you and you must accept them when they do. Is that clear?'

'All is made clear, my Lord,' the celestial prince smiled. 'It will be a challenge to train a guard of mortals in the high art, but I will do my best.'

The Rigden rose from his throne. 'Your final orders will be given to you both at Aggartha by the united body of sages. One last instruction: when you leave Shambala for Aggartha and the mortal world, do not carry anything with you, save the clothes on your back. Now you have my permission to withdraw.'

The princes bowed low as the Rigden walked out of the audience hall and into his inner chamber. Then they left for their own apartments.

IV

Dusk was giving way to a fragrant autumn night. Prince A-KarO heaved a great sigh. He was dressed for the evening in a white brocade jacket over a pale cream tunic edged in silver and loose cream pants held in place by a leather belt. He turned and beckoned to Tashi who hurried over.

'You have done an excellent job with my clothes, boy,' he declared. 'Now fetch my sword and dagger from the table.' Placing his sword in its scabbard and fastening it at his hip, the prince tied his dagger in place at his waist and said, 'You may rest now, Tashi. Take your dinner as soon as I have left and do not stay up for me afterwards. Go to bed. I will let myself in. Don't forget that you start the day early tomorrow at the practice grounds.'

Tashi bowed low and A-KarO left the room.

The prince walked rapidly down the familiar corridors till he was standing outside the queen's court which overlooked a lovely courtyard surrounded by an elegant garden. The fragrance of nocturnal blossoms hung over the garden, perfuming the air. A-KarO looked about him with interest. Then he caught sight of her, hidden, as usual, behind a trellis of fragrant flower-bearing vines. She was seated in the shadows, her slight form, as alluring as ever, merging into the darkness. Yet again, the prince felt the pull of attraction and was annoyed with himself for acknowledging it; this was an attraction which always went nowhere. However, destiny had taken a rather interesting turn; by divine ordinance, the eternal maiden had to take a consort now. Prince A-KarO suppressed a sly smile and made for the hidden recesses of the garden.

As he approached, her consternation was apparent. A-KarO smiled to himself again as he beheld her obvious discomfiture. Another step and he was in front of her.

'Dakini, why are you sitting alone in the dark?' he asked. 'May I escort you inside?'

Yeshe bristled at the suggestion. 'Prince A-KarO,' she said with cold politeness, 'please do not trouble yourself for my sake. I enjoy the dark. I will not keep you from going wherever you were bound. I am truly happy on my own here.'

A-KarO seated himself beside Yeshe. 'Ah, Golden One, it is beautiful here! The night is young. I hope you won't mind my joining you?'

Yeshe shifted on the bench. 'The night is beautiful indeed,' she responded, 'but I am sure the queen awaits you as do the ladies of the court.'

'Be that as it may, I would like to spend some time with you, Yeshe,' the prince smiled.

'I think there is no need.'

'Nevertheless, Dakini, I have something of import to convey to you – if you can spare me a few moments.'

'All right, I am listening,' said Yeshe, her hands fisted in her lap.

Prince A-KarO laughed. 'Am I so intolerable, Golden One?' he asked.

Yeshe tossed her head. 'You have always been intolerable. That I cannot stand you is not news for you. Now get to the point and let's get this over with.'

A-KarO shrugged. 'So impatient, Yeshe! Yet by orders of the Rigden, I am now one of your suitors.'

'A suitor for me? You? Let us be done with this farce!' Yeshe snorted disdainfully. 'For an entire millennium, I have been a celestial maiden, steadfast in my worship of the Goddess and the one eternal being, the father of creation. I will never entertain a suitor. So be gone, suitor!'

A-KarO laughed again, his mirth spilling over. 'And yet, Yeshe,' he went on, 'you have been given a poor choice in the matter of this divine motherhood that is to be bestowed on you. Your choice of mate is limited to Narasimha and me. And as we both know, Narasimha is already in love with Mimaki and spoken for. So you are left with me.'

'Left with you! No! I will not be the one to make a choice. A-KarO, let the situation unfold as it will and if this is how you seek to win me over, then your prospects are poor indeed. I would rather share Narasimha with Mimaki, than have you.'

'Do you think I am wooing you, Yeshe?' the prince said softly. 'In that case, a question arises – can you be wooed, celestial maiden?'

In response, Yeshe tossed her silken tresses back. A strand of her hair caught in Prince A-KarO's jacket. 'Now look what you have done!' she exclaimed, her distress evident.

The prince smiled slyly. 'But Yeshe, your tresses know they belong to me,' he said. 'I have not reached out for them, have I? Yet they have become entangled with me.' With that, he freed the silken strand of Yeshe's hair from his jacket and lifted it to his lips.

Before he could plant a kiss on it, however, Yeshe caught the prince's ear and pulled it hard.

'Release my hair this instant!' she ordered. 'Or I swear by all that is holy that I will gut you and leave you to dry!'

A-KarO laughed heartily. 'Yeshe,' he said, 'you may as well resign yourself to my company. We will be spending a lot of time together from now on, my dear.'

'I will leave you to your delusions,' Yeshe said sarcastically. 'I don't entertain any myself. Now will that be all or is there anything else?'

A-KarO turned serious now as he turned towards her and captured her stray strand of hair between his fingers. 'A moment, Dakini,' he said, 'do hear me out. I came to warn you that you are in danger. The Asur have begun their machinations. In fact, we have intelligence that they are already on the move. I have been told that the threat to you from the Asur is imminent and that you are not safe from them either in the mortal world or even here in Shambala. Dakini, you must alert your personal guard while you are still here. For the next two days, ensure that they are on high alert and vigilant at all times. Also, Yeshe, it is imperative that your psychic shields are in place and fully active, as are your wards. The moment we step out of Shambala, I will take over your security and you need not concern yourself with it anymore. Till then, however, I cannot take any action, for the Rigden has tied my hands. But please, Yeshe, be sure to maintain your own vigilance and state of preparedness. Be wary.'

A-KarO now encircled the dakini with his arms. 'Yeshe, you have heard me,' he said. 'Promise me you will be careful.'

Yeshe slapped his arms away. 'Unhand me this minute!' she commanded. 'I need no warning from you, A-KarO. I am a deity of compassion. I never go on the offensive. You know that well. However, I will take care and maintain my wards and warn my personal guard.'

Prince A-KarO inclined his head in acknowledgement. 'I will be keeping an eye on you, Yeshe. All you have to do is be careful for the next two days. Then I, along with Narasimha, will take over.'

Yeshe inclined her head and shook out her hair. 'Now kindly be gone,' she said curtly. 'I am sure you are late for your dinner engagement with the queen.'

Prince A-KarO stretched out his legs and sprawled on the bench. 'I can always say you delayed me, hmm, Yeshe? Just think of the comments my words will provoke at court.'

Yeshe jumped up from the bench and thundered, 'Don't you dare, A-KarO! If you know what is good for you, you will not breathe a word about this meeting to anyone. I don't want anyone getting the false impression that I favour you over Narasimha. Now if you won't depart, I will, you shameless creature!'

Prince A-KarO blew Yeshe a kiss. She stiffened at the gesture and, turning her back on him, marched out of the courtyard garden. Prince A-KarO followed her to the courtyard and, from there, made his way to the queen's court.

V

The celestial prince entered the queen's audience chamber and immediately scanned his surroundings, looking for Narasimha. Pearls and polished turquoise covered the walls of the opulent room, while its pillars were made of lapis lazuli. Suspended from the centre of the ceiling was a huge chandelier of glistening moonstone and light shimmered over the many silken couches from overhanging lanterns of coloured crystal.

Queen Rinchen, the Rigden's consort, was seated on a throne made of sapphires. Her raven-black hair, arranged in a crown over her head, was set off with a simple gold circlet encrusted with diamonds. She was dressed simply in a rose-hued skirt and a silver tunic embroidered in silver thread. A stole of silver tissue completed the ensemble. Her elegant silver jewellery – necklaces, armbands, bangles and anklets – was devoid of gems.

Prince A-KarO bowed low before the queen, pressing his hand to his heart in a gesture of humility.

The queen gave the prince a keen look and said, 'It is after a long time that you visit us, Prince A-KarO. Your presence here has been greatly missed.'

The prince smiled. 'It goes without saying that I too have missed my many discussions with you, Your Majesty,' he responded, 'but as you well know, I have been in Amravati the past couple of years, engaged in the defence of the eastern quarter of the universe that falls under the Lha forces. I returned to Shambala only this week and came to you as soon as I could, my Queen.'

'It has been many years since we last saw you and then you were but a lad,' the queen smiled. 'What news of your mother, Queen Nilamani?'

'My mother sends you her regards, Your Majesty. She has also sent a missive for you,' Prince A-KarO said, handing the queen a scrolled letter. 'As for the Lha king, my sire sends you his best wishes. King Ragen SakarO has sent a letter and many gifts for the Rigden. I myself have conveyed this to the Rigden.' Again, the prince bowed low before the queen.

Queen Rinchen smiled and signalled to her attendants for a couch to be placed near her for the prince. 'Prince A-KarO,' she said, once her command had been obeyed, gesturing for the prince to be seated, 'from time to time, my ladies and I have heard of your many exploits, adventures and accomplishments from our ambassadors and other sources. The last time that you were here was well over twelve years ago. Since then, all I know about you is mere hearsay. Now tell me in your own words what you have been up to and how the years have treated you.'

Prince A-KarO smiled and seated himself on the couch to the queen's right. 'Your Majesty,' he began, 'there is not much to tell. After I went to live with my sire, the Lha king, many centuries ago, and was later appointed his heir, I have been serving as General of the eastern Lha forces. In that capacity, I have been engaged in active combat with the Asur and other demonic forces. I have fought across the eastern celestial frontier, right from the border-worlds of Khos, Kansa, Rijek and Shamuk to frontier outposts like Aao, Lo and Doran. In fact, my Queen, since I left you and Shambala twelve years ago, there has been little in my life other than ceaseless battle with the Asur across the frontier, with occasional forays into Amravati to report to the Lha king. It was only on a recent visit to Amravati, a month back, that the Lha king ordered me to report to the Rigden in connection with a mission to Earth. My services are required to help provide a defence against the Asur. So here I am, my Queen, after an interval of twelve years.'

'That, Prince A-KarO,' smiled Queen Rinchen, 'is a toned-down account of your great achievements that does them little justice. Now I have heard that you will be leaving for Earth shortly and wish you all the best in your mission. While in the mortal world, you will undoubtedly be engaged in battle with the Asur once again, Prince A-KarO, but under no circumstances are you to feel that you are alone. We, in Shambala, will be sending you aid and messages from time to time.

'Now, to bring up another matter, I wonder whether you have met the dakini, Yeshe Nam Lha? She is accompanying you on the mission, as you know, and if the two of you haven't met already, I need to introduce you formally to each other.'

'There is no need for an introduction, my Queen,' Prince A-KarO smiled. 'I am well acquainted with the dakini and have met her from time to time, both in Amravati and here in Shambala. In fact, I just met up with her before coming to see you. The dakini was gracious enough to receive me.'

Queen Rinchen laughed. 'Aha! So she did have words with you, our Yeshe! The maiden is known to avoid interacting with males. She will not make it easy for either you or Narasimha. Courting her will be a rare challenge for you, my Prince.'

'And what, my Queen, is life without a challenge?' the prince countered.

'In fact, I find the situation very interesting. Yeshe will certainly prove a challenge, but one I am sure about being able to meet.'

Queen Rinchen looked across the room at Yeshe sitting in the shadows. 'No, Prince A-KarO,' she persisted, 'I don't think she will prove easy for either you or Narasimha. I am most curious to know what will actually happen between you.'

Prince A-KarO stood up to take his leave and bowed low before the queen. Then his eyes scanned the room for Narasimha – in vain.

He picked up a goblet of wine from one of the trays arranged around the chamber and circulated among the queen's courtiers, exchanging greetings and polite nods with them. Then he felt his gaze being drawn like a magnet to Yeshe's quiet figure sitting in a corner of the room. He started towards her, making his way through the crowds. Yeshe threw up her head in consternation and swiftly rose to her feet, making a beeline for the exit. In moments, she had left the room. Prince A-KarO tossed back his wine, laughing softly to himself. Then he too made for the exit.

Chapter 10

ASUR

I

Dawn broke slowly over the snow plains in rays of gold. Its soft, flattering light fell on the thick forest of firs and pines bordering the sprawling Asur fortress complex that stood a mere 10 leagues from Inkala, the headquarters of Asur royalty, whose members enjoyed the highest rank in demon hierarchy. Huge snowdrifts were piled by the roadside and snow had collected on the trees of Inken Forest that stood near the fortress of Bakala, just 50 km from Inkala, which was also the capital city of the frozen world of Inka, the leading planet of the demoniac Asur confederacy that held sway over the cold planets of the eastern span of the universe, a realm populated entirely by demons, save for the border-worlds, where beings of mixed blood resided.

Riding his horse, Spigol, bred from a unique line of Asur demon steeds, the Asur demon prince, Arden Ti Nazer Basher, made swiftly for the rather bleak-looking grey fortress of the infamous sorcerer, Nikas dom Bakala. A troop of guardsmen followed the prince in a disciplined formation.

There was the usual chaos outside the sorcerer's fortress, as Arden handed his mount over at the stables and walked swiftly down into the fortress's inner courtyard. There, a functionary from the sorcerer's household was waiting for him.

Bowing low, he said, 'We were informed that you would be arriving early this morning, Prince Arden. The sorcerer, Nikas dom Bakala, awaits you. I am to take you to him. Please follow me.'

Arden looked about him with disdain while unbuttoning his collar as the blast of heat from the roaring fireplaces of the keep's great hall hit him. Apart from the sorcerer's colours and coat of arms and his tribal sigils, which were proudly displayed on the walls, the hall was sparsely furnished with dark mahogany tables and benches. A formal wooden seat carved out of rosewood stood in one corner and was undoubtedly the sorcerer's ceremonial chair. The fortress floors were paved in grey marble and huge urns, stacked with wood and greens, stood near the doorways. Many of the sorcerer's acolytes and novices-in-training walked in the hall wearing dull grey robes. The occasional palace guard was visible, dressed in distinctive grey livery.

As he was led through the fortress, Prince Arden looked around him without interest. Well over seven feet tall, he had a lean frame that rippled with muscular strength and agility – the hallmark of the Asur royal household of Nazer Basher. His dusky complexion glowed in the gloom and a swirl of red light lit up the depths of his black eyes. His features were sharp; high cheekbones, a straight, narrow nose and thin lips hinted at ruthlessness. His black hair, tossed about by gusts of wind, fell straight to his shoulders. On his forehead gleamed a slim coronet of gold.

Prince Arden was the third son of the reigning monarch, Narman Ti Nazer Basher, whose clan enjoyed sovereignty over the eastern realm of the universe, home to the ice planets of the Asur demonic confederacy ruled by the Nazer Basher dynasty. Unrivalled as a warrior prince, Arden's battle strategy was the pride of the dynasty. As General of the border-land fleet, he had been engaged in active combat with the celestial Lha empire, which shared its frontiers with the demon Asur worlds. Arden straightened his fur-lined cloak and followed the sorcerer's functionary deeper into the fortress. After walking past a flight of stairs and through a twisting corridor, he was shown into the sorcerer's study.

A throw rug on the floor and a massive desk in one corner, with a chair behind it, contributed to the chamber's austere appearance. Books and papers lay scattered all over, lending the place a look of disarray. Two chairs had been placed in front of the fireplace, where a fire had been lit. And standing with his back to it was the Asur sorcerer, Nikas dom Bakala.

He smiled thinly as Prince Arden was shown into his presence. Nikas was just over six and a half feet tall – small by Asur standards – and had a thin, wiry body. His flowing white hair hung around his head like a corona and his eyes, pale pink with reddish glints, had a tendency to look bloodshot when he was under stress. The sorcerer was dressed simply in a robe of the deepest blue that almost verged on black.

'Your Highness,' he said, addressing Arden, 'I have received your message and, accordingly, have everything in readiness for your journey. When would you and your troops like to depart? I will open the portals for that precise hour.'

Arden inclined his head. 'Bakala, I believe you were briefed on my mission which, as you know, is of the first importance,' he said. 'I set forth with the intention of stealing the golden swan of the gods. A troop of twelve Asur will accompany me. It is also imperative that you join us on this mission. You will be required to open the portals for the chaos paths and lead us by the shortest route to Shambala. I will especially require you to open a path into the Rigden's palace so that we can gain access two evenings from now. On the way, we will halt in the world of Jubal, where we have an errand to run. Am I clear?'

The sorcerer pressed his lips together in a smile that was no smile at all. 'Your Highness,' he said, 'you wander into perilous territory. How will you disguise your presence when you step into Shambala?'

'It is all arranged,' Arden smiled. 'You, Bakala, are merely concerned with the work of transporting us there and back.'

The sorcerer smirked. 'Your Highness, could you share the details of your mission with me?' he asked.

Arden inclined his head and replied, 'Bakala, we go to abduct the dakini, Yeshe Nam Lha, from the Rigden's banquet, which is being held two evenings hence. We will travel by the chaos paths that the gods fear to use, but which are favourable to us.'

'So it begins, Your Highness,' Bakala sighed. 'The great battle dawns; the golden eagle flies in the skies. I shall have the portals opened.'

Arden smiled as he gazed into the warming glow of the fire. 'Get it opened now, Bakala,' he ordered. 'My men wait impatiently outside your study. Have one of your acolytes fetch them.'

Bakala gestured to one of the slim young Asur women who stood half-hidden in the shadows. 'Get the captain and the troops here,' he commanded.

Smirking, the sorcerer stepped up to the sparking fire and flung a black powder into the flames. Incense filled the room. Bakala smiled, his body writhing in ecstasy as he uttered the chaos incantation. The words rang through the room powerfully and the incantation continued for several minutes. Those who heard the chaos incantation being recited were swept away on a wave of ecstasy, as the chaotic forces of the universe flooded them, filling their beings with the intoxication of power. Then, just as suddenly, the wave of ecstasy subsided and the portals to the chaos paths slowly opened in the fire, looking like the silhouette of a doorway in the flames.

Bakala looked at Arden now, his eyes unnaturally bright. 'It will hold for a few minutes,' he said. 'Step through, Prince Arden, and let the men follow.'

Arden looked at Bakala and said, 'After you.'

The sorcerer frowned. Then assuming a serene expression, he stepped into the flames and was sucked into chaos.

Arden glanced at his captain, Sapher Nmaldris, who had led the prince's troops into the room. 'Order the men to fall into line, Captain, and follow me,' he commanded.

With that, Arden stepped into the flames and was engulfed by chaos. He was followed by his troops and the captain, who brought up the rear. An ice wind was blowing over the snowfields that stretched away as far as the eye could see. The skies were a leaden grey, promising more snow, and the snow plains stretched away into emptiness.

Prince Arden rubbed his hands together, warming them against the sharp drop in temperature. 'We march now, Captain Nmaldris,' he declared. 'Get the men into formation. There is no time to waste.'

It took mere minutes to get the twelve men to fall into arrow formation and Nmaldris then set off on the arduous march across the snow plains. Prince Arden smiled with pleasure; the snow was his element, the ice winds his friends.

The chaos paths chosen by the Asur had existed since the beginning of time, along with their brothers, the sacred path favoured by the gods and the paths of the winds, used from time to time by the forces of both gods and demons. The chaos paths crossed entire star systems and opened portals into different worlds. All three paths criss-crossed the universe, shortening the duration of travel through the subtle void and opening portals into gross worlds. The subtle and magical art of travelling too had existed since the beginning of time, but its custodians had been either the gods or the demons The decision was made following the treaty of Amravati, that was signed between the Gods and the demons following a battle that lasted five hundred years between the two sides. The treaty was signed a century ago since when an uneasy stalemate prevailed between the two sides. Following the treaty the chaos paths were controlled by the demons, the sacred paths by the Gods and the path of the winds was shared by both sides.

II

Time in the subtle void defied calculation; the chaos paths were beyond time. Prince Arden looked around the endless snowfield and sighed. They had been marching for eight hours straight. Ahead of them, against the snow line, he sighted the village of Cue, populated by the Quevasis, a tribe of lower demons who lived in the chaos paths and were beings of chaos, but owed their allegiance to the Asur.

The sorcerer, Bakala, who had been walking beside Arden, paused. Flinging out a hand, he pointed to the village. 'There, Your Highness!' he said, 'that's Cue. We can halt there for the night. Though the village seems to be close by, it is still a two-hour march away. The distances in this dimension are fraught with error and nothing is actually what it appears to be.'

'Still, it is on the horizon now,' Arden smiled. 'The men will find that heartening. Also, dusk approaches. I would prefer not to traverse the snow plains at night when the wild wind blows and the furies rage across the skies.'

He smiled at the Asur behind him and said, 'Cue on the horizon; not far to go now.' Then he signalled to Captain Sapher Nmaldris. 'Order double pace,' he commanded. 'I want to make Cue before nightfall, if possible. Give the men one shot of *ditche* each. Then we set off again.'

Captain Sapher Nmaldris smiled, his golden eyes glowing. An Asur demon of middle years, he was over seven and a half feet tall and massive in build. His complexion was a wheatish shade of brown and the depths of his golden eyes had a red tinge to them. His brown hair was tied back in a queue and his golden horns shone in the failing light of evening. His uniform consisted of the standard pale grey fur-lined tunic and pants and a thick grey cloak which was held together by a silver badge displaying the insignia of Inka. Like the uniform worn by the troops, the captain's too was magically charged with the power of taking on the colours of the Asur's immediate environment. Nmaldris dug out a huge silver flask of the elixir, *ditche*, and doled out a small measure to each of the twelve Asur who were marching with them. A fiery liquor made more potent with medicinal herbs, it was commonly used by the Asur during journeys and especially when they set off on long marches.

Arden gave the signal for resuming their journey and the men soon fell into the regular rhythm of their march. The prince and his men had been marching silently for a while when Bakala, who had been keeping in step alongside, suddenly stirred by his side and raised his staff.

'At Cue, we should arrange for transport through the snows, Prince Arden,' said the sorcerer. 'We will need two large sledges with a capacity of seating six people each and a team of snow wolves to pull them.'

Arden inclined his head and said, 'I have already had messages sent to Cue and Arisanthe. We will be provided with transport at Cue to take us through the snows and, at Arisanthe, there will be horses for us to ride through the barren plains. Arrangements are in place for our journey back as well. There will be no marching on the way back; we will have transport all through.'

Bakala nodded. 'That is good,' he declared. 'It is a pity the Quevasis did not meet us at the gates for this journey, but it does not matter. However, I wonder, Your Highness, if you have pondered the matter of the journey back, when there is every likelihood of pursuit by the gods.'

Prince Arden contemplated the cold evening light painting the frozen plains with its vivid colours. The biting wind that had started blowing sliced through his heavy fur clothing and made him shiver.

'Pursuit is inevitable,' he responded, 'but everything in this terrain is to our advantage. The elements and the denizens of these plains will fight the gods every step of the way – that is, if they dare to embark on the chaos paths.'

Bakala smiled craftily. 'I have had word sent to the furies to hound the trail of the gods if they cross into the chaos paths. Also, I have communicated with the snow wolves and the *quosharn*, the snow leopards, directing them to attack them. I agree with you, Your Highness, that pursuit by the gods is inevitable and that they will undoubtedly follow our trail, but the terrain will turn against the trespassers.'

Prince Arden smiled. 'As ever, you plan well, Bakala,' he remarked. 'Though the Quevasis in Cue and the Santhis in Arisanthe have already been apprised of our plans, I will be communicating further with them and will direct them to place obstructions in the path of the gods.'

Bakala shrugged and quickened his pace. His thin body, a hazy mirage in the snows, looked as though it might vanish, but the malignant glint in his bloodshot eyes left no doubt that this impression was dangerously deceptive.

Dusk was falling as Prince Arden and his troops neared the village of Cue. A delegation of Quevasis stood on its outskirts, waiting to receive them. The villagers were stocky and under four feet tall, but their sturdily built bodies were heavy with muscle and their nut-brown faces shone. The headman, Vasis Colearthis, a short, sturdy Quevasis demon with neat brown features, a pot belly and thick, muscled legs, stepped out of the snows in thick garments of fur and animal skin. His white hair was stiff, like straw, and the multicoloured tribal headband he wore marked him out as the delegation's leader and brought some semblance of order to his wild mane.

Colearthis bowed low before the prince. 'Your Highness,' he began, 'we welcome you here in the wilderness. It has been years since a prince of the royal house visited Cue. We are honoured by your visit and your interest in us. We have made arrangements for your stay in Cue.'

Arden inclined his head and said, 'Lead on, Colearthis. My men and I are weary. Once we have refreshed ourselves, we will hold talks with your people.'

'Your Highness,' Colearthis smiled, 'we have prepared the guest-house for your stay. I hope our humble efforts meet with your approval. Once you have refreshed yourself, dinner will be served for you at my humble abode. Arrangements have also been made for the troops' dinner. Do grace us with your presence, Your Highness.'

Arden inclined his head and said, 'We accept your hospitality with pleasure, Colearthis,'

A turn in the road brought the tired Asur to Cue. The village roads were lined with Quevasis, their women dressed in fur trousers and long, colourful fur tunics, with a white veil over their hair which was tied back in a becoming fashion. The public bowed low as the prince's party passed. The prince sighed as he smelt the woodsmoke rising from hearth fires inside the large wooden huts that lined the roads. All the huts had sloping roofs and a single window. Arden stopped outside a large house over which flags fluttered. The guest-house's caretaker and cook came out and bowed low in welcome, as Colearthis led his royal guest in, with the troops following in his wake.

A pleasant surprise awaited Arden when he walked into the spacious room the hut opened into. A crackling fire burned in the hearth and the room felt warm and cosy after the severe cold outdoors. The prince looked about him with curiosity. The main room led into four smaller ones. Peering into them, he found that in each, four straw pallets had been laid out and a lively fire burned in the hearth. He made his way to the armchair positioned by the fire in the main room, while the caretaker handed out steaming cups of a herbal brew to the visitors.

III

After a refreshing bath in steaming hot water, Prince Arden felt rejuvenated. He stepped out of the large room assigned to him and signalled to Captain Sapher Nmaldris to join him.

'Captain Nmaldris,' he said, 'please summon the sorcerer, Bakala, and your first officer, Jace Pegomse, and join me for a meeting in my room right away. I will be going over the details of our mission and strategy with all of you. After the meeting is over, you may address the men.'

He returned to his room and pulled his armchair closer to the fire. Within minutes, Captain Nmaldris and the rest of the core group had joined him.

Arden nodded to the group as he took his seat and looked at Captain Nmaldris. 'As you all know, we are here on a very sensitive mission at the behest of the highest authority. Allow me to inform you at the very outset that there is no room whatsoever for failure; we can only succeed. As you are aware, we are heading right now for the world of Jubal in the Regan system. This is the heart of enemy territory and the utmost caution and care are called for in your dealings.

'Jubal and Shambala, as you all know, are situated in the same corner of the universe; their portals lie in close proximity along the chaos paths. We will first travel to a remote mountainous area of Jubal, a highly underdeveloped world, to make contact with a source for our operation against Shambala.' Arden looked at Captain Nmaldris intently. 'We will reach the vicinity of the portals to Jubal by early evening tomorrow if we travel according to plan. Captain Nmaldris, I plan to send you and Jace Pegomse into Jubal tomorrow. Sorcerer Bakala, I will expect you to make no errors in your calculations when you open our path of access through the portals at the heart of the Iratse mountains in western Jubal. Now, Captain Nmaldris, you and your first officer, Pegomse, will be dropped at the location to make contact with the witch, Dar Lei Shar, for reasons I will explain shortly.

'Captain,' Arden went on, 'to navigate your way to the contact point on Jubal, you and Jace will be provided with horses. You will also be equipped with a mind map of the surrounding terrain in which the exact contact point is marked out for you. As soon as this meeting is over, you and your first officer must report to Sorcerer Bakala, who will provide you with the mind map I mentioned.

'At the contact point I referred to, Dar Lei Shar will hand over a sealed potion, along with some identification documents, which you will bring back to me. This vital potion, which will provide us with a body and spirit camouflage and enable us to pass ourselves off as celestial citizens of Shambala, will be effective for no more than twenty-four hours. I repeat: twenty-four hours; not an instant more. Within that span of time, not only must we complete our mission, but we must also cross the border and be back in Inka. Also, the portals will remain open for you at the exact place from where you enter, but just for ten hours. You should plan to cross them on your way back well within that time.'

Arden looked at the others, but focused especially on Jace. The captain's deputy was a wiry Asur demon standing tall at seven feet, with a slender, compactly muscled form that was sleek like a mountain cat's. His dark complexion was set off by arresting black eyes that gave off a reddish glow. His dark hair, tied up in a bun at the back of his head, was crowned by a pair of pointed black horns. His brows and his beard were just as dark and merged into his coal-black skin. Jace wore a feral look that was heightened whenever his razor-sharp claws assumed their protracted position.

'Now for the actual mission,' Arden went on. 'Its purpose is to infiltrate Shambala, the Rigden's palace and then swoop down at night for the Rigden's banquet. Our force of twelve élite Asur warriors will stand in readiness at a predetermined point just outside the Rigden's banquet hall, while Captain Nmaldris, his first officer, Jace Pegomse, and I will infiltrate the banquet. Once there, I expect you to move fast. You will appear to mingle with the guests, as I make directly for the dakini, Yeshe Nam Lha, and, on a pretext, lead her out of the banquet hall. You will follow me. Once we are near the exit, I will abduct her and we will rejoin the force held in reserve outside. We will then travel through the portals and transport her to the chaos paths. The entire action has to be over within an hour. Once on the chaos path, we will follow the shortest route to Inka. Is that clear?'

Captain Nmaldris smiled and said, 'Indeed it is, Your Highness. So the mission is to apprehend the dakini, Yeshe Nam Lha, thus aborting Shambala's plan in one stroke and carrying away the prophesied mother of the divine child. What a master plan!'

Arden smiled back at him. 'Well, this is it. As I said earlier, we will be taking twelve troopers with us as reserve and they will take up position at a previously identified location near the banquet. They are to be deployed only if absolutely necessary. I trust that this is clear. In order to seize the advantage, we have to ensure that we move fast. Now, Captain Nmaldris, address your troops and familiarize them with the plan. Then the three of you should get ready for the dinner. It is being served in the village headman's hut.'

IV

The first stars of late evening were peeping through the mass of clouds obscuring most of the dark skies, when Prince Arden stepped out of the guest-house for dinner at the headman Vasis Colearthis's hut. Captain Nmaldris flanked him on one side, while on the other, the sorcerer, Bakala, walked along with swift strides, his slender form almost merging with the night but for the glint of his hungry red eyes. Arden made for the centre of the village, where the headman's large residence was lit up with lanterns. Colearthis himself stood at the door to welcome his guests.

As Arden approached, the headman bowed low. 'Your Highness,' he said, 'your presence here bestows rare honour on me and mine.'

The prince smiled and followed Colearthis into a large, colourful wooden chamber, with a fire roaring brightly in the hearth. Woollen rugs lay on the floor and the skin of a huge bear graced one wall, its pristine white fur shining in the firelight. The headman escorted Arden to a large armchair placed near the fire. A flagon of *ditche* stood on a table by the fireside and a plate of nuts sat next to it. The rest of the troops settled on benches placed at vantage points across the room.

'Your Highness, I have some *ditche* of fine quality from Inka for you,' said Colearthis. 'Or would you prefer the local beer brewed here?'

Prince Arden looked around the room, enjoying the warmth of the roaring fire. 'Some *ditche* will do just fine,' he murmured.

Colearthis handed the prince a silver goblet of *ditche,* then poured some of the wine for the captain and his first officer. Bakala had asked for a tumbler of hot spiced milk. Settled in his armchair by the fire, he smirked to himself.

'What brings you so far out on to the chaos paths, Your Highness?' Colearthis enquired.

Prince Arden sipped at the fiery liquor. 'We travel in stealth,' he told the headman. 'Word of our passage must not filter out. Tell your people, Colearthis.'

'As Your Highness commands, no word of your passage will be breathed by a single villager in Cue,' the headman promised.

Prince Arden looked directly at him now. 'Tomorrow, we leave at first light. Colearthis, you will have to keep in readiness two large sleighs for our use and harness them to snow wolves. We will use them to travel up to the boundary to the plains. Also, have a message sent with a runner to Arisanthe for the Santhis to meet us with horses – fourteen in all – at the border where the snow plains meet the barren plains.'

Colearthis smiled obsequiously. 'Arrangements have already been made for the sleighs and the teams of snow wolves, Your Highness,' he declared. 'I have them ready for your use tomorrow. I will also have a runner sent to Arisanthe right away so that arrangements can be made in time for the Santhis to meet you with horses.'

With that, the headman stood up and left the room. Prince Arden settled back in the armchair and gazed into the fire's dancing flames. At that moment, Madame Colearthis entered the room. Slender of build, she had a perfect figure and pale brown hair that fell to her waist. She was dressed in loose trousers and a long tunic, complete with a fur jacket. Bowing low before the prince, Madame Colearthis smilingly set a plate of kebabs before him.

'Your Highness, may I entertain you with a recital of the *zitara*?' she asked.

Arden smiled at her and nodded. The demoness picked up a pipe-thin, reed-like musical instrument and began playing it, its shadow strains softly breaking into the night. The prince looked at her in surprise; she was, he realized, more than just a competent player. The *zitara* was a difficult instrument to master and a good player could render ecstasy through its haunting refrain.

Colearthis made his way back into the room at this moment. 'Your Highness, the runner has left for Arisanthe,' he announced. 'Is there any other way in which I may be of service to you?'

'Indeed, there is,' the prince smiled. 'On our return journey to Inka, we anticipate being pursued by the gods.'

Colearthis looked confused. 'The gods, Your Highness? But they never use the chaos paths,' he said.

Arden nodded. 'Believe me, this time they will. But do not be alarmed, Colearthis. It will, most likely, be a small group of celestials in pursuit. Now this is what you must do: delay them in one manner or the other by creating obstructions in their path and making them lose their way here.'

'In short, make mischief, Your Highness,' the headman smiled. 'Yes, indeed! We shall create much mischief for the celestials and delay them. From tomorrow itself, I will have traps set for them, clever traps to catch them unawares. Never fear, Your Highness! We will deflect them from their path of pursuit and cause them to go astray so they are lost in the wilderness.'

Arden inclined his head and said, 'Keep yourselves alert and create mayhem when they attempt to cross through these parts.'

'Your Highness,' Colearthis ventured, 'it is not my place to advise you on such matters, but if I may make so bold, perhaps the furies should be roped into service.'

Prince Arden sighed. 'All is in readiness, Colearthis,' he said. 'Word has been sent to the furies and to other denizens as well. Just do your job.'

'It is an honour to serve you, my Prince,' the headman murmured.

The haunting music of the *zitara* rose and fell and Arden found himself unwinding. He sighed softly, his abstracted gaze lingering in the depths of the dancing flames.

V

Mid-afternoon was long past and evening was approaching, when Prince Arden finally sighted the barren plains stretching away endlessly to the horizon. The snow plains had begun to thin out and slush and puddles of water from melted snow were visible by the side of the path. The speed of the sleigh had also slackened as the snow wolves carefully negotiated the new terrain. The sun was waning in the heavens when the sleigh driver finally called for a halt and brought the sleigh to a stop, signalling to the second party following them to do likewise. They had been travelling for more than nine hours since dawn.

'Your Highness, the sleighs will go no farther,' the driver announced. 'The snow layer has thinned out considerably. Your Santhis escort will be awaiting you with a team of fresh horses by the blue shadow stone at the boundary to the barren plains, a mere five miles from here. I will lead the way till that contact point, before taking your leave, Your Highness.'

Arden inclined his head and said, 'We have made good time, Lepei. I thank you for your offer to escort us till the blue shadow stone.'

The Asur now dismounted from the sleighs and fell into formation for the march. Then in a disciplined manner, the company started marching out of the snow plains, with Prince Arden in the lead and the sorcerer, Bakala, walking alongside. The ice-cold wind cut through Arden's furs and he found himself suppressing an involuntary shudder as he marched on. As they neared the boundary into the barren plains, the terrain became slushier still. The plains ahead were filled with shadows and rocks that had weathered in unusual ways so that they bore strange patterns and shone in iridescent hues, predominantly of pink and purple. The soil there was hard and cold and hostile to every form of vegetation.

The company marched into the plains and Lepei led them towards the right, moving into a thick, rocky belt and on to a channel-thin path that negotiated many sharp turns as it zigzagged its way between large boulders.

The sun was setting when the company approached the blue shadow stone, a huge stone that glowed a midnight blue in the failing light like a strange beacon and, what was stranger still, cast long blue shadows that extended for well over a mile. As the company drew closer to it, Arden spotted the waiting group of horses and two Santhis standing vigil over them.

The Santhis were a very different breed of lower demons. If the Quevasis were short and mischievous, the Santhis held magical powers and were pure evil. Arden made his way to the waiting horses and the two Santhis, who bowed low to welcome him, their reed-thin bodies swaying in the icy breeze of the plains.

'Arise,' said the prince.

'Your Highness,' one of the Santhis began, 'the horses are in readiness and both of us will serve as your guides. The daylight hours are fast dying and night approaches. Perhaps it would be best to retire to the Santhis village.'

He had a pale complexion and straw-coloured hair and his green eyes shone like a cat's.

Arden shook his head. 'I am afraid we will not be visiting your village,' he told the Santhis. 'We are in a hurry. Tonight, we will camp on the plains. Now I need you to head towards the east. We are to travel to the heart of the twisted wood, where the portals we seek are located.'

The Santhis smiled. 'As the crow flies, the twisted wood is fifteen leagues from here. That is not far. If we leave right away, we should reach it by midnight. The horses are fresh and rested and we can be off whenever you wish, Your Highness.'

Arden smiled. 'By the way, please introduce yourself, Santhis, and your friend as well,' he said.

The Santhis bowed and replied, 'I am Felt, Your Highness, and this is my son, Kelpin.'

Arden signalled to his captain and announced, 'We will have an early dinner now, Nmaldris. Then order the men to mount the horses. We are to ride straight to the twisted wood and the portals of Jubal.' Now the prince addressed the older Santhis. 'You and your son may join us for dinner now, Felt. Then we leave for the twisted wood.'

Felt bowed and murmured, 'As Your Highness commands.'

'Felt, I have a letter with some instructions for your chief,' Arden added. 'Please pass it on to him and give him my message that the instructions are to be strictly followed. If he performs his duties to my satisfaction, he, along with the villagers, will be duly awarded.'

Felt nodded. 'I will convey your message, Your Highness.'

Arden seated himself on a rock beside Bakala, who handed him a platter of hard bread and mutton kebabs, along with a chunk of cheese. Evening was deepening along the horizon and the first stars began appearing in the azure darkness of the night sky.

VI

A fast, cold wind was blowing as the prince cantered carefully over the midnight-shrouded plains. Across the horizon, the twisted wood appeared as a darker shadow in the night.

Felt drew his horse near Arden's. 'The twisted wood nears, Your Highness' he said. 'It is merely a league away. What are your orders now?'

'Sorcerer Bakala will now take the lead. We make for the portals in the heart of the wood.'

Felt saluted the prince and rode ahead, with Bakala following him to the front of the column to take the lead. Arden wrapped his furs tight around him and kneed his horse to move at a faster clip. The group trotted in silence over the barren plains till the twisted wood was almost upon them. The whispering of the wind in the trees produced an unnatural sighing sound. As they drew closer still, the pale twisted trunks of the trees shone in the night and their light leaves rustled loudly.

Prince Arden rode ahead until his horse was flanking Sorcerer Bakala's. They were now moving into the wood at a slow pace. Deep darkness lay under the trees and the canopy of trees overhead obscured the night sky. Fireflies glinted in the darkness giving off a jewel-like shine in the shadowy wood. The sickle moon in the heavens threw a faint light in the thick clusters of trees. The canopy of branches overhead obscured the night sky and barred entry to the faint light of the sickle moon; impenetrable darkness lay below. From time to time, the sounds of wildlife came from the depths of the wood – the keening cry of a nocturnal bird, the sawing call of a panther.

Sorcerer Bakala raised his hand and the group halted. Addressing Arden, he said, 'Your Highness, I need to examine the path that lies ahead. I shall now call forth a searchlight that will illuminate the way to the portals of Jubal.'

The prince nodded his consent. Bakala flung a shining powder into the air and began muttering a low chant. The aroma of musk oranges permeated the air and grew stronger, till a star-shaped point of light, shining brighter than the heavens, sprang into being at Bakala's fingertip. As the sorcerer chanted a few more words, the star shot ahead, describing an arc and carving a path for itself in the darkness, dancing between the trees, hovering in the wind and throwing off scintillating shards of light to beckon the group forward.

Bakala raised his voice and declared, 'Your Highness, we will follow the star. It will lead us to the portals.'

The mounted company followed Sorcerer Bakala through the shadowy, night-black wood and into greater darkness. The witch light danced through the trees, illuminating the path ahead. As Arden rode alongside the sorcerer, he took a sip of the fiery *ditche* from his hip flask to keep exhaustion at bay. The horses stumbled occasionally as they felt their way in the dark and, after what seemed to be hours of wandering in the shadows, the group came upon a huge oak tree in the very heart of the wood. The oak had a gigantic trunk that reached up into the heavens and its crisp green leaves sang their own refrain as they swayed to the rhythm of the night breeze. The dancing witch light came to a stop at the base of the oak, throwing sparkles into the night.

Arden sighed. 'We seem to have reached our destination,' he declared. 'Company, we halt here.'

He helped the frail sorcerer to dismount. Bakala stood erect, then walked up to the glowing star.

'Your Highness, the portals to Jubal are located here,' he announced. 'I shall forge an access path.'

Arden signalled to Captain Nmaldris and his first officer to take up position. 'Captain Nmaldris and First Officer Pegomse,' he said, 'ready yourselves and your horses for the journey to Jubal. The portals will open any moment and remain open for ten hours, awaiting your return. I expect you to make contact with the witch, Dar Lei Shar, accept the package she delivers and return at the soonest.'

'Your Highness, the sorcerer, Bakala, has given us the mind maps of the exact location,' the captain and his deputy said in response. 'The journey through the forest, starting from the place where the sorcerer is opening the portals to the witch's cavern, will take us an hour. We estimate being back within three hours – four, at the very most.'

With the witch light in his hand, Sorcerer Bakala stood near the base of the oak. 'Your Highness, I am about to open the portals. May I proceed?'

At a sign of assent from the prince, Bakala began a long, rolling chant, holding the star of witch light near the base of the oak all the while. Suddenly, a spark of light shot from the tiny star to the oak, illuminating the tree trunk. Another ray shot to the tree trunk and outlined a smoky, silver-tipped door, created entirely of witch light. The door began at the base of the trunk and rose to well over six feet. Bakala's chant continued, limning the door in smoky light. Slowly, the door opened on to a misty blaze of silver light and the sorceror signalled for the men to move through the door. Captain Nmaldris and First Officer Pegomse led their horses in through the silver door and were swallowed in a blaze of light.

Bakala moved off from the glowing silver portals that gave off a misty light. 'Your Highness,' he said, addressing Arden, 'the portals stay activated for ten hours. Now we will await the return of the captain and his first officer.'

Nodding, Arden issued an order to one of the guards standing behind him. 'Make camp under the trees,' he said. 'We will await Captain Nmaldris here. Also, tell the cook to get a meal going. The men are exhausted and hungry. Tell each trooper to see to his horse's needs first, before resting.'

The prince sat tiredly on a log of wood lying under one of the trees, as the men began putting up his tent. Sorcerer Bakala walked around the perimeter of the camp, setting up a warding that would prevent a wild animal or unwelcome presence from entering the camp. Arden yawned as he walked up to the blazing fire and pulled out his flask of *ditche*. Taking a long swig, he felt the liquor rolling off his tongue and blazing a trail into his depths.

VII

The first thing Jace Pegomse felt as they touched ground was the icy crispness of the air. They were standing in a clearing in the midst of a thick snow-clad forest of huge trees that stood several leagues tall. Jace looked around him, getting his bearings, and dragged in breaths of clear air.

'It's such a pity that we have come here during their winter,' he said. 'Else, we would have seen the verdant summer these worlds are famed for.'

Captain Nmaldris grunted, shaking his golden horns. 'Forget the summer and start moving. There is no time to waste. And you just might manage to enjoy a precious taste of summer in the paradise world of Shambala.'

The cold worlds of the Asur confederacy were snowbound all through the year and knew no summer, not even a few rare days of it.

Jace shook his head. 'If we survive Shambala, Captain, if we live to see it and talk about it,' he said, 'it would then be the single successful infiltration of the paradise world after two thousand years. For well over a millennium have the shining ones, the gods, debarred us from the warm worlds, leaving us to moulder in the ice and darkness of the eastern span, the frozen worlds of the universe.' The first officer looked at his silver grey horse that stood patiently waiting for him. 'Let's get moving, Sir,' he sighed.

While Jace mounted his steed, Captain Nmaldris accommodated his huge bulk on the back of his sturdy chestnut-brown horse. In an instant, Jace had seen a flash of the mind map that clearly revealed the path ahead. Soon, they were crossing the snowbound forest at a brisk trot, the horses navigating their way between the trees and rushing towards their destination. The deeper they moved into the forest, the more keenly aware they became of the sounds of nature surrounding them – the water dripping from trees, the warble of the birds, a melody to which Jace had never been exposed, and the many little noises of the forest that broke into the silence from time to time. Mile upon mile of forest flew by on either side, until they came upon a river rushing through. The horses followed its course as it unwound like a ribbon into the heart of the forest. The deeper they ventured, the dimmer the light grew until the trees were so thickly crowded together that the sky was hidden from sight.

In a little while, snow started falling softly until they could see another clearing in the dense growth. The smell of woodsmoke assailed Jace's nostrils as the horses made it into the clearing and he reined in his steed and brought it to a stop before a shadowy cave whose opening was completely screened off with entangled vines. The dancing light of a wood fire shone from within.

Captain Nmaldris grunted, 'This is the place. We are to wait for the witch.'

Jace dismounted and looked around him curiously. Suddenly, a wizened old woman stepped out from behind the curtain of vines and approached Captain Nmaldris. Her sharp green eyes stood out against her dead white skin and her stringy hair was tied back severely. Painfully thin, the old woman was dressed in a patched shirt of a greyish hue and a long black skirt that had seen a lot of use. Leaning heavily on a stick, she now approached them.

'Ah, Asur! So you have come! You are bound for Shambala, but who will allow you to set foot in the world that is the pride of the gods? Ha ha ha!' she cackled. 'Let this be a lesson to them for growing complacent. When the guard sleeps, the shadows grow.'

Captain Nmaldris bowed stiffly to her. 'Are you the witch, Dar Lei Shar?' he asked.

'Shar, beware of Shar, Asur!' said the old crone. 'Beware of your own folly.'

Captain Nmaldris found himself growling under his breath. 'Witch, I am waiting for the package,' he reminded her.

Dar Lei Shar frowned, then flicked her hands in a particular gesture. A small crystal decanter containing a colourless, smoky potion appeared in her hands.

'Two drops for each Asur that goes to Shambala,' she specified, 'not a drop more. Its effect will last for twenty-four hours. Take care.' Then the woman handed over a folder of papers. 'Identification papers for all of you bound for Shambala,' she explained. 'Now what news do you bring from the confederacy?'

Captain Nmaldris first tucked the decanter into a pouch and hid it away inside his jacket. Then he accepted the folder of papers and handed it to Jace for safekeeping.

'The Asur are on the move, witch,' he told the old crone. 'The monarch's priority has shifted to hands-on engagement with the gods. The long years of stalemate are over. War clouds hover along the borders separating the eastern span from the Lha kingdom.'

The witch shook her head. 'So Arden is going to head the operation on Earth, is he?' she asked.

Captain Nmaldris inclined his head and replied, 'I do not know whether there will be any need for an operation on Earth, witch, it is unclear yet.'

'Mark my words,' the witch cackled, 'all of you will winter on Earth and probably spend the next decade there. Tell Arden that it is to the mortal world that he is headed, as are the two of you.'

Captain Nmaldris shook his head, refuting her predictions. 'We are bound for Shambala, as you well know,' he persisted. 'Then we return across the border and go back to Inka.'

'Give Arden a message from me,' the witch smiled. 'Tell him to beware of the dakini, the golden one, Yeshe, for therein lies his doom.'

Captain Nmaldris blanched, stepping back involuntarily. 'We had best be off, witch,' was his brusque response.

The witch looked at Jace closely. 'There is more to you than meets the eye, young Asur,' she observed. 'When the dice falls, be prepared.'

Then she moved away and walked swiftly back into the cave.

VIII

Arden had barely woken up after half a night's rest and was sipping some strong herbal brew, when Captain Nmaldris and Jace rode back through the portals, back into the paths of chaos and twisted woods.

The prince looked up and asked, 'You have the potion and the papers? So you made contact?'

Captain Nmaldris bowed low before the prince. 'Yes, Your Highness, contact was established successfully. The witch was there on time. Here are the potion and the papers.'

'Good,' said Arden, taking charge of the package, 'everything is proceeding smoothly. Now report what happened there.'

Captain Nmaldris clicked his heels together. 'Your Highness, we established contact successfully with the witch, Dar Lei Shar, who immediately handed us the potion and the identification papers. She informed us that two drops of the potion were to be given to each member of the group entering Shambala. As for the papers, they provide identification for all of us who are bound for Kalpa.'

Arden inclined his head and said, 'Pray continue. What else did the witch say?'

'Your Highness, the witch spoke in a very obscure manner and her words might not be easy to interpret. However, she did say two things of note: one, that Your Highness and the entire team would be spending the next decade overseeing operations on Earth. She implied that despite our efforts, our mission might not reach a conclusive end now. Also, Your Highness, the witch asked me to warn you about the dakini, Yeshe Nam Lha. She urged you to beware of her, for the dakini – I beg your pardon, Your Highness, for uttering such words – would apparently prove to be your doom.'

'Interesting,' Arden smiled. 'The witch, as ever, talks in riddles.'

'That is all, Your Highness.'

Arden nodded. 'Now listen carefully. We will be leaving in an hour to find the portals for Shambala, located in this very area. An hour's distance separates them from the portals of Jubal. Captain, you will address your troops for the last time before our departure and tell them to be battle ready by six p.m.

'At that precise hour, we will enter Shambala and land just inside the Rigden's palace near the venue of the banquet. The force will wait in readiness in the Amber Courtyard. Only I, accompanied by the two of you, will infiltrate the banquet, which is being held in the royal gardens. We will have just fifteen minutes to mingle with the guests and make contact with Yeshe. You will ensure that you do not lose me in the crowd and are by my side all through. I will lead Yeshe out to the Amber Courtyard, where we will seize her and move through the portals and out to the paths of chaos. Is this clear?'

Captain Nmaldris held his hand to his heart and bowed low. 'Absolutely, Your Highness.'

Arden managed a tight smile. 'The entire operation should not take more than an hour,' he went on. 'You will assist me in luring Yeshe away from the banquet before we move to the portals and into the paths of chaos. Also, guile and deceit will be our most lethal weapon, rather than arms, for no amount of combat, however valiant, will be of use to us if we are caught. Even mere suspicion could spell disaster. You will dress in the formal black clothing that has been issued to you. Wear light armour underneath, carry your sabre and your knives concealed on your person. No other weapon will be of any use to you.

'Now, Captain, go and address the men. They are simply to serve as a fall-back measure, should our plans go awry. Our troops are to pass themselves off as guards patrolling the walls of the Amber Courtyard. The kits issued to them are designed to make them invisible at night. Make it clear to them that they must remain undetected and do everything possible not to attract attention to themselves. You may stand at ease now.'

Captain Nmaldris and Jace bowed low before the prince and left the room.

Prince Arden gave the command for the camp to be dismantled and for the company to start moving. A strange thrill ran through him; he felt more alive than he had in a long time; his claws itched to protract from his skin.

Smiling to himself, he turned to the sorcerer. 'We will set off in ten minutes,' he announced. 'Once we reach the portals we will halt there till five p.m. You can keep the portals open for two hours and no more. Even that is a risk. I do not want the gods to sense the chaos energy.'

'Your Highness, don't worry,' Bakala said reassuringly. 'They won't sense that energy. The portals I intend opening will be small and I will use powerful spells to keep the doorway concealed.'

'Then everything is in order,' the prince smiled.

The camp had been efficiently dismantled by now and the men formed a marching line. Prince Arden and Bakala took the lead, as they set off into the frozen wood. A chill wind blew through the sighing trees as they made their way through the shadowy forest towards the portals for Shambala.

CHAPTER 11

THE DANCE OF SHADOWS

I

Tashi woke up with a start, immediately alert to his bearings. He looked out of the window near his pallet and beheld the grey, pre-dawn skies heavily overcast with a thick cloud cover. This merely meant that the day's combat practice would be held in the indoor stadium in the palace's western wing. Tashi groaned; he would miss the crispness of the air outdoors and the sight of the rising sun. He rushed through his ablutions and dressed himself in a navy blue woollen tunic and trousers. He quickly tied on his boots, his fingers fumbling over the laces, and raced into the kitchen to heat some tea. It was still dark when Tashi took his breakfast of thick, crisp flatbread, along with the steaming tea. A sigh escaped his lips as he reminisced about the hot noodle soup with butter tea that he had so enjoyed at Demazong Gumpa, the hidden monastery.

Finishing his meal, the boy tiptoed into Prince A-KarO's room and was unsurprised to find the prince seated in the lotus posture on his meditation seat on the floor, his face glowing in the darkness with an amazing serenity. Moving on noiseless feet, Tashi began laying out A-KarO's clothes for the day and placed his highly polished boots next to them. Then he set a tea tray with a light morning repast with which the prince would break his fast and quietly withdrew from the room, picking up his bow and sheaf of arrows before leaving the apartments.

Few people were up at this hour and the corridors were largely empty. Tashi negotiated them at a slow run as he made his way to the covered stadium, a vast circular room that looked like a hall, with a wrestlers' pit in the centre. An indoor range had been set up for archery practice with set targets and plenty of space had been allocated for sword work and other sports.

When Tashi entered the stadium, it was milling with the Lha. Most of them were already beginning their warm-up and exercises before the prince joined them. Tashi made his way to the drill-master. Master Topen was shouting orders at the top of his voice to a band of young novices, when Tashi presented himself and bowed low before him.

His powerful body rippling with muscles, the drill-master eyed him for a moment. 'You are late today, boy,' he said sternly. 'You should have been here ten minutes earlier. Anyhow, I want you to stand there – not far from me, mind – and begin your loosening-up exercises. Then follow them up with the opening exercises of the Lha drill that you have been taught. I will join you in a moment.'

Tashi made his way to the indicated spot and first stood utterly still as he had been taught. He let his awareness expand, taking in the silence underlying the dawn hour. Then slowly, all the sounds from the stadium, of others working at their exercises, drifted through his consciousness and he became aware of the inherent unity of silence and sound. Tashi raised himself on his toes and, cat-like, held the position as he stretched, letting the silence seep into himself. Each movement, born of silence, made him descend into deeper silence. Tashi felt his mind settle down become stationary in the oneness and then he began the opening exercises of the Lha drill.

Master Topen joined him. As he spoke, his voice sounded to Tashi's heightened sense of hearing as if it were amplified many times over. 'Remember, boy,' the drill-master's words boomed, 'each move flows from the silence, from the source. You move not with the body or even with the mind but you move from that which is beyond; you move with the silence.'

Fluid, harmonious and aesthetic, Tashi's moves flowed, one step into the next. He executed what seemed like impossible turns, his movements slow and economical, yet grand.

Master Topen clapped his hands. 'Yes, you have got it!' he declared approvingly. 'Now remember, this is nothing. Here, in Shambala, you are executing these moves in your spirit form. The real challenge will come when you must return to the mortal world and perform the same Lha drill with your mortal body. Remember, never give up, boy, no matter how impossible the task may seem.'

Tashi stilled his movements and looked at Master Topen alertly.

'You have managed the opening moves of the Lha drill,' he said. 'I will now introduce you to the next move called "moonlight over flowing waters". Still yourself, boy. Allow yourself to attain a deeper level of awareness and observe with both your naked eye and the eternal eye.'

Master Topen demonstrated the move, executing it faultlessly. It was a rippling movement of the body between the air and the ground, impossible even to envision, let alone witness.

'Now carefully follow my instructions,' he said. 'Place your right foot in front. Then describe a perfect arc with your body, kicking up into the air and launching yourself. Let your body flow through the air and twist thrice, like a ribbon, before landing with precision on the arch of your right foot. Now let me see you do it. This is your first exercise for lifting off the ground and dancing in the air.'

Tashi stood utterly still and allowed his inner calm to deepen. Then he stepped on to the arch of his right foot and kicked out into the air, only to collapse in a heap. Mortified, he scrambled up and found Prince A-KarO standing there and shaking his head in amusement.

'You may go now, Master Topen. I will take over,' the prince announced. Then he turned to Tashi with a stern face. 'Tashi,' he said, 'for this move to be successful, you have to let yourself first sink deep into unity. The move is not an action originating in the body; it flows from the source. So let yourself go; immerse yourself in your inner silence. Then only can you begin.'

Tashi let the stillness within grow, till he had become one with his body, one with the room and all that surrounded him. The deep inner vibration of the silence increased, drowning out everything else. His eyelids began drooping halfway over his eyes.

'Now!' said Prince A-KarO.

Tashi literally flew off his right foot and danced into the air. His body twisted once, twice ... But his growing sense of excitement broke his concentration and he fell, his sweat-soaked body slamming on to the floor. Tashi felt pain jolt through him.

Prince A-KarO smiled. 'Practise,' he exhorted. 'For today, this is your task. Stay at it. You will get it sooner or later.'

The prince moved away and Tashi sank into stillness again. The sweat rolled off his body as he practised the move, but each time, the third twist eluded him. His concentration simply did not extend beyond two turns in the air.

From the time Tashi had begun learning the Lha drill, one day had followed the next in an endless pattern of hours spent on efforts to train himself in it. It loomed large before him, this seemingly insurmountable task, but he was determined to master it. Tashi shook his head in frustration now, as his concentration fractured and his muscles trembled in pain. The hours flew by as he practised with dogged concentration, repeating the schedule of the past week, his muscles clenching with pain.

It was late morning and the sun was bright overhead when he made his way to the water pitcher, splashed water over his face and then drank his fill. Ti Shan, his only friend among the Lha guards, smiled and made his way over to the boy.

'Do not be discouraged, friend,' the warrior told him. 'It can take a long time to perfect the Lha drill and you are but a mortal. It will come. Just give it time.'

'I cannot believe I have been at it all morning and in vain,' Tashi told him. 'And now I cannot practise archery either. The hour has grown late. I had better hurry back. The prince will soon be needing his midday meal.'

'Let me accompany you back to your room,' Ti Shan suggested. 'So, young Tashi,' he went on, 'I hear you have been invited to the banquet this evening? You must be excited about it.'

Tashi grinned. 'Oh! I had almost forgotten about it,' he said. 'Of course I am looking forward to the banquet, especially as I will be meeting my old master, Lama Ozer, there. I have not seen him at all since I moved in here with the prince.'

He looked around the hall and saw that Prince A-KarO had already left. He hurried out of the stadium, with Ti Shan trailing behind him, and they were soon lost in the dim palace corridors.

II

Later in the afternoon, Tashi headed towards the palace stables. His chores for the day done, he now needed some well-deserved leisure. Whistling cheerfully, he raced through the corridors towards the east gate that led to the stables. This was one hour of the day that he really looked forward to, because it offered him time alone with his only friend, the wind horse, Chetak. He had been setting some time aside every afternoon to spend with his steed and see to his needs. Tashi checked the bag on his shoulder; as usual, he was carrying two apples for Chetak. Tashi soon stepped out into bright sunshine and, nodding to the gate guards, raced towards the stables – huge, sprawling area that had many grooms and helpers in attendance. The Rigden was very particular about his horses and collected them from far and wide.

Soon, Tashi had stepped into the dimness of the stables. At this time of the day, there were few grooms about. With their morning work done, many of them had retired after their midday meal. Tashi worked his way towards the section that was screened off for the special use of wind horses. Tashi made his way to his stall and smiled as he beheld Chetak's familiar gleaming black coat.

'Ah, Tashi! I have missed you so! What have you brought for me today?' Chetak's disembodied voice rang out, communicating with the boy through mind speech.

'Today, you are really lucky,' Tashi smiled. 'I've got you two red apples.'

'This is a real treat, Tashi!' Chetak neighed, nuzzling the boy's hand with his velvety black mouth.

As the steed munched on an apple, Tashi picked up the brush and began grooming him, brushing him with gentle, regular strokes.

Chetak tossed his head back and neighed, 'This feels so good, Tashi! Now tell me what has been happening with you since we last met. It is so dull here! I spend most of my time munching on oats and simply waiting for you. By the way, please don't forget to take me out for a run. That is the one thing I most look forward to.'

'Well, a lot has been happening actually,' Tashi replied. 'Last night, I had to get the prince ready for his visit to the queen's court.'

'The queen's court? Ah! Did you visit it too?'

Tashi shook his head. 'Of course not, Chetak. I am just an apprentice. While out on his visits, the prince does not allow me to accompany him everywhere. Still, I do get to see a lot.'

'That is a pity,' Chetak remarked. 'The queen's court is worth visiting, Tashi. Its splendour is famed throughout the galaxy and the queen herself, who is the Rigden's second wife and Prince Narasimha's mother, is renowned for her beauty, wit and large heart. I am sure it would benefit you greatly to meet her. You should ask the prince to take you for an audience with her. I do think, however, that you will get to see her at the banquet tonight.'

Tashi laughed. 'I don't doubt the queen's court is magnificent,' he said, 'but then, Chetak, the entire palace is magnificent. From what I have seen of it – and I have now seen quite a bit – the place is unbelievable. Now there is something else I have to tell you. This morning, I suffered my first setback while learning the moves in my exercise. The prince had gone beyond the preliminary exercises and introduced me to a move called "moonlight over flowing waters". It involves three full twists, executed slowly and smoothly, a league up in the air. I managed two, but the third, no matter how hard I tried, completely eluded me.'

'The Lha drill is one of the most impossibly hard drills the universe has produced,' Chetak neighed, 'and it is from the moves of this basic drill that the legendary Lha sword work and fighting skills stem. It is no easy task, boy. Give yourself time, be patient and you will prevail. Of that I am confident. Now, about tonight; are you excited about this banquet? I know I am. Tashi, you must take me with you! I will guide you on how you should conduct yourself there.'

Tashi frowned. 'Take you with me? Chetak, don't be absurd! Even a wind horse cannot go to a banquet.'

'Do this for me, Tashi,' the steed implored. 'I feel this strong urge to be there. Something is compelling me to be at the banquet tonight and I never ignore my instincts. They have often saved a difficult day.'

Tashi shook his head. 'You know, Chetak, when you put it like that, I cannot deny you. But how will I get you in? I don't think they will allow a wind horse entry.'

Chetak neighed and tossed his mane. 'But they don't have to know, Tashi, that we have another way of travel at our disposal,' he reminded the boy. 'I will travel in spirit form in your heart.'

'Ah!' Tashi smiled. 'Of course you can travel in spirit form! Are you sure no one will discover you within me?'

Chetak shook his head. 'This is the prerogative of a wind horse and it has saved many a day. If I want to conceal my presence, even a god will not be able to detect it.'

Tashi frowned. 'An ordinary god may not,' he said, 'but what about Prince A-KarO? He is an adept. He will surely see you.'

'Trust me,' Chetak neighed. 'I can hide even from the prince, unless he is focused on tracking me down.'

Tashi frowned and said reluctantly, 'All right. So be it. But you will have to come with me right now, because I cannot return to the stables to fetch you. I have to attend on the prince.'

'At last some excitement after days of boredom!' Chetak neighed. 'Come, boy, let us be off.'

Tashi looked at him intently. 'But what about you?' he asked the horse. 'Won't you be missed at the stables by the grooms?'

'All you have to do is tell the groom you are taking me out for the night.'

'All right,' Tashi sighed, 'come on, then.'

With that, he led Chetak out of the dim stables and into the evening light. Nodding at the groom, Tashi told him, 'I'll be taking him out for the night. He will be back early tomorrow morning.'

Chewing on a betel nut, the groom nodded. 'All right,' he said, 'I'll tell the stable master.'

After walking some distance, Tashi and Chetak stopped in a shady arbour.

'Quick! Transform yourself into spirit form,' the boy urged. 'I am already late. I need to hurry and finish my evening chores before the prince arrives.'

Even as Tashi looked at Chetak, the horse started shimmering, then condenced his form to a spot of pulsing light which landed pat in his hand. Slowly, the boy carried the wind horse's essence into his heart.

'This feels great!' said Chetak's disembodied voice. 'Now let's be off to the palace, Tashi!'

Tashi strode towards the palace gates and disappeared into the familiar corridors, negotiating the turns swiftly as he raced towards Prince A-KarO's apartments. Inside him, Chetak was busy singing a rowdy song, with many neighs thrown in, and Tashi was ready to clap his hands over his ears to shut out the noise, except that the racket was within him.

III

Sunset was a splash of colour in the skies as the golden dakini, Yeshe Nam Lha, went on her evening stroll around her estate. Yeshe walked in a leisurely manner, a sense of sadness and isolation growing within her usually serene self. She eyed the blushing skies painted dark pink and purple with an inner pang; it could be years before she set eyes on her home again. Tomorrow, she was heading out to Aggartha with the rest of the company of travellers and, from there, to Earth. Yeshe sighed as the sound of the temple bells, so familiar, yet strangely poignant, rolled over her. The future stretched before her, alien and mysterious. Perhaps she ought to consult the oracle?

Yeshe walked steadily towards the lake in whose depths lay her underwater abode. With a graceful motion, she dived into the gently lapping waters and sank towards her abode. She smiled at the fish and the richness of colour around her, letting her mind settle into its usual serenity and discarding the last traces of sadness. Gently, she alighted on the outer veranda of her underwater palace, which shimmered pink in the dim light.

Yeshe walked towards her room, her feet dancing on the shell-inlaid floors, which glowed with a silvery hue. Entering her room, she found her matronly silver-haired nurse seated there, with a tea service set before her.

'Ah, golden flower! I have been waiting for you,' she said. 'I've got some hot tea ready. Should I pour?'

Yeshe sank on to a low-slung chaise longue. 'Ah, Sumaki,' she said, 'some tea would be nice. I am so tired, I just want to spend my last evening at home quietly. Who knows when I can return here? I shall miss you, Sumaki. You have been with me since I was a baby. How will I manage in the mortal world, in a mortal body, and away from Shambala and my divine mother's presence? My heart is heavy, Sumaki, a new experience for me altogether, for I have never known such sadness before.'

Sumaki poured tea into a sliver-fine mother-of-pearl cup and handed it to Yeshe. 'Never fear, my golden child,' she reassured the dakini, 'this will be a new experience for you. Your divine mother and the rest of us will be with you, in essence, awaiting the day your task is done and you can return home.'

Yeshe stretched out on the chaise longue, slowly sipping the steaming-hot tea. 'Sumaki, the weight of the future hangs over me,' she confessed. 'For too long have I been a maiden; I have become set in my ways. This change, it creates confusion within me and arouses strange feelings. I have feelings, Sumaki, that I have never known before.'

'It is only by experiencing feelings that you can conquer them,' Sumaki explained. 'After all, you could not have remained a maiden for all eternity. Now the choice of consort rests with you and you can take your time choosing him from between the two princes. Also, motherhood will help you to mature. It is only through tasting the life of a mortal that you can achieve mastery, the unique chance for total liberation rests in human birth. Great though your achievements are, golden flower, for you, who were called eternal maiden, it is now time for change and growth as well as for learning. If life on the mortal plain is harsh, as it is meant to be, it will prove to be both your testing ground and a great lesson for you.'

Yeshe sipped her tea and sighed. 'You are so right, Sumaki,' she murmured. 'I am overcome by an urge to visit the oracle today. Will you bring forth the dice? I would like to consult them on what the future holds.'

Sumaki sighed. 'Yeshe, you have the banquet to attend,' she reminded the dakini. 'Are you sure you have time for the dice? You need to start getting ready soon.'

'I am sure we have enough time to consult the oracle,' Yeshe smiled.

'All right,' Sumaki agreed, 'I will summon the dice of probability and possibility. Mind, they only show a glimpse of the future. And that I will interpret for you.'

Sumaki sat up erect and whispered a mantra. The air began to shimmer and a strange tension seemed to be building. Then a well-worn board with dice appeared before them. Sumaki spread open the board, which shimmered with energy and colour, and picked the two tiny white dice.

'Be ready, I am about to cast the dice,' she announced.

With that, Sumaki straightened her back, rolled the dice and cast them on the board. They landed in a shadowy corner of the board, over which hung an impenetrable haze of darkness, and rolled to a stop. Both dice bore the same number: three.

The nurse shook her head and sat back on her heels, the colour draining from her face. 'This is bad news,' she said grimly. 'You are on the threshold of a journey into darkness. That much is clear. You will have nothing but your resources to rely on. There is great danger.'

She rolled the dice again. Again, they came to a stop in a shadowy section of the board, but this time, with a golden sword of fiery light in their midst. Both dice displayed the number six.

Sumaki grimaced. 'This is slightly better,' she said. 'You are still in danger, but you have a protector, a very strong protector. The two sixes denote renewal, a new future.' She looked at Yeshe and declared, 'I will now cast the dice for the last time.'

She focused and then cast the dice again. Suddenly, the board blazed with light and a leaf-green shoot appeared in the centre, flanked by two swords.

Sumaki smiled. 'This is the first piece of good news. It gives a clear indication of a birth, a birth of light and plenty. Also, it indicates victory after intense struggle.'

Dazed, Yeshe shook her head, then laughed. 'It seemed grim, at first,' she said, 'but it all came out right.'

'My dearest, it gives but an image,' the nurse told her. 'Now I think we had better hurry. You have a banquet to attend. Now what will you wear?'

Yeshe sighed. 'Lay out my light yellow skirt and girdle and the orange blouse, Sumaki,' she replied. 'And no jewellery, please. Just flowers and that, too, orange ones only.'

'So simple, Yeshe?' the nurse smiled. 'Still, I ought to be grateful it is not white, as usual. A little colour never harmed anyone. I have already prepared the flowers and your clothes will take but a moment.'

Yeshe smiled and relaxed on the chaise, as Sumaki produced her garments from thin air.

'Come now, golden one, bestir yourself,' the nurse urged.

Yeshe stood up and Sumaki began dressing her. She made the dakini step into the golden yellow skirt, arranged the girdle tight around her slim, bare waist and added a garland of orange flowers around it. Then she helped her slip on the woven orange blouse. The nurse combed out the dakini's shining raven tresses and twisted them into an elaborate arrangement, which she decorated with saffron flowers. Next, she arranged garlands of saffron flowers around her neck and slipped a loose bracelet of flowers around her wrist, adding an armband of yellow flowers. Yeshe stepped into shining low-heeled slippers and shook out her pale yellow stole of fine silk which she arranged over her shoulders.

She looked around the Azure Palace and her underwater realm and was filled with a deep sense of contentment. It was time to go to the banquet and face the evening and what it would bring.

IV

Tashi rushed through his evening chores. Dusk was falling and the prince would be arriving any minute. He whistled as he cleaned the prince's boots lovingly, polishing the leather till it gleamed. He was highly excited. This evening, he would attend the banquet and see Lama Ozer after a ten-day break. And tomorrow, he would finally see action. For along with the rest of the select band bound for the mortal world, he would be departing for Aggartha before the journey to Earth. Tashi yearned to return home, to visit Demazong Gumpa once again and meet all his old friends. He finished polishing the boots and laid out the prince's evening finery. Finally, he set a decanter of dark wine and silver goblets near the prince's bed. Having completed his chores, Tashi sighed and repaired to the small kitchen in the apartment to heat a cup of tea for himself.

At this point, Chetak came awake within Tashi and declared, 'The banquet begins punctually at eight and it is already close to that hour. The prince should be arriving.'

'Oh, he'll come,' Tashi grinned. 'The prince is never late. I am really, really excited! Do you think the Buddha lords will be there?'

'No chance!' Chetak neighed. 'It is not the Council, after all. The Buddha lords only visit when the Council gets together. And that, too, as you have witnessed, occurs in another dimension beyond space and time. They do not grace banquets or royal functions, unless a major religious ceremony is involved. Even on such occasions, not all of them are present at the same time.'

Tashi asked, 'Then who is likely to be there at this evening's banquet?'

Chetak's disembodied voice replied, 'This is a court function. So it is Shambala's nobility who will be present, along with nobles from neighbouring worlds. Also, some of the higher gods and the Lha, representing Amravati and Zansa, will attend. You can expect quite a diverse crowd. The evening should be entertaining.'

Tashi smiled and said, 'What I am really looking forward to is meeting my old master, Lama Ozer. I just hope the lama is in good health. He is not too good at taking care of himself.'

'Boy,' Chetak neighed, 'now listen carefully to what I have to say. While at the banquet, you must follow my instructions. I will guide you around and tell you what to say and to whom. This should be interesting, Tashi. I have not attended a banquet in many a long year and, in Shambala, not at all.'

Tashi contemplated the wind horse's words as he slowly sipped his tea and hungrily polished off a bowl of steamed noodles.

Suddenly, there was a sound. Prince A-KarO had entered his apartments with his escort. Tashi swiftly gulped down the rest of his tea and rushed into the prince's chamber. He bowed low before him and handed him a goblet of wine.

'You take good care of me, Tashi,' Prince A-KarO smiled. 'I see that you have readied my evening kit. Now help me quickly into my garments and then you can get dressed yourself. Here, this is for you.' A-KarO handed Tashi a package. 'A set of ceremonial garments for you to wear to the banquet,' he explained.

The prince tossed back the contents of his goblet as Tashi bustled around him, helping him into his white silk tunic and pants and his pristine over robe, with its silver threadwork. Then the boy rushed through the rest of his chores, his heart beating with a wild inner fire. It was almost time to leave for the banquet. Prince A-KarO took one last look at himself, then strapped his dagger to his waist, shoving another dagger into his gleaming boots. Smiling, he looked at Tashi.

'I am off, boy,' he announced. 'Follow as soon as you are ready. Do not tarry. Also, carry your Garuda's feather with you. The Garuda himself will be there today and has asked that you present yourself to him at the banquet. He will bless the feather and mark it with his breath.'

At the mention of the Garuda, Tashi forgot himself and whooped in delight.

Prince A-KarO smiled. 'Don't delay, Tashi,' he reminded him, 'and don't forget to wear your better pair of boots. I hope you have polished them? See you later, then.'

After the prince had left the chamber, Tashi literally tore through the apartments, tidying up the rooms. Then barely pausing, he ripped open the package A-KarO had given him. Out tumbled a fine woollen navy blue tunic, with silver-cord detail at the collar, and a pair of matching pants. Chetak was now neighing a lusty song within Tashi and, keeping time to it, the boy threw on his clothes and changed his boots. He took precisely two minutes to slick back his hair with oil and tie it back with a black ribbon. Whistling merrily, he stepped out of the apartments and raced through the corridors, heading for the royal gardens where the banquet was being held.

V

Velvet night had descended over the gardens and a canopy of bright stars gleamed in the heavens, when the golden dakini, Yeshe Nam Lha, arrived for the banquet. The place was decked out in twinkling lights and glowing lanterns and silken couches had been placed inside bright pavilions. The fresh fragrance of a thousand flowers floated in the air. Yeshe looked around her warily and her gaze strayed to the elegantly attired guests. Women in flamboyant silks and gauzy tissue stood out as bright splashes of colour. Courtiers mingled with each other. This was going to be a huge bore, Yeshe thought. She hesitated for a second, then stepped forth to join the throng. Might as well get this over with, she told herself. Her plan was simple: to pay her respects to the Rigden and the queen and the leading courtiers, before withdrawing to a secluded corner, from where she could observe all, unseen.

The sound of laughter and chatter rose around her. Yeshe nodded to guests here and there and stopped to exchange a word with a few, as she made her way to the royal pavilion. The Rigden was seated on a silken couch, his silver hair shining in the night. He wore a deep wine-coloured robe with a gold chain bearing his official insignia and his crown gleamed on his forehead.

As Yeshe stepped before the royal couple to make her bow and offer the token gift, the Rigden smiled.

'Ah, golden flower, it is delightful to have you here!' he exclaimed. 'This evening is really in your honour, Yeshe, as it is for your companions. Tonight, we behold you in our midst and your presence must sustain our hearts for a while to come, as you leave tomorrow and we will not see you again for a good many years. Know this, golden one. You will be sorely missed.'

Yeshe looked at the Rigden and smiled. 'Your Majesty is very gracious,' she murmured. 'I, too, will miss you both greatly. And Shambala.'

The Rigden sighed. 'Do not think, child, that I will lose touch with you once you leave,' he reassured her. 'We will constantly monitor your progress from here. From time to time, I will also be sending my messengers to you with necessary communications. We are not sending you out alone, Yeshe. I have entrusted my own heir, Prince Narasimha, with the duty of accompanying you; he will safeguard you through your journeys. Similarly, the monarch of Amravati, the Lha king, has spared his son – none other then Prince A-KarO – to travel with you and keep you secure and focused. It is, however, your own role which is the most crucial of all; it could change all our futures. We wish you luck, daughter of the Goddess. When you have given birth, Yeshe, I myself will come to visit you to bless the child. We have great hopes for you, golden one.'

'I will do my best, Your Majesty,' Yeshe smiled. 'Rest assured that I take the responsibility I have been entrusted with very seriously. It is my only priority.'

The Rigden smiled. 'You have set my mind at ease, Yeshe. Remember, all our hopes travel with you. And now you must have a word with the queen. She has been desirous of your company.'

Yeshe made her way to the queen's side and the ladies-in-waiting parted to make space for the dakini. Bedecked in sparkling jewels, the queen looked regal in a fucshian pink skirt with a cream girdle. A silver-spangled stole covered her upper body. She smiled serenely at Yeshe when the dakini bowed low to her.

'Yeshe, golden flower, I am delighted to see you here!' declared the queen. 'It is rarely that you come to one of our gatherings. And now you are leaving. I will miss you greatly, child. Do take care of yourself.'

Yeshe bowed low again. 'I will, Your Majesty,' she said.

'I wanted to tell you, Yeshe, that you have been a maiden for long,' the queen said with a tender smile, 'but now change has come. You must accept it, golden flower. Do not fight it. Remember, the wise oak bends with the storm. Choose wisely, child. Get to know the two princes first and then make your choice. Do not delay unnecessarily. Do not neglect your duty. Else, it will come knocking on your door and time will take the choice out of your hands. Don't drag your feet, Yeshe. Make your choice.'

The dakini smiled. 'You always speak wisely, Your Majesty.'

The queen smiled. 'You and Narasimha have known each other since you were children, even if in recent years, you have neglected to keep up with each other. Get to know him, Yeshe. He is gentle and kind-hearted. We chose him as one of your suitors, because he is worthy. The Lha prince's reputation, on the other hand, is legendary. He is a celebrated hero of the first world. His reputation with women may make you wary, but know this, golden flower: there is no one who cannot be tamed by one with skill. I chose your two suitors; now make your own choice wisely, Yeshe.'

Discomfited, Yeshe itched to get away. 'I will, Your Majesty,' she said obediently.

'With you rides the hope of the universe, Yeshe,' the queen smiled. 'May you have all the luck, child.'

'I thank you, Your Majesty.'

The queen sighed and turned her attention to one of her ladies. Yeshe took that as a signal to make her exit. Bowing low, she withdrew and escaped from the royal pavilion.

The dakini had barely stepped out, when she ran into Prince Narasimha. The heir-apparent bowed low and matched his step with Yeshe's.

'Golden flower, I was looking out for you,' he said. 'What luck to run into you like this!'

Yeshe frowned. 'Well, you seem to have found me.'

Prince Narasimha smiled and his dark brown eyes twinkled. 'Surely, my presence is not quite so repugnant, Yeshe?' he teased. 'We used to be quite close when we were children.'

The dakini walked on swiftly. 'Childhood has been gone a while, Prince Narasimha,' she replied, 'in case you haven't noticed.'

The crown prince laughed. 'You have not changed much, Yeshe!' he declared. 'Still the ice princess, forever on her ice mountain.'

Yeshe smiled. 'You know, Narasimha,' she said, 'I love ice, snow and cold winds. They are among my many delights. As for you, Prince, are you ready to brave the ice wind to climb the ice mountain?'

Prince Narsimha looked at Yeshe and smiled. 'For you, golden flower, anything!' he declared. 'All this while, you were the eternal maiden, forever beyond my ken. But now, circumstances have changed and I can hope, at least, can I not?'

Yeshe smiled sweetly. 'Then live on in hope, my Prince,' she murmured. 'By the way, are you all packed for our journey tomorrow?'

Prince Narasimha shrugged. 'All I am carrying is my case of herbs and medicinal potions. I may be bound for the mortal world, but I intend to practise there as a healer. They are not letting us carry anything from here, but I am going to ask the sages for permission to carry my medicines.'

'I wish you luck, Narasimha,' Yeshe told him. 'I myself am not carrying anything from here. To tell you the truth, I hate the very thought of leaving Shambala.'

'It is not easy for me either,' the crown prince sighed. 'I leave much behind.'

'And what of Mimaki?' the dakini asked.

'Mimaki is distraught. The future changes, Yeshe, and none of us can control it or predict the outcome. I thank you for giving Mimaki the dark mirror; it has filled her with hope.'

'When you have Mimaki, why would you court me, Narasimha?' Yeshe asked him. 'Do not tell me you were ordered to do so?'

Prince Narasimha frowned. 'Know this, golden flower,' he replied, 'I was not forced into it. Courting you is a joy, not a duty. I have cared for you since our childhood days and I feel we could get along well.'

'But what of Mimaki, Narasimha?' Yeshe repeated.

'I don't see the problem,' Narasimha replied. 'The two of you can surely live with each other, can you not?'

'Know this, Narasimha,' Yeshe said curtly, 'I find both you and A-KarO insufferable.'

'At least, I am the lesser of the two evils, Yeshe,' Narasimha said with an amused glint in his eye. 'Where I am concerned, there are only the three of us – Mimaki, you and me. With A-KarO, on the other hand, there are thousands of concubines to contend with, not forgetting the *apsaras*. If you choose him, you will be reduced to a nonentity.'

Yeshe was exasperated by now. 'Narasimha,' she declared firmly, 'both you and A-KarO can disappear, for all I care. With such options before me, I would prefer not to make a choice at all.'

Prince Narasimha smiled. 'Yeshe, let's just be friends and forget all this for now,' he cajoled. 'We will not think of choices and decisions. All we must keep in mind is that tomorrow marks a new beginning and we will look ahead.'

'That is certainly a better perspective, Prince Narasimha,' Yeshe agreed. 'Now, if you don't mind, do fetch me a glass of wine. My throat is parched.'

Prince Narasimha departed and before he could return, Yeshe beat a hasty retreat. Spotting a dark corner behind a magnolia shrub, she made for it, intending to hide out for the rest of the evening.

VI

Tashi wandered around the banquet, mesmerized by the lights and the company. He had had a tough time tearing himself away from the tables laden with delicacies. After feasting to his heart's content, he had made his bows to the royal couple and then hastened to search for Lama Ozer. After walking around for some time, he sighted Prince A-KarO standing among a group of courtiers and deep in conversation with a silver-haired one.

Chetak's disembodied voice came across, nice and clear: 'Don't wander that side, Tashi. We do not want to encounter the prince. Else, we will be stuck by his side for the rest of the evening. Why not head towards that group of royal priests? Your Lama Ozer may well be in such company.'

Tashi drifted towards the group of priests and made his bows. Towards the back of the group, he sighted Ozer standing in the shade of a sprawling jacaranda tree. The lama was busy conversing with an elderly priest. Tashi walked up to Ozer, fell to his knees and touched his feet in a show of respect.

Lama Ozer looked down distractedly. 'Ah, Tashi!' he exclaimed, 'at last we meet again! Boy, have you been behaving yourself for the past few weeks that we have been separated?'

Full of enthusiasm, Tashi sprang to an upright position again. 'Yes, Lama, I have been on my best behaviour and have been following your instructions as well as the prince's orders,' he replied. 'I have been serving the prince well, Lama.'

'Ah!' Ozer observed with a smile. 'That is a new tunic, Tashi. And you are wearing silver cording! Boy, you are looking quite grand, I must say.'

'These garments were given to me by the prince for attending the banquet,' Tashi explained with a smile. 'Tell me, Lama, how have you been and how is your health?'

'I miss you, boy,' Lama Ozer sighed. 'You took such good care of me. Still, I have been managing just fine. I have been busy with my studies, both at the temple and at the library. Indeed, I have learned much on this trip. But how goes your training, boy? Tell me all about it.'

'Lama, I have learnt so much,' Tashi said excitedly. 'I am being trained in the Lha's celestial drill. It is a highly difficult martial-art form, but under the prince's guidance, I am making good progress. Also, Lama, the prince has been giving me instruction in archery, which I simply love and seem to have an innate talent for it. I am picking it up very fast.'

Lama Ozer clapped his hands. 'Archery, boy? That is good news!' he said with enthusiasm. 'Now you know, Tashi, that we depart for Aggartha tomorrow. Please be ready on time and remember not to pack anything. We cannot carry anything from Shambala with us.'

'Lama, do you think we will be stopping at Demazong Gumpa when we return to the mortal world?' Tashi asked eagerly. 'It will be great to go back home.'

Lama Ozer smiled. 'To go home would be a blessing, boy, but we must not ask for it. If it happens, it happens; that is all there is to it. Time will reveal all.'

'Still, Lama, our bodies are lying at the fortress in Qiang,' Tashi reminded Ozer. 'Don't you think that should be our first destination?'

'There is a strong possibility of us entering the mortal world from Qiang La, but we cannot speculate over it at this time. All will be made clear by the sages at Aggartha.' Lama Ozer held out his hand. 'Now run along, boy, and mind your manners at the banquet. I have much to discuss here with the wise Karica, an expert on herbs and medicines.'

Tashi bowed low and made his departure. He wandered out into the crowd of guests and floated around aimlessly for a few minutes, quaffing down a goblet of wine.

Then Chetak's disembodied voice floated out to him. 'Now, boy,' the steed told him, 'there, to your right, standing in solitary splendour, is the Garuda. You were supposed to meet him, remember?'

Tashi sighted the Garuda at once. He stood in a blaze of golden-red radiance, surrounded by a group of dakinis. The boy swiftly made for the celestial messenger, a being so glorious to behold that for a moment, his mind stilled in the presence of his immense divinity. The Garuda's celestial form was that of a golden youth with chiselled features, honey-gold eyes that blazed with divine fire and fiery, golden-red hair that tumbled down his back like a cloak of flames. Although he was tall and slender, his muscled form shone with vitality.

Tashi bowed low and fell to his knees before him. 'My Lord,' he said, 'I am most humbly beholden to you.'

The Garuda smiled and a pair of enormous transparent golden wings took shape behind his back. 'Tashi, child of fire, I have been awaiting you,' he declared.

The boy smiled and stood upright again. 'Lord, I thank you deeply,' he said fervently. 'It was your intervention which saved my life and that of Lama Ozer on more than one occasion. But for your grace, we would never have made it to Shambala.'

The Garuda held up his hand in a gesture of beneficence. 'My blessings are with you, Tashi,' he said. 'It is after an entire aeon that I have intervened in the life of a mortal. But so it is and my grace is with you. Now, child, listen carefully. You head for the mortal world soon. You will face many challenges and harsh days there. The Asur have established a strong presence on Earth and will try to thwart your mission. Pay heed to my words, boy. When the times are hard, remember me. When your strength fails, remember me. When the situation is dire and all else fails, draw forth my symbol, the feather, and I shall answer your call. Do not, however, call forth the power of the feather, unless the situation is truly dire and you are in extreme peril. I repeat: do not draw it out in vain or for fending off a paltry threat. Learn how to manage such problems on your own.'

Tashi bowed low and promised, 'Lord, I will obey.'

'There are dark days ahead and they may begin sooner than you imagine,' the Garuda warned. 'Remember, Tashi, you have a role to play. Never let your courage fail, no matter how harsh the adversity.'

Tashi bowed again.

The Garuda held up his hand. 'Now tell me, Tashi, how goes your training with Prince A-KarO?'

'I have been learning the celestial Lha drill and am making progress,' Tashi said excitedly. 'The prince has also started me on my lessons in archery. I simply love the sport!'

The Garuda smiled. 'Archery? So that is your special talent! The celestial art of archery is highly advanced, boy. A single arrow fired from the bow of emptiness can lay waste a kingdom or even an entire world. Learn well the art and perhaps we will have some adventures together on that score. Ningma, the last mortal I had taken under my wing, used to fire arrows while sitting astride me in battle. The two of us would cause immense havoc. So train well, Tashi, if you want to ride into battle astride me.'

'This will make me train even harder, my Lord,' Tashi promised.

The Garuda smiled. 'Now place the feather, my mark, on my palm. I will bless it for your use.'

Tashi complied. The feather blazed on the Garuda's palm with a reddish-gold radiance, emitting fiery sparks. The Garuda brushed it with his other palm and returned it to the boy.

'Now, when you want to communicate with me,' the Garuda went on, 'simply meditate on the feather and call out my name thrice. My communication will come forth through ether. You may use this process whenever you wish to consult me.'

Tashi bowed. The Garuda held aloft his hand in blessing and then dismissed him.

The boy wandered away into the crowd, aimless.

Chetak's disembodied voice called out, 'That was interesting work, boy! But it was thirsty work, nonetheless. Now let's head for the tables where the delicacies are laid out.'

So Tashi made for the nearest table of sweetmeats and busied himself filling up his plate.

VII

Escaping from the crowds at the banquet, Yeshe entered into a secluded arbour created by ornamental floral bushes and settled down on a bench to quietly watch the guests at the banquet. This was an ideal refuge from where she could observe everyone unseen and thereby escape unwanted attention. Smiling mischievously to herself, the dakini thought of Prince Narasimha returning to the gardens bearing refreshments for her, but finding her gone. It was at this moment that a tall, dark shadow fell across the arbour.

In the darkness, Yeshe made out the form of a tall celestial being, over seven feet tall. His long, dark hair was tied back in a queue, but what arrested the dakini's attention were his eyes. Shaped exactly like a cat's, the golden orbs gleamed with a dangerous light; and was that a red glow in their depths? Yet the celestial was no more than a shadow in the dark night. His clothes were dark and he was covered in a swirling cloak of shadows that contained every hue from dark grey to black. Yeshe looked at the man, fascinated.

Having caught her attention, he bowed low and spoke in a whisper. 'I hope I am not disturbing you, Dakini,' he murmured. 'I was but looking for a dark corner to rest my feet. Do you mind if I share this corner with you?'

Yeshe indicated with a gesture that he could. 'By all means,' she replied. 'You may rest here a while, but stranger, do introduce yourself, won't you?'

'I am Prince Arden, Dakini,' the celestial smiled. 'We are a minor dynasty. My home world is in an obscure system; it is a border world in the eastern span of the universe.'

'Ah!' Yeshe smiled, 'A prince from the border worlds! But many of them are under Asur control, are they not, though some remain with the gods?'

'Dakini, my world is a border planet,' Arden answered. 'We are in the frontline of the battle between the gods and the Asur. Our population consists mainly of Lha, with some Takhin and nomads thrown in.'

'You are a long way from home, Prince Arden,' Yeshe smiled. 'What brings you here, so far into the western span and the paradise world of Shambala?'

Prince Arden settled back on the seat and looked into Yeshe's eyes. 'I head a force of border rangers,' he replied. 'I wonder whether you have heard of them here?'

'Of course, Prince!' Yeshe said. 'I am not so ignorant as to not have heard of the valiant contributions of the rangers who police the wild border with the Asur. So tell me, Prince, what is your tale?'

Arden said earnestly, 'Dakini, I am on a mission, a quest, you could say. I cannot share its details with you, but I will naturally be discussing them with the Rigden when I have succeeded in getting an audience with him. But now that you know all about me and have an advantage over me, do introduce yourself, fair one, won't you?'

'Certainly, Prince Arden,' Yeshe said. 'I am the dakini, Yeshe Nam Lha, daughter of the Goddess Tara. Now, Prince, do tell me how long you have been here.'

'I have been here a month, Dakini,' Arden smiled, 'and allow me to say it is a rare privilege to meet you. I have heard all about you and your mission. You are to depart tomorrow. Am I right?'

'Yes,' Yeshe confirmed, 'tomorrow, I am bound for Aggartha with my companions and then we leave for Earth. So tell me, Prince Arden, have you seen much battle at the borders?'

Arden stretched his limbs and sighed. 'Dakini, from where I come, there is only battle and severe cold,' he replied. 'The cold freezes our bones and ceaseless strife is our eternal companion. One day to the next is a story of survival and little else. I have been at war, Dakini, since the age of twelve. That is the only life I know.'

'I have heard that life is very harsh in the eastern span and the border worlds,' Yeshe said in a grave voice. 'Tell me, what are these worlds like?'

'You, from the paradise world of Shambala, cannot even begin to understand the sheer hell the eastern span and the border planets represent, Dakini. The place from where I come falls in the eastern span and is a border world. We are snowbound all year round. Instead of green grass, we have permanent snowfields. Some of the major cities are encased in temperature-controlled bubbles, but the others are exposed to the elements. Food has to be imported and ceaseless warfare makes this a difficult process. In our world, survival is the bottomline and only the strongest survive. Then there is constant warfare. I myself run three sorties a day to keep the border clear of infiltration. Life is harsh, Dakini, but we manage.'

Yeshe looked at Arden, her expression full of concern. 'That sounds so bleak. Surely, there must be a positive aspect to life there?'

Arden's lips twisted in a smile. 'There is no benefit to living in the border worlds. Survival is the only reward. Dakini, I have a small wish that only you can fulfil.'

Yeshe looked at him, interested. 'Name it,' she urged. 'If there is anything within my power to aid you, I will.'

Arden said, 'Dakini, I have an artefact; it is rare. I would like you to bless it. Our priest assured me that if your hand fell on the object, it would greatly benefit our struggle.'

Yeshe looked at him. 'But I have very little time,' she said. 'I leave tomorrow. Could you, perhaps, fetch it now?'

'Unfortunately, I cannot do so,' Arden replied earnestly. 'Moving the artefact right now would be a problem. But my man has kept it under guard in the Amber Courtyard. If you agree to accompany me, all we have to do is walk out of the banquet and head for the courtyard. I will escort you there and back. I do hope you will come, Dakini. It will make a big difference to our efforts.' His tone was imploring.

'But of course I will accompany you, Prince Arden,' Yeshe said graciously.

Arden rose instantly to his feet. As he smiled with satisfaction, a red glow surfaced in his eyes. 'My two aides will escort us, Dakini,' he told Yeshe. 'I hope you will not mind?'

Yeshe shook her head and accompanied Arden, as he stepped out of the arbour and walked swiftly through the crowds, disappearing into their depths. The dakini matched her pace with his and soon, they were making for the exit into the gardens.

On the way, Prince Arden turned to Yeshe. 'Dakini,' he said, 'it is so kind of you to express an interest in my artefact and even take the trouble of blessing it. I cannot thank you enough.'

The dakini smiled back as she kept pace with him. 'It is the very least I can do for you and your brethren in the border worlds,' she responded graciously. 'In fact, Prince Arden, the border worlds have forever fascinated me. I have often wanted to visit them, but somehow, my travels have never taken me there.'

'If you ever decided to visit my homeland, the border worlds, Dakini,' Arden said, 'it would be my privilege to escort you there and introduce you to my people. Your grace would be a boon to them.'

Yeshe sighed. 'Prince Arden,' she said regretfully, 'as you know, I am bound for the mortal world now and a century or more may pass before I can even think of visiting the border worlds. For that, too, I would have to petition the Rigden for permission.'

'But Dakini, your kind – the higher deities and their band of dakinis – rarely, if ever, visit what we call the battle lines,' Arden reminded her. 'Still, there is life there. My people endure their existence bereft of the bounty and grace you enjoy here in Shambala. There is little hope and cheer to sustain them. But they are people, nonetheless, and must struggle in the harshest of conditions to eke out a living.'

Yeshe looked at Arden and a blush stole across her pale cheeks. 'Still, Prince,' she murmured reassuringly, 'where there is hope, there is life.'

'The problem, Dakini,' Arden sighed, 'is that my people are disdained as an inferior class of beings, because the blood of both demons and gods run in their veins. Dakini, would your compassion extend even to us, who live in darkness and have taken on its attributes? Is there any real hope for us? The gods shun us, except as cannon fodder in war. For them, we represent the frontline of battle and nothing else.'

Yeshe paused, extended her hands and clasped Arden's. The Asur stopped in his tracks, an expression of shock on his face.

'Not all of us shun the borderlanders,' the dakini reassured him. 'My heart goes out to them and I would gladly work in their midst if I were allowed to.'

Prince Arden clasped her hands tightly in his own. 'Dakini, would you have compassion for even those who walk in darkness?' he asked. 'Would you bring light to their eternal darkness, balm to soothe their eternal pain? Would you quench their endless thirst? Do you have such a golden heart, Dakini?'

'What do you mean?' Yeshe asked, bewildered.

Arden shook his head. 'It's an impossible dream,' he sighed. 'Please forget I ever asked, Dakini.'

The Asur's two aides hurried after them as Yeshe and Arden passed through the exit and made for the Amber Courtyard. As they neared it, the dakini looked around her and saw guards standing at every five paces.

She turned to Arden. 'Have you noticed that the guard has increased here?'

'Dakini, there is nothing to worry about. These are my own guard,' he reassured her in soothing tones. 'I had instructed them to wait for me here.'

Yeshe shook her head to clear it. She felt as if she were in a state of enchantment, under a spell, and, for a minute, she panicked. Just what was she doing here, she asked herself, alone in the dark, with an unknown celestial and his guard? As the thought crossed her mind, Prince Arden looked at her reassuringly.

'There is nothing to worry about, Dakini,' he repeated. 'Are you sure you want to go ahead and bless my artefact? If you are having second thoughts, I could always escort you back to the banquet.'

Yeshe made an effort to shed her uneasiness and smiled at Arden. 'Of course I am ready, Prince Arden,' she said. 'Now that we are in the Amber Courtyard, where is this artefact you mentioned? I don't see it anywhere.'

The red glow in his eyes intensified, as Arden said, 'Place your hand in mine, Dakini, and allow me to lead you to the artefact which is right there in the shadows.'

VIII

Tashi had just finished eating his eighth fruit tart, when he saw the golden dakini, Yeshe, moving swiftly through the crowd of guests. Escorting her was a tall man, who was mostly a shadow, his dark cloak swirling about his legs. In a moment, the two of them had disappeared from view and were cutting a direct path towards the side exit into the gardens. Tashi was shaking the crumbs off his tunic when he heard Chetak's disembodied voice.

'Tashi,' said the steed, 'you've eaten enough, boy! I think you need to go and acknowledge the dakini with a bow. After all, you will all be travelling together as a team from tomorrow. She walked past just a moment back. It's just a gut feeling, boy, but I think you should follow her. When the opportunity arises, you could make your bow to her.'

'I've had my fill, Chetak,' Tashi sighed. 'I might as well make my bow to the dakini. Here we go.'

Straightening his tunic, the boy brushed off the last crumb and stretched his legs. Then he began walking swiftly in the direction the dakini had taken. Tashi looked around at the crowd of nobles and dignitaries as he went, crossing a group of brightly dressed dancers with translucent veils, who were busy enthralling the audience. Fascinated, he paused for a moment.

'Chetak,' he entreated, 'the dakini has disappeared from view. Why don't we just watch the dancers for a bit?'

The wind horse's disembodied voice was curt. 'Don't be an oaf, boy,' the horse admonished him. 'Follow the dakini. Move fast! Something tells me we shouldn't lose track of her.'

Tashi looked around in bewilderment as he realized that the dakini and her escort were nowhere to be seen. They seemed to have vanished into thin air. Confused, the boy halted.

'Chetak,' he said, 'she seems to have disappeared! Now how do I find out where she's gone?'

'Tashi,' said Chetak's impatient voice, 'Don't worry, I'll guide you. Just head for the eastern exit leading out of here. And run! Something tells me we have no time to waste.'

Tashi doubled his pace. 'Don't you think we are getting worked up for no reason?' he queried.

'My instinct, Tashi, says we have to follow the dakini,' Chetak's disembodied voice replied.

Tashi hurried through the crowds, making for the eastern exit. He nodded to people here and there, though no one took much notice of him. Soon, he had passed through the exit and left the banquet behind him.

'Quick! Ask the guard if the dakini came this way!' Chetak urged.

Tashi sighed. 'Okay,' he agreed, 'but you are being a pain, you know.'

Saluting the guard, the boy said, 'A good evening to you. I was wondering if, by any chance, you saw the dakini, Yeshe Nam Lha, pass this way with an escort some time back.'

'A good evening to you too, young Tashi,' the guard smiled. 'Yes, the dakini did pass by, not five minutes ago, with a tall celestial. If you hurry, you might catch up with her. She went that way, towards the Amber Courtyard.'

Tashi broke into a run as he headed in that direction.

'Hurry, boy!' Chetak said anxiously. 'This does not sound good at all. What is she up to? I have a strange feeling about this and it's scaring me.'

Tashi asked curiously, 'Strange feeling? Why? Are you sure you are not overreacting?'

'I keep forgetting that there is so much you simply do not know,' Chetak snorted. 'We wind horses are famous throughout the universe for our intuition. Now hurry! There! You seem to be catching up. That's her and, yes, her escort too. But wait! There are two more celestials with them and they seem to be heading directly for the Amber Courtyard. Now move as stealthily as you can, Tashi. Step into the shadows. I will use them to camouflage you and then we can spy on them without being seen.'

Tashi sighted the dakini and her escort, which had now increased in number to three, as they turned into the Amber Courtyard. Approaching the courtyard, he noticed an additional contingent of guards posted at every five paces and slunk into the shadows, from which Chetak created a misty grey screen that would veil the boy from view.

Tashi heard Chetak's voice from within himself. 'No, Tashi,' the wind horse said, 'I do not like this one bit. Something very strange is going on. Now sit down here, so we can look directly into the Amber Courtyard from our vantage point.'

Tashi and Chetak settled into a shadowy niche, observing the dakini and her escort who stood in the centre of the courtyard, chatting quietly.

IX

Yeshe had barely placed her hand in Arden's, when the world became a blur of grey and was reduced to nothingness. In moments, the dakini had been transported to the chaos paths. A cutting wind was blowing and Yeshe wrapped her flimsy stole tightly around her to ward off the cold. She looked around her, bemused, taking in her changed surroundings. The forest was filled with shadows and the pinpricks of light emitted by fireflies failed to relieve its relentless darkness.

Yeshe blinked in confusion and turned to Arden. 'Where are we?' she asked. 'Where is your artefact? Just what is happening here?'

Prince Arden smiled and bowed low. 'These are the chaos paths, Dakini,' he announced. 'Your wish has been fulfilled. You will now see the eastern span.'

Shocked, Yeshe looked back at Prince Arden. Then her eyes went to his guards. They were preparing to move and had discarded their celestial guise. They were clearly demonic beings, with their sharp clawed hands and glowing horns.

With dawning horror, Yeshe whispered, 'Asur ... I have been taken by the Asur.' She took an involuntary step back and pointed a finger at Arden. 'Who are you?' she asked.

'I am Prince Arden Ti Nazer Basher, commander of the Asur borderland armies, at your service,' Arden replied with a smile. 'I never did hide anything from you, you know. Come, Dakini, we must leave for my home planet, Inka. We have a long journey ahead of us.'

Yeshe felt pure fury burn in her veins, 'Duped, that's what I have been!' she raged. 'You have me in your clutches now, but this is not the end of it.'

The dakini took another step back and flung out her arms, chanting a mantra of great power. Instantly, everything around her within a radius of five feet cleared. The air expanded and was compressed, leaving Yeshe surrounded by a glowing aura of light.

Prince Arden yelled in fury, 'The shield of ether! That won't protect you for long, Dakini!'

'I am not without means, Prince Arden,' Yeshe responded with a bitter smile. 'I have my own system of defence. Moreover, do not think you can carry me away without consequences. The Rigden will send a rescue team after me. The shield I have erected around me will serve for a sennight. And by then, I expect to be well away from you.'

Prince Arden stared at Yeshe. 'Now that I have you, no one can take you away from me, Yeshe,' he declared grimly. 'I would like to see them try.'

X

Tashi scanned the deserted courtyard in growing confusion. 'Chetak, just what has happened here?' he asked, agitated. 'Where is the dakini? She seems to have disappeared into thin air with that celestial.'

With that, he ran out of his hiding place and into the middle of the Amber Courtyard. 'She was here not a moment ago. And now she is gone?' Tashi said, incredulous. 'What should we do, Chetak? Should we wait for her here?'

The wind horse neighed loudly within Tashi and his disembodied voice rose in panic. 'Run, Tashi!' he urged. 'Run to Prince A-KarO and tell him what has happened. He urgently needs to know. Get one of the guards to stand vigil in the courtyard while you're gone. I strongly suspect foul play. I have a terrible feeling the dakini won't reappear. She has been carried off by force.'

Tashi shook himself out of his confusion. 'Did you notice the number of guards with that celestial who accompanied the dakini?' he asked Chetak. 'Who was he? His face was in shadow and that prevented me from getting a good look at him.'

'I didn't get a look at him either,' Chetak snorted, 'but I did see the guard. Did you notice anything unusual about the guard?'

Tashi thought carefully. 'Their faces were also in shadow and I did not get too good a look at them, but I did remember thinking they were very tall. And yes, for a brief moment, I thought there was a red glow emanating from the eyes of the guard nearest us, but I could have been mistaken.'

'This doesn't bode well, boy,' Chetak neighed. 'Now do hurry and inform the prince. He should be able to come up with some answers.'

Assigning a guard the duty of keeping an eye on the Amber Courtyard, Tashi raced out into the gardens, heading for the banquet where he hoped to find Prince A-KarO. A strange sense of urgency gripped the boy as he rushed through the crowds of guests at the banquet, searching desperately for the Lha prince. He finally spotted him standing in the shade of a tree, deep in conversation with an old man who did not look to be a courtier. Tashi rushed up to the prince, gulping in fresh air as he gestured wildly to draw his attention.

Prince A-KarO raised a sardonic eyebrow as he turned to Tashi. 'You have been missing the whole evening, Tashi,' he remarked, 'and now you turn up, quite out of breath and clearly out of your head. Have you had too much wine, young one?'

Tashi frantically gestured again. 'Your Highness,' he gasped, 'please spare me a moment. Something has happened and I need to tell you about it urgently.'

Prince A-KarO excused himself from the guest he had been chatting with and stepped aside. 'What is it, Tashi?' he enquired. 'You look panic-stricken. Are you feeling ill? Because if you are, you have my permission to retire from the party.'

'Your Highness,' Tashi persisted, 'please hear me out. Something terrible has happened. The golden dakini, Yeshe Nam Lha, has disappeared. I fear she has been abducted or that something foul has befallen her.'

Prince A-KarO seized Tashi by the front of his tunic and shook him. 'Come to your senses, boy!' he snapped. 'What nonsense is this? Now take a deep breath and tell me slowly all that has happened.'

Tashi sighed. 'I will start at the beginning, Your Highness, I am afraid I am not here alone today. Chetak has accompanied me...' Tashi recounted the incident he had just witnessed and ended with, 'That is why I came running to you.'

Prince A-KarO let loose a string of curses and then began running in the direction of the Amber Courtyard. 'Come, Tashi!' he urged, as the boy struggled to match the prince's pace.'We must make for the site where you last saw Yeshe. I will try tracking them through heat and body signatures. Let's see what it yields. Since not much time has elapsed since they left, their vibrations should still be intact and strong enough to trace.'

Tashi tried to keep up with Prince A-KarO as the latter raced through the gardens, making for the Amber Courtyard. As they approached it, Tashi saw a single guard standing just outside the entrance. A-KarO halted and the guard saluted and bowed low before him.

'Did you see anybody in the courtyard or passing through it?' the prince asked him.

The guard bowed again and answered, 'There has been no movement here, Your Highness. I have seen no one come or go.'

The prince stepped into the Amber Courtyard and froze. Tashi stopped abruptly in his tracks.

'Don't step in here, Tashi,' Prince A-KarO warned him. 'I am going to try and read the signs. I need silence.'

The prince took a step forward and a bright luminescence filled his body. He held aloft his hand and a brilliant white light lit up the courtyard, transforming it into a space filled with pure energy. Tashi saw thousands of energy signatures floating in the air. A clear emerald radiance emanated from the surrounding plants, sheathing them in green energy. The birds and insects in the courtyard gave off a golden glow, but already fading towards its centre were fainter purple splotches, strangely limned in golden light. At the heart of the purple cluster was a deep blue stain that glowed with light and, next to it, a white blaze of energy, like lightning. Prince A-KarO let out another string of curses, then followed it up with a single word: 'Asur.' Hearing it, the guard paled. The prince's form blazed with white light and as he stepped out of the courtyard, the light died.

A-KarO's expression looked grim in the moonlight. 'Tashi, we must see the Rigden right away,' he announced. 'You will report to him all that you have witnessed and then I will apprise him of my conclusions. This is the worst possible thing that could have happened. The Asur have kidnapped Yeshe. The signs point towards portals that were opened here to the chaos paths, but I cannot imagine how they kept the gateway hidden. Also, they succeeded, somehow, in camouflaging themselves with the semblance of a celestial aura. That is how they escaped public notice. That kind of deceit is typical of the Asur, but I would like to know who, in Shambala, helped them. Also, at least one member of the Asur royal family was in charge of the operation. Undoubtedly, he was Yeshe's escort. I am keen to find out his identity.'

Prince A-KarO turned to Tashi. 'Now be quick, boy! Run and locate Prince Narasimha, then bring him to the Rigden,' he directed.

'But what will happen now, Your Highness?' Tashi asked, baffled.

Prince A-KarO smiled. 'Now the chase begins, boy. We are about to launch a rescue mission. In an hour's time, I intend heading out to find the dakini. Now run and fetch Narasimha and meet me at the Rigden's pavilion.'

XI

Tashi raced through the gardens and back to the banquet. Soon, he was scanning the crowds for Prince Narasimha. He spotted him standing at ease and conversing with a group of courtiers.

Tashi ran up to him and bowed low. 'Your Highness,' he said, 'There is an emergency; the prince has asked that you join him at the Rigden's pavilion.'

Prince Narasimha looked concerned. 'An emergency, Tashi?'

'The prince will reveal all at the pavilion, Your Highness. You must hurry. The situation is dire. Now do excuse me. I must rush.'

With that, a breathless Tashi walked swiftly through the crowds and made straight for the Rigden's pavilion. Once he had arrived, he pushed his way through the crowd of courtiers to find Prince A-KarO already there and in conversation with the Rigden.

Tashi pushed himself towards the front to hear what was being said.

'Your Majesty,' Prince A-KarO was saying, 'I beseech you to place the paradise worlds under red alert. An emergency must be declared; there has been an incursion by the Asur into Shambala. A band of them not only trespassed into our world through portals they opened in the Amber Courtyard, but infiltrated the banquet too and abducted the golden dakini, Yeshe Nam Lha. We must move fast, Your Majesty. Please arrange for all our outposts and stations across the paradise worlds to be alerted. Also, blockades must be activated across the celestial plane. A rescue mission for Yeshe must be launched without delay.'

On hearing the news, the Rigden's face lost all colour. 'I insist on a detailed report on the incident right now,' he demanded. 'Please start from the very beginning.'

Prince A-KarO bowed low and said, 'Your Majesty, the story begins with Tashi. I am asking him to depose before you now.'

Tashi stepped forward and bowed low before the Rigden. Then he began to give a detailed account of all he had witnessed.

When he had finished, the Rigden turned to Prince A-KarO. 'A rescue mission must be launched immediately, Prince A-KarO, and I entrust you to lead it. Prince Narasimha will accompany you and so will a company of the élite corps. You must leave at once if you are to track the Asur who have abducted Yeshe along the chaos paths. Please remember to have a tracker accompany you. I would recommend Carlioni Iao, famed throughout the celestial realms for this skill.'

The Rigden turned to his first counsellor, Nishant Ariman. 'Have my commands conveyed immediately to both the tracker and the élite corps. They must be ready to move in two hours. Tell them to report to Prince A-KarO. Also, have the Lha monarch and Amravati notified of the breach of security and trespass by the Asur and request them to have alerts sent out across the empire. Similarly, notify all our outposts on the sacred paths, our way stations on all the paths, including the chaos paths, and the allied worlds. They must be prepared to provide aid to the rescue mission, intercept the Asur abductors, if necessary, and report on their movements.'

'Your Majesty,' Prince A-KarO intervened, 'I have a request. I would feel infinitely more reassured if I were to have my own élite Lha company with me. Also, please do allow me to take the boy, Tashi, along. He is my apprentice and has to stay with me at all times.'

The Rigden inclined his head in acceptance, but his expression was one of concern. 'So be it,' he said, 'I give in to your request, for something tells me that this is your mission. I must also warn you that you will have to travel the chaos routes used by demonic forces and we have almost no access to aid on these highly dangerous paths. However, we do have one functioning hidden way station. Messages will be sent out to them to provide you with all possible aid. Also, Amravati has its shelters on the chaos paths. They will be notified of your mission and will get in touch with you while you are on those paths.'

Prince A-KarO inclined his head. 'Notifying these shelters will be enough. I am well aware of their location, for I have travelled the chaos route twice,' he said. 'So do not worry, Your Majesty. We will acquit ourselves well.'

'There is no time to waste,' the Rigden reminded him. 'Every minute is precious. You must be on your way, Prince A-KarO, and best of luck.' The Rigden now looked directly at Prince Narasimha. 'The time has also come for you to depart, Narasimha. I want both of you to leave Shambala at the soonest.'

Both princes bowed low before the Rigden, then stood erect before withdrawing from his presence. Soon, they were striding out of the banquet and heading straight for the palace. Tashi raced alongside as the two entered the palace and walked down the corridors.

Prince Narasimha looked at A-KarO. 'We will go our separate ways from this point, but I will meet you in two hours outside the main palace entrance.'

Prince A-KarO inclined his head in agreement.

Tashi followed, as Prince A-KarO entered Captain Arif Leman's room.

'Tashi,' said the prince, turning to him, 'please pack my clothes for the journey and yours as well – and be quick about it. I will need two sets of fur-lined tunics and leather pants and don't forget my fur cloak. Pack your winter garments and don't worry about a cloak. I shall be getting one for you. While you are busy, I will have a word with the captain. Meet me at the main palace entrance in two hours' time.'

Tashi bowed low to the prince and left at a run.

XII

It was almost midnight when Tashi stepped out into the chill of the night. The palace courtyard was bustling with men and movement. The Lha company stood ready to move, dressed for battle, with many of the warriors wearing armour beneath their navy blue cloaks. All of them were armed to the teeth. All the warriors who could be rounded up were in the process of mounting their steeds. Tashi scanned the courtyard, looking for Chetak, when his eyes fell upon the familiar face of Ti Shan. The Lha trooper was standing in one corner, busy adjusting the stirrups on his horse.

Tashi walked up to him. 'Ready to see some action, Ti?' he asked.

The Lha smiled as he went about his work. 'This is your first time, Tashi,' he remarked. 'Are you nervous?'

'Not really,' Tashi replied. 'But I do admit all this has happened too fast and taken me unawares. I hadn't expected something like this to happen so soon, especially not here in Shambala.'

'With the Asur, anything can happen at any time,' Ti grunted. 'One always has to be prepared. The Lha have maintained this level of alertness for aeons. But so far, all action had been restricted to the borderlands. This recent incident marks the Asur's first major incursion into our realm in many years. It seems they have grown exceedingly bold.' Ti's steely grey eyes glinted in the night. 'However, you need not worry, young Tashi. Just stick close to the prince and you should be fine.'

Tashi frowned and murmured, 'I know I am a novice. I have just begun my training. Still, the prince did say that I had a talent for archery. I think if the situation warrants it and we see action, I can rely on my bow to carry me through.'

'For a novice, you use the bow with a fair degree of skill,' Ti acknowledged, 'but I hope you are carrying something more than just the bow with you?'

'I have two knives that were given to me by the prince, but I am still learning how to use them. I am not as confident with them as I am with the bow.'

'You'll do,' Ti said with a nod. 'Just stay close behind the prince when the situation warrants it and you should manage. By the way, Tashi, I hope you are carrying the famed mark of the Garuda whose bearer you are?'

The boy smiled and patted his tunic pocket. 'Right here.'

Ti finally finished with his chores and turned to the boy again. 'You are going to need a cloak, Tashi,' he observed. 'It will be freezing cold on the chaos paths.'

'The prince said he would get one for me.'

'That's fine,' Ti responded before asking, 'don't you think you need to locate Chetak and load your bedroll and luggage?'

Tashi nodded. 'I was just thinking of doing that. Well, I had better go and look for Chetak.'

Ti pointed. 'He's right there with Master Topen and the prince's steed.'

Tashi waved to the Lha trooper and disappeared into the crowd of warriors, cutting a direct path towards Chetak. Making his way to Master Topen, the boy bowed low before him.

'Master Topen,' he said, 'here is Prince A-KarO's luggage. Is there anything else you need me to do?'

The drill-master frowned. 'About time you got the prince's luggage here,' he said with some asperity. 'Don't bother about loading it. I will get one of the troopers to do it. Now you had better ready your horse. He has been waiting for you for quite some time.'

Tashi busied himself for the next few minutes in tying on his bedroll and fixing his luggage. He had barely finished and was adjusting the saddle straps, when there was a sudden commotion and Prince A-KarO emerged from the palace entrance. He was draped in a pristine white fur-lined cloak and wore a helm made of a shining white metal that glowed in the night. Underneath the cloak, he was wearing armour. The prince strode up to his wind horse, Storm, and mounted him quickly. Magnificent in size, the steed had a beautiful white coat that glowed in the night. His neck and chest were protected by armour in the same shining white metal as his master's. The prince accepted the salute from his élite Lha company. Captain Leman, a tall, slender Lha celestial with a very serious face, followed him.

Prince A-KarO signalled to Tashi who ran to do his bidding. The prince handed him a large package.

'That's your cloak and there's a mail shirt too, made of a rare metal called irithrin, produced here in Shambala. Now don both quickly and lead your horse into position right behind me.'

Tashi lost no time in unwrapping the package. Inside lay a dark blue cloak, lined with fur, and a shining white mail shirt. The metal was very light and warm to the touch. Donning it quickly, he draped the fur cloak around his shoulders and fastened it. Then mounting Chetak, he quietly led his horse into position behind Prince A-KarO's.

The soldier flanking him on his left looked at him. 'You look ready for battle, Tashi,' he observed. 'Do you know what that mail shirt is made of? It is pure silver irithrin, warded metal that will deflect any weapon it encounters. It is so rare that it is almost priceless in Shambala and the paradise worlds. Once upon a time, mail shirts fashioned from irithrin were only given to royalty. So the prince has done you a great honour.'

Tashi smiled, 'Thank you for informing me. I must thank the prince, yet again, for his kindness.'

Having swiftly fallen into cavalry formation, the company was ready to begin the long march. But for a huge grey wind horse that stood riderless.

'Narasimha is late,' Prince A-KarO said to Captain Leman. 'This is most unusual, Arif. We will wait another five minutes. If he is not here by then, we leave without him.'

The captain nodded and said, 'I am sure Prince Narasimha will be here shortly.'

The atmosphere was tense and Tashi could make out that the prince was anxious to be off. At that very moment, the crown prince entered the courtyard from the side gate, followed by two huge warriors. Prince Narasimha was also dressed in a mail helm of irithrin. Under his brown cloak, edged with fox fur, he wore light armour. The heir-apparent smiled as he hailed Prince A-KarO, then mounted his wind horse, Akash, known for his strength and speed.

'Sorry to keep you waiting, A-KarO,' Narasimha told the prince, 'but the Goddess Tara asked to see me. She sends her blessings and a message for you. She says our face-off will be with the dark prince of the Asur, Arden Ti Nazer Basher. It is he who has abducted Yeshe and carried her off into the chaos paths. He has a lead of some six hours. So we had better be on our way.'

'Ah, Arden!' A-KarO exclaimed. 'That changes the picture completely. Now that I think of it, no one else could have pulled off this operation so smoothly. We don't have a moment to lose.'

'I agree. I have brought two of my men along and they will take their place behind me,' Narasimha added.

In minutes, the company was on the move. Tashi led his horse carefully through the royal gardens, making for the Amber Courtyard, where the company halted, still in formation. Prince A-KarO led his horse, Storm, to the exact spot from which Yeshe had disappeared and called for Captain Leman.

'Get the warriors ready, Captain,' he commanded. 'I am going to open the portals at this very spot. Also, summon the tracker. He must scent the trail to determine the path ahead of us.'

Captain Leman called for Carlioni Iao, who rode up to the front and began sniffing the air. Tashi watched as the spry little man tested the air before nodding his confirmation.

'I have it, Your Highness,' Carlioni declared. 'The stench of Asur is strongest at this point and underlying it is the distinctive vibration of portals into the chaos paths.'

A-KarO inclined his head and launched into a chant that would open the portals, enunciating each of the sacred syllables in a clear voice. The sound of a single bell was audible as a sharp ray of light appeared, forging a path and carving a wide gateway in the air that opened into a scene straight from hell. Dark, twisted trees appeared and a foul wind, biting cold, blew through the gate. Captain Leman issued the command for the company to march. The two princes were the first to enter the portals, closely followed by the captain. The tracker rode alongside on his dun-coloured horse. The four of them disappeared through the portals and Tashi followed with the rest of the company.

Chapter 12

YESHE AND THE PATHS OF CHAOS

I

Yeshe crouched on a large rock and pulled her stole tight around herself to ward off the wind chill. It was bitterly cold and, clad as she was in light garments, she could not control her incessant shivering. The heat energy she had managed to generate and store in her body through meditation while on the move had been dissipated and she was too exhausted now to make fresh efforts to raise it. They had been travelling for the past eight hours and Arden had just called for an hour's halt for dinner. While he had left Yeshe seated a little away from the Asur soldiers, the prince had ensured that a guard of five surrounded her.

Taking deep gulps of breath, the dakini looked around her wearily and a feeling of utter despair overwhelmed her. Her distraught gaze flitted around her, seeking a means of escape, and came to rest on the burly guard of five Asur encircling her. Even if she managed to evade them and flee, she could not allow herself to forget that they were on the chaos paths. Harpies hunted in these skies and she would not survive for long. Yeshe's only hope lay in the rescue party that would surely be sent from Shambala to find her. The dakini shivered. During the aeons she had lived in Shambala, she had never known fear or panic, but now the feelings had crept into her. She felt that if she did not make a valiant effort to control them, she would lose the only defence she had at her disposal – the hastily erected shield of ether.

The shield shook as the first cracks began to appear in it. In desperation, Yeshe lifted her head and looked straight into the night sky, into the dark emptiness of space, unrelieved but for the faintest glimmering of faraway stars and planets. Bereft of choice, she now embraced the darkness and the cold, weaving them into a shield which she draped around her being. The cold crystallized and settled around her quivering belly and the sound of 'Om' rose from it. As she felt the mantra reverberate in the darkness, control returned to her and she wove a mantric shield around her heart, encasing it with the reverberation of the single word, 'Om'. Unbidden, the name of the one God, the creator, rose within her. Yeshe spun a shield of sacred fire and cast it around her mind. Lastly, she offered up a prayer to the Goddess Tara, thanking her for the inspiration and the help. Slowly, of its own accord, her being opened itself to the dark fathoms of space and stilled, creating its own net of luminosity. The shield of ether steadied and the cracks that had appeared in it vanished. Her panic subsiding, Yeshe was her calm self once more.

With her tranquillity restored, Yeshe reflected that she was not entirely helpless against the Asur. She could certainly build her own defence against them. The dakini extended the etheric shield around her and set the meat stew and water that had been brought for her by the guard outside the space it protected. She would have to avoid contamination by neither eating nor drinking anything prepared by the Asur. Yeshe drew a single line of luminosity around her that formed an effective barrier and demarcated the shield's boundary. By uttering a single syllable, she created a floor of darkness across the shielded space and conjured up a mat of ropes woven out of dried grass, on which she then seated herself. The whiff of the grass evoked memories of Shambala and she basked in their calming influence. Exhausted she might be, Yeshe thought to herself, but she was not disempowered. The golden dakini was not without means.

Then a memory rose, in Yeshe's mind of having held Arden's hand. She knew she could not touch any of the Asur if she were to retain her purity and her powers. It was clear to her that she would have to undergo a rigorous cleansing process when she escaped from them. The dakini contemplated the options that lay before her now. She was certain that a rescue team had been despatched from Shambala, but could she, in some manner, direct its members to her location? Could she, perhaps, establish psychic contact with them? It might be worth a try, but first, she must rest for a while and recharge her energy. Yeshe lay down on the mat and closed her eyes, willing her mind to fall back into the darkness of space. She would form a dark mirror in the mind, she told herself, and see what it yielded. Her breathing fell into a regular rhythm as she drifted into a light sleep and a soothing darkness embraced her mind.

II

The dakini had barely managed an hour's sleep when the sound of Prince Arden's voice woke her up. She opened bleary eyes to the sight of the Asur prince urging her to get moving. Yeshe sent up a silent prayer that thanks to the shield she had erected, Arden could no longer touch her or come too close. It was a pity, however, that the shield did not extend beyond her shadow. The Asur prince was still too close for comfort. Yeshe rose to her feet shakily, wrapping her stole tight around her to ward off the sting of the icy wind that was making her shiver uncontrollably.

'I have a cloak for you, Dakini,' Arden offered. 'It is cold here. Also, I observe that you did not partake of the meal your guard brought you. If you deny yourself sustenance, you are unlikely to survive on this plane.'

Yeshe looked at him calmly. 'Prince Arden, you know well that I will not touch a morsel of the food your guard serve me,' she declared. 'I would much prefer starvation to contamination. As for the cloak, thank you, but I do not require it. Know that I will accept nothing from you.'

Arden's eyes glinted with barely leashed anger and the red glow in them intensified. 'If you starve yourself, Dakini, you will not survive either here or in Inka,' he declared grimly. 'If you refuse to eat our food, I would suggest that you use your powers to conjure up your own, whatever you can manage. It should sustain you. You have five minutes to mount your horse. We are about to move on.'

Yeshe nodded and followed Arden and her guard to the horses. As they approached the chestnut mare she was to ride, she contemplated conjuring up a cloak to protect herself against the severe cold of the chaos paths, but felt too enervated to do so. The numbing cold and her own exhaustion were taking their toll and the dakini doubted she could summon even a stick right now if she wanted to. Supporting herself on a raised stone,

Yeshe mounted her mare. Once she was seated, she sat back and took several deep breaths. Waves of dizziness engulfed her. This would not do, she told herself firmly. She could not afford to weaken. Not once in the aeons that she had lived in Shambala had she ever experienced ill health; this must be the influence of the Asur. Yeshe shook her head and inhaled deeply; she must get herself under control.

Silently, she launched into *tummo*, the yogic breathing practice that leads to the generation of higher levels of heat energy in the body. She struggled through the first few breaths, then settled into a rhythmic pattern. As her concentration on her breathing increased, Yeshe grew oblivious to her horse's movements and the presence of the Asur around her. After 10 minutes of *tummo* breathing, she felt calmer. Her shivering subsided as her body temperature rose and soon, a sheen of sweat covered her face and arms. Yeshe smiled; she had conquered her first challenge, the cold. And now, with the renewed power of *tummo* coursing through her body, she decided to conjure up all that she needed.

The first object she drew out of the black void by summoning the power of the word was a thick, dark cloak, plain but serviceable. Even though Yeshe felt no urgent need for it in her present state, she decided to be practical and wear it, as the effect of *tummo* would not last beyond a few hours. Her next requirement was nourishment, for the level of weakness to which her body had been reduced could not be allowed to persist. Yeshe uttered a word of power and summoned some hot flatbread and cheese out of the void. She began eating the food and after finishing her repast, settled back on her horse and looked around her. She realized that they were nearing the boundary to the ice fields. The barren plains were giving way to fields of snow, which stretched out as far as the eye could see. High in the skies, a flock of harpies could be seen flying towards the barren plains. Yeshe shivered at the sight. Whichever rescue party of celestials was following her into the chaos paths would face many dangers here on the chaos plane, dangers that the Asur were immune to, thanks to an ancient alliance they had forged.

Prince Arden rode ahead, leading the party with his captain and the Asur sorcerer, Bakala. Around Yeshe, the guard of Asur rode in a disciplined formation. The dakini calculated that it was the time just before dawn, when the night is at its coldest. They must have been on the move for over 10 hours. She wondered if she should try establishing contact with the rescue party that had surely been despatched from Shambala to search for her. Exercising extreme caution, she used a silent chant to ward her mind so that neither the Asur prince nor the sorcerer riding with him would be able to read her intentions. She took one last look at the latter's thin, sinister form as he rode in front, seemingly deep in conversation with Arden.

Satisfied that he was too preoccupied to pay any attention to her, Yeshe let her mind travel back down the chaos path, retracing the barren terrain they had covered and scanning it for the slightest sign of a celestial's vibration. As she wondered from which point the rescue party might have entered the chaos plane, her instinct guided her; it would undoubtedly be the same place from which she herself had been abducted. The dakini's mind zeroed in on the twisted wood. And then she sensed a glimmer, a knot of celestial vibrations. She had found them! Yeshe was elated. More heartening still was the fact that the vibrations her mind had picked up suggested a substantial group of celestials, not a mere handful.

The dakini's mind focused on the knot. And then she saw it, the pure blue flare of a Ningma warrior. It was Prince A-KarO. His tall form came increasingly alive on the spirit plane as it strode towards her. The pale blue light grew sharper and more intense as the Lha prince's spirit form drew closer. Yeshe's spirit flew out towards it. A-KarO's spirit form drew her into an embrace as they met.

'Yeshe, are you all right? They have not harmed you, have they?'

Yeshe looked at A-KarO and tears welled up in her eyes. 'You must find me quickly, A-KarO!' she implored. 'I am doing my best to hold out against them and have raised the shield of ether so that they cannot touch me. However, the shield will only hold till the full moon. After that, I will be at their mercy and compelled to do their bidding. You must save me before that happens.'

'Take heart, Yeshe,' A-KarO told her. 'I am coming to rescue you, come what may. We are on your trail and are traversing the barren plains at the moment. Now can you give me some indications of your current location?'

'We have just moved out of the barren plains and are now on the snowfields,' Yeshe informed him. 'A-KarO, I must warn you that the devil, Arden, who is holding me, has an Asur sorcerer with him. I think his name is Bakala.'

'Never fear, Yeshe,' Prince A-KarO said with a reassuring smile. 'I will get you out of their clutches. Now return to your body. You are not safe.'

Yeshe smiled and embraced the prince's spirit form before withdrawing from the spirit plane and retreating into her body.

As she rode on, the dakini felt life return to her celestial body. However, spirit travel had drained it of all heat energy generated by *tummo* breathing and, once again, she found herself at the mercy of the elements and shivering from the intense cold. Yeshe wrapped her cloak tight around her. The snowfields, she noticed, stretched endlessly. As dawn splashed a rose and gold colour across the horizon Prince Arden signalled for a halt. Not far ahead, two small demons stood near a pair of huge sleighs harnessed to a pack of snow wolves. Reining in her horse, Yeshe dismounted and stood shivering in the snows, yearning for the lost heat energy from *tummo* breathing. But her heart was full; Prince A-KarO was coming to rescue her.

III

Yeshe was stretching her limbs after the long ride, when Prince Arden approached her.

'How are you feeling, Dakini?' he enquired. 'We are making good time and are almost halfway through our journey. From this point onwards, we will travel by sleigh. That should make things easier for you. Tonight, we will be staying over in Cue, a village inhabited by a magical race of lower demons called Quevasis. They can be quite enchanting and some of them have great musical talent. I feel this part of the journey should be interesting for you.'

'I am ignorant of the hierarchy among demons and have little knowledge of it,' Yeshe responded. 'It should be interesting to encounter the Quevasis.'

Prince Arden smiled, his skin golden and his sharp features prominent in the sunlight. 'Yeshe, your wish to see the eastern span is about to be fulfilled and I feel honoured to guide you through it.'

Yeshe glared at him. 'It had never occurred to me that what I so innocently articulated would come true and in such a manner,' she said. 'What you do is no honourable thing, Arden. You have carried me off by force and I do not intend to forgive you for that.'

Arden's eyes grew intense. 'Dakini, I have heard you are a deity of compassion,' he told her. 'Do you not find it in your heart to feel some compassion for my race, some stirring of tender feelings? We have been damned for ages, as you know. Do we not deserve some empathy, some healing?'

Yeshe looked away to gaze at the horizon. 'Your race, Arden, is a race of demons, the architects of evil,' she declared. 'The only compassion your kind deserves is that of the dark sword of the void. Your passions run amok and no healing is right for you, other than that of extermination, so that your being can return to the mystery of essence.'

There was bitterness in Arden's expression as he said, 'So speaks a daughter of the heavens. No hope for the dark scourge of the Asur, is there? I had expected more from you, Yeshe. We are beings too. We have hopes, dreams and loves, just like all other creatures of existence. We are consciousness too. So why are we picked out to be damned? I ask you, Yeshe!'

Yeshe stared at Arden and her expression hardened. 'You want to lock me in a golden cage and yet you talk of compassion, Arden? The Asur are a degenerate race. Tyrants and killers, they are the creators of mayhem, the purveyors of disease, the scourge of the universe. Don't seek compassion from me, Arden! My compassion is not for the damned.'

Arden held out his hands. A dark, malevolent energy spiralled about him and, for a minute, Yeshe held her breath. He was the prince of the damned and she could feel his power and sense his barely leashed lust. It burned like a bonfire within him, drawing her inexorably to its heat – the lure of an Asur prince trying to hold her in thrall.

Yeshe shook her head and tried to fight the pull. It would be all too easy to let down her defences and give in to him, to stumble and fall. But she was a daughter of the heavens. Yeshe girded herself for resistance. She turned her eyes away from Arden's to clear her head. In her mind, she saw A-KarO's familiar face like a light out of darkness. Yeshe latched on to his memory and turned her back on the Asur prince even as the latter's aura drew her to him and threatened to overwhelm her.

'Come, Yeshe,' Arden called out, 'the sleigh has been readied.' With that, he escorted her to the sleigh and held out his hand. 'Please let me assist you on board, Yeshe. I beg you for this honour.'

Yeshe looked at him and, for a fleeting moment, was gripped by an overpowering urge to place her hand in his. She knew that once she voluntarily touched Arden, the protective shield she had erected would fall away, leaving her exposed and vulnerable. She told herself that she must fight the urge with all her might. Yet again, she felt his heat reach out to her, searing her face with a burning intensity. Yeshe recognized this as the power of his spell and fought it.

'Stop this charade at once, Arden!' she snapped. 'You know well that I will never place my hand in yours.'

Arden's lips twisted in a smirk. The red in his eyes swirled, emitting smouldering glints like those from a fire. 'Ah, you break my heart, Yeshe!' he drawled. 'Remember that moment in the Amber Courtyard, when you did put your hand in mine?'

Yeshe used both her hands to pull herself up on to the sleigh. She seated herself and turned to the Asur prince.

'Your ploy is not going to work, Arden,' she told him firmly. 'Go trouble someone else.'

'You deny me, Yeshe,' he said with a mocking smile.

The dakini was overtaken by a sudden rush of heat and felt a strange sensation within her. What was he trying to do to her? What *was* this?

Arden read her mind and smiled knowingly. 'Confused, Yeshe? What you feel is what you are drawing out of me. It was never my conscious intention to hold you in thrall, but this is what is happening, nevertheless. And it is mutual. What I do to you, you do to me. I lie at your feet, Yeshe.'

The dakini shook her head vehemently in denial. 'This is nothing but a sham, a delusion, a mockery! Begone from my presence and leave me in peace!'

A strange fire lit Arden's eyes. 'Ah!' he smiled, 'I am unacceptable, Yeshe. Yet do ask yourself why this is happening to you. I shall leave you in peace for now.'

The Asur prince strode off with a swagger in his gait. Yeshe cursed him under her breath. How dare he try to hold her in thrall? Slowly, she allowed herself to settle back on the seat of her sleigh and savour the comforts it offered. It was covered in furs and there was even a blanket to put over her knees. She sighed and looked around her, noting that the Asur company was boarding the sleighs and the snow wolves seemed eager to be off. As usual, Arden was engaged in conversation with the sorcerer, Bakala, who eyed Yeshe speculatively and appeared to be reprimanding the Asur prince. The dakini looked curiously at the two Quevasis. They were odd little creatures, short and dark-skinned, with long hair and thick beards. They wore strange, primitive garments made of fur and skin and their language seemed to be very basic. Yeshe wondered whether they were a purely demonic race or of mixed blood, like many lower demons.

Suddenly, one of the little men approached Yeshe and bowed low before her. 'It is rare for us to meet someone of your world, Goddess,' he smiled. 'Do you need more blankets?'

Yeshe smiled back and thanked him.

By now, Arden and the sorcerer had also climbed aboard, with the prince taking his customary seat in front of the Asur company. At a signal from him, the sleigh drivers pulled at the reins and the snow wolves set off at a run. Yeshe settled back, comfortable under the blankets.

IV

Prince Arden smiled as he felt the rush of cold air like a rejuvenating charge through his body. He slid a glance towards Yeshe, as she sat huddled in the blankets and gazed at the endless expanse of snow. He could hardly deny the strong attraction he felt for her. Giving her one last, intense look, Arden deliberately turned his eyes away, only to meet the reproving gaze of Nikas dom Bakala.

Raising an eyebrow, the sorcerer warned, 'You are playing with fire, Your Highness. Do restrain yourself.'

Arden looked at him coldly. 'What if I cannot? Or, better still, will not?' he challenged.

Bakala frowned disapprovingly. 'The dakini is the emperor's, to do with as he pleases. You, Your Highness, cannot have her. So I would advise you not to hold her in thrall. I would hate to see you thrown into the dungeons for wilful misconduct.'

Arden raked his hands through his hair to subdue its wild abundance. 'It was never my intention to hold her in thrall,' he declared. 'Such a thought had never entered my mind, but Yeshe draws it out of me. Bakala, it happens of its own accord when I am in her presence.'

Bakala sighed. 'You must rein yourself in, Your Highness,' he said. 'If you surrender to this attraction, you might be inviting disaster. After all, we do not know what the emperor plans for her.'

'Do you think I am not aware of the dangers?' Arden said in frustration. 'But the moment I set eyes on Yeshe, I cannot help myself.'

Bakala said sternly, 'You have already begun to mark her and place her in thrall. You know well that few can resist the spell of an Asur prince. I do not approve of this at all.'

Arden gazed out at the snowfield. The expanse of white stretched for miles around them, silent, uninhabited. Not a single living creature could be seen anywhere.

Bakala looked at Arden and asked, 'You are aware, Your Highness, are you not, that the celestials are in pursuit? Their troops have already encroached on the chaos plane.'

Arden smiled, his eyes glinting. 'Oh yes, I am,' he replied. 'I sensed it the moment they breached the chaos plane just after midnight. But they pose no threat to us. We have an advantage of ten hours or more over them. Besides, they will be sorely afflicted here. I saw a strong group of harpies making for the barren plains; they would have sensed the presence of the celestials.'

The day was waning, with late afternoon giving way to evening. They had been travelling through the snowfields for over eight hours.

'They won't be able to catch up with us on the chaos plane,' Arden chuckled. 'If we go by my calculations, we should make the village of Cue by evening. We'll allow for a two-hour halt for dinner and then continue till we reach the portals site, another eighteen hours away. If we travel through the night, we could be there day after tomorrow by dawn. We need that halt at Cue to rest our company. The soldiers cannot continue at this pace indefinitely.'

Bakala nodded. 'I don't expect the celestials to get you on the chaos plane either,' he said, 'but what are your plans after that? Where will you hold the dakini?'

Prince Arden looked at Bakala. 'Once in Inka, we will make straight for the royal palace, where rooms have been prepared for her.'

'So you won't need me any more then, will you?' Bakala asked.

Arden shook his head. 'On the contrary, I carry your orders,' he replied. 'You have been assigned to me to assist in case there is any action.'

Bakala cursed under his breath. 'This is just what I needed!' he said in frustration. 'An interruption in my work and duty at the palace.'

Prince Arden shrugged. 'By the way, talking of our pursuers, the Ningma warrior, Prince A-KarO, accompanies the celestials. I have sensed his presence.'

Bakala nodded. 'He is probably leading them. We can expect trouble, for they will catch up with us sooner or later.'

'Once we are at the palace, I will send out troops to eliminate them,' Arden told him. 'That should pose no problem – save for the presence of the Ningma warrior. I suggest you retrace through your magic the route we have used thus far and track their exact position. Then report back to me.'

'Consider it done,' Bakala said.

The sorcerer now lapsed into silence. Closing his eyes, he went deep into himself. For the next 10 minutes, there was neither sound nor movement from him. Then Bakala returned to the present. He opened his eyes slowly and drew in a deep breath.

'The celestials are still over ten hours behind us,' he announced. 'They are nearing the blue stone and will be at the boundary by dusk. They are unlikely to catch up with us on the chaos plane, but I would suggest moving out of Cue fast.'

Prince Arden nodded in agreement. 'We will spend as little time as we can for dinner in Cue and then make straight for the portals. We will fit in what rest we can manage en route.'

Along the horizon, the silhouette of Cue village was beginning to take shape.

'Captain Sapher Nmaldris,' Arden commanded, 'get the driver to double the pace. We are very close to Cue and have just one hour in hand for dinner before setting off again. Tell the men to move fast.'

Captain Nmaldris saluted the prince and issued the orders in a booming voice. Soon, the two sleighs were racing across the snows and heading for Cue.

V

Prince Arden sighted the village of Cue as the hazy clutter of hutments in the distance became visible. The sleighs sped towards the village and down its broad central thoroughfare, making straight for the guest-house. A small delegation of Quevasis, led by the headman, Vasis Colearthis, stood waiting to greet them.

Colearthis bowed low as the sleighs came to a stop and Arden alighted from his. 'Your Highness,' he said, 'it is an honour to welcome you again to Cue. A feast has been prepared for you in the guest-house.'

Prince Arden nodded to the headman and strode into the guest-house. A bright fire was roaring in the hearth and Arden threw himself into a sturdy armchair next to it. Colearthis poured him a mug of fiery *ditche*.

Arden summoned Nmaldris. 'Has the dakini been settled in her chambers?' he asked the captain.

'Yes, Your Highness,' the Asur replied. 'She has a guard of five Asur and arrangements are being made for her food and drink.'

Arden nodded. 'See to the soldiers,' he ordered. 'They must be ready to move in two hours' time. We will not be spending the night here, but will make camp after covering half the distance to the portals.'

'Your Highness, the soldiers are tired,' the captain informed him. 'Even the snow wolves pulling the sleighs are weary. Their handlers urge that we stay the night here.'

Prince Arden shook his head emphatically. 'It is simply too risky,' he declared. 'We have a ten-hour advantage over the celestials and I have no intentions of losing it by sleeping here. We will stop at the cliffs of Dharen.

We should be reaching there a little after midnight. From there, we have a straight run to the portals. We should be there by dawn.'

Nmaldris bowed and murmured, 'As you wish, Your Highness.'

At this moment, Madame Colearthis walked in and placed a plate brimming with meat curry, bread and potatoes on the table for the prince.

Arden looked at her with a twinkle in his eye. 'Madame,' he said, 'I thank you for your hospitality. We have, it seems, kept you busy in the kitchen.'

Madame Colearthis smiled at him. 'It is an honour to serve you, Your Highness. Is there anything else I can do for you?'

Arden smiled back at her. 'Just send your husband in to me, Madame,' he requested. 'I would like to have a word with him.'

As the headman's wife left the room, Arden dug into the food, savouring the rich taste of the gravy. A server appeared at his elbow soon after, bearing a platter of rice. Arden took a serving and turned to Colearthis, who had just appeared by his side.

'Ah, Vasis,' he said, 'I was wondering whether you had followed the rest of my instructions.'

Colearthis smiled obsequiously. 'Your Highness, I have followed your instructions to the letter,' he said. 'We have set up several elaborate traps in the snow for the celestials. As you know, my people are not fighters, but they are certainly clever and their traps are bound to take their toll on the rescue party. Also, we have been in touch with the harpies. They will launch an attack the moment the celestials enter the trap zone.'

'Well done!' Arden told the headman. 'Any word from the Arisanthe on the developments at their end?'

The little demon nodded. 'The Arisanthe have sent a messenger for you, Your Highness. Should I call him in?'

Arden nodded as he poured himself another glass of *ditche*. 'Immediately,' he replied.

Colearthis left the room and escorted the messenger in. Arden settled back in his armchair.

'Your Highness,' said the messenger, 'I come bearing news from the Arisanthe. A company of Lha celestials, led by the Ningma warrior, Prince

A-KarO, has entered the chaos plane through portals set within the twisted wood. They have crossed into the snow plains. The village of Arisanthe stood united in putting up a valiant resistance to the celestials, but the demons we had sent out were routed. The Lha company has also had to face resistance from the harpies, who have been running air sorties against them. However, to the best of my knowledge, the celestials have suffered few casualties and are moving fast.'

Prince Arden nodded and turned to Colearthis. 'See to it that this Arisanthe gets his food and drink.'

The sorcerer, Bakala, now sidled up to Arden. 'They are moving fast, Your Highness,' he said urgently. 'I do not expect them to be impeded in their progress on the chaos plane, but they will certainly have to put up a fight and suffer casualties. I suggest we move now. I would much prefer a confrontation with the celestials in Inka, where the odds are with us, than here.'

Prince Arden nodded and signalled to Nmaldris. 'Round up the men and get the dakini seated in one of the sleighs,' he commanded. 'We are moving right away.' He got up and stretched, savouring the sharp warmth of the fire for a moment, before turning to walk out. 'Now Colearthis,' he said, pausing before the headman, 'best of luck in your endeavour. I don't expect your men to fight, but I do expect your traps to be nothing short of lethal.'

Outside, the snow had started falling. Arden could not help casting a longing look at Yeshe as she sat huddled in one of the sleighs, wrapped in her cloak and some blankets.

VI

The dakini was utterly exhausted by the time dawn appeared on the horizon and the sleighs cut a straight path towards the cliffs of Dharen which had appeared in the distance. It had been an excruciatingly difficult eight-hour journey since they had left Cue at midnight. The cold wind cut through the dakini's blankets, cloak and light garments. The sleighs finally rolled to a stop as they neared the first cliff. Under the shadow of an overhanging ledge that overlooked the turbulent waters of the ocean of the Deep Void, Arden finally gave the much-awaited command for setting up camp.

Yeshe got off her sleigh wearily and stretched her cramped legs. Her escort of five led her into the centre of the camp, which was bustling with activity as the Asur soldiers set up tents and got around to preparing a meal. The dakini yawned as she was led into a fur-lined scarlet tent. A pallet, with furs piled high on clean sheets, had already been laid for her. What disturbed Yeshe was the sight of a second pallet that had been laid alongside hers. She suspected this was Arden's tent and dreaded the thought of what would follow. Once again, she thanked the guardian deities that her shield was holding firm against all odds.

The dakini had just wrapped herself snugly in the furs and sat back, stretching her legs on the tent's rich silk carpeting, when an Asur guard entered and set down a platter of meat curry, boiled potatoes and rice before her.

Yeshe waved the dish away. 'I will not be eating this,' she told the guard. 'I do not consume flesh. Please take it away.'

The Asur glared at her and withdrew, leaving the food where he had set it down. Yeshe shook her head, picked up the platter and placed it outside the tent. She simply could not abide the smell of the food. Sitting down again, she allowed herself to relax and immersed herself in the practice of *tummo* breathing. Within 10 minutes, she was hot as a furnace and brimming with energy. She used that energy to conjure up for herself a meal – hot flatbread, a bowl of fruits, sweet potatoes and a carafe of wine. Yeshe offered prayers to the divine Buddha and slowly began to eat her food. Warmth trickled into her like honey and she found herself relaxing after the day's trials.

The dakini calculated that they had been travelling without pause for nearly forty-eight hours. This halt at Dharen was the first real rest stop. Arden must be confident of reaching the portals soon. It was time she got in touch with Prince A-KarO again to find out how far behind the rescue party was. Yeshe took one peep out of the tent. Arden was busy in discussions with Captain Nmaldris and some of his troops. She had some time in hand.

Yeshe lay down on a pallet and let her spirit fly free. She scanned the open countryside as, in spirit form, she retraced their steps to Cue. The snow plain lay deserted for miles, empty of people and habitation. After wandering around for some time, her spirit form spotted the smoke line of Cue. The celestials had not yet reached the village. She roamed the back trails and then, halfway to Cue, suddenly came upon the group of celestials. They had made camp on the snow plain. Yeshe made her way into the camp and entered Prince A-KarO's tent. He was sitting on his meditation seat, resting his mind in the flow of the word. Tashi was asleep in one corner of his tent.

As Yeshe approached A-KarO, he emerged on the spirit plane quite suddenly, his tall form striding towards her.

'Yeshe, how are you?' he enquired.

His gaze, full of concern, filled her with hope.

'So far, I am well, A-KarO,' she replied with a smile. Then her expression grew grave. 'Now listen to me carefully,' she told him. 'Arden and his group of Asur are way ahead of you. They are camped on the cliffs of Dharen. This is the first camp the Asur prince has set up in forty-eight hours. I think he is confident that the portals are now within reach.'

A-KarO answered, 'Never fear, Yeshe. I will get you out of their hands soon.'

The dakini went on, 'You will have to be careful, A-KarO. They have set lethal traps for you on the snows near Cue. Also, the harpies are planning to attack you at the very same place. Beware!'

A-KarO smiled. 'Yeshe,' he said reassuringly, 'the harpies and the traps are a mere nuisance. Just delaying tactics, no more. They cannot touch us.'

'A-KarO,' the dakini continued, 'the soldiers at the Asur camp are exhausted and will soon be asleep. I was thinking of taking the opportunity to make an escape attempt and try to reach you.'

Prince A-KarO shook his head firmly. He caught Yeshe's hand in his own and said, 'Promise me you won't indulge in such foolishness. There are many dangers out there. The traps could get you and so could the harpies.'

'I have my shield, A-KarO,' Yeshe reminded him with a smile.

A-KarO shook his head again. 'Promise me, Yeshe, that you won't try anything of the sort. If you subject your shield to such pressure, it may fracture, leaving you exposed to danger. Have patience. Wait for us to reach you. Help is coming soon.'

Yeshe smiled forlornly at the prince. 'I promise to wait for you, then, A-KarO. Now I had better be off. Arden will retire to his tent any minute.'

Prince A-KarO gave Yeshe a quick hug before her spirit form retreated. Within moments, it was back in her body. Yeshe sighed with relief as she found her tent empty. She poured herself some wine from the carafe by her pallet. Her hands trembled with exhaustion. The *tummo* heat had fled her body and all that remained was the cold and an overwhelming feeling of fatigue.

Yeshe had just about settled down on her pallet when the tent's flap lifted and Prince Arden entered.

'Still awake, celestial maiden?' he smiled. 'Ah! What is this I see? Contraband? Some Shambala wine? Will you share that with a damned soul, Dakini?'

Yeshe frowned and handed Arden the wine. 'Be my guest,' she said curtly.

Arden poured himself a glass of wine and sat back to unwind. He took a sip and closed his eyes. 'The bounty of summer, Dakini,' he murmured. 'Ah, it has been aeons since I tasted this. I have almost forgotten its flavour out here in this desolate corner.'

'Summer is not for the likes of you,' Yeshe told him coldly.

'So says the daughter of the heavens,' Arden smiled. 'Now only if you would let yourself relax a bit, let down your shield, smile at me ...'

Yeshe's eyes blazed. 'My smiles are not for such as you,' she snapped. 'Don't try anything you'll regret, Arden.'

The Asur prince smiled, his eyes glinting. Then he settled down on his pallet next to Yeshe's. 'You are stuck with me, Dakini, whether you like it or not. For tonight, I am yours.'

Yeshe shrank back into the corner. 'Shame on you, Arden!' she exclaimed. 'Bear in mind that you are answerable to your emperor. Shift your pallet out of this tent at once – or away from mine, at least.'

With a smile, Arden flung a silken sheet around Yeshe and drew her closer.

'Unhand me this minute, Arden, or you will live to rue the day!' Yeshe told him.

'I have you now, Dakini,' Arden grinned. 'I cannot touch you, but I can surely touch your sheet.'

Yeshe struggled in vain to free herself.

'Feel my heat, Dakini,' the Asur prince murmured, 'feel what you have rejected for so long.'

A panic-stricken Yeshe glanced into Arden's eyes. As their gold depths ensnared her, she felt heat coursing through her, arousing her senses. She looked around her frantically, desperate for a way out of his clutches. If she touched him of her own accord even once, the shield she had erected would melt and fall away, leaving her entirely at his mercy.

Arden placed a corner of the silken sheet over her lips and moved in. 'I may not be worthy, Dakini. I may be damned, but one kiss I will certainly take from your lips. The rest is up to you,' he said with a smile rich in innuendo.

Yeshe shook her head in disbelief. This could not be happening to her. 'Arden, you will not do this!' she said sternly. 'This gift is mine to offer, not to be taken by trickery.'

Arden smiled slyly, his eyes lighting up with unholy glee. 'Would you ever give this gift willingly to one like me, Yeshe?' he asked. 'You would not. So tonight, I will resort to trickery.'

Arden manoeuvred the dakini on to his lap and deliberately touched her silk-covered lips with his own. At his touch, a river of molten hell broke loose within her. Despite the silken sheet between them, Yeshe was lost as heat reverberating from his lips seemed to singe her own. She fought to retain her equanimity, but silent, forbidden desire welled up in her. It took all her strength and resolve not to surrender to it. As she felt the pressure of his lips again on the sheet covering her own and almost opened her mouth, help arrived.

Bakala stepped into the tent, took one outraged look at Arden and upended a carafe of *ditche* on his head. Seizing the prince by his collar, the sorcerer tore him off Yeshe. A roar of frustrated rage rose from Arden and as he turned his wrath on Bakala.

'How dare you, Your Highness!' the sorcerer growled. 'How can you risk everything we have worked towards for years simply for the sake of satisfying your lust?'

In response, Arden emitted a howl of uncontrollable fury. Bakala took one look at Yeshe's white face and told her, 'Leave the tent, Dakini. The soldiers have been issued fresh orders. They are to allow you to sleep in my tent. I will share Prince Arden's.'

Shivering in reaction to all that she had endured, Yeshe hurried out of the tent barefoot, carrying her boots in her hands. Her guard of five Asur immediately ringed her and led her to Bakala's tent, which had been erected some distance away from Arden's. The Asur prince's howls and curses followed Yeshe into the night. She shook her head to clear it. What had just happened to her? How had it happened? Never had she imagined that the shield could be breached in this manner. Without losing a moment, she poured her fury into rebuilding it, restoring it to its original, inviolable form. Relief swept over her when she realized how close it had been to collapse.

Yeshe shivered and entered Bakala's tent, a standard navy, like that of the troopers. Inside, a single pallet had been laid on the side, with woollen sheets, instead of the silk ones on Arden's pallet, and a couple of fur blankets. Shivering with cold, she wrapped herself in the sheets. She felt shaken. Her trust in the sanctity of the shield was gone. How would she survive like this, she asked herself. The Asur prince would try his best to seduce her and she had to resist him at all costs. She had to reach Prince A-KarO and fast. He would surely be able to help her. Her energy, however, was utterly depleted. But with the blush of dawn touching the horizon, morning would be here. It would help her regain her strength. Yeshe resolved to get in touch with A-KarO the moment that happened. With that thought, she lay down on the pallet and sank into the dark void of exhausted slumber.

VII

The morning air was crisp and cold as Yeshe rose from her pallet and went through her morning ablutions. She swiftly buttoned her cloak and pulled on her boots. Then running her fingers through her long hair, she stepped out of the tent. Her guard of five Asur surrounded her and escorted her to her sleigh. Yeshe instinctively checked on her shield; it was holding, but this morning, it did not give her any sense of security. Nervous energy burned in her as she took her customary place in the sleigh. The Asur were already packed into it. Those yet to board were Prince Arden and the sorcerer, Bakala, who stood engrossed in conversation. Yeshe eyed the Asur prince and tried to contain her feelings of panic. He had managed to breach her defences the previous night and shown her with what ease her shield could be fractured. Yeshe's thoughts went to Prince A-KarO whom she would have to contact at the earliest. Then Arden came on board the sleigh with Bakala and gave the signal for departure. The handlers of the snow wolves tugged on the reins and off they went, pulling the sleighs along.

As soon as they had set off, Yeshe slowly began focussing on the breathing technique of *tummo*. Its familiar rhythm calmed her and in 10 minutes, she was brimming with heat, energy and vigour. She stole a quick look at Arden, who was busy issuing instructions to Captain Nmaldris. Then she allowed herself to relax and let her gaze focus on a single point. Gradually, her spirit form left her body and flew towards Cue. She spotted the celestial group breaking camp and swiftly made her way to Prince A-KarO, who was in conversation with Prince Narasimha. Yeshe's spirit form hovered in the air near A-KarO until he sensed her presence. Signalling her quietly to wait for a moment, he made his way to a large rock buried in the snows. There he seated himself and almost instantly, his spirit form reached out to Yeshe's essence.

The dakini was trembling with anxiety by the time Prince A-KarO reached her.

'Yeshe, you have returned sooner then I expected,' the prince began.

She held her hands out to him imploringly. 'A-KarO,' she said, 'something has happened. I desperately need your help.'

Prince A-KarO's eyes glinted with concern. 'What is it, Yeshe?' he asked. 'What bothers you so?'

'My shield, A-KarO,' the dakini replied. 'It was almost breached last night. I know now that it is not the protection I had thought I could rely on.'

A-KarO gripped her hands and pulled her closer. 'What happened, Yeshe?' he asked gently.

The dakini's eyes were haunted as she answered, 'Last night, Arden succeeded in laying his hand on me. He threw a sheet over me and then kissed me. What am I to do, A-KarO? How do I keep him away?' Her voice was full of despair.

Prince A-KarO cursed under his breath. 'Did he do anything else, Yeshe?' he asked grimly.

The dakini shook her head. 'Luckily, Arden was interrupted by the sorcerer who entered the tent and took charge of matters,' she explained. 'I managed to escape to another tent. The fact remains, however, that my shield was rendered ineffective. If this happens again, how will I protect myself, A-KarO? I feel so defenceless!'

The prince gave her a reassuring hug. 'I will protect you, Yeshe,' he promised. 'Don't be afraid. I will erect your shield again and render it invincible. Now just sit down on the snow while I go about it.'

Yeshe sat back on the snow, her face forlorn. Prince A-KarO began a chant. The words fell rhythmically and then surrounded her. The prince glowed with light as he extended his hand and a bright ray emanated from it and surrounded her life force. The dakini sensed incredible heat and light building within her. Then suddenly, they subsided.

'Neither Arden nor anyone else will be able to touch you now, Yeshe,' the prince said grimly. 'Fear not. The shield will not yield or fall away under any situation other than during the full moon. Then it will vanish and will have to be erected afresh the next day. Don't worry, we are not that far behind and I will have you safely away before the full moon.' Prince A-KarO smiled at her. 'Now Yeshe,' he said, 'this is important. Have you any idea where they plan to take you?'

Yeshe nodded. 'From the talk around the camp, it is clear they are taking me to Inka. The portals open at Sorcerer Bakala's fortress. From there, they mean to take me to the royal palace, I think. That's what I picked up from overhearing conversations among my guard, but I will keep you informed on further developments.'

Prince A-KarO took her hands and gripped them tightly. 'You had better go back, Yeshe,' he urged. 'You mustn't give them cause to suspect what you are about.'

Yeshe nodded and her spirit form withdrew from the prince's presence, flying back across the ice plains to her body. She opened her eyes slowly and looked around her. The sleigh was flying across the snowbound landscape. She relaxed in her seat, reassured that she was safe for now.

Prince Arden turned around and looked at her, his golden eyes glinting. 'So you have finally woken up, Dakini,' he observed. 'The portals are not far off now. You will be reaching your destination soon.'

Yeshe ignored him and gazed out at the snow. A fast, cold wind was blowing and she shivered. All the *tummo* heat had slipped out of her body. She hugged her cloak and blanket and hunched into her seat.

VIII

It was close to midnight and they had been on the move for almost 14 hours. The night was heavily overcast and it had begun snowing. An icy wind pierced Yeshe's garments, making her shiver uncontrollably. She was wondering just how long this benighted journey would endure through the endless snowbound wilderness, when Prince Arden suddenly called for a halt. She realized that they were standing on high, snowbound cliffs. Dark ocean waves pounded the snowbound beaches.

The sorcerer, Bakala, held aloft his hand and declared, 'The portals are located here, Your Highness. I will begin the ritual for opening the gateway.'

Having said that, he walked to the edge of the cliff and lit an incense lamp, placing it on the snow.

Meanwhile, Prince Arden had given the command to dismount and the Asur were falling into position before they crossed over. Lightning crackled in the skies and sleet fell heavily. Yeshe wrapped her cloak around her and stood quietly next to Arden. The sorcerer had begun a low chant. The dakini could sense the fell sorcery of the Asur as the chant resounded around her. Bakala offered a blood gift to the ocean by slicing open his hand and letting the wind carry his dark, shining blood over the cliffs. As the chant went on, waves of ecstasy built in the air, enveloping the Asur and flowing over Yeshe. She felt the soldiers around her sway with it, this sensation that was like the heat of a bonfire, moist air on a summer day, a lover's touch. Yeshe marvelled at how it transformed the Asur while she stood in the centre of her shield, immune to its power.

Prince Arden smiled at her, his gaze ecstatic. 'Soon, you will alight in Inka, Dakini,' he announced. He held out his hand to her, but it rebounded on her shield. He shook his head. 'So this nonsense continues, does it?' he sighed. 'How long can you make it last? All shields are made to shatter sometime or the other.'

Yeshe looked away as his turbulent energy spread around her, the sheer magic of his spell pulling at her. Suddenly, a violent bolt of lightning split the skies and a huge gate made of light started opening in the air at the edge of the cliff. Yeshe looked with curiosity into the grey murk that was Inka. All she could see was a haze. She shivered at the sight; it did not look promising.

The sorcerer, Bakala, inclined his head. 'All is ready, Your Highness,' he announced proudly.

Prince Arden gave the command to march and gradually, the Asur troops vanished into the haze. Yeshe stepped lightly through the grey mist and looked around her. The land was snowbound for miles. Ahead of them, a grey fortress rose above the mist, gleaming with menace. The troops assembled in the snow and the slush. To the right, a huge forest of tall evergreens stood clad in white. It was morning in Inka, but the sunlight was feeble, the land swathed in mist and gloom. Yeshe shivered again as the troops marched towards the fortress.

Prince Arden inclined his head and said, 'Welcome to Inka, Dakini. Not a very inspiring sight, is it? But you can now see for yourself how the other half lives. And yes, we thrive.'

At that very moment, there was a flurry of movement as the fortress gates were thrown open and the troops were led into the outer bailey. The steward at the fortress came out to greet them in Bakala's grey livery.

'Your Highness, my Lord,' he said, addressing both Arden and Bakala and bowing to each, 'the royal palace in Inkala has sent an escort to conduct the dakini there. The escort awaits your pleasure, Your Highness. Refreshments have been prepared and served in the hall.'

Prince Arden nodded and looked at the sorcerer. 'I would like to leave right away, Bakala,' he announced. 'It is still a two-hour run to Inkala and I need not remind you that we are being pursued.' He turned to the steward and ordered, 'Please have the escort fall in line immediately. We leave right away without delay.' Then he turned to Bakala again. 'I suggest you accompany me,' he said. 'We will have to give our report to His Majesty very soon.'

The escort arrived in the black and gold colours of the Inken royal family. Their commander, Istekan Salubis, bowed and said, 'Your Highness, allow me to congratulate you on your success. The company is ready to move. We await your command.'

Prince Arden acknowledged his words with a curt nod. 'Get the soldiers in position to move to Inkala right away,' he ordered.

Yeshe looked around her curiously. All over seven feet tall, the Asur looked like an exotic breed of beings as they stood out starkly against the grey mist. Their polished black or gold horns shone in the dim light and their eyes were fierce as they sat astride pure black stallions brought in especially for Prince Arden and his soldiers. Demon steeds, they stood almost eight or nine feet tall and had protruding fangs instead of teeth and fearsome claws on their hooves that resembled the paws of a lion.

Arden led a huge black stallion up to Yeshe.

She shook her head, protesting furiously. 'I cannot ride this beast,' she said firmly. 'Definitely not!'

The Asur prince grinned at her. 'Its bark is worse than its bite, Dakini,' he told her. 'These horses are tame.'

The horse threw back its head and neighed furiously. Yeshe calmed down as she looked at the creature's eyes. They were a golden brown and fringed with long lashes. The horse looked at her imploringly and Yeshe could not help but smile. For such a feral-looking creature, it was strangely tame. Fascinated, the dakini continued gazing at the stallion.

'How do I mount the steed, Arden?' she asked, 'Is it not too high for me?'

Prince Arden smiled disarmingly and held out his hand. 'I am here to help you, Yeshe,' he said.

Yeshe looked at him and shook her head. 'You know that's impossible.'

Prince Arden sighed. 'Then it can't be helped,' he said. Turning to the stallion, he commanded, 'Down, Mischief.'

To Yeshe's surprise, the great horse went down on its four paws and lowered its head. The dakini clambered on to its back and smiled as she took up the reins and the horse got back on its feet immediately.

'Now he is going to be a challenge,' she remarked.

His eyes gleaming, Prince Arden said, 'He will carry you, Dakini. You need not do a thing.'

Yeshe sat back on the horse and, within moments, the troops were off. The stallions moved at tremendous speed down the broad road leading away from the fortress into Inken Forest. The dakini lightly patted her horse and felt the unusual warmth of his hide under her hands. At her touch, the charger threw back his head and neighed, his joy reaching out to her.

IX

The horses galloped through Inken Forest at terrific speed, following the winding road that cut through it and climbed steadily, before descending again on the other side. Her head covered with a stole that veiled her face against the bite of the wind, Yeshe gazed at the snowbound forest and sighed. She had to admit that it had a wild beauty of its own. Tall evergreens stood proudly together, their branches weighed down with layers of snow, from which water dripped incessantly. Yeshe spotted wandering deer and on the branches of trees perched strange birds with multi-coloured plumage and sharp, elongated beaks. Two hours later, they had left the forest behind. The road broadened as they neared the capital city of Inkala.

Mist hung heavy over the ground, trails of it floating everywhere. The sunlight faltered and the land lay shrouded in shadows. Yeshe was gripped by the surreal feeling of moving on horseback through a great void. Suddenly, out of the grey mist, the silhouette of Inkala was visible on the horizon. On its outskirts appeared the flat mud dwellings of the poor. Their roofs were made of timber and the houses huddled close together, their surroundings mired in slush and snow and sheer filth. Tall Asur males could be seen going about their work. Beyond the shantytown lay a deep moat that ringed Inkala and further on, the city walls stood tall, with guard posts built along them at regular intervals and manned by the Asur city guard. The gates leading to the inner city were manned by a section of the city guard whose members saluted Prince Arden's entourage and waved them in. The inner city was well planned, with broad intersecting roads and multi-storeyed buildings of yellow sandstone. Yeshe looked around her with open curiosity as the cavalcade passed through many crowded marketplaces and residential areas.

The inner city gradually gave way to the citadel where the emperor's palace was located. Another moat ringed the citadel and high granite walls surrounded the palace complex, with guard posts visible at regular intervals. A huge iron gate appeared in the walls. It was manned by the royal Asur guard, which immediately recognized Prince Arden's entourage and welcomed its members into the royal citadel. Yeshe looked around her in amazement. Made of pure black granite, the Asur royal palace was surrounded by sprawling ice gardens. The snowfields had been used to full advantage by the Asur, who had created massive, though strangely aesthetic ice sculptures, including fountains and tall spires. The Asur royal palace complex was a sprawling area dotted with arches, minarets and filigreed overhanging galleries of marble and granite.

The arched main gates opening into the palace were inlaid with intricately carved panels of granite and marble studded with precious gems. The huge bronze doors were beautifully embossed with figures of flying demon horses. They opened into a vast hall, marked with arches and pillars of granite. The flooring was of polished green stone. As Yeshe entered, taking in the sights with a sense of wonder, she had to concede that while the Asur royal palace did not match the perfection of Shambala and Amravati, it had an eerie beauty and a charm of its own. The hall was crowded with male Asur courtiers dressed in silks and expensive furs who stared with avid curiosity at the dakini and Prince Arden's entourage. The Asur women were conspicuous by their absence.

The palace steward, Asak Dumane, a very tall, slender Asur with pure black skin and cat's eyes, came forward and bowed low before Arden. 'Your Highness,' he said, 'we have been expecting you for some time. The emperor has been asking after you almost every day for the past week. I will lead you to the special warded chambers that have been prepared for the dakini. Also, I have been instructed to tell you that tonight, at the eighth hour, His Majesty is expecting you and Sorcerer Bakala in his inner audience chamber.'

Yeshe felt a frisson of unease as the Asur's cold, cat-like gaze lingered on her.

'Your Highness,' Dumane went on, 'the dakini has been assigned a contingent from the royal palace guard. Your guard will no longer be required for the purpose.'

Asak nodded at the waiting gold-and-black livery-clad Asur royal guard, whose members immediately surrounded Yeshe. Arden gave the command for his own guard to disperse. Then he and Sorcerer Bakala went ahead with the palace guard.

Yeshe noted with curiosity that the twisting palace corridors were full of Asur men. The steward led them through the corridors to the palace where the narrow passage they walked through opened into a heavily guarded section on the ground floor in the North wing. Yeshe guessed that her rooms would be located somewhere in this area. A tall, arched bronze door opened into a spacious apartment with granite walls and marble floors. Yeshe entered what she realized would now serve as her living space. Silken rugs lay on the floor. Low couches stood about and a hanging lantern gave off a green light. Candleholders occupied niches along the walls. Another arched entranceway opened into the bedroom, where a double bed, laden with furs, stood in the centre. Here, too, silken rugs lay on the floor. A fire blazed cheerfully in the grate. Looking around her luxurious surroundings, Yeshe realized she would now be held in a gilded cage.

Prince Arden followed her into the bedroom. 'This is where you will stay, Yeshe,' he told her. 'You will have two maids attending on you and seeing to your every need. I trust you find your apartments comfortable.'

The dakini narrowed her eyes. 'I am not fooled, Arden,' she said. 'However luxurious this apartment may be, it is still a cage.' Yeshe eyed the wide windows that were provided with her bedroom that overlooked a small courtyard attached to her apartment. The sitting room also overlooked the frozen, almost bare, courtyard and had two wide windows and a door that opened into it. However, as Yeshe peeked out she saw two sentries on duty in the courtyard and the high walls surrounding it had the unmistakable hum of warding. The entire apartment and corridor outside were heavily guarded and warded. The Asur were clearly taking no chances.

Arden smiled, his eyes glinting a rich gold in the lantern light. 'I shall leave you now, Yeshe, but I will be back. I am to report to the emperor. He will send for you later, but I don't expect that to happen very soon.'

The dakini followed Arden out into the sitting area. Sorcerer Bakala stood there, impatiently tapping his foot. He and the prince filed out and the bronze doors swung shut ominously after them. Yeshe sat down on a couch and looked absent-mindedly at the iced courtyard where a single dried fir tree threw long shadows in the waning afternoon light. The day was already giving way to evening. She slumped against her couch and gazed at the dancing flames of the fire. They gave her hope, and she smiled wanly.

CHAPTER 13

THROUGH THE SNOWS

I

Tashi gazed at the snowbound wilderness through which they were riding. He scanned the skies carefully. There were no harpies in sight; nor was there any other sign of an imminent threat. It seemed they had been given a brief reprieve. How long it would last was anyone's guess. The party of celestials had been on the move now for 14 hours without a break. They had crossed the snow line five hours back, resisting repeated attacks from the harpies through the night. Tashi glanced at Prince A-KarO. He was also scanning the horizon and his face looked grim in the afternoon light.

Pointing into the distance, the prince said to Narasimha, 'That's Cue on the horizon. I will call for a stop here, because from this point onwards, we have to move cautiously.' He turned to Captain Leman. 'Arif, tell the men to halt so they can break bread,' he directed. 'Then we will resume our journey. Send the tracker, Carlioni Iao, to me. We need to plot our course from here with the utmost care.'

The captain saluted and, in a booming voice, called for a halt.

Tashi dismounted from his horse wearily. The afternoon light was sharp, but devoid of warmth, and a cutting wind blew over the snow plains. He noted that despite the shooting that had taken place through the night, all his arrows were intact. He checked his knives. Then huddled in his cloak, he took out a stone and some oil from his pack and sat down to sharpen his blades.

Ti Shan approached, bearing a plate of cold potatoes, cheese strips and a roll of bread. 'Eat when you can, Tashi,' he urged. 'We will be on the move soon.'

Tashi accepted the food gladly and dug into it. 'I pray the harpies leave us alone tonight,' he said. 'I was hoping the prince would issue orders to make camp. We seem to have been travelling through this wilderness for ever.'

Ti smiled. 'The prince drives his warriors hard,' he admitted. 'It is his way. But there is, indeed, much need for urgency.'

As Tashi ate his food, he observed the two princes, A-KarO and Narasimha, who seemed to be deep in discussion. The boy had barely set aside his plate when Prince A-KarO, who was sitting on a boulder with his legs outstretched, summoned him with a gesture. Tashi sprang to his feet and ran up to him, buckling on his newly sharpened knives as he went.

'Tashi, bring the tracker here to me,' the prince directed. 'He has been waiting for me for quite sometime.'

Tashi bowed and moved away, his eyes alert as they sought out the short, wiry form of Carlioni Iao. His build notwithstanding, the tracker was an astute being and had been guiding them through the snows with confidence. Tashi escorted Iao to the prince and hovered nearby as they spoke.

'Iao, we need to move fast,' Prince A-KarO told the tracker. 'The dakini, Yeshe, has been carried out of the chaos plane and on to Inka. During my most recent contact with her a few hours back, she informed me that they were travelling to Inka. By now, however, she will have left this plane and will be in Inka. She is evidently being transported to the royal palace in Inkala, where the Asur will keep her in captivity. Given the circumstances, we cannot afford to tarry on this plane longer. We need to move fast.'

Prince A-KarO's gaze veered from Iao to Prince Narasimha and back. 'The dakini has already warned me of danger near the village of Cue, which is now visible on the horizon,' he told them. 'From what I have learnt from her, we should anticipate a harpy attack and be simultaneously prepared for traps set up by the Quevasis. Now, Iao, I need you to take us by the shortest route skirting Cue. Then we will get back on the dakini's trail. We should set a pace that will get us to the cliffs of Dharen by midnight. We can make camp there. Then at dawn, we start for the portals.'

Iao nodded. 'Yes, Your Highness,' he said. 'I will take you by the shortest route around Cue right away. Hopefully, we should be able to evade the traps. Then we will set course for the cliffs of Dharen.'

'Good, let us move, then,' the prince responded.

Iao bowed himself out of the princes' presence. A-KarO turned to Captain Leman.

'Arif, get the troopers to move,' he commanded. 'I want them in position right now. And warn them that they must be on full alert. There is danger all around us.'

Tashi rushed forward to hold the reins of A-KarO's horse, as the prince vaulted on to the saddle. Then the boy mounted his own steed and moved to his customary position behind the prince.

Prince Narasimha turned to A-KarO. 'Are you sure Yeshe is off this plane?'

'Yes, she has been moved,' the prince replied. 'Inka is where she is now. Her essence has grown very faint. I can barely sense her presence on the spirit plane.'

Prince Narasimha acknowledged the information with a nod. 'You know what that means, don't you?' he said. 'She won't be able to communicate with us till we reach Inka ourselves.'

'It cannot be helped. All the more reason for my urgency.'

Tugging on Chetak's reins so that the horse settled into a measured trot, Tashi sat forward in his saddle, straining to eavesdrop on the conversation between the two princes.

'I don't like this at all,' Narasimha said, shaking his head vigorously, his hair flying from the queue he had bound it in.

Tashi had just relaxed in his saddle when an eerie wail rent the skies and, with a great flapping of wings, harpies without number began swooping down on them in aggressive formation like a swarm of locusts. With the upper bodies of old women – shrunken dugs, wrinkled necks and the long, sharp beaks of carnivorous birds – and the lower bodies of huge carrion birds, they presented a terrifying sight. As they approached on rapid wingbeats, Tashi quickly nocked an arrow into his bow and waited for the perfect shot.

11

As the celestial Lha warriors moved to resist the attack with their spears and swords, the skies reverberated with the shrieks of the harpies, while the screams of the wounded and the dying rent the air. Blood and gore spilled on the pristine snow. With the Garuda's feather in his pocket glowing red and throwing off tendrils of auburn light, Tashi felt charged with a strange energy. The lust for battle coursed through his veins as he let fly arrow after arrow, downing one harpy and wounding others. Yet another one, flying low, closed in on him. Tashi instantly pulled out his knife and slashed at it wildly, aiming to disembowel it. He struck the neck and cut through cord and tendon, lopping off its head. Yet another harpy closed in for the kill and Tashi felled it with a well-aimed arrow. Next to him, Ti Shan was hacking away at the creatures with his sword. Tashi was momentarily distracted by the sight of the Lha trooper disembowelling one harpy as it swooped down for the kill.

It was at this moment that another harpy launched a lateral attack, knocking Tashi off his saddle and pitching him on to the cold snow. The boy stumbled and then righted himself, pulling out his knives in a clean move. The harpy swooped low, aiming for Tashi with its cruel beak. The boy ducked low as it came for him, its massive wingspan casting a shadow over him, then thrust the knife upwards and straight into the harpy's stomach with all his might, opening it up from neck to claw. As its bloody entrails tumbled out, the creature screamed in agony and plummeted to the ground.

Ahead of Tashi, Prince A-KarO, a sword whirling furiously in each hand, galloped straight into the harpies, cutting a clean swath through their ranks. The boy took shelter behind a snowdrift and watched the prince quell the harpy attack. Then he nocked an arrow into his bow. As he took a step back to get into position, Tashi found himself hurtling into an abyss. For the first time, he felt fear grip him and the battle lust within died away. He had fallen into a deep pit.

Tashi had barely got his bearings when he saw snakes crawling over his boots. The pit was filled with the reptiles and the boy shuddered with fear and revulsion. His mind numb with terror, he shouted for help. He felt a snake sink its fangs into his leather-clad leg. The sting was hot and sulfuric and the searing pain seemed to travel like lightning through his nerves. Tashi shouted again. Then suddenly, Prince A-KarO's worried face appeared at the mouth of the pit and looked down at him.

'Stay calm, Tashi,' he urged. 'You just walked into a trap, but I will get you out of there right away. Don't move under any circumstances.'

The prince mouthed a word of power and held his hand over the pit. There was a blinding flash of light and, suddenly, the writhing snakes froze and became utterly still. Tashi flexed his knee and shook off two snakes that had crawled up his leg. By the way they fell limply to the ground, he knew they were dead.

Prince A-KarO looked down at him anxiously. 'Have you been bitten, Tashi?' he asked. 'Just hold on. I will have you pulled out immediately.'

Tashi nodded sluggishly, for a sudden feeling of weakness had come over him. There was an excruciating pain in his leg and a cold sensation was creeping up from the snakebite on his foot to the rest of his body. Feeling faint, he found himself slumping against the pit walls, his body bereft of all strength.

'Tashi, are you feeling ill?' he heard Prince A-KarO ask, the voice seeming to come from far away.

Tashi swayed in the pit, holding his head in both hands. 'Your Highness,' he slurred, sweat beading his brow, 'I feel very ill. All my strength seems to be seeping out of me and I am unable even to stand.'

Having uttered those words, the boy lost consciousness and collapsed in the snow at the bottom of the pit. Meanwhile, Ti Shan had lowered a rope into the pit and was slowly climbing down into it. When he reached the bottom, he dropped down on his knees next to Tashi and tried to rouse him, but to no avail.

'Your Highness,' he told A-KarO who was watching the proceedings from above, 'he is unconscious; he must have been bitten by the snakes. I will send him up.'

Ti Shan carefully tied the rope around Tashi's waist and gave the signal for his fellow troopers to haul him up. Inch by tedious inch, the

Lha warriors raised the rope and pulled the unconscious boy out of the pit before laying him out on the snow.

Prince A-KarO gave Tashi a gentle shake in an effort to revive him, but he was evidently in a deep state of unconsciousness. His forehead felt clammy and feverish and involuntary shivers racked his body.

The prince turned to the warriors next to him. 'Send for Prince Narasimha immediately,' he commanded.

Fortunately, the harpy attack had been beaten back for the moment and the Lha troopers were busy ministering to the wounded among them. Prince A-KarO pulled off Tashi's shoes and examined his foot and ankle; there were four snakebites.

The crown prince now approached, his cloak flapping in the wind. He carried his bag of medicines and herbs. 'What's wrong with young Tashi?' he asked, concerned.

'Four snakebites, as far as I can tell, but there could be more,' Prince A-KarO replied. 'He fell into a pit filled with snakes.'

'Hmm,' said Narasimha. 'Luckily, I am carrying the antidote for snake venom. I shall mix the ingredients and feed him the potion, but he will still run a fever through the night. I expect it to break tomorrow morning at the earliest, but it could take longer.'

Prince Narasimha now pulled out a small bottle of potion from his satchel. Mixing it with water, he parted Tashi's lips and slowly poured the liquid down the boy's throat. Some of it spilled out, but most of the potion went down. The prince mixed some more of the antidote in water and poured it into a bottle which he handed to Prince A-KarO. 'Tashi has to be given a measure of this mixture every four hours,' he explained. 'He must finish the contents of the bottle by dawn.' Next, he cleaned the bites with water and applied a salve, instructing Ti Shan how to tie a bandage around each. Then he carefully examined Tashi's legs and torso. 'That's it,' he declared. 'There are no more bites.' He turned to the Lha prince. 'Now A-KarO,' he said, 'there are others I have to attend to. At least three of our troopers fell into traps and five were wounded by the harpies. So far, we have suffered no casualties.'

Ti Shan carefully bound Tashi's leg and straightened his clothes. 'Your Highness,' he said, addressing A-KarO, 'since the boy will run a fever, do we carry him along on a stretcher as we travel?'

The prince shook his head. 'All our wounded, including Tashi, will be tied on the backs of their horses. We will not be making camp before reaching the cliffs of Dharen. We leave right away.'

The prince turned to summon Captain Leman with a gesture and as the young captain rushed up to do his bidding, said, 'See that the wounded are tied securely on the backs of their horses, Arif. We leave now. We will move slowly and cautiously till we have crossed the trap zone. We are not out of danger yet. Prince Narasimha and I will lead the way, clearing the path through the traps. Get our warriors to fall into formation and order them to follow in our footsteps, ensuring that their horses tread carefully.'

Captain Leman bowed low to the prince. 'Your Highness,' he said, 'though we have inflicted great losses on the harpies and they have retreated for the time being, I am anticipating another attack from them somewhere ahead of us.'

Prince A-KarO acknowledged the information with a nod. 'There is that. They will certainly be back, but I think they will give us some respite for now. Tonight, I expect us to make the cliffs of Dharen. We will make camp there and I will set up a powerful warding to keep the harpies away.'

Having said that, the prince carried Tashi to Chetak and held him in place as Ti Shan tied the boy securely to the wind horse's back. A-KarO felt Tashi's brow. It was hot and he had still not regained consciousness. The prince uttered a word of power and light flared around Tashi. A warding appeared around his aura.

'This warding should keep all evil away from him if we are attacked again,' A-KarO explained.

Chetak neighed and tossed his head. 'Your Highness,' he promised, 'I will bear him as carefully as possible so that no harm comes to him.'

Prince A-KarO nodded and patted the great horse's silky black hide. Then he murmured another word of power and a warding appeared around Chetak. The horse fell into place behind the two princes and Captain Leman gave the command for the column to move. Slowly, the celestial troops moved through the snows, cutting a direct path out of the trap zone.

III

Dusk was approaching when Prince A-KarO called for a halt. The men had been on the move for many hours now. Burning with fever, Tashi was restless as he lay across Chetak's saddle. Ti Shan carefully untied him and laid his semi-conscious form on a blanket which he had spread on the snow. He bathed Tashi's forehead and used an ice pack to bring down the fever. The boy tossed and turned on the blanket, muttering incoherently and calling for Lama Ozer.

Prince Narasimha approached Tashi, his face grim, and sat down beside him to feel his pulse. 'The fever is high,' he observed. 'I expect it to continue through the night.'

Then the prince began a low chant as he fed the boy some medicine he had mixed with gruel. The moment the chant was over, he turned to Ti Shan. 'Stay with him and continue to bathe his face and brow as long as we are here. Also, feed him this gruel, a little at a time. I have mixed a medicine in it that should help his fever subside. I am expecting it to break sometime towards dawn.'

Ti Shan nodded and bowed low as the prince moved away to attend to the wounded warriors.

The Lha trooper picked up the bowl of gruel and proceeded to feed Tashi. The boy fought the food at first, but Ti Shan was as persistent as he was patient and managed to make him consume the entire contents of the bowl.

Not long after, Prince A-KarO gave the command to move. Ti Shan carried Tashi back to Chetak and tied him in place on the steed's back. Soon, the party was moving rapidly through the snowbound wilderness. Tashi stirred, caught in the grip of pain and delirium. His dreams were confusing. At times, he was fighting for his life against an Asur. At other times, his mind drifted to the hidden monastery and he was attending on Lama Ozer. Then the Rimpoche was scolding him and, again, he was running after Lama Ozer, trying to keep pace with him. For a few fleeting moments, Tashi regained consciousness and was perfectly lucid as he gazed up into the blushing skies of evening and wondered where he was. Then suddenly, he was jolted on the saddle and, with a cry of pain, relapsed into unconsciousness.

Dusk gave way to night as the party sped towards the cliffs of Dharen. Ti Shan edged his horse closer to Tashi's as they rode in position behind the two princes so that he could keep an eye on the boy. Suddenly, the night echoed with the screams of harpies. They were circling overhead, ready for another attack. His senses on full alert, Ti Shan eyed them warily. Then his gaze dropped as he realized that their party was surrounded on the ground by packs of demon wolves. At that moment, the harpies gave one fell cry and swooped down for the kill. Ti Shan positioned himself in front of Tashi and pulled out his sword. A huge wolf leapt at him, snarling viciously, its yellowed fangs bared, its red eyes glinting in the night. Leaping back in a classic Lha defence posture, Ti Shan sliced his sword through the beast's neck, severing its head clear from the body and leaving it hissing in the night.

The Lha warrior took a quick look at Tashi. Both the boy and his great horse were safe, protected by the force field of the powerful warding set up around them by Prince A-KarO. He looked up, just in time, to see a huge harpy swooping down on him and leapt high into the skies with a fearsome yell, blinding it with his sword in one smooth manoeuvre. The creature let out an enraged shriek and raked him with its claws. Ti Shan slashed at its legs, severing them from the body, till the harpy tumbled from the skies, screeching in agony. The Lha warrior now went in for the killing blow, lopping off the harpy's neck. Black ichor sprayed out of the dismembered remains and drenched Ti Shan. He looked around him and saw Prince A-KarO dancing with both his swords held out in front, laying waste to harpies and wolves alike. As suddenly as the attack had been mounted, the harpies wheeled and retreated, shrieking into the skies. The demon wolves, on the other hand, stood their ground until they had all been cut down.

Ti Shan wiped his sword on a rag and cleaned his arms and neck with water from his flask. Without wasting a moment, the party fell into position and moved off swiftly into the night. The cliffs of Dharen were now a five-hour ride away and Prince A-KarO was determined to reach them before midnight. Ti Shan cast a worried glance at Tashi. He was still restless on his saddle. The horses continued to move at a measured pace through the night. They had been on the move for almost two days, a feat of endurance that only Shambala's celestial horses could accomplish. But now, even the great steeds were exhausted and Ti Shan began looking forward to camp and a meal. He cast another worried look at Tashi; the boy continued to be restless and mumbled in his delirium.

IV

It was almost midnight when the celestial troops halted under the shadow of the overhanging cliffs of Dharen. Mist was thick on the ground when Prince A-KarO gave the order for the troops to dismount and set up camp. There was a flurry of activity as the exhausted warriors rubbed down their horses and gave them their feed. Still others were busy setting up tents for the troops. The navy blue tents for the princes were set up in the centre of the camp. Ti Shan carried Tashi into Prince A-KarO's tent. Thick woollen rugs had been spread on the ground and a trooper had already made up two pallets, lined with fur and piled high with thick quilts. Ti Shan tucked the boy into bed and felt his brow. It was still warm, but he was sleeping easier. The Lha warrior fed him some medicine, then left him to rest.

Prince A-KarO stood outside the tent, engrossed in conversation with Prince Narasimha. 'I think the portals are not far now,' he said. 'With Iao's help, we should be reaching them tomorrow. Now what bothers me is the location in Inka where those portals open and whether we should even try gaining access through the very same gateway that the Asur party had used earlier.'

Prince Narasimha's pale brow was furrowed with exhaustion. 'I don't think it would be wise to use the same point of entry as the Asur party,' he said. 'We might be walking into an ambush. I suggest Iao open the portals into an area in the vicinity of the original gateway.'

Prince A-KarO agreed. 'All such decisions will, of course, have to be taken once we reach the site,' he said. 'I am also worried about Yeshe. It's been an entire day since she last established contact.'

'Once we are in Inka, we will be in a better position to establish contact with her,' Prince Narasimha assured him.

Prince A-KarO nodded. He could still sense Yeshe's presence, but it was faint and far removed. 'I will try to reach out to her tonight,' he told the crown prince. 'I doubt I can communicate with her from here, but I might manage to see where she is being held.'

Carlioni Iao approached them, his light eyes glinting in the night. 'Your Highnesses, what time do you plan to move in the morning?' he asked.

'We leave at dawn,' Prince A-KarO replied. 'I expect us to reach the portals tomorrow. What is your own assessment of the situation, Iao?'

The tracker smiled briefly. 'Your Highness, we will definitely make the portals by tomorrow and, possibly, by afternoon. I can sense its location. It is not far.'

'Tomorrow afternoon will do just fine, Iao,' the Lha prince said with approval. 'That should give us some daylight hours in Inka to plan our journey ahead and see the lay of the land.'

'Your Highness, I will need to examine the portals,' the tracker told him. 'Could you spare two scouts to accompany me as I move ahead of the party to see if it is safe for the rest of you to follow?'

Prince A-KarO shook his head. 'Your services are needed, Iao. I cannot risk your journeying ahead alone.'

Prince Narasimha turned to the tracker and said, 'Prince A-KarO and I were just discussing the portals site and concluded that it would be dangerous for us to enter Inka through the same access point as the Asur had used.'

Iao nodded. 'Do not worry, Your Highnesses,' he reassured the princes, 'I have already thought this through. I will open the portals at a site which is in the general vicinity of the one used by the Asur, but at a safe distance from it.'

A trooper now appeared with a table and two stools, which he set down nearby. Then he began laying out dinner for the two princes – a platter of steamed rice balls, a plate of potatoes, vegetable stew and breads. Iao bowed and withdrew. The two princes sat down to their meal. The trooper appeared at their elbow with goblets of ruby red wine which he proceeded to serve. Prince A-KarO swallowed a liberal mouthful of the wine and Prince Narasimha tucked into his meal, his eyes wandering over the camp to ensure that everything was as it should be. He had already attended to the wounded and they now lay resting. Most of the troops were gathered around campfires, eating their meal, while others prepared to turn in for the night.

Prince A-KarO finished his meal and rose from the table. 'I suggest you retire early tonight, Narasimha,' he said. 'You will need your full strength tomorrow. I will now walk along the perimeter of the camp and set up wards against possible nocturnal attacks.'

The prince then proceeded to walk along the camp's perimeter, chanting mantras and building a series of wards as he went. As he completed the ritual, there was a flash of light and the wards fell into place. A-KarO now walked back to his tent and entered it. Tashi lay on his pallet, his quilt thrown aside, muttering in his sleep. The prince felt his brow; it was clammy. His fever was beginning to break. He gave the boy his last dose of medicine for the night, then tucked his quilt snugly around him. At last, he turned to his own pallet. Pulling off his boots, he sat down in the meditation posture.

Prince A-KarO allowed his mind to settle into silence. Once he had achieved stillness within, he brought forth his inner resolve; he had a spirit journey to make. The prince's spirit flew out of his body and travelled by spirit roads to Inka. He passed through a void filled with grey storm clouds till, at last, he sighted through the spirit gate the vast snowfields of Inka. A-KarO's spirit form now set foot in the demoniac world of Inka and felt assailed by the miasma of demon vibrations. He camouflaged his spirit presence and flew towards the city of Inkala, travelling through leagues of snowbound terrain and evergreen forest. Silently, he floated over the city, making for the royal palace visible in the distance. Lit up by torches fuelled with special oils that were routinely replenished, the palace rose up from the grey predawn mist, the contours of its arches and minarets prominent in the night.

Prince A-KarO now floated into the royal palace in his spirit form. Parts of it were submerged in darkness as the Asur slept, but the guards were vigilant, going about their duties. The celestial prince sent out a communication to Yeshe's spirit presence and it suddenly registered in his inner eye as a flicker of luminescence lodged in the heart of the palace. He drifted towards the eastern wing and reached a heavily guarded corridor. It was clear to him that the Asur were not taking any chances. Yeshe was being held in an apartment made entirely of plethium, an indestructible metal that was impossible to penetrate. Not only were the entrance gates to her apartment made of plethium, but the walls, too, were lined with it.

Prince A-KarO cursed the Asur in frustration as he realized that his spirit presence could not enter a space surrounded by plethium. Nor would the dakini's spirit form be able to leave the room and join his own. Focussing on her essence, A-KarO saw her in the sitting area of her apartment. Utterly still, she sat in a meditation posture, her form blazing with light as she merged into oneness. The prince's expression softened as he beheld her. Then taking note of her guard, his spirit form returned to his body. Prince A-KarO now allowed himself to relax, letting life flow back into him. Finally, he lay back on his pallet and surrendered himself to the soothing embrace of sleep.

V

Dawn came much too soon. Tashi stirred, then woke up with a sigh. His fever had broken. He was conscious, but felt weak and exhausted. He forced himself out of bed and completed his absolutions. Then he stepped out of the tent.

Ti Shan was waiting for him. 'I am glad to see you recovered, Tashi,' he said. 'There is no time to waste. You had better eat your breakfast. Then I will give you your medicine. Prince Narasimha says it will help you get back your strength.'

Tashi accepted his steaming-hot tea and bowl of porridge and slowly sat down to eat. The very smell of food nauseated him, but he forced each morsel down his throat.

Ti Shan smiled at him. 'You look much better today, Tashi,' he observed. 'That's just as well, because we have a long ride ahead of us. We will be reaching the portals today and crossing over into Inka. Now take your medicine. And then we had better see to the horses.'

Tashi drank the golden-hued potion and felt strength returning to his limbs. Then he hurried up to Chetak.

The great horse neighed on seeing the boy approach and tossed back his head. 'You look fine today, Tashi,' he said. 'I don't think they will need to tie you to my saddle any more. Now quick, mount me. Captain Leman has already given the command to mount. Then we must fall into position.'

Tashi patted Chetak's shining black hide and was astride him in a moment. The wind horse manoeuvred himself into position behind the princes' horse. Soon, the company was moving. A biting cold wind stung Tashi's face as Chetak moved effortlessly through the snow, a strange luminescence emanating from his hide. The boy noticed it and wondered at its source.

Then he heard the horse's disembodied voice in his mind. 'What you are looking at, Tashi, is the warding. We were attacked repeatedly yesterday and during one of those episodes, you were unconscious and needed protection. Prince A-KarO in his magnanimity warded both of us. So now we are safe from demoniac attacks of any kind.'

'I must thank the prince at the first opportunity,' Tashi said gratefully. 'In fact, I must thank both the princes. Had it not been for Prince Narasimha's timely medical intervention, I would not be back on my feet now.'

Chetak snorted and lengthened his stride, covering the miles with ease. Huddled in his cloak, Tashi settled back in his saddle. The wind was freezing cold and the sunshine was devoid of warmth. Hours flew past as they raced over the snows, making for the portals. By early afternoon, they had reached the portals site without any further trouble from the harpies. The wind chill had increased and the skies had become overcast when the tracker, Carlioni Iao, called for a halt. The flat snowplains stretched out before them, seemingly without end.

Iao led them for a short distance eastwards before stopping and pointing several furlongs ahead. 'This is it, Your Highnesses,' he said. 'There, slightly farther to the east, lies the portals site.'

Prince A-KarO vaulted off his horse, as did Prince Narasimha, and the two accompanied the tracker to the location of the site to examine it.

As he reached the site, Prince A-KarO began chanting, his voice undulating with the wind and rising from low to high. Carlioni Iao joined in, then handed the prince a cup of water. The latter now breathed over the water, chanting mantras all the while. Suddenly, the water evaporated, leaving behind shards of light. A-KarO flung them into the air. Gems and rich jewels came down in a shower and, suddenly, the portals were unveiled as the outlines of a filmy grey gate that opened into Inka.

Iao moved up to the gate and chanted low mantras. A vision unfolded in his mind, showing him the locations of the different sites where the portals opened.

The tracker held up his hand. 'Your Highness,' he said, addressing A-KarO, 'the portals had opened for the Asur at the fortress of Bakala. For obvious reasons, we cannot use that route. I will search for a site, not too far from there, which lies near the road to Inkala.'

'I rely on your instincts to select the best one,' the prince told him.

Iao continued to chant mantras in a low voice. Without warning, the gates opened into a vista of grey mist and evergreen trees.

'Your Highnesses,' the tracker said, ' I have found it. This is a secure but hidden site located in Inken Forest. It is a two-hour run from the fortress of Bakala and not too far from the Inkala road. I hope you deem it an appropriate accessway.'

Prince A-KarO nodded. 'The party will wait here,' he ordered. 'Iao, you will accompany me into the portals and we will check if the site is secure.'

The prince and the tracker rode in through the portals and soon disappeared in the folds of grey mist. A-KarO looked around him. The first thing that struck him was the eerie silence. They were in the midst of an evergreen forest. A counterpoint to the silence was the roar of a waterfall that plunged from the heights into a small pool near where they stood. Iao and A-KarO wandered around, checking for signs that would suggest the site had been used, but there were no demon tracks. The prince finally gave the command for the company to move through the portals and Prince Narasimha and Captain Leman led the celestial troops into Inka.

Tashi inhaled a breath of fetid air and looked around him cautiously. He was in the middle of an evergreen forest. The trees were very tall, their branches laden with snow, and the land, undulating in waves, was covered with snow. A thick layer of grey mist hovered over the ground. An icy wind blew through the forest. The deep silence was broken by the roar of a waterfall that plunged into a small pool nearby. Tashi wandered up to the pool and hunkered down on its edge to wash his face and hands.

Prince A-KarO called the boy urgently to his side. 'I hope you didn't drink that water?' he asked, concerned, when Tashi approached. 'Don't, till it has been checked by us. Remember, nothing here is what it seems. Even the trees and the undergrowth, the animals and the birds are tainted. You must proceed with the utmost caution. Now send Captain Leman to me.'

The captain approached and bowed low to the prince. 'Your Highness, what are your orders?' he asked.

'Firstly, send out scouts with Iao to check the path he is thinking of taking into Inkala. They must also undertake a careful survey of our surroundings. Secondly, I am expecting Reman Luskar, our man in Inkala, to establish contact with us soon. Keep a watch out for him. Thirdly, get the water in this pool checked. If it is safe, the troopers may use it. Also, have lunch served to them. Just a cold lunch. Nothing more.'

Captain Leman bowed and withdrew. Prince A-KarO sat down carefully on a rock and summoned Tashi with a gesture.

The boy hurried to him and remarked in a voice of wonder, 'Your Highness, there is no sunlight here. It's so dim.'

'Tashi, it is always dim in Inka,' the prince explained. 'There is no light, no cheer. Now I don't want you getting into trouble. So I need to forewarn you. Do not eat or drink anything you may find in the forest here, until Prince Narasimha and I have examined and approved it. Now I want you to fetch my meal for me and ask Prince Narasimha to join me.'

Tashi bowed and said, 'Prince Narasimha is attending to the wounded warriors, Your Highness. By the way, there is some good news. Most of the troopers, except for the three who have suffered fractures, have recovered sufficiently to be back on their feet.'

Prince A-KarO nodded in acknowledgement and Tashi moved off, making his way to Prince Narasimha, who was working on one of his patients. Looking around him, Tashi smiled. At last they had reached Inka! He felt better after the previous night's ordeal, but he was still rather weak. His spirits, however, were high and he expected to be completely back to normal by the following morning.

VI

Prince A-KarO took one more carefully manoeuvred turn through the snowbound forest and sighed as he recognized the familiar clearing. It was just another turn ahead. They had been riding through the forest for the last couple of hours. As evening approached, an icy wind had begun to blow. One more turn through the frozen forest path and the prince had given the command to halt. They were in the middle of a small clearing, with a stream cutting through it. Thick trails of mist swirled around them, obscuring the forest.

A-KarO turned to Captain Leman. 'We go no farther today,' he announced. 'This is a safe and convenient site and will serve as our base camp. Inkala is no more than a two-hour run from here and there is a forest path that leads right up to the city's outskirts. That is the path we will use. I have camped here before and used this trail in the past. Get the men to set up camp now. No fires are to be lit. They would be easily detected. Get the cook to serve the food cold.'

Prince A-KarO vaulted off his horse and handed the bridle to Tashi. 'You look all in, boy,' he remarked. 'Lead my horse to one of the troopers and get him to rub him down. Then come back here for your medication. The moment my tent has been set up, you will rest.'

Tashi had barely led the steed away when Prince A-KarO turned to Captain Leman. 'There is another matter that needs to be taken care of immediately, Arif,' he said. 'Tell the warriors to use spiritual glamour to conceal their presence here.'

The captain understood that the prince was referring to that subtle, bewitching grip of illusion which masqueraded as reality.

'The Asur must be prevented from sensing our celestial vibrations,' the prince went on. 'I intend, of course, to set up some warding that will camouflage those vibrations, but the troops should, nonetheless, use glamour to do the same and do it right now.'

Captain Leman nodded. 'I should have thought of that myself, Your Highness,' he admitted. 'However, I cannot help thinking that we will need more protection than the kind mere glamour affords to travel to Inkala without hindrance.'

'Don't worry about that, Arif,' Prince A-KarO told him. 'I will use such fine artistry to transform their appearance that our soldiers will, to all intents and purposes, look like the Asur themselves. This of course I will do after they have used their own rough glamour, I will simply refine it. Also, as a precaution, I don't intend sending more than two or three troopers into town initially. Now sometime tonight, I expect Reman Luskar, our contact in Inkala, to reach us. Please inform me of his arrival. But right now, I have work to attend to and do not wish to be disturbed for at least an hour. I repeat, I am not to be disturbed for the next hour.'

The campsite was abuzz with low-key noise and activity. Some of the warriors were in the process of setting up tents, while others attended to their horses. A lean-to shelter had swiftly been erected for the horses under the trees and the cook had set up his tent to the rear of the campsite. Prince A-KarO walked quietly along the camp's perimeter, mouthing wards. Chanting low in his throat, he carefully set up the three mature wards of concealment first. He proceeded, then, to the creation of the next three subtle wards that would transform celestial vibrations into subtle energy. Settling the concealing wards first, he went on to the subtle wards and arranged them into an orderly pyramid. Then he spoke a word of power and fixed the wards in place. A bright ray of light flashed around the campsite and was absorbed into nothingness. Lastly, Prince A-KarO fixed the wards of warning so that if any Asur or demoniac animal presence approached the campsite, he would receive advance warning. Having completed these important tasks, the prince made his way to his tent which had, as usual, been set up in the centre of camp.

He entered the tent and found Tashi waiting up for him with a flagon of wine.

Prince A-KarO looked at him sternly. 'Why are you still up, boy?' he asked. 'Did I not say that you should rest?'

Tashi bowed and replied, 'Your Highness, I will rest soon enough, but I have to see to your needs first.'

'Have you taken your medication?'

'Yes, Your Highness, I have,' Tashi replied. 'Ti Shan saw to that a while back.'

Prince A-KarO nodded and settled down on his meditation seat. 'Now Tashi,' he said, 'I want silence. And you had better rest till dinner.'

Tashi nodded. As he lay down on his pallet, he felt fatigue overtake him. He realized then that his body still needed to heal.

Prince A-KarO allowed his body to assume the diamond posture before letting his mind flow. Slowly, the silence within grew as all thought processes stilled. He let the subtle mantra vibrate in his mind. A picture formed. Then his spirit left his body and flew towards Inkala. Through subtle paths, the prince's spirit form made its way, moving into the shantytown in the outer city where Reman Luskar lived. The prince made his way through the narrow, crowded lanes and entered Luskar's small workshop, moving from the outer room, where he worked as a stonemason and carver, to the small inner chamber, where he kept the tools of his trade. A-KarO was in luck. Luskar was sorting through his tools and looking at designs. The stonemason felt a sudden wind on his shoulder and sensed Prince A-KarO's presence. Immediately, he stilled and his spirit form left his body to rise and meet the prince's, bowing low before the latter.

'Your Highness,' Luskar said, 'I have been expecting you the past few days. I have news for you. But by being here, you endanger yourself. An Asur sorcerer will sense your presence in the city.'

'Fear not, Luskar,' the prince reassured him. 'I am heavily warded now. You know the campsite, the same one I used last time? I expect you there this evening at eight sharp. We will talk at length then. Right now, I must attend to another matter.'

Luskar bowed low and murmured, 'I will be there at the campsite as agreed, Your Highness.'

Prince A-KarO's spirit form drifted away and made its way out. The prince then reduced his spirit presence to the size of a thimble and converted all his celestial energy into its subtle form. Then warding himself powerfully, he made his way to the palace.

Alighting on the palace roof, he drifted in through a window, taking care to note the exact route from the guards' gate to Yeshe's apartments in the North wing. The corridor leading to her rooms was heavily secured and lined with Asur guards. There were twelve guards in all and Prince A-KarO took careful note of their number and their positions.

He knew he could not step into Yeshe's rooms, because the apartment was encased in plethium, but his spirit form sensed her presence and he visualized her sitting in front of the fire, leafing through a book. He was relieved to note that her shield was still intact. He willed her to look at him and, slowly, she raised her head and did so, her gaze direct. She began to rise to her feet, but realized that the maid sent by the Asur to attend on her was watching her. Yeshe settled back with her book, but a small, hopeful smile now played on her lips.

Prince A-KarO realized that it would be dangerous to linger there. He had sensed that the maids were not ordinary creatures, but sorceresses in their own right. His spirit form drifted out of the corridor and away on to the palace roof. From there, it flew towards the camp and returned to his body in the tent.

Prince A-KarO slowly unlocked his stiff limbs and looked around him. Night had fallen and Tashi lay fast asleep on his pallet, the covers thrown off his young body. Smiling, the prince gently covered the boy and sat down in a chair, stretching his legs and pouring himself a much-needed glass of wine.

VII

Sometime in the night, Tashi finally woke up. He was alone in the tent. Stretching his limbs, he got off his pallet and stepped out. The two princes were sitting just outside the tent, deep in conversation.

Ti Shan walked up to Tashi. 'So you are finally up, my friend!' he said. 'You should be feeling better now.'

Tashi nodded. 'I am, indeed, much better, thanks to your care,' he said gratefully.

Suddenly, there was a commotion as a tall, thin Asur stepped into the clearing. Tashi eyed him with fearful curiosity, wondering at his presence. Accompanying him was Captain Leman, who led him straight to the princes. The Asur bowed low from the waist as he was ushered into their presence. Tashi moved forward, eager to hear what was being said.

Ti Shan whispered, 'That Asur is not what he seems, Tashi. Do not be fooled by his appearance. He has used glamour to disguise his true identity. He is Reman Luskar, a celestial spy and our man in Inkala.'

Tashi nodded and looked on in awe.

Prince A-KarO called out to the boy. 'Tashi,' he said, 'Luskar has travelled far today. Go and get a flagon of wine and glasses and inform the cook that he should serve Luskar a meal before he leaves.'

Tashi immediately left to carry out the prince's orders.

Meanwhile, A-KarO had invited Luskar to take a seat next to him. 'So Luskar,' he began, 'what is the news that you bring from the palace?'

Reman Luskar smiled, his dark eyes glinting. 'Your Highness, there is much of import that is happening just now,' he replied. 'My palace sources inform me that the dakini, Yeshe, is in good health and, so far, untouched. She is being held in the North wing of the palace in a specially fortified apartment that is virtually impregnable. There is a two-pronged ring of twelve elite Asur guards around her. There is a change of guard every twelve hours, at dawn and at dusk. The two maids appointed to serve her are Strani sorceresses; nothing escapes their notice and they can be lethal when calling their powers into play. The overall responsibility for ensuring the dakini's defence and well-being continues to lie with Prince Arden.'

'This much, at least, is not news to me,' Prince A-KarO said. 'I had already ascertained this and you have merely confirmed it, Luskar. Now what more do you have for me?'

'Your Highnesses,' Luskar went on, addressing both the princes, 'time is running short for the dakini. Palace sources inform me that the Asur emperor has taken the decision to have her impregnated with Asur seed. The Asur firmly believe that the divine child whose birth has been prophesied must come from a celestial-Asur union. Should such a union be successful, the divine child will become a deliverer for their race and a great Asur conqueror-monarch. This belief is strongly prevalent among the Asur royal family and based on their prophecies.

'According to intelligence I have received, the emperor has nominated Prince Arden to serve as the dakini's Asur mate. They have plans in place for her deflowering. And tomorrow, in a widely publicized gathering at court, the emperor will entrust Prince Arden with the duty of taking the dakini as his consort.'

Prince Narasimha's expression had grown grim. 'The news you bring us is terrible, Luskar,' he said. 'This means we have even less time to act then we had assumed. Yeshe will be under severe stress and we must rescue her at the earliest.'

'Anything else, Luskar?' A-KarO asked in a brusque tone.

Luskar nodded. 'Your Highnesses, from tomorrow onwards, the dakini will be under unbearable pressure. The emperor is keen for the impregnation to take place on the night of the full moon. I need not remind you that it is also the night that her shield will weaken. As the prophesied mother of the divine child, the dakini is a prize for them and they will not let her go easily. This entire issue is a sacred one for them and has long been carefully planned. Now please tell me, Your Highnesses, in what way I can help.'

'I have a plan,' Prince A-KarO said, inclining his head. 'Narasimha is aware of it. We have thought out a stratagem to get the dakini out of the palace. Now I need you to arrange for twelve élite guard uniforms from the palace, along with the a dozen identity papers of the élite palace guard. Prince Narasimha and I will need the uniforms and identity papers of two captains in the élite guard. The plan I have devised is exceedingly simple and therefore easy to implement. It will move fast.'

'What you ask for will not be easy to procure, Your Highness,' Luskar stated, 'but I will manage it. By when do you need all this, Your Highness?'

'The sooner, the better. Say, in three days' time?'

Luskar nodded. 'Your Highness, I will have everything ready for you at the soonest. Anything else?'

'Over the next two days, I will be leading some of our troopers down to the palace to observe and familiarize ourselves with the routine of the guards,' A-KarO replied. 'Their task will be simply to observe. I will need your help to get us into the palace, at least on the first day.'

'That should not be a problem,' Luskar told him. 'On which day do you plan to organize the dakini's rescue, Your Highness?'

Prince A-KarO smiled. 'Don't worry about it. That's for me to decide. Just get us what we need and arrange for our troopers to get into the palace.'

'Everything will be done in conformity with your instructions, Your Highness,' Luskar said with a smile

Prince A-KarO returned his smile. 'Now go and eat your dinner before you leave, Luskar. And take care.'

The spy stood up and bowed low from the waist to both the princes before withdrawing from their presence.

A worried Prince Narasimha looked at A-KarO. 'Things are going to get rough for Yeshe, A-KarO,' he said urgently. 'We must move fast.'

'I am keeping three to four days in hand for observation and preliminary preparations,' A-KarO told him. 'On Sunday, when the full moon is to rise, we will move in for the rescue. In other words, I hope to get Yeshe out of the Asur's clutches in precisely one week.'

Prince Narasimha nodded. 'I suppose we could not have managed it any sooner,' he said.

Prince A-KarO stretched out his legs and sighed. The night skies were dim and overcast. Fog had rolled down into the camp, obscuring the view and trails of it floated here and there. A pair of Lha troopers walked up smartly, bearing dinner for the princes on loaded trays. They laid out a crisp white tablecloth, carafes of wine, vegetable stew, steamed fish wrapped in leaves, flatbread and bowls of fruit. As Prince A-KarO served himself, he felt the familiar excitement coursing through his veins – the excitement of the hunt.

CHAPTER 14

DESIRE

I

Yeshe awoke to the sound of a lone bird crying plaintively in the courtyard outside. She saw it was morning. Furtively, she looked around her. She was alone. The fire burned low in the grate and the cold was bone-chilling. She threw off the covers and got out of bed, noticing that her clothes had already been ironed and laid out for her. Not wanting to attract the attention of the two maids in the adjoining room, she tread as lightly as she could. The marble floor beneath her bare feet was cold and absorbed the sound of her footsteps. It had been almost a week since Prince Arden had confined her to her room. Yeshe took deep, calming breaths as she prepared to complete her ablutions. She approached the two buckets of water that had been left for her use and dipped her hand into them. She sighed with relief; the water was ice-cold and refreshing.

Yeshe stepped out of her clothes and, holding her breath, slowly poured a pitcher of water over herself, chanting the age-old hymn meant for the cleansing ritual. The shock of the freezing-cold water made her shiver, but she continued to chant in her lilting voice, as the original hymn gave way to others invoking the sun, the Goddess Tara and the Lord Buddha. As soon as she had finished her bath, she drew on her clothes; first, the black silk tunic and black woollen overshirt, followed by the long grey woollen skirt that went with them.

Stepping swiftly out of the bathing chamber, the dakini sat down on a chair and began brushing the tangles out of her long hair, smoothing it down to her satisfaction before twisting it up in a knot and fixing it with pins at the back of her head. The moment she was dressed and ready, a surge of panic swept through her; it was the second-last day before the full moon. From that very night, her shield would begin to weaken steadily and, two days hence, would have disappeared completely, leaving her at the mercy of any and every Asur in Inka.

Taking deep, calming breaths once more, Yeshe tried to contain her panic. Perhaps, she reassured herself, nobody would trouble her. After all, Prince Arden had not visited her even once in the past week. She had been fortunate. But she doubted that her run of luck would hold forever. At that moment, Aao, the older of her maids, entered the room. An Asur Strani sorceress like her twin who had also been assigned to guard Yeshe, Aao was seven feet tall, with swarthy skin, cruel grey eyes and straight black hair that fell down her back in a shower. Her younger sister, Dei, was identical in appearance, except for her uniquely mismatched eyes – one grey, the other green – which gave her a strange, feline look.

Staring at Yeshe, Aao remarked, 'I see you are up, Dakini. I have brought you your breakfast and you are to eat it without a fuss.'

Yeshe frowned 'You know well enough that I do not partake of the meals you bring me,' she said coldly. 'Why, then, do you insist?'

The second sorceress, Dei, now entered the room. 'This meal has been especially prepared for you on Prince Arden's orders,' she announced. 'It contains neither meat nor spices. You will eat it, Dakini, or else, I will force it down your throat.'

Eying the flatbread and vegetables Aao had placed before her, Yeshe sighed. 'I cannot,' she began, but Dei took a step towards her and the dakini felt assailed by a wave of foul sorcery that rose around her. She felt the sorceress's anger like a force assaulting her. Yeshe shook her head violently, trying to rid herself of the foul wave threatening to choke her, but could not prevent it from ramming itself down her throat and creating a stench in her body. She gasped and retched, panic rising within her as the foulness continued to consume her.

'This foulness will contaminate you more surely than any food from the palace kitchen,' said Dei, her green eye burning a bright emerald in the light. 'Give in, Yeshe. Else, I will keep this foulness coming at you in full force. Perhaps your shield will then collapse even before the full moon, which is no more than a day away.'

Yeshe threw up on the floor, then raised her hand. The flow of foulness ended. She took a deep breath. Slowly pulling herself upright on weak legs, Yeshe swayed and dropped into a chair.

Dei threw a cleaning rag at her. 'Now clean up this mess you have made and then eat!' she ordered.

Yeshe fell to her knees immediately and began mopping up her vomit. After cleaning the mess, she washed and sat down before the food she had been served. Offering up a whispered prayer over the meal, she began eating slowly. With each bite she took, she felt her strength drain away. Warily, she tested the shield as she ate. It still held, but from tonight, it would begin to weaken.

Yeshe had barely finished her meal and swallowed a mouthful of cold water to wash it down when Dei said in a satisfied voice, 'You should know that this is the first time vegetarian food has been prepared here in the palace. If the prince shows you his favour, it is only fair that you respond to it in the appropriate manner. Now you may follow me out for your morning walk.'

Yeshe got up at once and followed the sorceress out into the little high-walled courtyard that adjoined her apartment. In her hurry to be outdoors, she had stepped out without her shawl, but she barely noticed it as she wandered around the small courtyard, soaking in the sunshine, despite its lack of warmth, and treading carefully on the slippery carpet of frozen snow. Yeshe smiled, feeling the fresh, cold wind on her face, and walked to the little fountain that stood in the centre of the courtyard. There was some snow melt at its base, but the fountain itself was frozen solid. Yeshe picked her way with care to the single bare-branched fir tree that stood in the corner. A little black bird with a plaintive cry had made its nest there. The dakini smiled as she held her hand over the bird's nest and let a wave of pure divine energy flow into the eggs. Then she carefully touched the tree trunk and sent a tingling flow of energy into the living tree it had once been. It had been her daily mission, from the time she arrived in the palace in Inkala, to try and bring the fir tree back to life. Finally, she walked to the well that stood in one corner of the courtyard and let pure divine energy flow into its depths. She sang a hymn to purify the waters before wandering away.

The sorceress, Aao, now approached Yeshe to say, 'Dakini, I have some news for you. This evening, Prince Arden will come to fetch you for your audience with Emperor Nisarn Jebrail Ti Nazer Basher. The prince will be here at your apartment promptly at five. I have laid out a robe and garments for you to wear for the meeting. You are to be dressed and ready by five. Under no circumstances must you delay.'

Yeshe's heart sank. 'I shall be ready,' she said.

'If you know what is good for you, you will behave,' the sorceress smirked. 'The emperor does not tolerate insubordination. So do not even try it, Dakini. This meeting will determine your future with the Asur. Now come back inside and sit in the parlour.'

Yeshe reluctantly made her way back inside and sank down on a couch. With the sorceress having relit the fire, the room was warmer, but still the dakini shivered, staring into the flames as she retreated into herself to search for Prince A-KarO. She was overcome by frustration when she realized that even in her spirit form, she could not break out of this room which was lined with wards of sorcery.

Yeshe sat back to ponder over her plight. Although she might not be able to communicate with him, she would make an attempt tonight to see through the flames and find out how Prince A-KarO was placed. Tonight, when the moon rode high, she would try and discover the situation in which the celestials now found themselves. Strengthened by her new resolve, Yeshe felt fresh energy and hope surge through her.

II

The shadows of evening were creeping across the snowbound courtyard and the evening skies were heavily overcast, when Yeshe smoothed down her black skirt and took one last look at herself in the mirror. She was ready for her meeting with the Asur emperor.

The sorceresses, Aao and Dei, her two watchdogs, eyed her critically.

'Your appearance is fine, Dakini,' one of them remarked. 'Now mind your manners when you walk into the emperor's presence. You must go down on your knees, bow low before him and hold that position, until he gives you permission to rise. This is standard court etiquette for all captives. You must show respect for him by demonstrating your unreserved subservience to his authority. Do you understand me?'

Yeshe remained silent, her mind calm, as she practised *tummo* breathing and felt heat flood her body.

Incensed, the sorceress pinched her face. 'Don't try to ignore me, Dakini! I asked if you understood me,' she said sharply. 'And look at me when I speak to you.'

Yeshe turned to look at Aao and raised one brow. 'I am listening to you,' she stated calmly.

The sorceress frowned. 'If you want to survive here, Dakini,' she said threateningly, 'I suggest you pay close attention to my words. I was speaking about your audience with the emperor. Once he has given you permission to rise, do so, but remember to keep your head bowed at all times and never to meet his eyes. Do not speak unless spoken to and under no circumstances must there be even a hint of defiance in your manner. Once he grants you permission to withdraw from his presence, you must again bow deeply before him.'

Yeshe felt waves of *tummo* heat flowing within her. Her sense of calm awareness grew stronger and she offered silent prayers to the Buddha and Goddess Tara and glanced at the sorceress who continued to lecture her on seemly conduct in the emperor's presence.

Aao pinched the dakini again, this time on her wrist. 'Pay attention, Dakini!' she persisted. 'I cannot overemphasize the importance of this meeting for you. It is most likely to be the occasion on which the emperor decides on your future. Now take care to follow my instructions and don't bring shame on me.'

There was a commotion at the door and the sorceress, Dei, rushed to open it. Prince Arden walked in.

His step agile, the prince smiled as he approached Yeshe and bowed low before her. 'Dakini, we meet again!' he declared. 'I trust you have been comfortable here.'

'As comfortable as circumstances permit, Prince Arden,' she replied.

The red in Arden's dark eyes swirled. 'We had better be on our way, Dakini,' he said. 'We cannot afford to delay.'

Yeshe fell into step beside him as they left the room and made their way down the corridor. She sighed from sheer relief at having got an opportunity to leave the confines of her room.

Arden glanced at Yeshe, a half-smile playing on his lips. 'So did you, perhaps, miss me, Dakini?' he murmured.

Yeshe snorted. 'I will not dignify that question with an answer, Prince.'

'So how do you like Inka, Dakini?' he asked.

Yeshe sighed, walking swiftly to match his pace. 'What have I seen of it so far, Prince, locked as I am like a pigeon in a cage, with two sorceresses to guard me?' she asked in turn.

Arden smiled. 'Once you settle in and accept your life here, I will take you around the city,' he promised, his intense eyes boring into hers.

Yeshe felt a strange warmth growing within her, like sunlight on grass.

Arden inclined his head and asked, 'I trust you are being looked after well?'

'I am fine,' Yeshe replied, 'but what was the need to assign sorceresses to keep watch over me?'

Arden smiled slyly. 'Well, you are special, Dakini, and a guard of sorceresses was the least I could arrange for you,' he replied.

Yeshe changed the subject and said graciously, 'I would like to thank you for having vegetables served to me, Prince. They must be rare in Inka.'

'So you noticed,' he smiled. 'You know you are my honoured guest and that is the least I can do for you.'

'Not your guest, Prince,' she corrected him, 'your captive.'

Yeshe looked around her curiously as they moved down the black granite polished corridor that ran twisting and turning through the heart of the palace and opened into a vast stark white hall with tall pillars, a vaulted ceiling and a marble floor so finely polished that it looked like a mirror. Asur courtiers dressed in furs and silken garments walked around or stood talking in groups, but when Yeshe passed them, conversation ceased and all eyes turned to her.

Prince Arden said to Yeshe, 'This is the formal throne room, but it is not our destination. We are expected in the emperor's personal audience chamber which is nearby.'

At the end of the hall was a huge throne placed on a dais. Made of iron, it was decorated with gold and a polar bear's pure white fur was thrown across it. Prince Arden strode swiftly through the hall, nodding to courtiers, and passed through yet another corridor which opened into a small white chamber with five arched doorways. A brass and glass lantern hung from the middle of the ceiling.

Arden opened the door to the right and whispered in Yeshe's ear, sending shards of warmth dancing down her veins, 'Be careful, Dakini. We are now about to enter the presence of His Majesty Emperor Nisarn Jebrail Ti Nazer Basher.'

Yeshe entered the room with the prince behind her and noticed the three people seated there. To the left was a rather rotund Asur in fine silks and a golden fur cloak. Golden horns sprouted from his russet brown hair. Seated in the middle was an old Asur male with a rather lean build, amber eyes and silken white hair that fell to his shoulders. He wore a robe of plain, very fine white wool over a black woollen tunic and matching pants. A pristine white cloak made from the fur of a polar bear was draped around his shoulders. On his head sat a circlet of gold encrusted with a huge black diamond. This was the Emperor Nisarn Jebrail Ti Nazer Basher. Yeshe was quick to observe that though his complexion was a ruddy brown, he, like Arden, had no horns, but a head shaped like a celestial's.

To the emperor's right sat an ancient-looking Asur with a reed-thin body and pointed black horns. His bloodshot eyes glowed in his dark, heavily wrinkled face. He wore a heavy gold chain over his rich brown velvet robe and his hands rested on a polished black staff with a huge diamond glinting on it.

Prince Arden bowed low before the emperor and whispered to Yeshe, who stood a few paces behind, 'Don't just stand there, Dakini! Bow!'

Yeshe walked into the room until she was next to the prince. She stood erect, her stance defiant, locking her gaze with the emperor's.

Arden chuckled quietly as he noticed her defiance. 'Unbowed, I see,' he observed under his breath. 'He won't like that, though.'

Yeshe glared at him. 'Is that the emperor in the centre?' she asked.

Arden whispered, 'Yes, that is, indeed, the emperor. To his right is the Perfecti, the highest authority among the sorcerers, and to the left is the first counsellor to the emperor.'

Utter silence reigned in the room. Then the emperor waved his hand and commanded, 'Step closer, Arden, and bring your captive forward.' He studied Yeshe intently before saying, 'So this is Dakini Yeshe Nam Lha, the prophesied mother of the divine child. Hear this, Dakini! The child you bear will be part Asur and the conqueror we have long awaited.'

Yeshe threw back her head and laughed disdainfully. She looked the emperor boldly in the eye and retorted, 'You speak too soon, Emperor. There is a chasm between what you hope and what will be.'

Enraged, the emperor held up his hand. 'Silence, Dakini!' he commanded sternly. 'Do not dare to question the power of my will. I do not tolerate insolence from my captives. Arden, after she leaves my presence, the dakini is to be whipped in the public hall. Fifteen lashes precisely. Next time she is brought into my presence, she will know how to comport herself.' The Emperor Nisarn frowned as he looked at Yeshe. 'Dakini, the only reason we have allowed you to live is this child you are prophesied to bear,' he told her. 'We, too, have similar prophecies in our writings. It is mentioned there that if the fated mother of the divine child gives birth in Inka and he is part Asur, he will be a boon for the Asur race and conquer the lands of the gods; and the worlds of men and all races will be subservient to his power. It is my wish that this child be born here in Inka and you would do well to reconcile yourself to your destiny. If you give me this child, Dakini, I promise to raise you to the status of Prince Arden's royal consort.'

Yeshe opened her mouth to protest, but the emperor held up his hand again. 'Listen, Dakini, and you too, Arden,' he went on, 'what I say now concerns you both. Arden, my son, I am giving you this dakini as your concubine. Now that the full moon approaches, take her in hand and break her in to her new destiny. The next time she is brought into my presence, I expect a change in her behaviour. Else, it will reflect on you, Arden.'

Prince Arden smiled. 'I am honoured by this duty you entrust me with, Sire,' he declared.

The emperor inclined his head and said, 'Consider the dakini a reward for your long service in the borderlands, Arden. But as the year ends, I expect her to give birth to the prophesied child. He must be ours, the perfect melding of the celestial and the Asur. He must be mine to shape and I will harness his great power for furthering our cause. He will be our future, the long-awaited one, the conqueror-king, the vanquisher of the celestial lands. Now, son, she is to stay within the confines of the palace for the next few years until she gives birth.' The emperor looked at Yeshe. 'Dakini, your future is in your hands,' he said. 'Bend your will to what is fated and accept it without reserve. Then everything will be yours. Defy it and you will face my wrath.'

Yeshe felt the terrible force of the emperor's will bearing down on her, but stood up to it bravely. 'Emperor of the Asur,' she said coolly, 'hear me! My son, who is long prophesied as a great saviour of the universe, will be no conqueror. He will be the child of immense purity, the hope of the universe, the fated messiah of the dark age, the fourth age and in that role will he bring blessings to all races, including your own. But mark my words, Emperor! He will be born only if the purity of his conception, as ordained by the universe, is attained. If that purity is tainted and the universal law betrayed, this sacred conception will fail, the birth will not take place and a great opportunity will be lost. Do not give me to Prince Arden, Emperor. Release me. Release me to fulfil the destiny for which I was born.'

The Emperor Nisarn roared with displeasure. 'Silence, woman! You know not what you say. Your destiny is with us, with the Asur. Reconcile yourself to it.' He turned to the prince. 'Arden,' he said, 'she is too defiant and free-spirited for her own good. Ensure that she is whipped tonight. Her spirit must be broken until it bends to my will. I give you one week to work on her, after which we will have another meeting. If I am not satisfied with her conduct then, it will be the dark room for her. Also, tonight is the full moon. This night is auspicious for our people to tame her and make her surrender to our will, my son. I want her with child before the month is over.'

As he finished speaking, the Wizard Perfecti rose from his chair and approached Yeshe. He examined her and turned to the emperor. 'She has great power, Your Majesty,' he declared, 'but it is all white power and benign. In other words, it is useless, as far as her own security goes, but it can be a boon for those around her.' He passed his hand over Yeshe's womb and said, 'She is healthy and will breed. There should be no problem in that respect.'

Yeshe concentrated on maintaining *tummo* heat and remaining calm within. She would not allow the sorcerer's words to affect her.

The emperor now turned to Prince Arden. 'Guard her well,' he commanded. 'Her security is yours to see to. I intend to have a word with you later, but for now, you may withdraw.'

Prince Arden bowed low to the emperor, but Yeshe simply turned on her heels and strode out of the room. Once outside the audience chamber, she felt as if life were returning to her body.

III

As Yeshe made her way back to her apartment, Arden matched her stride so that he was walking alongside.

'Now look what you have ended up doing, Dakini,' he chided her. 'You have provoked the emperor's displeasure and earned yourself fifteen strokes of the lash. Would it have been so very difficult for you to bow to him and remain silent? Did the sorceress not brief you at all before your audience with him?'

'Don't blame the sorceress, Prince,' Yeshe replied. 'She did all she could to make me comply with your court etiquette. But I am adamant about not submitting to your emperor's dictates. He does not know what damage he does by insisting on carrying out his plan. For that matter, neither do you.'

The prince sighed. 'You will not listen to reason, Dakini,' he said regretfully. 'Somehow, I knew you would be difficult. And now you must bear the consequences of your obstinacy and endure the punishment the emperor has decided on for you.'

'Let me go before it is too late, Prince,' Yeshe advised.

He took her hand and kissed it. 'Yeshe,' he murmured, 'you are my treasure and mine alone to hold, not to release.'

Outside, the moon had risen and dark night was visible from the windows of the hallways they passed. Yeshe disengaged her fingers from Arden's grip. The shield, she realized, was weakening faster then she had anticipated.

'Yeshe,' Arden began, concern in his voice, 'you do realize, do you not, that with the full moon set to appear tomorrow evening, your shield has already weakened considerably? Without its protection, the lashes of the whip will hurt. I cannot do anything to countermand the emperor's orders, but I will tend to your wounds myself, after it is over.'

Yeshe felt nervous tension building within her as Arden led her through the many corridors and halls towards a section of the palace she had never seen before. She was led into a huge hall lit up by torches. Its walls were made of grey stone slabs and the floor was grey marble. Apart from the odd noble Asur courtier, the hall was packed mostly with people who looked to be commoners. Asur soldiers patrolled the place or stood around in groups.

Arden led Yeshe up to the captain of the guard seated behind a wooden desk in one corner. The captain sprang to his feet at the prince's appearance.

'Captain,' Arden began, 'I bring you a royal command that is to be obeyed without delay. This is the dakini, Yeshe Nam Lha. By order of the emperor, she is to be administered fifteen lashes.'

The captain stood at attention, saluted the prince and replied crisply, 'It will be done immediately, Your Highness. I shall get Tora Bilak to attend to it right away. Is this order to be carried out in the public hall?'

Arden nodded. 'Get it seen to right now,' he commanded.

The prince seated himself, while the captain moved away to make arrangements for the public flogging before returning to join Arden. Yeshe found herself standing alone. She took a deep breath and concentrated on building *tummo*, feeling the waves of heat energy spreading from her navel and her calm returning.

Tora Bilak, a huge Asur with rippling muscles, entered the hall. His dark hair was tied back with a thong. As he approached her, Yeshe had a sudden vision of Prince A-KarO. She held on to the image as Tora secured her hands tightly with a rope and led her to a post located in the centre of the room. He removed Yeshe's overcoat and flung it aside before tying her to the post. The dakini was left standing there in her thin black silk tunic. She focused on raised breathing and let her mind slip into a trance-like state. Tora now returned with a long, coarse leather whip, which he slowly raised and brought down viciously on Yeshe's back. A burning pain flooded her body, but she continued to focus on *tummo* and let her mind drift. She watched Prince A-KarO 's visage come ever closer and focused on it. The whip fell repeatedly, ripping her back each time, but Yeshe's mind drifted in a *tummo* haze, gazing at the rolling pastoral fields, golden with corn, in Shambala, the waves of the silver ocean crashing on the beach and the cherry blossoms surrounding her home. On and on they came, the beautiful, comforting images of home.

Yeshe's eyes strayed to the window. The moon glowed brightly. A sudden rush of cold air snapped her out of her trance-like state. The tenth whiplash struck her back and the pain was almost unbearable. Yeshe stiffened, but would not allow a whimper to escape her lips. She gritted her teeth and focused again on A-KarO's image which seemed, somehow, to lend her strength. The whip continued to rise and fall, leaving a searing trail of pain across her back. As the last of the lashes fell, Yeshe collapsed and slumped to the ground, unable to summon the strength to rise.

Prince Arden now approached and, with gentle fingers, brushed her hair off her face. Then he lifted her up in his arms and, nodding to the captain, carried Yeshe out of the hall. The dakini felt people staring at her as the prince carried her out of the room.

'So, Prince,' she murmured, 'now that I have been suitably punished, are you satisfied?'

'Yeshe,' Arden sighed, 'I cannot warn you enough about the need to be circumspect in your behaviour at the palace. The emperor will have you watched constantly and will arrange for regular reports on your conduct to be delivered to him. Please ensure that you do not incur his wrath, for he can be utterly ruthless in dealing with insubordination. And in that eventuality, I will be powerless to help you.'

Yeshe slumped back in his arms and a shiver went through her body that was now racked with pain. Her back seemed to be on fire. In her misery, she scarcely noticed that they had reached her apartment.

The two sorceresses hovered around her, curious about her condition.

'What has happened, Your Highness?' Aao enquired. 'Did the dakini invite the emperor's displeasure?'

Arden laid Yeshe on the bed, face down, and cut open her silk tunic. Her back was criss-crossed with whiplashes.

'She was administered fifteen lashes, sorceress,' he answered quietly. 'Now I must tend to her wounds. Bring me some salve to apply on them.'

Aao moved away to a wall cabinet from which she brought out a dark bottle and handed it to the prince. Arden first cleaned Yeshe's back by gently dabbing it with a damp towel. Then he dipped his finger in the murky ointment and applied it carefully to her wounds, massaging it in with infinite care till it had been absorbed into her skin. Yeshe felt golden warmth dripping into her skin and she forgot the pain and sheer pleasure seeped into her wherever he touched. It felt almost as though sunlight was falling into her skin. Yeshe groaned low in her throat.

Arden laughed, continuing to massage the ointment into her back. 'Ah!' he exclaimed, 'so you feel something other than pain, do you, Yeshe? Never fear, I will return tomorrow morning to check the condition of your back and apply the ointment again.'

As he continued massaging the ointment into her back, Yeshe cursed the prince silently, realizing that he had worked a powerful spell on her that seemed to be steadily tightening its grip.

'You can now lie on your back and rest, Dakini,' Arden advised her. 'Within a few days, you should be all right.' He turned to Aao. 'Now sorceress,' he said, 'get the dakini her dinner. Make sure it is prepared in accordance with my instructions and see that she eats it. After she has partaken of her meal, leave her in peace and see to it that she is not disturbed.'

With that, Arden got to his feet. Taking a last look at Yeshe, he left the room.

The dakini watched as the sorceress brought in her dinner on a tray. It was a small feast. There was saffron rice and potatoes in gravy, lentil stew and salad, as well as a bowl of sweetened yogurt. Yeshe sat up in bed and crossed her legs. She stifled a yawn as she sat down to eat. Despite the pain, she felt hungry. She took a bite of the food. It was delicious, but had a weakening effect on her. She ate quickly, musing that somewhere outside, Prince A-KarO and the celestials waited to rescue her. Yeshe sighed as hope surged through her. She vowed she would seek the Lha prince through the flames that very night.

IV

Midnight came and went as Yeshe waited for all activity at the palace to cease. Without making a sound, she got out of bed and took a furtive peek into the darkened parlour. The fire burned low and the two sorceresses appeared to be fast asleep, with Aao snoring softly. Yeshe looked at them in wonder, for her two jailers always slept with an ear cocked for any suspicious sound from her bedroom and looked in on her all through the night. Just to be sure, Yeshe checked their state in the etheric plane; they were, indeed, in deep slumber, as if under a spell. But if that was so, the spell was too subtle for the dakini to detect.

It was at this point that a strange feeling came over Yeshe; someone was out there in her courtyard, a tall, subtle form, a shadow against the shadows. The dakini sensed the white light pouring from it, the light of a Ningma warrior. Prince A-KarO had come.

Yeshe sensed the moment he became aware of her focus on him. He signalled for her to step out. She looked into the darkened parlour once more. Her guard was fast asleep. Excitement coursed through her as she made her way to the small doorway that led out into the courtyard and stepped through it. Immediately, she felt Prince A-KarO's hand on her arm. He drew her into the shadows, put a finger on her lips and hugged her. Yeshe felt tears of relief well up in her eyes.

A-KarO, however, was alert to the dangers around them. He gestured for silence and slowly began to chant under his breath. Then he whispered, 'Now we can talk. I have erected wards against anyone who might eavesdrop on us or become aware of our presence here.'

Yeshe nodded in silence, unable to believe her eyes and ears.

'I felt you focussing on me desperately this evening, Yeshe,' the prince told her. 'You were calling out to me. I am quite surprised that the Asur sorcerers failed to pick up the vibrations. What happened to you? Are you all right?'

'I am fine, A-KarO,' Yeshe smiled. 'Now that you have come, I am fine. Just take me away from here, I beg of you! '

'You do not sound fine to me,' the prince observed. 'Tell me, Yeshe, what happened to you? Did someone touch you? Were you … ?'

Yeshe shook her head. 'No, nothing like that,' she assured him. 'I have not been violated, though it surprises me that I am still untouched in that respect. However, I was whipped under the emperor's orders.'

A-KarO's expression froze and his fingers curled into a fist. 'By the gods, they will pay for this!' he said through clenched teeth. 'I will know no rest till their blood has answered for this grievous wrong!'

Yeshe put her fingers to his lips. 'Don't take such an oath, A-KarO!' she implored. 'Promise me that you won't bring blood and revenge into this.'

'You ask the impossible, Dakini,' the prince sighed. 'Your abduction by the Asur will trigger another great war and there will be no peace for ages to come.'

'Have you then come to take me away?' she asked. 'Is it to be done now?'

A-KarO shook his head. 'Not tonight. I merely came to apprise myself of your situation. Tomorrow, after midnight, we will be here. Remember the hoot of a white owl. It is the signal marking the commencement of your rescue. Everything is in place. May the universe be with us.'

'You cannot imagine how hopeful that makes me, A-KarO,' Yeshe told him. 'I will wait for you.'

The prince looked at her. 'To whom has the emperor promised you, Yeshe?' he asked.

She took a deep breath and expelled it in a sigh. 'Arden.'

A-KarO looked at her strangely. 'Then he is marked,' he said. 'As of this moment, he is one of the walking dead.'

On hearing him utter those words, Yeshe felt a strange pang and crushed it immediately.

The prince took her in his arms and kissed her lightly on the cheek. 'For luck, Dakini,' he murmured. 'Now go back to your apartment. The sleep spell I had cast on your keepers and your guard will soon dissipate and suspicions will arise about what had come over them. You will need to handle that in the morning. Now I will watch you go back in before I leave.'

Yeshe smiled as she looked at A-KarO. 'Till the charmed owl hoots,' she said.

A-KarO laughed. 'Till his mistress calls,' he added.

Filled with hope, an effervescent Yeshe walked to the door and looked back. A-KarO had disappeared, a shadow against the wall. The night had grown old and dawn would come soon. Yeshe entered her apartment and threw herself on the bed. 'At last, a contact!' she told herself. She sent up a silent prayer to the Buddha, the Goddess Tara and the guardian deities, entreating them to protect A-KarO and his celestial band of rescuers. Then sleep overtook her and, still smiling, she surrendered to it. Outside, the skies had greyed. Soon, the pink blush of dawn crept over the snowbound horizon. A fresh wind rose in the north, danced through Inka and ruffled Yeshe's hair as she slept. The name of that wind was hope.

In the adjoining room, the two sorceresses stirred. Wearing identical expressions of bewilderment, they sat up, having been roused from their magic-induced sleep. Suddenly, panic struck. With one fear driving them, they raced into Yeshe's room and sighed with relief when they found her fast asleep.

Aao turned to Dei. 'Sister, when did you last see me sleep like that?' she asked.

Dei thought for a moment. 'Never,' she answered.

'This slumber was not natural, not ordinary,' the older sorceress mused. 'Something strange happened to us. Should we report it to His Highness Prince Arden?'

'Have you lost what little wit you possessed?' Dei snapped. 'If we report it, it will be our heads on the block. No, we will ask the dakini about it. Let the celestial wake up. Then we shall see.'

'You're right,' Aao agreed. 'We shall question her and intensify our vigilance.'

The twins then explored the two rooms, trying to sense the telltale traces of alien magic, but failed to detect even a lingering essence of it. Finally, they stepped into the courtyard. Aao raised her head, her nose to the air, and circumscribed a circle, but could sense nothing at all. Neither could Dei. Confused and feeling sheepish, they finally walked back in.

'Perhaps it was nothing,' Aao mused, 'just sleep catching up on us.'

'Don't be a fool!' Dei said sharply. 'Just because we failed to sense it does not mean that something didn't happen.'

Aao nodded. 'You could be right. It's odd that we should both fall so deeply asleep at the same time. The chances of that happening are nil.'

'Go and draw the dakini's bath and lay out her clothes,' Dei instructed her twin. 'His Highness Prince Arden will visit her soon after breakfast. He will want to examine the condition of her back.'

'That one!' Aao said resentfully. 'She can twist the prince around her little finger, but she thinks nothing of him. We are no more than dirt for her. These celestials!'

V

Yeshe woke up smiling. She lay in bed for a moment, remembering the events of the previous night, and was filled with a pleasant sense of anticipation. Slowly, she roused herself, got out of bed and went into the bathing chamber. The two sorceresses glared at her; they seemed unusually hostile this morning. Yeshe hummed as she settled down to her bath. She played with the especially heated water for some time, praying over it and slowly feeling it slither down her back. She stretched with relief as the heat relaxed her stiff, aching muscles. Finishing her bath, she wrapped herself in a dry sheet and stepped out of the room. The sorceress, Aao, helped her into a sage-green tunic and a flared skirt of heavy wool in a dark shade of forest green that fell straight to her ankles. Then she handed Yeshe a fine woollen over-tunic of sage green. After the dakini was dressed, she brushed her dark hair and tied it back in a ponytail with a green silk ribbon.

Yeshe had barely finished, when Aao served her breakfast. It consisted of warm flatbread, two kinds of pickles, butter, fruits and a glass of warm milk. The dakini savoured the warmth of the saffron-flavoured milk and sat down to the rest of her repast.

Dei glared at her and remarked, 'Despite your injured back, you appear to be in a very good mood this morning, Dakini. Perhaps something special happened last night, hmm? Surely your high spirits have nothing to do with Prince Arden's anticipated visit?'

Yeshe stiffened. 'What are you trying to imply, Dei?' she asked.

A half-smile lit up the sorceress's face, but it did not reach her eyes. 'This is the first morning since your arrival that I have heard you humming and actually singing,' she said. 'We are not fools, Dakini. What have you been up to?'

Yeshe looked at Dei innocently. 'What do you mean, sorceress?' she enquired.

Dei narrowed her eyes. 'Tell us what happened last night,' she persisted.

Yeshe felt bands of pressure around her head, as though someone were squeezing it. 'What could possibly happen, Dei?' she asked. 'I really don't know what you are talking about.'

Dei snorted, her scepticism obvious. 'My sister and I both fell fast asleep last night. This has never happened to us before. In fact, we hardly ever sleep. So something out of the ordinary must have happened. What was it, Dakini? What have you been up to? Tell us or else this pressure around your head will only get worse.'

The pressure now bore down on Yeshe's head, until she could hardly endure it and tears of pain welled out of her eyes. At that very moment,

Prince Arden entered the room. Confusion registered on his face for an instant until he realized what was happening. Then he gave vent to his rage.

'Sorceress!' he thundered, 'how dare you torture the dakini!'

Aao and Dei immediately fell to their knees. 'Your Highness, please forgive us!' they begged. 'The dakini was being uncooperative and mutinous.'

The prince could barely contain his fury. 'Leave immediately!' he commanded. 'You are dismissed! Report to the captain of the guard. Tell him that I have ordered twenty lashes each for the two of you. When your punishment has been meted out, you will both return to the Strani quarter and be reassigned to other duties.'

The twins scurried out of the room to do his bidding.

Arden turned to Yeshe. 'Have they troubled you a great deal, Dakini?' he enquired. 'This is inexcusable! New maids will be assigned to you immediately.'

'It is a trifle, Prince Arden,' Yeshe said with a smile, 'please spare them punishment.'

Arden took her hands in his own. 'My dear,' he said, 'as it is, they are getting off lightly. But don't worry. Their replacements will come soon. Now how is your back? Do the muscles feel stiff?'

'It is better,' Yeshe replied, 'but yes, it is stiff and it hurts. But don't worry, Prince Arden, it is not so unbearable that I cannot tolerate it.'

The prince brought out a bottle of shining oil from his side pocket. 'Turn your back to me and relax, Yeshe,' he advised. 'I have procured some clean oil for your wounds from my sorcerer. It works miracles with bruises and will take away both the pain and the swelling.'

Sighing, Yeshe turned her back to him. 'I did not expect the Asur to be so considerate,' she remarked.

Arden laughed. 'We are a race like any other,' he told her. 'Of course we are demoniac and driven by strong passions. We are capable of cruelty. But we can also love and care for others and be stirred by deep emotions.'

Yeshe felt self-conscious and bashful as Arden lifted the back of her tunic and spread the shining oil on her bruises. The touch of his fingers unleashed feelings of ecstasy within her. Wherever his hand came in contact with her skin, she felt warmth pouring into her and she sighed with pleasure.

Arden chuckled as he continued massaging the oil. 'You do realize what is happening, don't you, Yeshe?' he said. 'This is no thrall. You are simply bonding with me. An Asur truly bonds only once in his life and you are he one with whom I am doing so.'

Yeshe recoiled from his touch, her mind fighting the intensifying pleasure in her body. 'What you talk of, Prince, cannot be,' she said firmly. 'So do not mention the subject to me ever again.'

Arden laughed softly, the sound of his mirth spreading through the room and the dakini found herself strangely drawn to his laughter.

As the prince continued to massage her back, Yeshe declared, 'You are wicked, Arden! This is simply your thrall working. Withdraw it and see what happens. Or do you not have the guts to do that?'

Arden laughed harder. 'The thrall you mention is a part of me, Yeshe,' he told her, 'and it affects you. I cannot help that, can I?'

Incensed, Yeshe tossed her head back and retorted, 'Not a moment ago, you said there was no thrall, Arden. And now you contradict yourself and say it is there. Liar!'

'What did you expect, Dakini?' the prince countered. 'I am Asur, a demon, and you expect me to speak the truth? Then you are more naïve than I imagined.'

Yeshe shook her head, trying to make sense of the magic his fingers were working. 'Stop toying with me, Arden!' she snapped. 'You are utterly despicable!'

Arden wiped the excess oil off with a cloth, then rolled down her tunic so that her back was covered again.

'Now is there anything else I can do, Dakini,' he asked, 'to be back in favour again?'

There was a hint of calculation in her eyes as Yeshe answered with a smile, 'Actually, there *is* something.'

Arden smiled. Taking Yeshe's hands in his own, he turned them and kissed the palms. 'Name it, Yeshe,' he said softly.

'Since I came here,' she said, 'I have seen nothing of Inkala. Take me for a ride into town, Arden.'

'Now that's a bit risky, is it not?' he said.

'Please, Arden, please!' she cajoled with a smile.

Arden gazed at her and then nodded. 'All right,' he agreed. 'Put on your cloak and boots. And ensure that you are veiled. Be quick about it and then follow me. I do not have all morning to wait on you.'

Yeshe clapped her hands in delight. 'Right away, Arden!' she said, rushing to her cupboard to pull out her fur boots and a cloak. Then rummaging around on the shelves, she spotted a pure white transparent veil, which she pulled out.

Soon, dressed and appropriately veiled, she was following the prince out of the room. The two disappeared down the dark corridors.

VI

The skies were overcast when Yeshe stepped out of the palace. A brisk, cold wind blew and she hugged her cloak for warmth, but her spirits were high. Nothing could dim her joy today. Tonight, she would be rescued and be forever free of the Asur.

There was a grin on Prince Arden's face as he walked along beside her. He signalled to a soldier who came running and bowed deeply to him.

'Have my chariot brought here immediately,' he ordered.

'Right away, Your Highness!' the Asur replied, bowing again before withdrawing.

The swirl of red in his eyes glowed prominently as Prince Arden turned to Yeshe. 'Remember one thing, Yeshe,' he warned her. 'Now that you have asked a favour of an Asur, there will be a price to pay. When we return from our ride, I will claim my reward.'

'I am not in a position to give you anything of worth, Prince Arden,' she smiled. 'Now if I had been in Shambala, it would be a different matter. Perhaps you could claim your reward in the future?'

On hearing her words, Arden frowned. 'So you expect to return to Shambala, do you, Dakini?' he asked. 'If you do, I would advise you to forget such pipe dreams. Know that I will never let you go. And if you do manage to slip away, I will hound your every breath till I get you back. So, Dakini, be prepared to reward me after we return to the palace.'

'Yeshe shook her head and adjusted her veil. 'The reality is that I am your captive, Prince Arden,' she told him. 'Under these circumstances, how can I be in a position to give you a fitting reward?'

Arden laughed. 'Don't worry, Yeshe,' he drawled. 'When the time comes, you will be in just such a position.'

At that moment, a groom drove the prince's chariot up to the doorway. Pulled by four magnificent black demon horses, it was a work of beauty. With an umbrella of carved wood topping it, the chariot was plain, but made with care and polished black to a high finish. Prince Arden helped Yeshe into the finely carved black seat. Then gesturing to the groom to stand in the rear of the chariot, he seated himself beside the dakini and picked up the horses' reins.

Pulling on them, he got the stallions to move effortlessly in synchrony and pick up speed. Yeshe adjusted her veil and looked around her in delight. Except for her visit to the emperor, she had spent over ten days confined to her apartment and was relieved to be outdoors. She gazed at the palace grounds, covered in snow, and admired the impressive ice sculptures dotting them.

'The ice sculptures are beautiful,' she observed, 'but it is a pity that there is no such thing as a thaw in your world. The snow never melts here. Or am I mistaken?'

Arden gave her a sideways glance and replied, 'For two months, a rather brief summer comes, but it is hardly the kind of summer you know. The snow melts into slush and sleet. Cold winds blow and the rain is incessant. Moreover, the temperatures are still too low for grass to grow. No real summer has come to Inka in decades. It is said by the ancients that when the land was pure at its birth, rolling grassy fields abounded in Inka. But as the Asur grew demoniac, the land gradually froze and became encased in ice. Now the farmers are able to harvest a single crop, that, too, only with the help of our sorcerers. Still, this brief summer is better than no summer at all.'

Yeshe continued to look around her with curiosity as Arden drove the chariot out of the palace gates and on to the broad thoroughfare outside. Under his skilled hands, the horses fell into a swift rhythm and soon they were moving at a brisk pace through the streets of Inkala.

'Dakini,' Arden said, smiling at Yeshe, 'Inkala is divided into three parts: the outer city, the middle city and the inner city. Today, I will take you on a tour of the inner city, which largely consists of the palace, the residential complexes of nobles and the royal bazaar.'

'Why not the rest of the city too, Prince?' Yeshe asked.

Arden shook his head. 'The outer city is home to scum. It would be dangerous for you to be seen there. The middle city, populated by merchants, is a sprawling area with many bazaars, but it is not safe for you, Dakini. Your celestial blood is a big draw for the crowds and if we step out of the inner city, you will need an escort of armed guards.'

'Where are we now, Prince?' she enquired.

'This is the first residential area for the high nobility,' Arden answered with a wave of his hand, 'and behind it is the residential complex for the lower nobility and the clergy responsible for ensuring the smooth functioning of the palace's day-to-day affairs.'

The chariot sped around a corner and Yeshe saw a sprawling and colourful market open up right before them. Flanking the road on either side was a labyrinth of shops and covered walkways. Yeshe itched to get off and explore the area.

'Could we please stop here, Prince Arden?' she entreated. 'I would love to explore the place.'

Arden shook his head. 'Content yourself with just looking at it today, Yeshe,' he suggested. 'And if you are good, I will, some day, consent to your coming here with your maids and some guards.'

Yeshe took in every detail of the market as they passed by. There were spice vendors, cook shops and big shops selling fabric, where young Asur boys advertised their wares in loud voices to attract customers. There was an entire row of jewellers and other shops lay beyond them in the shadowy interiors. Heavenly fragrances wafted out of a small perfumery that stood in the corner and Yeshe was overcome by a great desire to explore it.

Arden looked at her eager face and smiled. 'That is a famous perfumery,' he informed her, 'but don't ask me to stop here, Yeshe.'

'These markets remind me of home,' the dakini explained with a smile. 'This is the only part of Inkala that, for a few moments, has made me forget where I am.'

'I will bring you here again soon so that you may explore it, but not today.'

Yeshe smiled to herself; she did not expect to spend another night in Inka, if luck stayed with her.

Prince Arden drove the chariot out of the covered market and back towards the palace. The icy wind struck Yeshe's face as they sped along the thoroughfare and it seemed hardly any time at all before they were back at the palace. The dakini thanked Arden as he led her in through the palace entrance, across the public hall and down twisting corridors and flights of stairs back to her apartment. Soon, they had entered her rooms. A bright fire had been lit in the sitting area. A silver carafe of wine stood on a low table, alongside a plate of nuts and fruits.

Yeshe's two new maids hurried into the room and bowed low before them.

Arden nodded an acknowledgement. 'This is the sorceress, Labin, and her assistant, Arbla – your new maids,' he told the dakini. 'They will look after your needs.'

Yeshe nodded, threw off her veil and sat down on the couch. Labin poured wine into two crystal goblets and handed them to the prince and the dakini.

Yeshe nibbled on some fruit and took a sip of wine.

'Now, Dakini,' Arden began, 'I will name my reward – a kiss from your ruby lips.'

Yeshe stared at him, aghast. 'That is out of the question!' she said.

Arden smiled in response and ordered the two sorceresses to leave the room.

The two maids hastened to comply.

With a languorous movement, Arden snaked his arms around the dakini. 'Just one kiss for a demon, Yeshe,' he said. 'Surely I don't ask for much?'

Yeshe clapped her hand over her mouth. 'No! This cannot be!' she exclaimed.

Arden trailed a finger down her cheek, smiling all the while. Then, without warning, he pulled her close and kissed her. A golden sensation of warmth unfurled within her. It was like sunlight pouring into the depths of her being, like golden dusk heralding the onset of night, a slow unwinding, a painful pleasure. Layer by layer, she felt herself unravel, come apart ...

As suddenly as it had begun, it ended. Arden drew back, a mischievous smile on his face. 'Whether you want to or not, Yeshe,' he told her, 'you rise to meet my ardour and I will not let you deny that.'

With that, he rose to his feet and left the room without a backward glance, whistling all the while.

Yeshe sank into the cushions, deeply shaken. Fear clutched at her heart. She had to get away. She sent up a silent prayer to the guardian deities that her rescue effort would go off tonight without a hitch.

Chapter 15

RESCUE

I

Tashi frowned with concentration as he strung an arrow on to his bow, then, taking careful aim, released it to find its mark. The arrows flew through the air and hit the target right in the centre.

Ti Shan clapped him on the back. 'You certainly have improved, Tashi,' he observed. 'This is the third time consecutively that you have hit the target right in the centre. It proves without a doubt that you are naturally skilled with the bow.'

Tashi smiled at the compliment. They were standing in a corner of the forest clearing where camp had been set up and he had been practising without a break for over two hours.

'Still, don't let this go to your head,' Ti cautioned. 'For a Lha soldier, this skill is but a beginner's and you have mastered no more than its physical aspect. There is a lot more to the high art of archery. You have yet to master the use of mantra and power, as applied to archery, and that is but the second step. What few succeed in mastering is the power of combining *astra* with archery – the celestial art of bringing to archery the benefits of different *astras* or magical weapons of great power that can level entire cities.'

Tashi picked up his bow and murmured, 'I wonder when the prince will introduce me to the second mantric phase in archery?'

'It will happen only when he deems you ready. And that can take time. The art of applying mantra to archery is based on power and not to be taken lightly. It is an art that comes with responsibility and only students considered worthy of bearing it are trained in it for the third level. In fact, very few – not more than two or three at a time in the entire Lha empire – reach this level.'

Tashi looked around him and realized that dusk was already setting in. 'I guess I had better curb my impatience, then,' he said. 'Only, this endless waiting is getting on my nerves. We have been holed up in camp this entire week. I wonder when the prince will decide to move. There is a rumour going around that it will be tonight. What do you think, Ti? Will it be tonight?'

'There is a good chance of that,' Ti Shan replied. 'Tomorrow is the night of the full moon and I don't think the prince will deem it wise to leave the dakini unsecured till then. Now we had better get moving, Tashi. You should get back to your duties. The prince might be needing you.'

Tashi nodded. 'You are right,' he said.

Securing the bow and the arrows, he set off at a fast pace, cutting a direct path through the camp towards the princes' tent. A-KarO and Narasimha were both seated outside when he arrived. Captain Arif Leman was standing facing them.

'Captain, I want the men to fall in right here and as quickly as possible,' A-KarO commanded. 'At midnight, we will move out of camp and make our way into the palace to secure the dakini. Please inform your deputy of my plan right away. Then I will hold another discussion with you before addressing the warriors.'

Prince Narasimha was busy whittling a piece of wood into the carving of an owl. 'So we move tonight as planned, A-KarO,' he observed.

The prince nodded. 'Everything is in place,' he said. 'We have the uniforms and the identification papers. There is no sense in waiting further. We are as ready as we can ever be.' Then he noticed Tashi hovering on the peripheries and summoned him with a gesture. 'Run an errand for me, will you, Tashi?' he said. 'Go fetch Reman Luskar, the spy, right now. He is here in camp.'

Tashi saluted and took off at a run.

Captain Leman, accompanied by Master Topen, now presented himself before the princes and saluted smartly.

'Arif,' Prince Narasimha began, 'we will be discussing the rescue plan in a moment. We're just waiting for the spy, Luskar, to join us.'

Leman was invited to take a seat as Prince Narasimha unrolled a white parchment and spread it out on the table before him. It was a plan of the palace in Inkala. Luskar arrived, with Tashi trailing behind him. The boy quietly pushed himself to the front and placed stones on the corners of the parchment to weigh it down. Then he hovered nearby to listen to what the others had to say.

Prince A-KarO now took out a bottle of red ink and a marker and addressed the captain. 'Arif,' he began, pointing to a spot on the plan, 'this is the dakini's apartment, located in the palace's eastern quarter. At midnight, we will leave for the palace, an hour's run from here. By two a.m. sharp, our troopers must be in position to infiltrate it. I will take ten of our warriors with me to get the dakini out. The rest will wait near the palace walls under your command, Arif. In addition to rescuing the dakini, I want the Asur palace torched. Once I give the signal, use the archers to do the needful and make use of the mantric arrows.

'I want you to order our troops into position right now, Arif. Once that is done, I will name the ten I intend to take with me into the palace.'

Prince A-KarO now turned to Luskar and asked, 'From which point do you think it best to infiltrate the palace?'

'Your Highness,' the spy replied, 'I would strongly recommend entering the palace through its sewers. You are aware of their location and those of our warriors who were sent out to the palace on a reconnaissance mission are already familiar with them.'

The prince nodded his approval. 'That is a sound proposal,' he said. 'I myself have used the sewers recently. They will serve as the perfect infiltration point.'

'It's a mere ten-minute walk from there to the dakini's rooms,' Luskar went on, 'but I deem it too risky to approach her apartment from within the palace. I would propose accessing it from outside.'

Prince A-KarO nodded in agreement. 'The interior of the palace is one big trap,' he conceded. 'Therefore, we will approach the palace from the outside. I will signal to the dakini to come out into the courtyard adjoining her apartment. And when she does so, we can spirit her away from the place. I want us out of the palace complex and making for the portals by four a.m.'

'Your Highness,' the captain now interrupted, 'the troopers are lined up now, ready for you to address them.'

'Now that both of you have got the gist of the plan, I will address our troops,' A-KarO declared.

II

The full company of Lha warriors, almost a hundred of them, had filed out according to rank and number and now stood waiting behind Captain Leman and his deputy, along with drill-master Topen. The light from flaming torches shone over their expectant faces.

Prince A-KarO faced them, waiting for the hum of conversation to die down. Then he began to speak. 'Our period of waiting is finally at an end,' he said. 'Tonight, at two o'clock sharp, we will launch our operation to rescue the dakini and wreak vengeance on those who dared to infiltrate Shambala and abduct her. The Asur palace is an hour's run from this camp. Ten of you – I will announce the names shortly – will enter it with Prince Narasimha and me. The rest will be assigned duties near the walls.

'Once the dakini has been taken out, I want the Asur palace torched,' the prince went on. 'At the appropriate signal, Lha bowmen will fire mantric flame arrows into the palace. These, as you know, will burn through any substance that comes in their way. I want to see the Asur stronghold turn to ashes. The bulk of our warriors under Captain Leman will act as our reserve force and wait at a designated spot near the outer wall. It is from there that they will fire at the palace. Let the flames roar our revenge!'

The Lha troopers let out a roar of approval.

Prince A-KarO held up his fist. 'The Asur will pay in blood for this great insult to our race! They cannot be allowed to prevail or chaos will follow in the seven plains of existence. The balance of power in the universe has to be maintained at all costs. If the might of the celestial armies and the shedding of Asur blood are required to achieve that goal, so be it! The Lha are the foremost shield of the gods and of the seven worlds.

We, as the guardians of the universe, will not fail in our sacred duty. My warriors, the blood price has to be paid by the Asur and that is why we are gathered here today.'

There was another roar of approval from the Lha.

'Now, listen carefully,' the prince went on, 'Prince Narasimha and I, along with the ten chosen warriors I have yet to name, will enter the palace through a hidden route located in the sewers and make our way to the apartment where the dakini is being held. Once she has been secured and chaos prevails in the Asur palace, we will leave the grounds and make for our camp and from there to the portals leading into the sacred paths. May truth guide us! May the guardian deities bestow their power and blessings on us as we move to fulfil our quest! May we be victorious in our mission!'

The men roared and banged their shields in unison as an expression of their solidarity. Tashi looked on, bemused, the prince's stirring speech still ringing in his ears. His heart beating with excitement, he waited for A-KarO to announce the names of the chosen men who would accompany him and Prince Narasimha for the rescue, praying hard that he, too, would be included in the group.

Prince A-KarO now held out a list. With a smile, he announced, 'Now for those who will accompany Prince Narasimha and me into the palace. The first is Reklan Sepak, our famous bowman.'

A tall, slender celestial raised his hand in acknowledgement. Tashi recognized him right away; the boy had spoken to him in camp many times.

'Next comes Hardak Simani, the swordsman.'

This brute of a man, almost as tall as an Asur and big built, was known for his fiery temper.

'Qui Deora, the veteran shield bearer and swordsman,' the prince went on.

Tashi stared in fascination at the tall, well-built celestial with piercing grey eyes and a calm manner.

'Lam Sutia, the bowman.'

This warrior was a small but agile man.

A-KarO then read out the names of Reman Luskar, the spy who would guide the special task force into the palace complex through the hidden route, and Ruslan Sipassan, the celebrated swordsman, a legend among the Lha, whose short stature was more than compensated by his sharp intelligence and lightning-quick reflexes.

Prince A-KarO now looked at those around him and smiled. 'My personal staff – my apprentice, Tashi Thendup, and Ti Shan, my aide – will also accompany us,' he announced. 'Now I repeat: my warriors, you are to be ready to move at two a.m. sharp. So say your prayers now. May the eternal being be with us. Remember, the portals into the sacred paths are located here in the camp and this will be our point of exit when our mission is complete. We must be back here by dawn, for it is at that hour that the portals will be activated. May luck be with us. You may rest now.'

Tashi accompanied the two princes back to their table. Captain Leman and Luskar followed.

'Before we leave, Narasimha,' A-KarO said, seating himself, 'I wish to have the portals set to be activated at dawn. That is, at four-thirty a.m. precisely. By then, the company should return to camp. I hereby entrust you with that responsibility.'

Narasimha stood up, stretched, and left to do the needful, nodding to both Captain Leman and Luskar. An excited Tashi hovered near Prince A-KarO.

The prince now sat back and addressed the captain. 'Arif,' he said, 'this mission will have to be carefully orchestrated. Make sure our warriors fan out along the wall so that they are in position to torch the palace from several vantage points. But see to it that they are not too far apart, because they will be expected to provide covering fire when we are on our way back from the palace.' A-KarO now turned to Luskar. 'The entire company will exit through the sewers,' he told him.

'Your Highness,' the spy said, 'we will have to be exceedingly cautious. There are at least three separate Asur patrols guarding the route to the dakini's apartment. They will have to be taken care of without alerting the others.'

'That is to be expected,' the prince said with a nod. 'Now Arif, the signal for torching the palace – three hoots of a charmed owl – will be given once and repeated thereafter. You alone will hear it, for it will resonate in your mind. The signal will indicate that we have got the dakini safely out of the palace and you may then begin torching it without fear of compromising our safety. Any questions?'

'None, Your Highness,' Leman replied.

'Then I suggest that you rest now,' said the prince. 'You too, Luskar. And the two of you should be here promptly at a quarter to two.'

Prince A-KarO now threw Tashi an amused glance. 'So, fledgling,' he said, 'excited, are you? Now go and arrange for dinner to be served for Narasimha and me. He should be back any time. Once that is taken care of, I want you to rest and catch what sleep you can manage. We are in for a long night.'

Tashi bowed to the prince and enquired, 'A light repast, Your Highness?'

Prince A-KarO nodded abstractedly. 'Very light, Tashi. Tell the cook there should be no wine served nor food prepared in rich, creamy sauces.'

Tashi nodded and ran through the camp, making for the tent that served as the kitchen. The warriors were relaxing, he noticed. Some played cards. Others were engrossed in games involving coloured dice. A solitary soldier sang tenor to the accompaniment of a stringed instrument that he strummed.

On reaching the kitchen tent, Tashi saw that the tray bearing dinner for the two princes had already been laid out. Irom, the cook, a heavily built Lha with a boisterous manner, was very busy and nodded to Tashi, explaining that he had prepared a simple meal for the royals, as was customary before battle.

'Nothing more than vegetable stew with flatbread and salad,' he said, pointing out the wine flagon in the corner.

Tashi picked up the heavy tray, looked at the flagon and shook his head. 'The prince has made it clear that no wine should be served tonight,' he said, remembering A-KarO's instructions.

Irom swiped the flagon away and put it aside. 'After you have served the princes, come right back here again,' he directed the boy. 'The troopers will have finished their meal by then, but I will keep some stew hot for you.'

Tashi made his way back to the princes' tent. Prince Narasimha was back and was busy sharpening his sword with a whetstone. Prince A-KarO was seated in his chair, his eyes half-closed. Tashi swiftly laid out dinner for them both in front of the tent and was about to withdraw, when A-KarO spoke.

'Tashi, lay out my light armour,' he instructed. 'Just the breastplates. Also, my pair of swords and the bow, as well as the brace of knives. And don't forget to wear your mail shirt under your tunic before we set out.'

'Certainly, Your Highness,' Tashi murmured. 'Your weapons are already sharpened and oiled. I will lay them out right away.'

III

Tashi entered the tent, his eyes lighting up as he spotted Prince A-KarO's two swords stacked together in one corner. Squatting on his haunches, the boy separated them carefully. Both swords were unadorned, their only embellishment an 'Om' carved on the hilt. Their blades honed to a fine sharpness, the swords were perfectly balanced and shone with a blue light. Their very simplicity hinted at the perfection they manifested when the prince put them to use. Tashi gazed at them in awe. Made at the dawn of the universe by master craftsmen, each sword had an ancient history, now lost in legend; it was said that they were made not from any substance, but from pure essence – the perfect weapon of the Ningma warrior.

Tashi laid out the two swords, then picked up the yew wood bow that stood in the corner. Its string taut, it had been fashioned with consummate skill. Tashi filled the quiver with an assortment of arrows, beginning with a number of ordinary black-feathered ones that had sharp, poison-coated metal tips. These were followed by the rosewood mantric arrows which, though innocuous in appearance, were arrows of power and used for mantric arrow work. Lastly, he inserted five silver *astra* arrows that shimmered with an unusual, ever-changing light and were rumoured to be made of pure essence. These were used for firing *astras* of great power. Having filled the quiver, Tashi picked up several boxes of arrows and placed them in a canvas bag. Lastly, he laid out the prince's set of throwing knives. Razor-sharp, they shone with a silver light that was visible in the dark.

Having laid out the weapons, Tashi unwrapped the package in which the prince's shining armour had been placed and stared at the silver breastplates in awe. Made of itheleum, a rare metal that was extremely difficult to procure, such armour had been crafted in ancient times by master sorcerers who reinforced it with ring upon ring of protective warding, making it impossible to penetrate. Despite the fact that its price exceeded the wealth of a large kingdom, such armour was much coveted by that group of individuals which enjoyed the exclusive privilege of owning it – celestial princes and Ningma warriors. Tashi laid out the breastplates and the armguards, along with the backplates. Finally, having completed his task, he left the tent and headed for the kitchen at a run, praying that the cook had managed to save some dinner for him. The thought of food made him hasten his pace.

Irom grinned when he saw Tashi.

'You are just in time, boy!' he said. 'I had almost given up hope of your return and was going to shut down for the day.' He placed a dish of stew and flatbread before Tashi and smiled as he sat down to brew tea. 'Join me for some tea, young Tashi,' he invited. 'You look as though you deserve it.'

Tashi gratefully sat down cross-legged and attacked his meal with enthusiasm.

Irom chattered on as he worked. 'Now pay heed to my words, Tashi,' he said. 'You will be seeing action with the Asur for the first time in your life. Don't do anything rash. Be cautious in your engagement with them. When you shoot your arrows at them, remember to aim carefully for the neck, their vulnerable point, or the eyes. That will kill them on the spot.'

Tashi nodded as he ate.

'You be careful, boy,' the cook went on. 'Stay right behind the prince. Don't lose your head or try to be bolder than necessary. You should be all right.'

Tashi wiped his bowl clean with the last of the flatbread and sat back with a smile. 'I will be careful, Irom, don't worry,' he assured the Lha.

'Also, you forget that I have the Garuda's feather to aid me. That is my great advantage.'

'Ah!' Irom exclaimed. 'That had completely slipped my mind. Call on the Garuda when you see action, boy. His help would be of vital importance to the celestials.'

Tashi grunted his consent, sipping the hot, sweet tea Irom had prepared for him. Then he asked, 'What about you? Will you be accompanying us?'

Irom emitted a snort of regret. 'Alas, Tashi, my days of seeing action are gone!' he replied. 'I have retired from the army. The prince has brought me along this time as his cook. Now finish your tea fast.'

Tashi gulped down the rest of his tea and thanked Irom. Then he rose to his feet and strolled back to his tent, observing the warriors as he passed them. Some were settling down for the night, while others attended to their weapons. In this ambience of relative harmony, Tashi reached his tent and prepared for some rest.

IV

It was pitch dark when Ti Shan shook Tashi awake. Disoriented, the boy looked around him and could not, for a moment, decide where he was.

The Lha trooper whispered in his ear, 'We have to hurry, Tashi! Get dressed quickly. The two princes are ready and waiting outside with the captain.'

Awareness dawned and Tashi's mind snapped back to alertness. He threw the bedclothes aside and sprang to his feet. 'Ti Shan, I am already dressed,' he said. 'Just give me a moment to pull on my boots and pick up my weapons.'

Properly shod, Tashi swiftly secured his knives to his belt. Then picking up his bow and his quiver of arrows, along with the sack containing the surplus arrows, he stepped out of the tent. The celestial warriors were gathered outside, many of them already mounted on their steeds. Others were drinking a quick cup of tea. Mist swirled about the trees as Tashi made his way to Prince A-KarO who was already mounted, as was Prince Narasimha. Both were engaged in a last-minute discussion with Captain Leman.

Chetak snorted as Tashi walked up to him and ran a hand over his dark, gleaming hide. The boy swiftly mounted. It was bitterly cold and he gratefully accepted the steaming cup of tea Ti Shan handed him.

'Tashi,' said the Lha trooper, 'the prince asked me to ensure that you were carrying the Garuda's feather on you.'

A suddenly panic-stricken Tashi thrust his hand into his breast pocket. Relief was writ large on his face as he brought out the Garuda's feather which gleamed brightly in the dark and sent out dancing tendrils of auburn light.

Satisfied, Ti Shan nodded. 'Keep it safe,' he urged, 'and remember to use it when the need is upon us. Now I had better mount my own horse. The warriors are already in position and the prince will give the command to move any time now.'

Tashi quickly gulped down his tea and disposed of the cup. Then he led Chetak to his customary position in the second row, behind the prince. Ti Shan soon took his place behind Tashi and Captain Leman, having finished his prolonged discussion with the princes, edged his steed into position alongside Tashi's. Absolute silence reined down the line of Lha horsemen. Tashi shivered, partly with cold and partly in anticipation of what lay ahead.

Prince A-KarO now raised his gleaming sword and declared in ringing tones, 'To vengeance and victory!'

The Lha let out an answering shout and the company began moving. The horses sprang forward and the group passed like phantoms in the night. A shivering Tashi hugged his cloak around him to ward off the bitterly cold wind, but to no avail. However, the excitement coursing through his veins took precedence over his discomfort; they were finally going to see action.

Prince A-KarO led the company through the forest, maintaining a punishing pace, but so effective was the magic he spun that the thunder of their horses' hoofbeats was inaudible and no one heard them approach. The prince whispered mantras under his breath and Tashi watched in wonder as he cloaked the Lha company in darkness and spread a protective net of warding, a powerful glamour around them, thereby transforming their appearance to make them look like Asur warriors. Tashi could hardly believe his eyes at the metamorphosis and was further startled at the changed appearance of his own hands; they now looked much larger and darker. He shot a quick look at Ti Shan, who now resembled an Asur. Even Prince A-KarO and Prince Narasimha now looked like Asur nobility.

Noticing the expression of shock on Tashi's face, Ti Shan smiled and drew his horse closer to Chetak. 'This is nothing but glamour, Tashi,' he explained, 'a camouflage to help us enter the palace and blend with the Asur inside without being detected.'

The Lha warriors, Tashi now observed, were all dressed in Asur royal guard uniforms that had been distributed earlier by Captain Leman. The boy now looked at his own uniform and discovered that his appearance was indistinguishable from that of the Asur.

Tashi concentrated now on the meandering forest trail along which Prince A-KarO led the company. The ground was uneven and the surrounding countryside wilder than anything he had ever seen. A biting wind continued to blow over them. Ahead, the path rose steeply uphill, winding its way through a thick shroud of mist. As they reached the summit, Tashi gazed at the country around him. A slim belt of forested land separated them from the flat plain beyond. Along the horizon, Tashi made out the walls of the city of Inkala. The horses charged through the forest and, in very little time, had left it behind. Tashi's curious eyes took in the trails of mist that hovered over the plain they were now traversing.

Suddenly, Prince A-KarO gave the signal to halt. In a disciplined fashion, the warriors reined in their horses and came to a stop.

The spy, Reman Luskar, rode up to the front. He got off his horse and bowed from the waist to the two princes. 'Your Highnesses,' he said, 'From here, I will take the lead, till we have reached the site of the palace sewers.'

Prince A-KarO nodded his approval and Luskar rode ahead. The Lha rode at a gentler pace now, their horses' hoofbeats muffled by the Prince's magic. Luskar led them unerringly across the plain, preferring to keep to the trails and away from the road. In the near distance rose the massive walls of Inkala. They rode through the hours remaining before dawn broke and approached a small village near Inkala. The country lay in darkness, its inhabitants deep in slumber.

Luskar led the company to a small hill on the outskirts of the village and halted at its foot. Then he approached the princes and announced, 'Your Highnesses, we have reached the entrance to the palace sewers.'

Prince A-KarO nodded and gave the signal for the men to dismount. The company did so in silence. Luskar led them to a gorse bush behind which lay a small tunnel. Water seeped out from it and into the hillside. Prince A-KarO began to chant softly, weaving energy and magic together, until a rudimentary shelter had appeared on the site. The horses were led into it and tethered. Then the prince placed a protective ring of warding along the structure's perimeter to make it disappear from view. As Prince A-KarO gave the command for the men to file into the tunnel, a cold wind began blowing furiously down the hillside. Before long, the Lha company had disappeared into the palace sewers.

V

It was pitch dark in the tunnel and Tashi paused for a moment, waiting for his eyes to adjust to the unrelenting gloom. Luskar, who was leading the company through the tunnel, lit a single torch and soon, the warriors let the light guide them. Tashi hurried to catch up with the two princes. The tunnel was ice cold and water dripped from the roof and lay in puddles on the ground. He shivered in his cloak, hugging it to his body, and moved forward stoically. For a while, the tunnel ran straight. Then, without warning, it split into three. Luskar halted and held the torch aloft, examining the openings to all of them, before choosing the narrowest one to the right. The air inside this tunnel was stale and damp and the ground was covered with water.

Tashi splashed through the water, following the light from Luskar's torch that glowed weakly in the darkness. Prince A-KarO continued to chant as he moved ahead, casting a net of subtle warding around the company that muffled all sound of movement and spread a veil of darkness around them so that they were not easily visible. Prince Narasimha walked by his side confidently and joined in the chanting, reinforcing and helping to maintain A-KarO's complex warding.

'Why are the princes chanting, Ti Shan?' Tashi asked the Lha warrior in an undertone. 'Surely we are sufficiently warded by now?'

Ti shrugged. 'Who knows what the princes spin with their chants, Tashi?' he whispered back. 'But I would imagine they seek to conceal our presence from the Asur sorcerers.'

As the tunnel walls gradually closed in, Tashi felt the first flutter of panic. The tunnel grew narrower still, till the Lha were crawling through it. As Tashi, too, began making his way in the dark on all fours, he felt the chill of the damp mud against his belly and panic gripped him. By then, Luskar's torch had long been extinguished and the boy felt the darkness envelop him like a shroud. He prayed to the holy Buddha to lend him strength and continued crawling.

An hour later, the tunnel suddenly widened out into a single artery, where the air was fresher. Tashi hoped that they were approaching the end of the sewer chute. Soon, the Lha could stand upright and walk through the tunnel and many sighed in relief. As Tashi made swifter progress through the tunnel, he heard the sudden flap of wings. A memory of the harpies sprang to mind immediately, but he discovered with relief that these were just stray bats winging their way in the darkness.

The tunnel ran on for some time, then narrowed again. The air remained fresh, but foul, slimy water flowed along the ground. Tashi held a piece of cloth to his nose to block out the noxious fumes and plodded on. The tunnel grew narrower still until the warriors were forced to move in single file and the tunnel walls brushed against their shoulders on either side. A sudden bend in the tunnel wall brought a whiff of fresher air. Inhaling deeply, Tashi surmised that the opening was not too far off. Another ten minutes and the sewer opened out into the night; they were inside the palace grounds.

The moment the Lha company had filed out of the sewers, Prince A-KarO signalled to Captain Leman. 'Spread the men out along the walls and keep your fire arrows in readiness,' he instructed. 'At my signal, begin shooting. Also, stay in place till you sight us. Then provide covering fire for us to get the dakini away safely.'

Tashi looked out around him. They were standing near the palace walls in a deserted, snow-covered stretch of the grounds. The dark contours of the palace's massive structure were visible from here. Prince A-KarO now gave the signal for the ten chosen Lha warriors to step forward. Tashi, along with Ti Shan, joined them and soon, the group, headed by the two princes, had separated from the bulk of the company. Luskar and the royals conferred in whispers, before the team began moving across the snowbound grounds like a shadow in the dark.

Prince A-KarO passed a message on to Tashi. 'Watch out for the Asur patrols,' he warned, 'and remember to take them swiftly and in total silence.'

As one, the group moved stealthily towards the palace, with Luskar leading the way.

VI

Tashi looked about him warily as he followed the two princes across the looming shadows of the palace complex. With the wards in place, A-KarO and Narasimha had ceased chanting and the group now moved in single file and in silence. Even the muffled vibration of their footsteps could no longer be heard. All that remained was the sigh of the night wind in the trees. They had barely walked for ten minutes when they spotted the first patrol – a party of seven Asur – making its way across the grounds.

As it drew nearer, Prince A-KarO held up his hand. 'Take them swiftly and in silence,' he commanded.

Drawing out one of his knives, Tashi followed in the prince's footsteps. The celestials waited for the Asur patrol to cross right in front of them before they attacked. With a quick slash of the sword, A-KarO decapitated an Asur and turned to another.

Tashi was right behind, deftly knifing an Asur in the heart and slitting his throat, before letting the body crumple to the ground. Prince Narasimha stood to Tashi's right, his sword dripping with blood as he disembowelled an Asur. The celestials dealt out death to each member of the patrol with consummate skill. Soon, all had been taken care of and the bodies were hastily buried in a snowdrift nearby. Then the celestials fell in line to continue on their way to the palace.

Soon, Luskar was leading them into the shadow of the royal palace and down a narrow pathway between two buildings towards the eastern wing. They crossed an open courtyard with a fountain in its centre that lay under the shadow of an overhanging palace galley. The Asur guards keeping vigil at each corner were swiftly despatched by the celestials with a silent knife-thrust.

The group moved confidently through the maze of sprawling palace buildings till they had reached a square that was brightly illuminated by two torches. A pair of guards stood smoking a pipe.

Prince A-KarO held up his hand, a signal for the party to halt, and turned to Luskar. 'The square is far too brightly lit,' he murmured. 'Is there another way?'

Luskar shook his head.

The prince nodded. 'This calls for bow work, then,' he declared.

With a gesture, he indicated that his two bowmen, Reklan Sepak and Lam Sutia, should step forward. Taking careful aim, they fired their arrows at the two guards, getting them between the eyes. The Asur crumpled to the ground. Prince A-KarO now pointed his finger towards the burning torches and chanted below his breath. A sudden gust of wind blew over the square, causing the torches to flicker and then die out. The prince now gave the signal for the party to move ahead. They crossed the square without incident. Luskar turned left and led them down yet another narrow path between palace buildings that ran straight for some time before turning right.

They entered and crossed a small courtyard, then scaled its high walls to find themselves in yet another square. In its centre was a small ice sculpture, shining in the moonlight. Two Asur sentries stood guard in the corners. Tashi swiftly shot off an arrow that pierced the right eye of the sentry on the right. The Asur fell to the ground, a hit to the eye was fatal for an Asur. Reklan shot off the next arrow that struck the second Asur, who also collapsed and was swiftly knifed by Prince Narasimha before he could do more than croak in his death throes. The celestial party now crossed the square and followed Luskar as he turned into yet another narrow pathway. Ahead lay a small, enclosed courtyard with a solitary leafless tree. Bright moonlight played across its naked branches.

Luskar turned to Prince A-KarO. 'We have arrived, Your Highnesses,' he murmured.

Prince A-KarO called for the party to halt. Silently, he vaulted over the walls of the courtyard and, within minutes, the shrill cry of a white owl rang out in the night. The prince mimicked the cry twice as he waited in the courtyard, chanting under his breath to ensure that the spell he cast by doing so would make the dakini's sorceress maidservants and Asur guards continue to sleep contentedly. The moonlight lit up the courtyard with its brilliance and Prince A-KarO clearly made out Yeshe's slight form as she stepped out of her apartment. The two guards on duty continued to slumber under the spell.

Yeshe held her hands out to the prince, 'You have come for me at last!' she whispered.

Prince A-KarO caught her in a swift embrace. 'Hush!' he whispered. 'We must be on our way.'

With an agile movement, he hoisted her up on the courtyard wall, from where Prince Narasimha lifted her off and set her down on the snow.

But as soon as the dakini's feet touched the ground outside the courtyard, there was a blinding flash of light and a piercing wail rang out from the ward that stood around the walls. Eerie in pitch and intensity, the sound was terrifying.

'Move!' Prince A-KarO exhorted, his tone urgent. 'The ward has gone off and the Asur are on their way!'

The party streaked down the frozen path, making for the small square. The two princes held the dakini between them and their warriors surrounded them as they left the square and made for the narrow gully beyond it. Racing down the gully with the others, Tashi saw sheets of flame envelop the eastern wing of the palace and smiled with satisfaction, realizing that the prince had already conveyed the command for torching the palace to Captain Leman and the second party of celestials waiting near the walls. The smoke thickened as fire enveloped the edifice, the flames licking its walls and invading the interiors.

Pandemonium had broken out within the palace, with a great number of Asur running out in panic, when Prince A-KarO's party left the narrow path and entered the large square, now brightly lit up by the glow from the flames. In the centre of the square, arms akimbo, stood Prince Arden, his sword standing erect before him, its point thrust into the snow. A full company of the Asur royal guard stood behind him.

The Asur prince greeted the celestials with a chilling smile. 'I was awaiting you, A-KarO,' he declared. 'This visit of yours is no surprise. Now hand over my consort immediately.'

There was the very devil in Prince A-KarO's smile as he responded, 'So we meet again, Arden!' Without moving his gaze from the Asur prince, A-KarO whispered to Tashi, 'Now is the time to use the feather, boy! We will need all the help we can get.'

Tashi immediately unveiled the feather. Auburn light streaked out from it and danced around the square, illuminating it with a golden glow.

Suddenly, the sound of beating wings filled the air, as a huge bird flew overhead. The Garuda had arrived and let out a trumpeting call. Then a golden youth with burnished wings stood before them, his form radiating a brilliant light, his innate divinity manifesting itself in a shower of dancing sparks of auburn. The Garuda cocked his head and stood by Prince A-KarO, then threw back his head and laughed in sheer delight. His resounding laughter struck terror into the hearts of the Asur.

He now turned to Tashi and said with a smile, 'You called and here I am! Come, young one, now we join the battle!'

With those words, he let out a great battle cry and pulled out his flaming sword. Then along with Prince A-KarO and Prince Narasimha, the golden youth fell upon the demon hordes.

VII

Running to keep up with Prince A-KarO, Tashi swiftly positioned his bow, even as he ran, and let loose a volley of arrows. Several of them found their mark and at least two Asur fell, never to rise again. Ahead of Tashi, Prince A-KarO had burst into the front ranks of the Asur, a whirling sword in each hand. With the two celestial princes and the Garuda fighting side by side, no obstacle could stand in their way. Tashi set aside his bow and pulled out his knives. His Asur opponent of the moment stumbled as the boy kicked out his legs. Then Tashi leapt into the air, unconsciously repeating a manoeuvre from the Lha drill, and thrust a knife deep into his opponent's chest. Even before the Asur had crumpled at his feet, Tashi stood ready for the next one, a giant covered in mail armour.

With the enormous axe he carried in one hand, the Asur took a swing at Tashi, which the latter adroitly sidestepped. The boy's knives were useless against his opponent's armour and, taking advantage of this unexpected opportunity, the Asur took another swing at him with the axe. Had the weapon found its mark, Tashi would have been in serious trouble, but he was quick to jump out of the way, causing the Asur to be carried forward by the momentum of the swing. Exploiting the moment, Tashi tripped him up. The moment he fell, Tashi pulled out his knife in one swift move and drove it into the soft tissue of the Asur's unprotected neck. Blood spurted from the wound, but the demon rose again and caught Tashi around the waist, squeezing it so tightly that the boy felt he would faint. With Tashi temporarily incapacitated, the Asur positioned his axe and prepared to swing it at him. Before he could do so, however, a knife whizzed past Tashi and buried itself in the Asur's left eye. The gigantic demon instantly crumpled to the ground and lay still. A dazed Tashi stood up shakily. Ti Shan, he realized, had saved him with a timely and accurately aimed throw of the knife.

The boy now looked around him, discovering that they were hopelessly outnumbered by the demons. The Asur guard fought with a ferocity that was hard to rival and a shocked Tashi watched helplessly, as the celestials drew themselves into a tight ring, with the dakini at its centre, and fought for their lives, while their opponents pushed them steadily back towards the palace wall, step by step. Had it not been for the brilliant swordplay of the two princes and the defence provided by the Garuda, the celestial group would have been massacred. A-KarO had let the wards fall and the celestials were revealed in all their brilliance and glory against the darkness of the Asur hordes. Tashi rushed to take up position behind the prince, then pulled out his bow and shot an Asur who was heading towards him. Even as the demon fell to his arrow, yet another Asur, big-built and in clothes smeared with blood and gore, came charging towards him.

Tashi quickly set aside his bow and pulled out his knife. Soon he was engaged in a battle of cut and thrust which seemed to go on for ever. Tashi kicked out at the Asur, causing him to lose his balance, and swiftly stepped into his guard and slit his throat. Blood spurted from the wound and the Asur stumbled and slowly fell to his knees. But his fellow Asur came on relentlessly, one taking the place of another who had fallen. Tashi felt his arm beginning to tire with the endless knife work. Ti Shan stood to his right, engaged in combat with a huge Asur, but he was fast and nimble with his sword. Tashi watched in horror as Lam Sutia took a fatal thrust to the heart and fell – their first casualty. Without missing a beat, Qui Deora took his place and closed the gap in the circle. His sword flew faster than the eye could follow, as the tall, sturdy celestial slew Asur after Asur, singing in a clear tenor that could be heard over the din of battle. Tashi positioned himself on a boulder and pulled out his bow, letting arrow after arrow fly, many of which found their mark. Ti Shan remained a protective presence by his side, keeping an eye on Tashi, even as he fought on. Yet nothing seemed to deplete the Asur numbers and they came on relentlessly, pushing the celestials, little by little, into retreat.

The Garuda's clear voice now rang out, chanting a mantra of great power. He threw out his hand and golden light streaked out from it, engulfing large numbers of Asur in the front ranks in flames. The rest of the Asur panicked and fell back, but Prince Arden's fearless voice rang out and drew them back into battle. It was at this point that the two celestial princes resorted to their special stratagem. Narasimha called up mist and fog, uniting them to draw a veil over the battlefield, till none of the Asur could see beyond it. A-KarO now summoned a dancing spark of brilliant eternal light that streaked ahead of them, cutting a path through the veil. Then he organized his Lha warriors into arrow formation and thus they progressed through the square, taking full advantage of the confusion that reigned among the Asur.

Prince A-KarO's voice rang out amid the din, addressing his warriors. 'Prepare for retreat!' he exhorted them. 'Follow the eternal spark which will lead us to the sewers. Run!'

Within moments, the celestials had left the square and were out on the narrow path beyond it. Tashi followed Prince A-KarO at a run, negotiating twisting gullies, moonlit squares and vaulting across courtyards. Prince Narasimha maintained the veil of mist around them as they stole through the night. With the Garuda moving alongside, the princes kept Yeshe protectively between them as they retreated through the narrow palace paths.

Prince Narasimha had, all the while, continued with a low-voiced chant, cloaking their passage in mist. Then, as they reached open ground, he pointed his finger to the skies and chanted in an undertone. Trails of mist and fog descended from the sky, surrounding them with a camouflaging curtain. Concealed by it, the party ran across the ground and reached the walls. Captain Leman saluted smartly as he sighted them and his warriors, waiting in readiness for the final move, let out a cheer.

Prince A-KarO's voice rose in command. 'Quick!' he said, 'start moving! Get the troopers into the sewers. The Asur are right behind.'

Prince Narasimha took Yeshe by the hand and led her into the sewers. The rest of the party followed. In minutes, the celestials had disappeared into the darkness of the tunnels without leaving a trace of their presence.

VIII

Tashi stayed close to the two princes and the dakini and stared at his surroundings. They were in a narrow tunnel and the way ahead was shrouded in darkness, but the air inside was still fresh. Luskar was in the lead again, holding a torch he had lighted. As they progressed, the air grew damp. Foul water trailed on the ground and a stench hung over them. The tunnel grew narrower still and closed in on them as they moved ahead. Soon, Tashi and the rest were crawling on all fours through the muck. Although he had been through this experience that very night, he could not help covering his nose with a rag and silently prayed to the Lord Buddha, the Goddess Tara and the guardian deities for help. A little way ahead, the tunnel opened up and Tashi was relieved to be able to stand upright again. The air was fresher here and he ran to keep pace with the two princes and the dakini.

Yeshe's feet barely touched the ground as she moved through the darkness. Tashi saw how her form glowed with an unusual luminescence and she seemed to float through the tunnel. After a while, they arrived at the point where the three tunnels branched off. With unerring instinct, Luskar chose the right one and the party followed him at a run. In the disorienting darkness, Tashi seemed to lose track of time. Then suddenly, the tunnel opened up and the air was no longer foul. It was at this point that Tashi noticed both the princes chanting softly, putting the wards of protection and concealment back in place.

Soon, the company was filing out of the tunnels and into the world outside. The dawn wind was blowing and it was the cold, lonely hour before sunrise. Tashi stumbled out of the tunnel and raced down the snowbound plain, making for the shelter where the horses were concealed. The company briskly followed and was soon leading the horses out.

Tashi beamed as he saw Chetak and felt his quiet presence touch his mind.

'I see you have got the dakini back,' the wind horse observed.

Tashi patted Chetak's gleaming dark hide as he led him out. 'We must ride fast now; the Asur are on our trail,' he told his mount.

Chetak neighed as Tashi swiftly mounted him and led him to his customary place behind the two princes.

Prince A-KarO held up his hand. 'We will head for camp and then to the portals!' he announced to the troopers. 'Ride like the wind! The Asur sorcerers have raised the alarm and are in hot pursuit.'

The wind rushed past Tashi's face as the company moved out into the fading night, the horses galloping across the plain. Dawn was breaking over the horizon and night retreated, as a pink blush spread across the skies and early morning greyness seeped into the landscape. Soon, the golden rays of the sun had lit up the frozen plain. Tashi gave Chetak his head and the great horse picked up speed, his midnight hide gleaming in the morning light. Ahead of them rode the dakini, flanked by the two princes and the Garuda flew in the skies, its wing-beats creating a draft for those riding below. Soon, the grey blur of Inkala Forest was visible on the horizon, stretching as far as the eye could see, like a great ocean. The rolling plains dipped into its grey shadows.

Tashi was enjoying the morning breeze whipping his face, when Chetak's quiet voice sounded in his ears. 'I hear the thundering of many hooves. The Asur are catching up with us,' he said.

Ahead of them, Prince A-KarO urged his warriors to drive their steeds harder still and so they did, racing across the wide plain and making for the shadows of the forest. Then Tashi heard the sound of hooves beating against turf as a large group of Asur horsemen approached. The celestial company spurred their horses to still greater speeds and galloped towards Inkala Forest. Tashi glanced over his shoulder and saw the black demon stallions of the Asur rise up like phantoms from behind the plain's incline. He calculated that the forest was at least 20 leagues away and there was no way they were going to reach it, before the Asur caught up with them.

Prince A-KarO led the celestials away to the shelter of a rocky outcrop that rose from the plain and called for a halt. Turning to Narasimha, he announced, 'We will confront and engage the Asur at this point as a diversionary tactic, while you ride on ahead with the dakini and pass through the portals. An escort of two warriors will accompany you. The rest of us will follow when we have taken care of matters and you are safely away. Now fly! They will be upon us any moment.'

Prince Narasimha shook his head. 'A-KarO, I am needed here!' he insisted. 'Send the dakini off with some other reliable escort.'

'This is no time to argue, Narasimha!' A-KarO reminded him, his voice tinged with impatience. 'You must be the one to take Yeshe through the portals to safety. I entrust you with this duty. Now hurry!'

Prince Narasimha bowed and then embraced A-KarO. Then, with the dakini alongside, he and two Lha bowmen rode on ahead across the plain, making straight for the forest.

Prince A-KarO organized the celestials into a classic arrow arrangement to face the oncoming tide of the Asur. Tashi strained to see across the plain. Then he detected the shadowy forms of the Asur approaching, their silhouettes growing more prominent and menacing as the distance separating them narrowed.

Suddenly, the Garuda was by Tashi's side in its celestial aspect. 'Quickly, young one!' he urged. 'Climb on, I want you on my back. Together, we will rain havoc on the Asur from above, with you using your skill with the bow to full advantage. Now follow me.'

The Garuda now walked ahead of the company and, with a nod to prince A-KarO, metamorphosed back into the gigantic form of the mythic bird with its huge protruding beak, massive armoured claws and many-hued, rainbow-coloured plumage. Its great fiery-orange wings glowed with touches of peacock blue and iridescent violet. Ti Shan tossed Tashi on to the Garuda's back where, strangely, he found a small seat made of tough material awaiting him.

The Garuda's strident voice rang out in Tashi mind. 'Quick, boy!' he urged. 'Strap yourself in and then we take off.'

Tashi worked his way into the saddle, strapped himself in and fastened the clasps to secure his legs and hips. The Garuda gave a trumpeting call and took to the skies in a mighty sweep of wings. Tashi felt pure exhilaration surge through him as the great bird flew in wide circles over the Asur who were hurtling towards the celestials on horseback. Tashi held his breath as the enemy came within range. Then sighting across his bow, he let fly an arrow into the oncoming ranks of the Asur. The arrow found its mark and an Asur riding in the first wave tumbled off his horse.

Then Tashi heard the Garuda's quiet voice in his mind. 'Not bad!' remarked the great bird. 'Now watch this.'

The Garuda swooped low over the Asur horsemen before showering flames over them that burned to a cinder those who came in its path. The demon horses riding alongside panicked, creating havoc in the Asur ranks.

Tashi gazed down at the flaming battlefield, noting that the Asur had brought a small army down to confront the celestials. Though some had fallen in battle, there were at least 2,000 Asur in full attack mode. They came in disciplined formation, as the celestials stood grouped together on the hillock in the classic arrow formation. Soon, the Asur were within range and, for a breath, the two sides were silent as the Asur horsemen raced towards the celestials.

Then, without warning, dark arrows hurtled across the skies as the two sides clashed and the Asur cavalry rode into the knot of celestials. The real battle had begun between the 2,000 odd Asur, on the one hand, and the 80 celestials on the other, an unequal conflict, if ever there was one – if one went merely by numbers. Tashi sighed with satisfaction as the Garuda swooped down, breathing fire and mayhem on the Asur advance. Tashi sighted across his bow and fired arrow after arrow into the Asur, but their numbers kept increasing, until the celestials looked like a small circle of light in a field of darkness.

IX

Yeshe's steed galloped through the shadowy forest, following Prince Narasimha's down the narrow trail. Behind her, in single file, rode the two Lha guards Prince A-KarO had assigned for her protection. The rays of the early-morning sun barely penetrated the thick canopy of trees that grew tall and in profusion on both sides of the trail. As they rode through the undulating terrain, Yeshe prayed fervently for the deities to protect Prince A-KarO and the celestial warriors who had remained behind to stave off the enemy, thereby ensuring that she herself could get away. Prince Narasimha rode fast and unerringly down the mountain trail, chanting softly as he wove together wards of protection and concealment. The dakini lent her own powers to his magic so that their passage would be virtually untraceable.

Narasimha led the way uphill as the land rose along the path. It was an arduous ascent and the horses had to slow down as they made their way carefully through the rocks and the brush. At last, they came to a rocky shelf from where the trail bifurcated, with one path leading to the summit of the hill and the other descending farther into the forest. Prince Narasimha reined in his horse, peering into the forest, then turning to gaze at the horizon. Yeshe dismounted and allowed the horses to drink water from her canteen, before quenching her own thirst. Then wiping the sweat off her face, she took a good look around her. She could just about make out the shadowy impressions of the battle in progress on the plain. She felt fear clutch at her heart as she saw the blazing light of the celestials surrounded by a dark sea of Asur. Would Prince A-KarO and his Lha warriors be able to get away? In these circumstances, with the unending ranks of Asur poised for a massacre, it seemed doubtful.

The dakini was abruptly brought back to her own situation by Prince Narasimha, who whispered, 'Yeshe, we must move, but with the utmost caution. I detect movement in the forest; some Asur are about. Now mount quickly so that I can lead you to safety. On no account must we squander the advantage we have been granted.'

Hardly moments had passed before they were riding cautiously down the hill, with Prince Narasimha in the lead and Yeshe's agile mare matching the pace he had set. As soon as they had descended to the foot of the hill, the forest closed in around them. The air was heavy with moisture and the trees had a malevolent air about them and seemed to be whispering to each other. Yeshe shivered, sensing the presence of ancient evil and the gaze of hostile eyes.

They were passing through the dense undergrowth of a rocky ravine with a rivulet running down its middle, when Prince Narasimha held up his hand to signal a halt. He indicated with a gesture that Yeshe should follow him.

'An Asur party is coming this way,' he murmured. 'This is the best place to take cover.' With that, he led the horses into the shadows behind a large clump of gorse bushes.

They had barely taken cover when Yeshe heard the unmistakable sound of hoofbeats. They sounded unnaturally loud in the silence of the forest. A faint luminescence emanated from Prince Narasimha, who kept a hand on his horse's mane and the other hand on Yeshe's mare as he chanted under his breath to weave his magic around them, till they had been encircled by wards of concealment. Then he ceased chanting and silence fell between them again.

Suddenly, a small party of Asur horsemen burst out of the forest. They were the escort guard for the sorcerer, Bakala, who was, no doubt, on his way to the battlefield to provide what assistance he could to Prince Arden. Despite the magic Narasimha had spun, the sorcerer immediately sensed something was amiss and called for a halt, looking around him with alert eyes.

'I sense a presence here,' Bakala said to his deputy, 'although it is very subtle. Have our surroundings thoroughly searched.'

Obeying the sorcerer's command, the Asur horsemen spread out, looking up into the trees and down into the undergrowth. Yeshe remained utterly motionless and silent as two guardsmen peered into their hiding place. Such, however, was the power of the magic Narasimha wielded that nothing was visible to the Asur but shadows and they soon retreated. Bakala, however, continued to look suspicious, his gaze sweeping over the surrounding forest as though he could track his prey by scent alone.

His deputy saluted him and declared, 'Sorcerer Bakala, the men have gone over the ground thoroughly and they report having noticed nothing untoward.'

The sorcerer shook his head, looking unconvinced. 'I still sense a vibration here. It could be the residue of past action. It is possible that magic was worked here not long ago. Anyhow, one last test remains to be carried out, before I can be absolutely certain.'

Bakala now held aloft his black staff and spoke a fell word of power. Instantly, there was a perceptible shift in the atmosphere. A ray of red light separated from the staff. Multiple beams spreading from it cut across the channel. One probing beam passed over the celestials, but failed to touch them, for Narasimha had murmured a mantra under his breath and managed to deflect it. The beams then coalesced into one and flew back into the staff.

'Ah, perhaps it is nothing much,' Bakala concluded. 'We are delaying needlessly. Let us be off.'

His frail form swayed on his dark steed and his fell eyes glowed blood red, as he led his men out of the channel.

Narasimha heaved a sigh of relief as the Asur company rode away.

He remained where he was for the next ten minutes. Once the hoofbeats of the demon horses had died away, he signalled to Yeshe to mount her mare and soon, they were riding like the wind through the forest. The ground had evened out and the air was less humid now, but the trees were still as thickly clustered as ever. This time, their journey was unimpeded. They came across no sign of habitation in the forest. Nor was there any hindrance in the form of more Asur parties.

Half an hour later, just as her mare was beginning to tire, Yeshe rode into the camp. With the tents rolled up and the equipment packed and ready to be loaded on horses, it was apparent that everyone was prepared for departure.

Narasimha smiled at Yeshe, but his expression was tense. 'Dakini, we are almost there,' he announced. 'The portals are situated near the waterfall behind the camp. Follow me.'

He led her to a much-used trail and, walking her horse down it for a few minutes, Yeshe heard the rush of a waterfall. Passing beyond the curtain of foliage that hid it from view, she came upon a small, circular lake filled with clear water. A cascade reflecting rainbow hues tumbled into it from the heights.

'Now don't stop, Yeshe. Just follow me as I cross over,' Narasimha urged.

Then having led his horse to the edge of the lake, he disappeared without warning. Startled, Yeshe paused for a moment and then followed in the prince's footsteps, reaching the exact point where he had stood before disappearing from view. Then she saw the portals located at the very edge of the water. Narasimha stood on the other side, awaiting her, his back to an oak grove. A highland meadow, dotted with glowing golden flowers, spread away behind him, stretching as far as the eye could see. For the first time that day, Yeshe found herself smiling. Then she entered the portals and stepped on to the sacred path.

X

The Garuda flew low over the masses of Asur in full cry. Tashi sighted across the Garuda and took aim, throwing his knife directly into the enemy.

One Asur guardsman fell letting out a scream of agony. Suddenly, the Garuda dived, letting loose a wild roar. A huge ball of fire burst from its beaks, burning many Asur to cinders. Tashi's eyes swept over the battle scene. The situation seemed desperate for the celestials who were now ringed in an ever-tightening circle by the Asur and being pushed inwards, step by inexorable step.

There was a sudden eruption on the Asur front. Bursting out of their ranks was a colossal beast that stood over 12 feet tall. Though its upper torso bore a vague resemblance to a man, the creature had a shimmering, scaled lower body and a long tail. Its razor-tipped black horns and protruding fanged teeth were designed to strike terror into the hearts of those who beheld it. The beast now broke through the ranks of the celestials, creating havoc in their midst. It lunged at and caught the famed swordsman, Hardak Simani, in its huge paw, crushing the life out of him before flinging him into the air. Simani's mangled form fell to the ground and lay still. The beast then went after Ti Shan.

Tashi's breath caught in his throat as he saw Ti fighting for his life. His nimble footwork and sword thrusts seemed to get him nowhere, for the beast caught the Lha trooper around his waist and lifted him towards its dark maw.

In desperation, Tashi cried out to the Garuda, 'Do something, Lord! That beast will destroy us all!'

The Garuda's answer came to him as a whisper in his mind. 'That fell beast is the Gorod and fire will not work against it. Only one thing will work: a mantrik power arrow, fired into each eye. Take the shot, boy! I will whisper the mantra in your mind.'

Tashi spread his hands, indicating his helplessness. 'But I have never been trained in mantrik arrow work!' he cried.

The Garuda whispered, 'You alone are in a position to take this shot right now, Tashi. The prince is engaged in keeping Arden at bay and I cannot help you. So focus on the mantra – "Lam". Fix your mind in the void, in emptiness; then release the arrow to the vibration of the syllable, "Lam".'

Even as the Garuda spoke, the beast, with Ti Shan still dangling from its paw, continued to trample warriors in the celestial ranks, crushing many to death.

Tashi fixed his mind in emptiness and let it quieten. As ecstasy rose within, he intoned the syllable, 'Lam'. At its first vibration, he shot off his arrows, one after the other. They flew home, striking the Gorod in the eyes. The beast emitted a terrifying roar of rage. Then swaying on its feet and lashing its tail, it slowly crumpled to the ground, landing on the Asur soldiers and crushing many as it fell.

Tashi let out a whoop of joy, but the thought of what might have happened to Ti Shan cast a shadow over his happiness and he began looking frantically for him. To his immense relief, Tashi caught sight of Ti standing upright with some support from his fellow warriors.

Meanwhile, taking advantage of the confusion in the Asur ranks as the great beast fell, the Garuda had swooped low and let out another immense roar. Flames burst from its beaks and consumed the masses of Asur crowding the front ranks. The Garuda now flew in circles over the battlefield, its gaze intent on the enemy.

Tashi scanned the crowd for a glimpse of Prince A-KarO and finally sighted him locked in a sword fight with Arden. The celestial prince's sword flew faster than the eye could see, as he parried each move by the Asur royal. Prince A-KarO feinted and stepped inside Arden's guard, but his thrust was blocked by the Asur prince. The celestial danced away, using his nimble footwork to advantage. Wary, but tireless, the two circled each other, one smoothly blocking the other's thrust. As Arden attacked again, Prince A-KarO met the onslaught with a smooth flip of his arm, switching to the classic swordsman's move of 'moonlight over flowing waters'. Arden tripped A-KarO. The latter leapt up in the air, going straight for the Asur prince's jugular. Arden immediately sprang aside and danced back, smoothly moving into the stance of 'spreading dusk' as he retaliated to A-KarO's attack. The two princes circled each other, their movements as light and effortless as that of dancers, engaging in combat and then separating. They were so evenly matched that neither could enter the other's guard.

Then moving with lightning speed, Arden flew at A-KarO. For a fraction of a moment, his fast-moving sword found purchase and nicked the celestial on the arm.

Prince A-KarO smiled in response. 'First blood goes to you, Arden.'

The Asur royal flicked back his hair, an arrogant smirk on his face. 'Wait and watch; the rest goes to me too.'

Without warning, Prince A-KarO soared up in the air and went straight for Arden's throat. The latter smiled slyly as he brought his sword forward and blocked his opponent's attack. A-KarO fell back and circled the Asur warily. Arden now attacked the celestial in a flurry of sword strokes, but A-KarO managed to parry each move. Then suddenly, he sprang aside and thrust his sword into his enemy's exposed shoulder blade, breaking skin and tearing ligament.

Arden grimaced as he fell back. 'So you've managed to draw blood,' he observed.

Smiling, A-KarO smoothly parried a thrust, then stepped back. 'I have no time in hand to see this through to its conclusion, Arden,' he declared. 'So it seems you will live to see another day.'

With that, Prince A-KarO stepped back and held his fist out to the sky, murmuring a word of power. As it vibrated around them, the air grew moist and heavy and a veil of fog descended on the battlefield, obscuring the surroundings. With the complete absence of visibility that ensued, the Asur soldiers milled around in confusion.

Prince A-KarO raised his voice to address his company. 'Warriors, we retreat to the camp at once. Each man makes for the portals.'

At a signal from the prince, the conch sounded the notes of retreat and the Lha stepped away from battle, spurring their horses towards the forest. The Garuda flew ahead, with Tashi now slumped tiredly on its back.

'I will fly us directly to the location of the portals and we will cross over, Tashi,' the Garuda told him. 'I only hope your horse makes it.'

Tashi felt the wind rushing past his face as the Garuda made straight for the shadow of the forest. Below, a dense, murky fog cloaked the ground. In no time, the great bird was flying over the Inkala Forest and towards the campsite.

XI

Tashi pressed his knees into the Garuda and held on as it flew on. Dawn had given way to morning and there was a freshness to the wind. Visibility had improved a little, though the forest below continued to be covered in a veil of mist that lay heavy on the ground, with the treetops swimming up through it like phantoms rising out of the ocean. An exhausted Tashi now took stock of his battle wounds. The dagger wound on his thigh throbbed with pain, but it was not deep. Blood oozed from it, however, and Tashi tore a strip of fabric from his shirt and bound it. He ignored the few shallow cuts along his ribs.

Tashi now sat back on the Garuda, enjoying the fresh, cold breeze that rushed past, praying that Prince A-KarO and the rest of the company had made it safely through the portals. There was a strong chance of pursuit by the Asur, but Tashi was confident that the heavy fog cover would stall them. It would not, however, be enough to hold the Asur sorcerers at bay. He peered down into the murky forest, wondering if he might spot any of the celestial company, but all he saw was mist. The Garuda now flew low over the forest and, at last, Tashi made out the familiar shape of the hill summit.

The Garuda's quiet voice sounded in his mind, 'We will alight on the summit, Tashi,' it said. 'We must look out for signs of the prince and his warriors.'

As the great bird landed on the summit, Tashi disentangled his cramped limbs and dismounted from the saddle, stumbling a little before he found his feet. Meanwhile, the Garuda had metamorphosed into his alternate avatar of a golden youth. He now held his hand out for the canteen of water which Tashi passed to him. The boy walked gingerly around the summit, trying to work the kinks out of his legs and gazing at his surroundings. Little was visible of the mist-shrouded forest around them.

The Garuda whispered a mantra and shut his eyes, maintaining silence for a few moments. Then he turned to Tashi and announced, 'Prince A-KarO and his warriors are just ten leagues or so away now. They are headed for the camp and riding full tilt. The Asur are on their trail, but the celestials have the lead and should be able to hold it, thanks to the mist that is impeding the enemy's progress. There is now a sorcerer in their midst, however, who is guiding them through it. Well, boy, it's time to fly again. So climb on.'

Tashi complied and within moments, they were airborne and heading for the portals site. He felt heartened by the news the great bird had given him and continued to offer up silent prayers for the prince's welfare.

A mere half-hour later, Tashi spotted familiar terrain. The forest had begun to thin out; the trees grew farther apart. The mist cover had lifted. Ahead of them was the clearing where their camp had been set up. The Garuda swooped down and alighted. Tashi immediately hopped off and strolled around, stretching his legs. The Garuda shimmered with golden light as he transformed himself into a youth. His golden brown eyes blazed with fire and he smiled at Tashi.

'We will await the prince and his warriors right here, boy, so we can offer what little assistance we can when they arrive,' he declared. 'Then we will cross through the portals with them.'

Suddenly, Tashi sighted the cheerful form of Irom, the cook, making his way towards them.

'About time you all returned! I was getting worried, Lord,' the Lha said, beaming with joy.

Bending his portly body from the waist, he bowed before the Garuda, who smiled serenely and held out his hand in beneficence.

The expression of worry returned on Irom's face. 'Where is the prince and the rest of the company, Lord?' he enquired.

'They are on their way here, Master Cook,' the Garuda replied. 'I expect them here within the next hour or so.'

'I have some hot tea ready,' Irom smiled. 'Would you care for some, Lord?'

The Garuda inclined his head and smiled. 'That would be very welcome.'

The Lha scuttled off to fetch the tea and Tashi flopped down on the grass and stretched out. 'I wonder how closely the Asur are pursuing them, Lord,' he pondered.

'They are not more than five leagues behind the celestials now, but the Lha company is riding hard,' the Garuda replied.

After resting for a few moments, Tashi sprang to his feet. 'I will fetch the prince's luggage and keep it ready for their arrival,' he suggested.

The Garuda shook his head. 'There will be no time for that, Tashi,' he warned. 'We will have to abandon camp and leave things lying as they are. The Asur are too close behind the company for comfort.'

The cook now approached carrying two steaming mugs of tea which Tashi and the Garuda accepted gratefully. Tashi took his first sip of the hot, sweet beverage and smiled. This is divine, he thought.

'Master Cook, have the dakini and Prince Narasimha already made the crossing?' asked the Garuda.

'Indeed they have, Lord,' Irom smiled, 'about two to three hours back. I witnessed it.'

Tashi finished his tea and approached the spot where his tent had stood. The dismantled tent had been rolled up and packed, as were the princes' bedding and luggage. Tashi carted the luggage up to the spot where he had been waiting for the celestials to return and put it down. He found the Garuda sitting on a prominent boulder and sunning himself. His eyes were shut and he was whispering softly to himself.

Curious, the boy approached him and asked, 'Any news, Lord?'

The Garuda opened his eyes and answered, 'They will be here soon, but the Asur are right behind them. There has even been an exchange of fire between the two groups. Be ready, Tashi, for they will be here any moment now.'

Having uttered those words, the Garuda transformed himself into his avian form. The great bird's golden plumage shone in the sun and Tashi swiftly climbed on its back, aligning his bow and arrow simultaneously. Moments passed before he heard the familiar thunder of hooves. Then the first few horses appeared. Prince A-KarO was in the lead and making straight for the portals. Right behind him flew Chetak and Captain Leman on his charger. A party of 20 hard-riding celestial horsemen followed the prince. The Garuda let out his trumpeting call and rose into the skies, flying overhead as another knot of 10 horsemen galloped in just five minutes after the prince and his party had passed.

The Asur were right on the heels of this smaller group of celestial horsemen, led by Qui Deora, the veteran bowman, and kept harrying it. Following Deora's steed was another carrying the grievously wounded Ti Shan tied to its back. Understanding the celestials' predicament and the need to provide them with covering fire until they reached the portals, Tashi immediately took aim and shot off arrow after arrow into the Asur horsemen, while the Garuda swooped low, breathing fire into their front ranks. The mythic bird let loose a final burst of fire and mayhem, then wheeled in the air and made for the portals. Tashi felt reality blur as they crossed over. Soon, they were flying low over a peaceful green meadow dotted with golden flowers that glowed in the sunlight. The Garuda trumpeted as they caught up with Prince A-KarO and landed in safety.

Tashi got off in a hurry and ran up to the prince, going down on one knee before him. 'Are you all right, Your Highness?' he asked anxiously.

The prince nodded, but Tashi noticed that his white cloak was bloodied and his clothes smeared with gore.

'We must wait here till evening to ensure that we are not abandoning any stragglers from among our troopers,' A-KarO declared. 'You have done well, Tashi. You may rest now.'

Tashi smiled and quietly made his way to Chetak, throwing his arms around the horse's neck. 'I am so glad to see you again, Chetak!' he said with feeling.

Chetak neighed in response and the boy rubbed his ears. The horse nibbled the grass contentedly, while Tashi enjoyed the warmth of the golden sunshine on his back. He was beginning to realize how much he had missed it.

CHAPTER 16
ON THE SACRED PATHS

I

Yeshe's forehead was furrowed with anxiety as she followed Prince Narasimha striding ahead of her.

'Narasimha,' she called out, 'I feel we should have waited for A-KarO and the warriors at the site of the gates. I just can't reconcile myself to this decision of yours to move on without them.'

'It was my duty to get you safely back to Shambala at the soonest, Dakini,' the prince replied firmly. 'We could not have waited at that site. I must repeat, yet again, that we are now near the monastery of Peur, where we will rest for the night. There is a strong chance of A-KarO and his men joining us there in a couple of hours. Then we can all leave together.'

'But I can't help feeling we should have waited at the gates, Narasimha,' Yeshe persisted. 'Surely, there was no danger in doing that?'

Prince Narasimha frowned. 'Dakini,' he said sternly, 'the magic of the gates is perilous. Its vibrations are a hazard for all beings. Moreover, even though it is unlikely that the Asur will follow us here, attempts to infiltrate into this realm have been made by them on more than one occasion. So we cannot afford to be lax, Dakini, and I have to keep you moving. Even our halt at Peur will be a short one – only till dawn. At first light, we will move on.'

Yeshe stubbornly shook her head and pleaded, 'I beg of you, Narasimha! Let's turn back.'

The crown prince looked at the dakini grimly. 'Yeshe, the sunset hour is almost upon us,' he reminded her, 'and it would be ill advised to return to the gates. Peur is just a little way ahead, less than a league from here.'

Then he looked at her agonized expression and his face softened. 'I have a suggestion,' he said. 'Why don't we both keep vigil at Peur? I will sit up with you for A-KarO's arrival.'

Yeshe looked ahead and glimpsed the distinctive grey stonework of the Peur Monastery as they turned a corner. The edifice perched atop a hill and its distinctive thatched roof shone in the sunlight.

'There it is, Yeshe!' Narasimha announced. 'We are almost there. We will await A-KarO at Peur. The monks there are also likely be keeping a watch over the gates and may have news of A-KarO.'

Yeshe nodded and they walked on until they came to the foot of the hill, where a delegation of monks had come to greet them.

Leading them was a tall, thin monk dressed in grey robes – the monastery's abbot. Lama Dorji bowed low before Prince Narasimha and Yeshe, then stepped forward to place *khadas* around their necks in welcome.

'Dakini Yeshe and Prince Narasimha, I welcome you to Peur,' he said. 'We are honoured to receive you here. Dakini, your very presence signifies the success of the mission. I offer thanks to the Lord Buddha and the Goddess Tara, as also the guardian deities, for your deliverance. Prince Narasimha, we have been awaiting you for the past week or so. Messages reached us from Shambala that you would be passing through in the near future. Dakini, we have a palanquin ready to carry you up to the monastery.'

Two monks now stepped forward and placed the palanquin on the ground. Made of polished cherry wood that gleamed with a reddish tint, the palanquin had a carved roof with a dragon motif and a seat upholstered in white silk. Red silk curtains screened the door. Tired from travelling for hours on horseback, Yeshe smiled her thanks and seated herself, letting herself lie back and relax. Two monks lifted the palanquin on their shoulders and began moving uphill.

Prince Narasimha matched his pace to that of the palanquin bearers and turned to ask Dorji the question that was foremost in his mind. 'Lama,' he began, 'do you have any news as to whether the rest of the party has crossed over or not?'

Dorji nodded. 'I have good news, Prince Narasimha,' he replied. 'Prince A-KarO, accompanied by thirty celestials, crossed over early in the evening

– our time. The Garuda accompanies them. They are maintaining vigil at the gates for possible stragglers from the celestial army. I expect they will move on soon. They should be with us a little after midnight or by dawn, at the very latest.'

Yeshe laughed joyfully, the light notes of her relief and delight dancing in the air. 'You bring good news, Lama!' she declared. 'For this, accept my humble gift to you.'

With that, she held out her hands and muttered an incantation beneath her breath. Instantly, a shower of gold coins filled her cupped palms. Turning to the abbot, she said, 'Please accept these as a humble donation for your monastery.'

'This is very kind of you, Dakini,' Dorji murmured in acceptance.

Yeshe now looked at Prince Narasimha with a grave expression. 'While this is good news,' she said, 'only thirty of the eighty warriors who set out have made it back. The rest are either dead or stranded in Inka.'

'There was always a high level of risk to this mission, Dakini,' Narasimha acknowledged. 'However, if the stranded troopers survive, they should be able to make their way back home with the help of our agents in Inkala.'

Looking pensive, Yeshe settled back in her seat. The monks carrying the palanquin reached the hilltop and passed through the wooden gateway of a very cheerful-looking monastery. It overlooked a neat garden carefully lined with flowerbeds where white blossoms and yellow poppies grew in profusion. They set down the palanquin in the compound and Yeshe alighted, looking around her curiously, her gaze going to the monks in grey robes who had all gathered to receive the visitors.

Entering the monastery, Yeshe found it clean and welcoming. On one side was a large hearth, where a cheerful fire burned. Swing-back chairs stood around a table and colourful woollen carpets lay on the floor. As Yeshe sat down, a monk stepped into the room bearing a tea tray which he carried around to each of the visitors. The dakini accepted a cup of tea and tiredly leant back against her chair. She was impatient for nightfall, when she could make contact with A-KarO through a spirit journey. She prayed silently for the celestials stranded in Inka and hoped they would make it across the portals. Outside, dusk was giving way to night and the stars had begun to peep out from the heavens.

II

Yeshe sat back on the wooden cot and let herself unwind, her gaze idly wandering around her rather modest room. The floor, bare of rugs, was of wood. The white-washed walls were adorned with a single *thangka* of the Buddha in a meditation posture. Next to her cot was a small table with a burning candle on it. Yeshe poured herself a glass of cool water and sipped it slowly, looking out of the window to gaze at the multitude of stars studding the heavens. Draining the tumbler, she collected herself and prepared to perform her last task before going to sleep. Seating herself in the lotus posture, she let her mind drift into the meditative state. When one-pointed calmness had permeated her entire being, she disengaged her spirit body from her physical form. Stepping out of her divine form, her spirit took shape in the air above it. Then strengthening her will, she flew out of the window and into the dark night, away from the monastery.

Travelling for miles over rolling meadows, Yeshe's spirit smiled. The wholesomeness of this realm invigorated her. Across many leagues she flew, until she had reached the portals. There, she found Prince A-KarO waiting with his troopers.

The moment she arrived, the prince sensed her presence, raised his head and gazed directly at her spirit form. Then leaving his body, his spirit form flew to meet hers.

Prince A-KarO enveloped the dakini in an embrace and said, 'Yeshe, I never imagined you would come!'

'But how could I not, A-KarO?' she said with a smile. Then her expression grave, she asked, 'How many of your warriors have made it through the portals today?'

'Not as many as I would have liked, Dakini,' he replied. 'Twenty riders came with me and ten followed subsequently. Then late in the afternoon, five more reached the portals site, but the enemy pre-empted them and blocked their path. The Garuda then took to the air in attack mode, providing a distraction, while some of the troopers who had already crossed over with me went back through the portals to help their fellow warriors. As a result of their efforts, all the five warriors made it across. Then for a while, no more Lha were to be seen. But just an hour earlier, three of my company tried to make their way across and managed with our help, but two were badly wounded in the process. They are in urgent need of healers and the nearest are at Peur. So is Narasimha.'

Yeshe's brow furrowed. 'Should I send Narasimha to you?' she asked

Prince A-KarO shook his head. 'No, don't do that,' he said. 'We have decided to give up the vigil by the gates. Now we will ask the monks at Peur to take over for some time. We will all be leaving for the monastery now. The wounded warriors will have to hold on till then. We should be with you by midnight.'

'So, from what you tell me, only thirty-eight warriors made it back,' Yeshe said. 'What about the ones who are still stranded in Inka?'

'They were briefed before we embarked on this mission,' A-KarO explained. 'Those stranded in enemy territory will seek out our local agents and lie low for a while. Their best chance of survival lies in staying hidden and seeking the protection our agents can provide them. The portals are being left open, though the monks of Peur Monastery will post a guard on this side and keep the gates under surveillance. The stranded celestials will bide their time and cross over at the opportune moment, when the alertness of the Asur guarding the portals slackens.'

'And what chances are there of the Asur themselves crossing over?'

'For the Asur, the sacred paths are anathema,' A-KarO explained. 'They cannot cross over so easily. And it is most unlikely that a large body of Asur horsemen will even attempt it. However, an Asur spy just might take the risk. Hence, the guard at the gates is essential. Don't worry about it, Yeshe. The Asur have played their hand for now. When we reach the mortal world, however, we can expect another attack from them.'

'That makes sense, A-KarO,' Yeshe said. 'Till later, then. I will keep vigil for our warriors. Now make haste and reach Peur.'

With a smile and a wave to the prince, Yeshe's spirit form departed. Her return journey was quicker and she flew over the glowing meadows and was soon back in her room in Peur.

The dakini felt life slowly returning to her exhausted body as she came back to herself. She poured herself another glass of water and sipped it, a little at a time. Then she stepped out of her room and into the narrow corridor outside, making her way through the monastery till she had come to the entrance hall. She found Prince Narasimha sitting alone, whittling away at a piece of wood. A single candle burned on a table.

Narasimha looked up when he saw her. 'Dakini,' he said, 'are you ready to join me in my vigil?'

Yeshe nodded. 'I have some news for you, Narasimha,' she told him. 'I have just communicated with A-KarO. Some thirty-eight celestials have made it back alive today. However, I fear for the rest who are stranded in Inka. What will become of them, should things not work out?'

Narasimha sighed and crossed his legs. 'They know what to do in this situation, Dakini. They will manage.'

'A-KarO also told me that some of the warriors who succeeded in making it back were wounded in the attempt,' Yeshe said. 'They will need attention the moment they reach Peur.'

Narasimha sat up. 'I am ready for that situation,' he told her. 'I have already prepared my supplies. Besides, there are healers among the monks here and they, too, have a well-stocked infirmary. We should be able to handle the situation. In fact, the main reason behind my vigil is to give the wounded immediate attention when they arrive.'

Yeshe sat on a swing-back chair and relaxed. The minutes ticked away. Narasimha poured some steaming tea out of a pot and handed the mug to the dakini. She sipped the herbal tea and felt life being restored to her exhausted body. Outside in the garden, crickets chirped merrily. Yeshe felt peace invade her being. At last, she felt safe, at home. Her eyelids drooped and as they closed shut, a pair of sly golden eyes appeared in her inner vision. Arden! She shuddered and shook herself awake. Shaken that her subconscious mind had somehow drifted to Arden, she shuddered again and sipped the hot, comforting tea. Wiping the sleep from her eyes, she sat up, alert, staring into the night.

III

Tashi smiled with pleasure as Chetak raced through the night. The beauty of the rolling meadows flanking the sacred paths reminded him of Yumsamedong and its high alpine meadows. He remembered the hidden monastery and was overcome with nostalgia. He would give anything to be back there, attending on Lama Ozer and going about his daily chores. Tashi forced himself to emerge from his pleasant daydream and looked ahead. The night breeze was cool against his face and the prince was riding hard in a bid to make it to Peur Monastery by midnight. They had been on the move for four hours now and the moon was already halfway up in the heavens. Tashi hoped their destination was not far off now. His anxious glance went to the seriously wounded Ti Shan who rode alongside, strapped to his horse. He was afraid Ti's wounds would start bleeding again because of the speed at which the horses were galloping along.

Looking stern as always, Captain Leman rode in silence next to Ti.

Chetak threw his head up and neighed, 'We are nearly there, Tashi. Just a turn in the road will reveal the lights of Peur Monastery.'

Tashi patted the wind horse. 'And about time too, Chetak,' he declared. 'We seem to have been riding forever.'

The horse crested a rise in the meadow and the lights of Peur Monastery appeared before them. Torches had been lit at the gates and a bonfire burned brightly in the courtyard. Lights shone from both floors of the monastery.

As the company approached the gates, the monk standing sentinel there blew a horn in three bursts. Many of his fellow monks who had been sitting around the bonfire now rose to their feet as the company approached and lined up with *khada*s for the prince and Captain Leman. A delegation of monks hurried forward to welcome the warriors as they poured into the monastery compound. A monk rushed forth to hold the reins of the prince's horse as he dismounted.

The abbot came forward and bowed low before Prince A-KarO, then placed a *khada* around his neck. 'You do us a great honour, Your Highness, by staying in our humble abode,' said Lama Dorji.

The prince smiled in response, then said, 'Lama, I have several warriors who are badly wounded. I am relying on the healers among your monks to attend to them.'

'But of course, Your Highness,' Lama Dorji assured him, 'we will have the wounded carried into the infirmary, where our healers will attend to them.'

A group of monks came forward and directed the able-bodied warriors to carry the wounded into the infirmary. Tashi balanced Ti Shan's weight on his shoulder, as he carried his friend in. Cots with clean bed linen had been laid out in the infirmary and the healers moved about, settling the wounded before treating them. Tashi laid Ti out on a wooden cot and gently poured some water into his mouth so he could quench his thirst. Prince Narasimha entered, followed by the dakini, Yeshe. By the time the wounded had all been carried in, most of the beds were occupied. Tashi followed Prince Narasimha around, eager to help.

'Tashi,' the crown prince requested, 'lead me to the most seriously wounded troopers right away. I must attend to them first.'

The boy immediately led Narasimha to Ti Shan.

The prince examined Ti and shook his head. 'This is a bad case,' he murmured. 'There is internal bleeding and the condition of his lungs and heart does not leave much room for hope. Let's see what I can do for him.'

Fear gripped Tashi's heart as he stared at Narasimha's expression.

The prince placed his hands on Ti's chest and let a trickle of blue healing energy flow into it, directing it carefully into his heart. Only when he felt the blockages clearing and the damaged valve regaining its strength did he turn his attention to the patient's lungs. Carefully directing a flow of violet energy into Ti's lungs, Narasimha literally reconstructed the damaged right one. The prince worked on Ti for more than an hour, reconstituting a large part of his collapsed chest and damaged heart tissues and cells. Sweat trickled from his brow, as he worked swiftly, efficiently and with complete focus.

Finally, when his work was complete, Narasimha looked at Tashi. 'I have done for him what I could,' he explained. 'Now it is up to his body to fight back. If he survives the night, he may well live.' Tying a poultice of healing herbs to Ti's chest, the prince moved on to the others.

The monks, meanwhile, had cordoned off the section where the critically wounded warriors had been laid out, hanging up sheets to separate them from the rest of the infirmary and setting up braziers of healing herbs. Tashi noticed the veteran bowman, Lam Sutia, on one of the beds and directed the prince to him. As Narasimha examined Lam, Tashi stood by patiently.

'He is in a bad way,' the prince declared, 'but his situation is not hopeless. There is a puncture to his left lung and his collarbone and ribs have been broken.'

Having said that, the prince swiftly began working on Lam. Yeshe assisted him by passing him the herbs he needed and handed him the required instruments for setting the broken bones. Tashi observed them for some time, then walked back to have a look at Ti. The celestial looked pale and lay utterly still. His breathing sounded laboured. Tashi wiped his friend's face with a towel dipped in water, then left him to rest.

Tashi's exhaustion was catching up with him when he made to step out of the infirmary and was hauled back inside. The monk who had grabbed him by the sleeve now led him firmly to a chair and made him sit down. Washing out the wound on Tashi's thigh with healing herbs, the monk applied a poultice to it, muttering all the while. He examined the boy thoroughly and attended to his other cuts and bruises before finally letting him go. Tashi walked tiredly out through the door and made it into the hall, where dinner had been laid out. He sat down to a repast of rice, lentils and green vegetables from the monastery gardens. Eating quickly, he finished dinner and found himself a pallet in an antechamber which was attached to Prince A-KarO's room. He settled himself on it, intending to wait up for the prince. Tashi thought of the past day and especially of the Garuda who had been invincible in action and smiled as he remembered the Garuda's leave-taking of the celestials. The messenger of the Gods had brushed Tashi's hair playfully and then disappeared, winging across the blue skies of the Sacred Paths. A smiling Tashi let exhaustion take over and by the time A-KarO came in, the boy was fast asleep.

IV

The morning sunshine was bright as the company set off for the portals, a mere two-hour ride away. A well-rested Tashi was looking forward to reaching Shambala and meeting up again with Lama Ozer. His mind wandered to Ti and he sighed with relief. His friend had managed to survive a rather difficult night. It had been touch and go for a while, but at dawn, things had taken a turn for the better. By late morning, Prince Narasimha had declared him out of danger and the Lha company had left Peur only after the prince had attended to the more critical patients and handed over their care to the monks.

As the company rode on, a small grove of shady, broad-leaved trees with small fragrant white flowers appeared ahead of them. Prince A-KarO immediately signalled to the warriors to slow down and led them at a leisurely pace through it. They came upon a small stream wending its way through the heart of the grove. The prince signalled for the company to halt, swiftly dismounted from his horse and began chanting in a low voice. His voice rose and fell as he continued to murmur incantations. Then suddenly, a blaze of light issued forth from his fingers and illuminated the outline of the portals at the edge of the stream. The portals grew larger, but all that was visible on the other side was a haze of green. The princes and the dakini then led their horses through the portals, with the rest of the company following. Tashi smiled as he found himself in the familiar environs of the Amber Courtyard in the Rigden's royal palace.

A trooper blew a blast from the conch thrice to announce their arrival. Tashi beamed with joy as the company now led the horses through the gardens at a gentle trot, making for the stables. A crowd of people had collected at the stables and began cheering the warriors as they approached. Grooms rushed forward to hold the horses as the party dismounted and lead them into the stables. Prince A-KarO gave the command for the company to disperse and the troopers swiftly set about returning to the comforts the palace offered.

Meanwhile, Tashi had led Chetak to his stall. He hung around while the groom entrusted with the wind horse's care examined the latter closely and clucked his tongue when he saw his hooves. Tashi helped the Lha curry Chetak, filling his bin with feed and water before picking up the grooming brush.

'I will take over from here,' the boy suggested. 'You had better see to the other horses.'

The groom shook his head as he continued to examine Chetak's hooves. 'These are in bad shape and will need to be soaked in a medicinal solution,' he explained. 'While I am preparing it, you may brush him down.'

Tashi nodded and proceeded to get on with the job.

Chetak already had his muzzle in the oat bin. 'Ah, Tashi!' he exclaimed between munches, 'you cannot imagine how wonderful this feels! It's so good to be back. I don't doubt I will be dreadfully bored in a while, but something tells me we will be on the move again. By the way, don't forget to come back tomorrow afternoon with all the palace gossip.'

Tashi scratched Chetak behind his ear and the horse nuzzled him in response. The grooming session over, the boy took one last look around the stall.

Meanwhile, the groom had walked in with a basin full of medicinal solution and strips of cloth. 'You may go now, Tashi,' he said. 'I will attend to the wind horse myself.'

The warriors had already dispersed as Tashi made his way out of the stables and towards the palace. He entered it and whistled as he strolled through the palace corridors that led to the prince's apartments.

Tashi entered them and was surprised to find it empty. The clothes that Prince A-KarO had travelled in were lying in one corner where he had apparently taken them off and discarded them. Tashi felt mortified that in his eagerness to be with Chetak, he had neglected his duty to the prince. He went about his chores until pangs of hunger drove him whistling through the palace's busy corridors to the royal kitchens. It was not yet lunchtime, but he knew the cook could definitely spare a snack for him. Entering the pantry, he saw the cook bustling about, seeing to an order from one of the royals. He looked up and smiled broadly when he saw Tashi.

'Boy, am I glad to see you back safe!' he exclaimed happily. 'You must tell me all about your various adventures and especially about your experiences with the Asur.'

'Only if you provide me with some victuals right now,' Tashi said with a smile.

The cook beamed. 'But of course!' he said. 'Here, have some cake. And I have some fresh lemon pie in the oven, ready to be taken out.'

With that, he pulled a steaming-hot lemon pie out of the oven and cut a thick slice for Tashi. Then he set out a jug of creamy milk and a glass for him to wash it down with

'Help yourself, boy,' the cook urged. 'But once you've finished filling your stomach, you must give me a blow-by-blow account of your adventures.'

Tashi sighed with bliss as he sipped the frothy milk and took a bite of the pie. 'No one can rival your cooking, Master Cook,' he said. 'You cannot imagine how much I have been missing it.'

The cook smiled as he settled down at Tashi's elbow, eager to hear a detailed account of his adventures and the boy obliged him between bites of cake and pie.

V

Yeshe sighed with relief as her horse galloped into familiar territory – the rolling grounds of the Azure Palace with their rich parkland, abundant with blossoming trees and neat flowerbeds. At last, she was home, even if it was to be for a short while. She would have to be content with that. Following her closely was the royal guard assigned for her protection, but even their presence could not detract from her happiness. Yeshe raced her horse to the very edge of the pool and dismounted. Then she dived into its cool, clear waters.

She sank into its lucid depths and made her way to the bottom. Then she strolled through the beautiful underwater garden surrounding the Azure Palace. Gently cupping in her palms the small fish that swam around her, she crooned to them, allowing a wave of divine energy to flow into them. She greeted the larger fish like old acquaintances and then wended her way through the colourful flora and fauna to her underwater retreat.

Dripping wet, Yeshe stepped into the magically dry air of the Azure Palace courtyard. Immediately, her maidens hastened to welcome her home, followed by her old nurse who came forward to enfold the dakini in a warm embrace.

'My child, golden flower, peerless Dakini!' she said emotionally, 'you have returned! My prayers have been answered.'

Handing Yeshe a steaming-hot towel to dry herself, the old nurse gestured to the maidens to withdraw. The dakini felt her exhaustion peeling off, as she stepped into her home.

'Yeshe, my child, let's go to your room,' the nurse suggested. 'I have a bath prepared for you.'

In a daze, as it were, the dakini allowed herself to be led to her room with its shell-inlaid floor. In the centre sat a large, round wooden tub, filled with hot water stained a delicate pink with cleansing herbs. Tendrils of steam rose from it invitingly.

The dakini experienced an overwhelming sense of relief as the nurse helped her slip off her clinging wet garments and step into the tub. She immersed herself in the hot water and felt her muscles relax instantly. As she let herself unwind, her old nurse bustled about her, chattering constantly.

'Golden flower, my prayers have been answered,' she said. 'All I asked for was that you return to us, safe and sound. But you have lost too much weight, golden flower. You are nothing but skin and bones. And there is no time either to fatten you up before you leave for the mortal world. I hear that you are spending no more than a day here before departing for Aggartha with the princes and your other two companions day after tomorrow.'

Yeshe forced herself to emerge from the stupor into which she had sunk. 'Oh?' she said. 'Then you surely know more than I do, for this is news for me.'

The old nurse smiled. 'Orders have come from the palace that you are to be present this evening for an audience with the Rigden at seven sharp,' she said. 'Moreover, it has been decreed that tomorrow you are to undergo a ritual cleansing at the Pegamse Monastery near the Half-Moon Lake. A carriage will come from the monastery at eight a.m. to pick you up.'

Yeshe let her body slump back in the water. 'So, tomorrow is my last day here in Shambala and I am obliged to spend it cleansing myself. Ugh! But then, I knew that was inevitable.'

'Child,' the nurse said, 'a trip to the Asur realm, Inka, would evidently necessitate the most rigorous cleansing possible. And you surely understand that it is for your own good. You are to bear the divine child, after all, and not even the slightest whiff of contamination can be allowed to linger in your body or in your psyche. And it is not you alone who must go through the cleansing process. The two princes, along with all the soldiers who accompanied them, have to submit themselves to it. However, I am told they will undergo their cleansing in the Riumse Monastery in the city.'

Yeshe slipped farther into the hot water, enjoying its warmth.

'Here, golden flower,' the nurse offered, handing the dakini a mug of fragrant tea, 'sip this herbal brew as you soak in the tub. It will relax you.'

Yeshe gratefully sipped the honeyed tea steeped in crushed marigolds, enjoying the floral fragrance that rose to her nostrils and feeling her muscles relax as the brew worked its magic.

When the water began to cool, the nurse coaxed Yeshe out of the tub and wrapped a thick towel around her which soaked in the moisture from her body. Then discarding the towel, the dakini stepped into a soft white robe.

The nurse was attending to her wet hair, when there was the sound of gentle footsteps and Yeshe looked up to find the High Priestess, Ina, the Goddess Tara's emissary, standing before her in all her perfection. The chief priestess for the goddess's worship wore a plain white shift and around her neck were several garlands of marigolds. Strings of marigolds entwined her arms. Swan-shaped beads of dew adorned her earlobes and a tiara of sparkling dewdrops sat on her head. The high priestess came forward and Yeshe went down on her knees and bowed low before her. Then leaning forward, she kissed her fingers and remained on her knees, her head bowed reverentially.

The High Priestess spoke. 'I bear a message from your mother, the Goddess Tara. Prophesied mother of the divine one, the messiah of the Fourth Age, arise. Your mother sends you her love and also expresses joy at your safe return. She sends you some healing to help restore you after your arduous journey. However, she cannot meet you now. She urges you to be strong and to fulfil your duty as expected on Earth.'

The High Priestess's expression grew grave. 'Golden flower, Yeshe! The goddess was greatly disturbed by the news of your abduction and imprisonment in the Asur palace in Inkala. She is more perturbed still by the fact that the defence you require to keep you safe cannot be arranged for you on Earth. Nor can a great host be sent from here for your protection in the mortal world. You are allowed no more than a few companions for your journey. Such are the terms set by the sacred guardians of the universe for the birth of the divine one.

'Given the situation, the goddess has prepared a gift for you that will safeguard you. Should there be danger, it will serve as your last defence.' The High Priestess held out a necklace made from tiny beads of dew that sparkled with an unusual lustre. 'This is a moon necklace,' she said. 'Created from dewdrops collected at midnight, the necklace was strung at the goddess's temple to the accompaniment of many sacred chants and accords its wearer the power of invisibility. Yeshe, the goddess bids you to wear it at all times. When in distress, you can make yourself invisible by breathing over the beads and chanting the mantra, "Om". All of us at Tirshangle hope that it will help you in a moment of dire need.'

The High Priestess smiled in farewell and vanished, her essence ebbing from the chamber. Yeshe picked up the necklace and put it on. Her old nurse clapped her hands in relief.

'Now mark my words, golden flower,' she said, 'that necklace will help you, especially on Earth, where your divine powers will no longer be at your disposal.'

Yeshe smiled. 'Do you think you can rustle me up some light food?' she asked. 'I find I'm hungry.'

Her nurse nodded. 'Of course, child. Your maidens have prepared a feast for you. Come break your fast with them.'

Yeshe smiled in acknowledgement, then left her room to head for the dining hall.

VI

Darkness had descended by the time Yeshe, riding her horse, Tirshan, reached the palace complex, accompanied by an escort of guardsmen. Lightly patting the steed, she made her way across the grounds to the stables. Then dismounting, Yeshe left the guard and entered the palace, making her way through the maze of corridors to the oceanic hall.

She entered this vast space with its azure-blue walls that depicted ocean waves and were studded with dark blue sapphires. The light that emanated from the gems provided the hall with its illumination and navy seats were placed at certain points. Yeshe was striding through the hall when a familiar voice hailed her.

It was Prince A-KarO, with Tashi trailing behind him. Yeshe felt faintly self-conscious at his attention, but smiled in greeting.

'Dakini, I am so glad to have met up with you here,' the prince said. 'You must be on your way to the Rigden's audience chamber. Come, allow me to escort you there.'

Yeshe inclined her head to indicate her consent. 'I hope I am not late,' she told him as they made their way to the audience chamber. 'I understand this meeting is important and concerns our immediate future.'

Prince A-KarO's eyes twinkled. 'Undoubtedly, Dakini,' he confirmed. 'I hope you found time to rest a bit? The past few weeks have not been easy for you.'

Yeshe shrugged. 'Rest does not seem possible in the near future,' she murmured. 'I understand we leave for Aggartha day after tomorrow.'

'That is so, but I still intend to enjoy every moment of my remaining days here before our departure. I do not expect to see Shambala for a long time to come.'

'Leaving Shambala is hard,' Yeshe sighed. 'I have always lived here and feel like I am being torn away from my home.'

Prince A-KarO looked at her, his gaze astute. 'I can quite understand how you feel, Dakini,' he said. 'I, on the contrary, have been on the move for a long time now, engaged as I am in battle along the border worlds to defend our territory from invaders. However, I will certainly miss my celestial life while I am on Earth. Are you reconciled to life as a mortal, Dakini? For that is what awaits us once the sages have briefed us before our departure.'

'I have come to terms with this reality,' Yeshe replied. 'It is a sacrifice demanded of us and I will try my best to honour the decision determining my destiny.'

'Don't forget, Yeshe, that Narasimha and I will be with you on this difficult journey,' the prince reassured her. 'We will do our utmost to keep you safe and help you fulfil the duty that all of us have been entrusted with, but which lies most heavily on your shoulders.'

Yeshe smiled. 'I may not always have given your words due respect, Prince A-KarO,' she admitted, 'but now I do value your advice as well as Narasimha's. I shall depend on both of you, but will try my best not to be a burden. Also, I have never been to Earth. I quite look forward to exploring it. Are you, perhaps, familiar with the mortal world?'

'Oh, yes!' the prince replied with a smile. 'I am more than familiar with it. I have made many forays into that world over the years and even have friends there. I quite look forward to going there again.'

They turned into yet another corridor and then came up to the bronze gateway leading to the Rigden's inner audience chamber. The two guards on duty saluted smartly and stood back for the Prince and Yeshe to enter, with Tashi trailing behind them.

'Ah! I see that all of us have been summoned,' Yeshe remarked. 'Narasimha and the venerable Lama Ozer are already here.'

As usual, the chamber was filled with nobles and dignitaries. Prince A-KarO stopped to talk to a group of nobles, while Yeshe made her way to one side of the room, intending to wait there quietly till they were called. She observed young Tashi running up to Lama Ozer and bowing to him. Then the boy broke enthusiastically into conversation with the lama. Yeshe's gaze moved to Prince A-KarO. Prince Narasimha had joined him and the two stood to one side, chatting amiably. Yeshe studied them intently. The two celestials could not have been more different. Narasimha was the gentler one, his overall demeanour unassuming. A-KarO's personality appeared to be darker, more dynamic. He seemed to blaze with barely leashed energy and Yeshe felt both thrilled by and wary of his presence. In his company, she felt uneasy, self-conscious and quite out of her depth. After the heroic rescue he had organized, spiriting her away from the Asur palace, she could not bring herself to snub him the way she had earlier. Yet she was wary of expressing warmth. Looking at them both, she felt helpless at the impossible choice she had to make. Of the two celestials, neither was suitable as her consort. One was impossible and the other already taken.

Shaking her head, she looked towards the Rigden, who was dressed simply in an ivory robe, with his silver hair tied in a severe topknot. His dark eyes glinted as he addressed the courtiers before him. There was a flurry of activity as the courtiers were given the signal to depart and Yeshe's name and that of her companions were called out. She nodded to Lama Ozer on her way to the dais and reached it just as the rest of her companions arrived. All five of them bowed low before the Rigden. Yeshe looked up expectantly at him.

'Ah, Yeshe! Golden flower, I am so glad to see you back with us at last!' the Rigden began, his pale countenance lighting up with a smile. Then he looked at the two princes and his gaze took in Tashi as well. 'I believe I owe all three of you a debt of gratitude. Prince A-KarO, you have, once again, fulfilled our hopes and helped us in our hour of need. Narasimha, you have done me proud. As for young Tashi, who brought doom to a Gorod, of all creatures, from what I hear, you are proving to be a worthy warrior.' Then the Rigden addressed Lama Ozer. 'Lama,' he said, 'your disciple, young Tashi, has done you proud. You have brought the youngster up well.'

The Rigden's tone grew serious as he said, 'But now it is time for all five of you to prepare yourselves for your descent to Earth. Tomorrow, you will participate in the cleansing ceremony. Each of you has been notified of the venues where it will be held. The day after, you leave for Aggartha at dawn. All of you are to make your way to the royal monastery, from where we will send you forth through the direct-link gate to Aggatha. There, the council of twelve sages will give you detailed information pertaining to your stay on Earth and explain what is expected of each of you. Shambala's hopes lie with you all. Yeshe, golden flower, innocent one! You are the prophesied mother of the divine child and much is expected of you, the first being to choose your consort from among the two princes accompanying you. Prince A-KarO, Narasimha and young Tashi! You are to protect the dakini from all perils and keep her safe. The sages will tell you the rest.'

'Your Majesty,' Prince A-KarO interrupted, 'I have a request to make.'

'Go ahead.'

'The dakini's defence rests with me, Your Majesty, and we know that Earth is not safe, for the Asur are sure to launch an attack on us there. You have already informed us that there are restrictions on what we may carry with us to the mortal world and our celestial forces will not be there to help us. However, please allow me to take select members of my trained Lha troops with us.'

The Rigden shook his head. 'I would be relieved to do so, Prince A-KarO,' he said, 'but unfortunately, we cannot allow the dakini more than four companions for this journey. Such are the conditions set for the birth of the divine one. However, you may recruit mortals on Earth to organize a guard for the dakini and we are confident that you will be able to train them sufficiently to be fit to face the Asur.'

A-KarO sighed with frustration. 'So be it, Your Majesty,' he said. 'This only makes our challenge all the greater.'

'However,' the Rigden continued with a reassuring smile, 'you will not be entirely without means for countering the obstacles you face. We have notified all the chiefs of the hidden communities on Earth as well as our agents there of your imminent arrival and they will come to your aid, should you need it. We have provided Lama Ozer with a list of their names. We expect you to make use of these persons and communities as and when required. You may, in fact, use whatever resource is available on Earth to protect yourselves.'

Prince Narasimha interrupted him. 'I, too, have a question, my Lord,' he said. 'I believe we are to be stripped of our celestial powers. Will this not compromise us further?'

'It is true that you will lose your celestial powers and status on Earth, but you will be more than mere mortals. You will retain your knowledge and are expected to use it to your advantage to survive on Earth and fulfil the duties with which you have been entrusted. Lastly, I would like to remind you not to carry anything from this realm for your stay on Earth, other than what is specifically permitted. You are expected to use your superior intelligence in the mortal world and be innovative when it is so required.'

'We will be at a clear disadvantage, my King,' A-KarO said in frustration.

Unmoved, the Rigden retorted with a thin smile, 'Only if you allow yourself to be at a disadvantage, Prince A-KarO, and I don't see that happening. Now I have said all that I needed to. You have my permission to withdraw.'

All five of them bowed low before the Rigden and were ushered out of the audience chamber. Yeshe smiled to herself. She was determined to make the most of what little time she had in Shambala.

VII

Dawn was stealing into her room, tinting the waves of the azure pool outside with gold, as Yeshe finished a light repast and rose from her seat. She wandered to the window and admired the golden light mingling with the azure waters, creating a scene of ethereal beauty. Yeshe was still gazing out of the window when her nurse bustled into the room.

'Golden flower,' she said urgently, 'it is time to get dressed. A carriage has already arrived from the monastery to take you there. Come now, this is no time to tarry. Hurry!'

Yeshe sighed, moving away from the window and making her way to the bed, where simple white garments had been laid out for her. Without wasting a moment, she stepped into the white skirt and slipped on the matching blouse, wrapping the light cotton stole around herself. Then she strode from the chamber and made her way to the veranda that overlooked the shining waves of water swirling around at the bottom of the pool.

As she murmured a word of power, her form shimmered and disappeared. The next moment, she was standing at the edge of her pool in the rolling grounds of her estate. An old wooden contraption, more cart than carriage, drawn by four mountain ponies stood waiting for her. Yeshe stepped in and seated herself. The driver cracked the whip and the carriage began moving. The dakini pulled the window curtains aside and inhaled the fresh morning air. Soon, they had left the gates to her estate behind them and were heading for the Half-Moon Monastery. Yeshe sat back and relaxed; it was going to be a long ride.

The coachman was a young monk who talked incessantly, badgering the dakini for an account of her adventures in the Asur realm. She bore the chatter for a while before deciding to ignore him completely. The monk finally took the hint and apologized.

'Dakini,' he said, contrite, 'I do apologize for tiring you with my chatter. My master tells me, time and again, that I talk too much. However, I need to tell you that my master asked you to practise raised breathing. This will help you to bear the discomfort of the cleansing ritual.'

Yeshe sighed and slowly began the practice of *tummo*. Gradually, her body temperature rose until she felt like a furnace and wondered if waves of heat were radiating from her. As her mind disengaged itself from the physical aspects of the exercise, waves of ecstasy started rising within her, filling her with a sense of emptiness, weightlessness and golden, effervescent joy that flowed through her like fine wine. Finally, holding her breath, she let her mind slip into *sunyata* or the golden void. Then she allowed the rhythm of her breathing to slow down and her heartbeats returned to a semblance of normalcy. The session drew to a close, but Yeshe's body and being were now charged with pure energy and she felt herself able to go through the ordeal of the cleansing that awaited her.

They were not far from the monastery now, with the serene silver waters of Half-Moon Lake flanking the road on one side, while a well-tended hedge ran along the other. A turn later, the Half-Moon Monastery became visible atop a small hill that overlooked the lake. The carriage picked up speed as Yeshe approached her destination and they were soon climbing the hill. Within minutes, the carriage had come to a halt in front of the monastery's entrance. Yeshe stepped out, gazing up at the classic structure in the shape of a crescent moon that had been painted in maroon and white – the colours of the religious order its resident monks belonged to. A pair of monks were waiting at the entrance to greet her and they led her away to meet the abbot.

A tall, thin man with a lean face and a straggly beard, the abbot rose to meet Yeshe and declared, 'Dakini, we must begin the cleansing rites immediately. A room has been prepared for the performance of the ritual during which I must request you to maintain absolute silence. Also, once we begin, you must abstain from food and drink. So if you are thirsty, Dakini, you may drink some water now. You should be aware that we will be taking you through the entire process, as you may have been exposed to contamination or worse during your stay in the Asur realm. Follow me, Dakini,' he directed her. 'We must begin without delay. I will preside over the ritual myself.'

With that, he led her down a long corridor to a solitary cell. 'A shift has been laid out inside for your use,' he told her. 'You may change into it.'

Yeshe entered the cell, changed into the thick white cotton shift and sat down on the single cot provided for her. The abbot came in shortly and surveyed her, nodding his approval.

He handed Yeshe a small glass containing a green herbal brew and said, 'Drink this. The first step in the process is to purge you.'

The dakini accepted the glass and swallowed its contents in one gulp.

The abbot now placed an empty bucket at her feet and handed her a basin of water, along with a towel. 'You will feel the effects shortly,' he told her. 'I will come in and check on you in a little while.'

Moments after the abbot had left the cell, Yeshe felt waves of nausea rising within her. And then she was throwing up violently into the bucket. For the next two hours, she vomited continuously. This was followed by a few moments of dry retching, until her stomach was empty and the nausea had passed. An exhausted Yeshe stretched out on the cot to rest. Two lay sisters now entered the cell with steaming towels. They wiped her clean and gave her a fresh shift to wear.

They had just finished ministering to the dakini, when the abbot came in bearing a goblet of fire water. The incandescent, fiery liquid frothed with bubbles.

'Drink this, Dakini,' he directed Yeshe. 'This will purge your spirit of all traces of contamination and restore it to its original state of pristine essence.'

Yeshe shook her head. 'I cannot abide fire water, Abbot,' she protested. 'Is there no other way?'

The abbot shook his head firmly and handed her the goblet. With an unhappy sigh, she downed the liquid and felt fire break out over her inner being. Yeshe felt waves of the most excruciating pain break out over her body and her essence and curled herself into a tight ball to withstand them. It was as if flames were licking at her insides and consuming them. The waves of pain rose and subsided, then rose again.

Yeshe curled and uncurled herself, shuddering uncontrollably as the pain devoured her, then burst into screams of agony. A dark, clammy sweat rose from within and spread over her thrashing body, sticking to her skin like a miasma. From time to time, the lay sisters mopped her face and her body with hot towels, but Yeshe was lost in agony, oblivious to everything but the fire raging within her. The hours went by and Yeshe's ordeal showed no signs of coming to an end. Then finally, a shimmering yellow aura spread over her.

Observing her, the abbot shook his head. 'This is not a good sign, Dakini,' he said gravely. 'You seem to have been contaminated in the worst way possible. The black sweat that has appeared on your body and the yellow aura of enthralment which is also visible around you have made it clear that an Asur noble had held you in thrall. I thank the goddess and the Lord Buddha that you were brought here in time. Your body and your essence are now rid of contamination, but complete purification and healing are not possible, because the shimmer of enthralment remains. We have done what we could to weaken its hold and its noxious effects will die away in time – provided that you do not encounter the Asur noble who worked his magic on you. But you will have to remain alert from now on and safeguard yourself against danger in the future.'

The abbot now handed her a goblet of blue healing liquid and asked her to drink it. Yeshe complied. Gradually, a soothing coolness spread through her body and spirit, extinguishing the flames of agony and affording her sweet relief.

Yeshe felt sanity return to her, little by little. 'I thank you, Abbot, for what you have done for me,' she murmured gratefully.

The abbot smiled, but his tone was grave as he warned, 'Beware, Dakini! Beware of the enthralment. Do not allow the Asur noble who cast the spell near you ever again.'

'He was Prince Arden Ti Nazer Basher,' she told him.

The abbot blanched at the name. 'You will not take that name ever again, Dakini, and I urge you to always be on your guard against him. I will also have to inform the Rigden about the outcome of the cleansing process so that he may warn your companions for the forthcoming journey to be extra-vigilant about possible encounters with this Asur noble. I am sure you understand that it is my duty to do so.'

Yeshe nodded, then followed the abbot out of the cell. She was surprised to discover that the sun had set and the stars were out. Her ordeal had lasted an entire day.

VIII

Dawn was breaking over the horizon when Tashi woke up. Instantly alert, he threw off the bedclothes and got to his feet. Then having hurried through his ablutions, he pulled on a crisp, navy blue tunic and matching trousers, slicking his hair back with oil and tying it neatly behind his head with a leather string. As he pulled on his boots, he was barely able to contain his rising euphoria. They were leaving for Aggartha today. From there, it would be back to Earth. Tashi nurtured the silent hope that they would somehow return to the mortal world through Sikkim and even manage a quick visit to the hidden monastery.

At that moment, there was a knock on the door and the boy rushed to open it. A minion from the royal kitchen stood there, holding a tray laden with the prince's breakfast. Tashi swiftly took the tray from him and carried it to A-KarO's room.

Already up and dressed, the prince was grooming his hair, when Tashi walked in.

'Breakfast, Your Highness,' he announced.

Prince A-KarO nodded. 'There is enough for two,' he observed. 'Tashi, fetch your plate and join me. We have little time in hand. I trust you are packed and ready, because we depart in ten minutes.'

'Yes, Your Highness,' he replied. 'I had packed your clothes as well as mine last night.'

'I hope you haven't taken too many things, Tashi,' the prince smiled, 'because we will be spending but a single night in Aggartha. The very next day, we leave for Earth and, as you well know, we are not allowed to carry anything from Shambala other than the clothes on our back. However, I do plan to carry my two swords with me. I also intend to collect Chetak from the stables, for he is my gift to you. I will petition the sages to grant you permission to take him along.'

'I will run to the stables and fetch him, Your Highness,' Tashi announced happily. 'I'd better be on my way.'

Prince A-KarO pointed to the breakfast tray. 'Eat, first, young Tashi!' he reminded the boy. 'Then you can carry out our packs and leave for the stables.'

Tashi nodded, waiting for the prince to begin eating, before he served himself some porridge. He relished the creamy taste of the milk and the sweetness of the porridge. He finished his meal in a hurry and was granted permission by the prince to leave for the stables. Tashi rushed back to his room and picked up the two light travel packs – his own and the prince's – containing no more than a change of clothing. Then he left the room and ran down the palace corridors, deserted at that early hour, racing out through the exit and across the grounds towards the stables, where he almost collided with a groom.

The man put out a hand to steady the boy and prevent him from falling and hurting himself. 'Careful, Tashi!' he cautioned. 'I suppose you have come for Chetak?'

Tashi flushed, embarrassed at having been caught running. 'Yes, Master Groom,' he answered.

The groom smiled. 'I have already groomed your wind horse and he is ready to be led out,' he said. 'I thought you might come for him, especially since you are leaving for the mortal world today.'

Tashi followed the groom into the stables and to Chetak's stall.

The wind horse had pricked up his ears when he sighted Tashi and let out a welcoming neigh. 'I did think you would come for me, boy,' he said. 'So I get to accompany you to Earth, do I?'

'Well,' Tashi replied, 'this much is certain; you are coming with us to Aggartha. There, the prince will petition the sages for permission to have you accompany us on our journey to Earth.'

'Of course I am coming with you, Tashi,' Chetak said confidently. 'And if they deny you permission to take me along, I will follow, nonetheless. I have my ways. So don't you worry.'

Tashi led the wind horse out of the stables and into the fresh air of dawn. Invigorated by the thought of their impending journey, he began whistling. It was a beautiful morning and there was a pleasant nip in the air. Tashi made his way across the palace grounds towards the entrance and stood by for the two princes to emerge. While he waited, he pulled out an apple from his pocket and fed it to Chetak. The wind horse had barely finished munching it when the princes appeared.

Prince Narasimha wore a brown woollen robe and a cloak around his shoulders. He carried nothing but a small bag of medicines which he held with great care. Prince A-KarO was dressed simply in his leathers. His white cloak lay draped around his shoulders and his only ornament was the legendary pair of swords strapped to his waist in matching black velvet scabbards.

Tashi bowed low to the princes before greeting them. 'A good morrow to you, Your Highnesses,' he said. 'Are we to leave now?'

Prince Narasimha nodded. 'Yes, right away,' he replied. 'Just follow us to the monastery. It is but a short walk.'

Tashi obediently fell in behind the royals as they walked ahead of him, straining to eavesdrop on their exchanges. But all he managed to catch was snatches of their conversation and he soon lost interest. He took one last, lingering look at the palace gardens and their beds of bright, multi-coloured flowers bedecked with shining dewdrops. The grass was a vivid green and springy under his feet. Once again, the boy could not help marvelling at Shambala's indescribable beauty.

They made their way across the gardens towards the Turquoise Courtyard, where Tashi gazed at the fragrant orange flowers and remembered the previous occasion on which he had been there – his first visit to the palace. Soon they had left the courtyard behind and entered a cultivated garden that fronted the beautiful royal monastery, an edifice the awestruck Tashi had never set eyes on before. Its roof was made of sheets of pure gold. Its walls had been hewn from rock and depicted intricately carved scenes from Shambala's history; peaceful tableaux of entwined lovers, of forest dryads sunning themselves, of nymphs cavorting in the moonlight were juxtaposed with scenes of battle, with air sprites rushing to engage in combat. The trio made their way to the gates of the monastery which stood open, with the abbot and a retinue of monks waiting by them to receive the visitors. As the princes approached, with Tashi in tow, the abbot stepped forward, greeted them warmly and placed *khadas* around their necks. Then he ushered them into the main hall. Tashi immediately spotted Lama Ozer standing to one side with the dakini, Yeshe.

Tashi bowed deeply to them both before embracing Lama Ozer. 'I am so glad to see you, Lama,' he said warmly.

'So am I, boy,' the lama responded. 'Now we will be together. No more separations. I hope you have served the prince well, Tashi?'

Tashi nodded. 'I have done my best, Lama,' he replied.

The abbot now interrupted them to say, 'Your Highnesses, Prince A-KarO and Prince Narasimha, Dakini Yeshe, Lama Ozer and young Tashi! It is good that you are all gathered here, for it is time now for your departure. In compliance with the Rigden's orders, you must leave Shambala by five this morning. With the link gates opening directly into Aggartha from this monastery, you will not have to endure the rigors of travel. I have set them at a prearranged point about which the sages have been informed and I will now lead you to them. The moment you make the crossing, they will contact you.'

Having said that, the abbot led the group out of the monastery hall and into a long corridor that led into a small chamber shimmering with incandescent light.

'The gates stand open,' the abbot announced. 'You may pass through now.'

Tashi's eyes hurt as he tried to focus on the blazing circle of ethereal white light at the far end of the chamber. Prince A-KarO moved towards it. Then he stepped into its brilliance and disappeared from view. So did Prince Narasimha and Yeshe. Lama Ozer gestured to Tashi, indicating that he should follow them.

The boy was about to comply when he suddenly remembered Chetak. 'Abbot,' he said, 'I must fetch my wind horse, Chetak. He is to travel with us.'

'Your horse is right behind you, Tashi,' the abbot smiled.

Tashi looked over his shoulder to find a young monk leading Chetak in. The boy accepted the horse's reins from him and led him to the gateway radiating light. Chetak neighed with joy as they stepped through. Lama Ozer bowed deeply to the abbot and the monks gathered there. Then, walking stick in hand, he made his way into the gates and stepped through, disappearing in a blaze of luminosity.

CHAPTER 17

AGGARTHA: THE HEART OF THE MYSTIC REALM

I

White light shone brightly and high mountains stood unveiled, their pinnacles merging with light-laden skies. A shining river, its banks strewn with gleaming, multi-coloured pebbles, flowed along the path on which the group of five was now making its way. Not a blade of grass sprouted anywhere and the silence was absolute. Not even a bird called. The members of the group now halted by the riverbank to wash their faces and hands. Careful, however, to preserve the pristine purity of the waters, none took a dip. Tashi gazed at his surroundings in wonder. In the near distance loomed a range of high mountains, purple in the morning light. Stretching away as far as the eye could see was a rolling plain, stark and bare, but for the stones scattered across its expanse that sparkled in the morning light, their colours ranging from a deep maroon to violet and dark purple.

Lama Ozer seated himself on the riverbank, gazing into the waters as they waited for the sages to appear and deliver their commandments. A restless Tashi paced the bank, his eyes straying to the shining watercourse. He could barely contain his excitement at having finally reached Aggartha, that etheric realm of great purity where the sages dwelt. None of the party, other than Prince Narasimha, had visited it before and they knew what a great honour it was for them to be here at all. Narasimha seated himself on a boulder and stared into the distance, his expression full of melancholy. Tashi wondered whether leaving Shambala had hit the prince hard; he seemed to be in a pensive mood. Meanwhile, Prince A-KarO was having trouble drinking the water he had scooped up from the river in his cupped palms. At every attempt, the water would slip through his fingers like glittering diamond teardrops. The dakini, Yeshe, was seated nearby. Her palms neatly folded in her lap, she was staring at the horizon. Tashi followed the direction of her gaze. Sure enough, there was a bright ball of diffused golden glory heading their way.

Hardly a moment had passed before a being of golden light, a sage, descended among them, his still nebulous form hovering just above the ground. In the silence that ensued, a clear communication took birth in the form of thoughts. The princes immediately went down on their knees and prostrated themselves. Tashi followed suit, as did Yeshe and Lama Ozer. As the group slowly sat back on their heels, the command came: 'Be seated, all of you. Your orders will be conveyed to you soon.' The voice continued, 'First, the collective will of the universe has ordained that you step forth and descend to Earth to fulfil your karma and meet the great need of the hour. The duty you are being entrusted with is equally a part of your own evolutionary journey and involves an engagement with the mortal world, rather than with the celestial realm. That journey will help you to grow further and realize your own true purpose.' The being paused and light, tinkling laughter flowed from his golden form. 'Next,' the voice went on, 'you have to create conditions suitable for the descent, yes the descent of a new age and the birth of one who embodies utter truth, naked truth, is at hand. He is the flame of truth, you have to form the chalice for him to take birth. This will only happen if conditions are fulfilled. It is for you to prepare the vessel for him to be born in. This will only be possible if the conditions laid down by the universe are fulfilled.'

As the five focused on the message, the words sank into their consciousness.

'To begin, step forth, Yeshe Nam Lha!' said the voice. 'Now what is required first, step forth Yeshe Nam Lha, now the time has come, I tear off the mantle of deity-hood that has sat upon you for countless ages past and send you down as a mere mortal woman. Shorn as you will be of all your attributes but compassion, you must rise to the demands of the challenge set before you, however difficult they may be. Disdain not this human birth, child, of which you are the instrument and the means, for it is unique, offering, as it does, a direct path to the zenith of the evolutionary process. Know, however, that many perils lie along this path.'

Yeshe took a step forward, her face impassive. The rising breeze tossed her hair about and made her form sway gently.

The being shimmered in the wind and his golden laughter flowed out in four directions. 'Here, hand me your garments, child,' he directed. 'From this moment onwards, you have surrendered much: your identity as a deity, your status in the higher realms and your immense wealth, treasures and estates. You are about to leave the Silverlode and descend to the mortal world with a new purpose.'

Yeshe, the mortal woman, stepped forth, slipped her clothes off her body and approached the golden being, naked and barefoot.

'This is your lot now,' the sage said, handing her a pale lemon shalwar and kurta, along with a white stole.

Yeshe slipped them on immediately.

'You accept this bond, woman?' the sage asked.

'I do,' she confirmed, her expression serene.

'Do you accept your identity as a humble mortal?' the sage went on. 'Do you submit to the sacrifices demanded of you and reconcile yourself to the loss of all that you were defined by earlier – your divine powers, the numerous *siddhis* that you, as a deity, were endowed with, the wealth and status beyond compare you had enjoyed as a dakini? Do you accept your spirit being stripped to its very core and losing everything familiar to be a guardian of the golden flame? Do you accept it all, my child?'

Yeshe's silken tresses unfurled and flew out like ocean spray. Trembling slightly, she went down on her knees and said stoically, 'I do, O Great One. I surrender everything I must and accept all that I have to. I open myself to whatever is ordained by destiny.'

The sage placed a glowing golden hand on her head and said, 'Child, you cannot imagine the extent of that which you surrender and that which you open yourself to, but I accept your word. The process of sacrificing all that you have been stands completed. I give you the grit and inner strength to achieve *Sat* – Truth – for the conditions to be fulfilled are punishing indeed.'

Yeshe shivered, but the golden light sustained her.

'As you have undoubtedly been informed, you are to select one of your two companion princes as your mate. That process must be completed within six months, following which an emissary from Shambala will contact you and convey your decision to us and to the royal court. Yeshe, you are the chosen mother of the divine child yet to be born. Your circumstances in the mortal world will be difficult, for the reign of Kalyug, the Fourth Age, is complete and the lot of women is a sorry one. There will be much for you to endure. However, you are not alone, but part of a group whose members are entrusted with the responsibility of taking care of each other. You have already been provided with all the knowledge you need for living in the mortal world. Also, your general appearance will be subtly altered.' There was a hint of a smile in the golden being's voice.

Yeshe smiled as the sage lifted his hand and she discovered that her skin was now lightly tanned and her hair fell in long, thick dark waves around her shoulders, curling at the edges. She had lost two inches from her height and her frame was slim, her carriage erect. Her eyes remained the same pale, translucent brown that changed with the light.

The golden being smiled and handed her a sword, well-worn, by the look of it, its handle made of plain silver, its blade sharp. 'A gift for you, child,' he said simply.

Yeshe accepted the weapon and held it with ease, spinning it out into the wind once before placing it at the sage's feet and prostrating herself alongside.

'Rise, child,' the sage exhorted her. 'Perfection never becomes irrelevant with the passage of time, although the mortal world has forgotten the use of the sword and a true wielder of the weapon has not existed for aeons. I pass this enchanted sword to you in blessing. It will empower you. Cover the weapon, guard it carefully and use it well, for you will need it to defend yourself when the Asur attack – as they inevitably will.'

Yeshe rose to her feet, smoothed down her clothes and adjusted the weapon in her hand.

'Now braid your hair,' the sage instructed. 'it is much too thick to be left loose. Take a step forward.' He drew her closer and lightly anointed her forehead with his grace. 'You are now ready, I think,' he said. 'A few practical matters need to be sorted out. This bag,' he pointed to the one in his hand, 'contains two sets of clothes for you and such necessities as may come in handy, including some money. Don't look so baffled, child. You will soon discover the use of money. Inside the bag is a basic medicine kit. Use it sparingly, for such medication is not available in the mortal world. A prayer book has also been provided. Read it slowly and commit its contents to memory.' The sage's form glowed brighter than the brilliant light of the realm. 'Now go and sit by the river. The rest of your instructions will follow when I address you all as a group. I will now make merry with the great celestial princes gathered here, not forgetting the earthbound young monk and his superior,' the golden being announced, laughing heartily.

His mirth was so infectious that Yeshe felt it infuse her being as surely as if it were a strange new intoxicant. She was free, free from all that she had been earlier. Then the thought struck her that the sage, this golden being, was more liberated than anyone or anything she had encountered.

The sage now turned to the princes. 'Ah, Your Highnesses, your turn has come. Are you prepared to step forth or would you rather not?'

Prince A-KarO glared at the being of light, his hands clasped together.

Narasimha smiled and stepped forward. 'We are both ready,' he announced.

Immediately, A-KarO, too, took a step forward.

'So you are!' the sage laughed, his mirth spilling over into the mountains. 'But Your Highnesses, for neither of you will it be easy, though you have really not been given a choice in the matter. It is ordained that you must step forward and the moment is here. Now you must divest yourself of your garments, your titles, your wealth and your powers and place them before me! Your weapons too. I know it is very hard. Now Your Highnesses, one at a time. First, Prince Narasimha.'

The crown prince stood silently for a moment under the luminous skies, motionless, his visage sombre and pensive. Then he stepped forward and, bowing deeply, prostrated himself before the sage. Then rising, he shed his garments, folded them neatly and handed the pile over, along with his sword, daggers, bow and sheaf of arrows. In silence, the golden being handed him a pair of khaki trousers and a forest-green shirt, an overcoat and a wallet containing plastic credit cards and some money.

'Narasimha,' the sage began, 'I see that you are ready, but have no idea what being truly prepared means. But your humility at this moment is appreciated. I shall no longer address you as "Your Highness", for in your mortal form, you will no more be heir-apparent to a divine royal lineage. You are neither to mention nor even contemplate the position you held in your celestial life till your task on Earth is complete and you have returned to your celestial responsibilities in Shambala. However, that choice is not yours to foresee now, for it lies in the future. Remember that all your vast accumulated *siddhis*, your celestial powers, your wealth, status and position in the celestial world are no longer at your disposal. But you do retain your innate wisdom and your vast knowledge. If you use them creatively, they will help you to deal with people and circumstances and to acquire power on Earth. Your deep compassion, your talent for dealing with beings of all kinds and your gift as a healer will serve the mission well.'

Narasimha had slipped into his new clothes by now. He stood erect, his height and dark complexion unchanged, but his eyes were now hazel brown and his hair was shorter than it had been. However, his mortal features were almost identical to his celestial ones.

'I am aware of the deep attachment that you share with your celestial consort, Mimaki,' the sage went on. 'She has petitioned us for permission to meet you while you are on your mission. On three occasions – no more – will she be allowed to visit you as a messenger bearing tidings from the Council. She will spend one night with you and then depart. You will not meet again till such time as your mission is over and your responsibilities as a man have been fulfilled. You will have to see at least one human lifespan through. We hope that you will accomplish your mission in that one lifetime, but then, you never know with such things.'

'I understand, Great One,' Narasimha said gravely. 'I do not ask for more.'

'Also, your designated role in the mortal world is chiefly that of a healer, emissary and purveyor of wisdom,' the sage reminded him. 'Thus, you may not, except in self-defence, raise your hand against anyone or take a life. I also make you a small gift,' the being of light went on, handing Narasimha a small pouch. 'This will offer you direction. Each time you open the pouch, you will find the answer you are looking for. But use it only when you or a member of the group is in dire need. For it will open only when the situation or circumstances are urgent enough to warrant its use. Now be seated, while I deal with the celestial prince, A-KarO.'

The sage turned his attention to the Lha prince, who stood straight as an arrow, his shadow falling long and dark on the river's shining surface. 'Now what are we to do with you, Your Highness?' the being of light mused. 'Magical being, spoiled beyond compare – note, I did not say "beyond repair"! Celestial god, prince of the higher gods, incomparable commander of many celestial battles, prince of intrigue, possessor of many magical powers, brilliant scholar and knowledge-bearer, with talents of the darker kind – should I list them, hmm? Will they stand up to scrutiny?'

A-KarO smiled, his silver hair spilling across his forehead. Then he went down on his knees and touched his forehead to the ground. 'Great Sage, Revered One!' he murmured.

The sage cut him short. 'No histrionics and no talk, Your Highness,' the golden one said clearly. 'You have but one duty now and that is to listen.'

A-KarO rose to his feet.

The glowing sage laughed, his golden form shooting beams of light in four directions. 'I herewith divest you of your past,' he said. 'Such baggage is irrelevant to your mission, for you are now a mere mortal, a speck in the universe. As you are well aware, this was ordained.' The sage paused, before continuing, 'Now A-KarO, you are being sent forth to forge a new destiny for yourself and for those bound to the yoke of the Fourth Age. As I mentioned earlier, you have been spoiled for too long. From this moment, you are divested of all your magical powers, your *siddhis*, your titles and your celestial palaces and estates. What remain with you are your innate wisdom, vast knowledge and sheer spirit. Your talent with weapons of war will come in useful. You will not only be able to wield any and every weapon, but create new ones and master the art of using them. You will retain your qualities as a commander of warriors in battle, but will be constrained to work through or around circumstances that are not of your making. It is imperative for you to understand that power, success, glory, wealth, titles and fame are of no use if you do not know how to love truly. Only through compassion that comes from the deepest love is the door – hidden alike to gods, men and lower beings – unlocked to the threshold of Truth. Few cross this threshold and the privilege always comes at a cost. So prince no more, but a mere man, A-KarO, find and unlock that door and cross that threshold.'

The sage's smile emanated shards of multi-hued golden light around him. 'This is your inner purpose, celebrated warrior,' he told A-KarO. 'From now on, be true to your vocation in the real sense. Your swords have seen many a celestial battle, but the real sword is wielded with mastery only by a true lover who understands that in battle, the sword plays, the arm moves, the body swings in the most perfect action, but the inner being stays immersed in the One. In war, heroism is seen in terms of conquest and victory. But true heroism is that which emerges from perfect inner harmony and few have achieved it in the Fourth Age.'

The sage's golden communication ceased. His essence permeated the group, creating a warm glow within. A-KarO stood in silence, absorbing its warmth.

The communication resumed. 'A-KarO, I look to you to extend all help to the group in as many ways as possible,' the sage went on. 'You are entrusted with the duty of protecting members of the group, especially Yeshe, as she will be particularly vulnerable, and the divine child she gives birth to. As for the details of your mission, I will elaborate on them later when I address the group collectively.'

A-KarO smiled, but his eyes, glinting with golden lights, were devoid of expression.

'Now, hand me your garments without delay,' the sage directed.

A-KarO took off his clothes and placed them in a neat pile near the golden being who now handed him an expensive, well-tailored shirt, along with dark, heavy trousers, a stylish fawn jacket, an expensive leather wallet and a watch.

A-KarO donned his new clothes, strapped on the watch and was examining the wallet curiously, when the sage said, 'There is money inside that wallet. I think you are more familiar than the others with the workings of the mortal world. In fact, if I am not mistaken, you have not only sustained a lively interest in it, but have made several trips there, defying injunctions against intervening in its affairs.'

A-KarO nodded in acknowledgement and said, 'I am aware, O Great One, that this wallet contains what would be considered a veritable fortune on Earth. And as for this watch, I admire your taste.'

The sage nodded, his golden effulgence lending the air a crisp, fresh feel. 'Other than a few changes, A-KarO, you will retain your original appearance,' he said.

There was a moment of silence before he continued, 'I expect you to maintain decorum while on Earth. You are to fulfil your mortal duties to the fullest and, above all, your duty to the group. There is one more matter, A-KarO. Surrender, one by one, the weapons you carry on you – those visible and those concealed.'

A-KarO grimly proceeded to lay out his twin swords, along with his bow and sheaf of arrows.

The sage smiled. 'And now, A-KarO, I take charge of your hidden weapons, hmm? Ha, ha, ha! Don't frown in that manner, mortal man! I know how much this hurts, but there is something else that will hurt still more.'

A-KarO stood motionless, his eyebrows knit together, looking askance at the golden being as he said, 'Revered One, we should be almost done now.' Brushing his waist-length hair firmly back from his face, he went on, 'If you will allow me, I must petition you for something.'

The sage nodded. 'Go ahead.'

A-KarO spread his hands. 'Revered One,' he began, 'would you cut off a warrior's hands by divesting him of his weapons? Those swords travel with me everywhere. I cannot survive without them. They are cast from my very lifeblood. Do at least grant me permission to carry them with me.'

'Son of the heavens, your wish is granted,' the sage said benignly. 'Now your second petition, for I know there is more to come.'

A-KarO's relief was visible on his face. 'Great One,' he went on, 'my second petition concerns the boy, Tashi, who is my student. I gifted him a wind horse, Venerable One, and the boy has grown to love him. His heart will break if he leaves the steed behind. Moreover, they have bonded so deeply that I doubt his horse can live without him either.'

The sage held up his hand in blessing and addressed Tashi, 'You may keep the wind horse, young one,' he said.

A-KarO bowed deeply to the golden being and murmured, 'I thank you, Revered One, for your kindness.'

'The time has come for me to address the older monk and his disciple,' the sage announced. 'But before that, I have a small gift for you, A-KarO, as I had for your companions.' The golden one handed the Lha a small book. 'The day you have worked out the puzzle in this book,' he went on, 'my gift will be visible to you. Make it a point to refer to the book whenever you are at a crossroads or in need of direction. It will guide you. Now be seated while I converse with the senior lama here. He has come a long way and I need to address him.'

A-KarO seated himself by the river and gazed into its brilliant depths. Yeshe lay on the grass. She seemed relaxed, her face serene, her breathing barely perceptible. Tashi was assisting the lama to his feet.

The great sage radiated waves of light as the lama came forward and prostrated himself before him. As the sage remained silent, Ozer spoke up.

'Should I hand you my garments, Great One?' he asked.

The golden being broke his silence at last. 'No, it is not necessary,' he replied. 'Your circumstances and the instructions that you will be given for the descent to Earth are different from those of the others. Lama, you will retain your original identity as well as your monk's robes. You have done well and shown remarkable perseverance. The time has come for you to rest. I instruct you, Lama, to return to your base at the hidden monastery. From there, you are to closely watch the circumstances that develop around other members of the group and send them messengers with advice that you deem appropriate and aid, as and when they need it. Your job is to monitor them closely and serve as their link to Shambala. Any questions, Lama?'

'Great One, it is not my place to question, only to obey,' Ozer replied. 'However, I do need to clarify how I will monitor them from so far away.'

'Once you reach the hidden monastery, denizens who serve us will get in touch with you. It is they who will keep you informed of the whereabouts of the group's members and the individual situations they find themselves in at a given moment. You may collaborate with these denizens to work out a system whereby they will bring you information about the group and serve as your messengers when you need to send out instructions or assistance. You yourself should avoid travel as far as possible. Your age and physical condition do not permit it. However, if you deem a given situation dire enough to warrant your presence, you may set forth, but I leave that entirely to your discretion and your judgement. Also, we will be in touch with you through our messengers. You will act as our intermediary for passing on our instructions and the little aid we can manage to the group from time to time. As such, you will be the only member of the group to remain in close physical contact with both the worlds.'

The lama prostrated himself, yet again. 'I am honoured, Great Sage,' he murmured.

The golden one smiled, tenderness emanating from him. 'My gift to you, Lama, is of a practical nature,' he declared, bringing forth an object. 'This is a seeing crystal through which you will maintain contact with the rest of the group and communicate with them. It also allows you to maintain contact with us and with the Rigden, as and when required. Now it is young Tashi's turn.'

The lama prostrated himself and withdrew. Tashi rose and approached the sage, bowing deeply to him.

'Do I hand you my garments?' the boy enquired.

'But of course, my child,' the sage smiled, golden light radiating from his presence, 'and be quick about it.'

Tashi swiftly took off his clothes and folded them neatly before handing over the pile. In their place, he received a pair of grey trousers and a crisp white shirt. He flushed with embarrassment as he fumbled with his new clothes in his hurry to put them on.

'Boy, relax!' the sage told him, his voice hinting at laughter. 'Take your time. If you are done, hold your hands together in your lap and give me all your attention.'

'Yes, Revered Sage,' Tashi said, smiling through his confusion, his face red from his exertions.

Golden beams emanated from the sage's amorphous form as he began. 'The time has come, Tashi, for you and Lama Ozer to go your separate ways. The lama will travel back to the hidden monastery and your duty to him is over. Your future now lies with the group in general and A-KarO in particular. It is to him, first and foremost, that you will now be duty-bound. Your first responsibility, from now on, will lie in helping A-KarO take the mission forward. Simply put, you will be a companion to A-KarO and help him in every way possible. You will look to him for your training, yet to be completed, in the Lha martial and spiritual arts, go about it with the utmost sincerity and give it your best. In the process, I expect you will evolve and learn much. You are the bearer of the Garuda's feather and will continue to remain so. Use it sparingly, however, and only when your lives are at stake.'

Tashi bowed again. The sage had fallen silent and the boy waited patiently for him to continue.

'You will all descend to Earth at Qiang La, the silver fortress, from where you must make your way to Sikkim,' the golden one went on. 'There you may rest for a few days before getting in touch with the local hidden communities for information. It is here that you will bid Lama Ozer farewell. Details of your mission will be revealed in a subsequent meeting that will take place tomorrow morning, when more of my brethren appear to convey their instructions and bestow their blessings.'

The sage fell silent, the golden glow around him spreading all the way across the horizon. And then he disappeared. The dazzling afternoon light had mellowed in the meantime and given way to evening. Tashi gazed up at the skies and smiled as the first star appeared. He sighed softly. Although the journey to Aggartha had not been an arduous one and the air here was so stimulating that it was impossible to feel tired, he felt overcome by sudden exhaustion. Now if only he could have a cup of tea!

While he was musing about it, the golden glow reappeared along the horizon and a crisp voice spoke into the magic of the night. 'Refreshments have been prepared for all of you,' it said. 'Please partake of them and rest for a while. With the light of dawn will I return, accompanied by my fellow sages. I will then address you as a group and explain the crux of your mission on Earth.'

For a second, the sage's form was clearly silhouetted against the night skies. Then it vanished into nothingness, leaving no more than traces of the dull golden light that had emanated from him. With his disappearance, a white sheet magically appeared on the grass before them. A cheerful fire crackled to their right, as heaped bowls of fruits appeared on the sheet – apples, bunches of bananas and grapes and a platter laden with sliced mangoes, pineapples and papayas. Two huge jugs of steaming-hot tea stood beside platters of rice and lightly sautéed sweet potatoes and a large bowl of lentil soup. Two enormous platters of green salad stood beside a bowl of sweet, fried cashew nuts. It was a veritable feast.

The sight of all that food revived Tashi's appetite in an instant. He could barely wait for the others to gather around the feast. Narasimha served Yeshe and himself portions of the fruit and poured steaming cups of tea for them both. A-KarO left the fruit untouched and heaped his plate with rice and sweet potatoes. Tashi first served the lama some fruit, then followed it up with helpings of cereal. It was only after Ozer had finished that the boy served himself some rice with lentil soup and heaped his plate with sweet potatoes. A great sense of satisfaction filled him as he settled down to his meal and it was only when he was relaxing with a cup of tea that his mind actually registered thoughts.

Gazing at his surroundings, he was filled with wonder. What an amazing place this was, with the dark range of mountains standing out against midnight skies, their snow-dappled peaks glistening in the gloom! The land was arid, devoid of much vegetation other than scrub, and dotted with rock formations. Nor far from where they sat, the river glowed silver in the dark. The realm of Aggartha was, indeed, unlike anything Tashi had ever seen. No cities seemed to exist here, but he had heard the company talk of nameless settlements run by the sages and their disciples. There had also been talk of dense forests, south of the mountains, which lent the barren landscape a verdant touch and provided refuge to communities that had lived on Earth long ago, but had subsequently migrated here to escape the rampant human degradation that had been the scourge of the Fourth Age.

Tashi rose to his feet to assist the lama, as was his habit after dinner, but Ozer held up his hand.

'No, boy, not tonight,' he said. 'I will manage on my own. You had better go and attend to the prince.'

Tashi bowed low before the lama and quietly made his way to A-KarO, who sat in the meditation posture. Not wanting to disturb him, the boy headed for the broad silver river that meandered through the countryside, inhaling the smells a refreshing gust of breeze wafted in from the waters. He strolled up to the banks and was just settling down for a good wash, when he spied Yeshe sitting on a rock that jutted out from the middle of the watercourse.

II

Tashi tried calling out to her, then waved frantically to attract her attention. All to no avail, for his voice was muffled by the rising wind which teased the waves relentlessly, causing them to toss and turn. A concerned Tashi whipped off his shirt and jacket. Tossing them aside and still in his pajamas, he dived into the river. The ice-cold water was like a knife through his flesh, yet amazingly refreshing. His focus riveted on Yeshe, he swam towards the rock in the centre. Unaware of his rescue attempt, Yeshe continued to gaze into the water. With broad, sure strokes, Tashi made his way through the water, slowing his pace only when he neared the rock. Yeshe continued to sit in silent serenity, a wistful half-smile on her face as she gazed out at the choppy waters. It was only when the boy drew closer that she stirred.

'Tashi, what brings you here?' she asked, surprised.

Breathless, the boy replied, 'Yeshe, the river is in turbulence at the moment. While bathing in it, I spotted you sitting here and grew concerned enough about your safety to swim across. The wind is making the waters choppy and the waves will only get rougher. Don't you think we should head back?'

'I suggest you head back yourself, Tashi,' Yeshe answered calmly. 'Do not worry about me. I can look after myself and, in fact, intend spending the night here.'

Tashi's heart plummeted. 'Here?' he said, incredulous. 'But this spot is far from safe. Besides, don't forget that you are no longer a celestial. Your mortal body is far more fragile than your earlier form.'

'How can I forget that, Tashi?' Yeshe said. 'I simply wish to test the limits of this body and grow used to it.'

Tashi shivered as the force of the waves made him bob up and down in the water. 'But surely you can't spend the entire night here, Yeshe!' he protested. 'Come back with me to the riverbank.'

'Dear one,' she said, smiling, 'it is rarely that one comes across a land of such perfection. And I doubt we shall be returning to Aggartha in the near future. I intend to spend the night exploring this fair realm. The sage has not prohibited us from doing so. Now I urge you to return to the bank and sleep in peace. I shall be back by three in the morning, well before the sages arrive at dawn.'

'I cannot leave you unprotected, Yeshe,' Tashi said firmly. 'So I shall stay with you.'

Yeshe's voice tinkled with laughter. 'If that is what you must do, Tashi, go ahead,' she declared, 'but being in the water must be uncomfortable for you and I have been sitting at this spot long enough. Let's swim to the opposite bank. I believe there is a forest just a few miles from there. Much has been said of the forests in this land which are apparently charmed and populated by ancient races, from whom we could have much to learn.'

With those words, Yeshe dived into the cold, clear water and began to swim with sure, confident strokes towards the opposite bank. Shaking off his fatigue, Tashi swam alongside. Soon, they had reached the other end and climbed out of the water. Yeshe slipped easily out of her wet clothes and wrung the water out of them before putting them on again. Tashi quickly averted his face and hung back for a moment to afford her privacy till she was dressed. Ahead of them, smooth grassland stretched for miles. To the west lay a dense wood, the treetops limned in bright moonlight. The wind, audible over the murmurs and sighs of the trees in the distance, blew in great cold gusts over the grassy plain, knifing through their shirts as Yeshe headed for the forest, breaking into a steady run, with Tashi just a step behind.

An hour or more later, they neared the first, shadowy row of trees from where the wood began and entered it. Yeshe called for a halt. She stood motionless and silent, her slim, lithe form merging into the shadows cast by the trees, chin raised and nostrils quivering as she sniffed the air. Tashi was simply glad for the chance to get his breath back.

'Hmm ... Mostly, forest smells,' Yeshe observed, 'but here and there, I am getting a whiff of something more. We will simply follow the path and see where it leads us,' she said in cheerful tones. 'I hope you ate well, Tashi, for this is going to be a taxing evening for you.'

Typical forest sounds became audible as the boy followed Yeshe into the depths of the wood along the path that ran ahead. Since his departure from Yumsamedong, Tashi had been missing the lure of a large natural forest and was excited by the very thought of entering one again. This one certainly looked promising. Shadows appeared to flick past as Yeshe, navigating by moonlight, led the way. After walking for half an hour or so, they came to a fork in the path. Without a moment's hesitation, Yeshe took the one to the right. Moving on, they sensed that the air around them was growing heavy with moisture.

'A river, surely, or a waterbody of some sort, hmm, Tashi?' Yeshe speculated. 'I feel it is quite near.'

The path broadened as they progressed along it and led to a vast lake that stretched away to the horizon. Tashi almost whooped in delight as he saw the silvery waves lapping peacefully in the moonlight. Both he and Yeshe half-ran to the shore and stopped in surprise as their gaze fell on a small, solitary boat moored there. It rocked gently with the rhythm of the waves lapping against its hull.

'Obviously, there is habitation somewhere around here,' Yeshe surmised. 'Where do you think the boat might head from here?'

Tashi pointed to a large mass of land in the centre that lay like a dark patch on the silver waters. 'To that island, I think,' he replied. 'Perhaps people use this boat to travel to and fro.'

'You took the words out of my mouth,' Yeshe told him.

Without another word, she stepped into the boat, with Tashi following a little reluctantly. A gentle breeze began blowing as Tashi pushed the boat away from the shore and began heading for the island.

'Look what I found here,' Yeshe remarked, 'a lantern! But we shan't light it. It might be used as a signal. Best to find out first what we are walking into.'

Tashi nodded, rowing steadily into deeper waters. Yeshe's gaze was now fixed on the island and as they approached it, she saw that it was thickly wooded. A high hill, wreathed in mist, rose from its heart. The closer they got, the harder Tashi rowed, his arms beginning to feel the strain. Eager now to set foot on land, the boy leapt across the waters lapping at the shore. Yeshe followed and, together, they tethered the boat to the protruding branch of a tree.

Standing on firm ground, they gazed at their surroundings. In whichever direction their eyes wandered, they found dense forest. Ahead of them, a broad path led into the heart of the island.

'Let's explore the place, Tashi,' whispered Yeshe, 'but we had better hurry, because the first watch of the night is done and we will soon have to head back.'

Curious despite his apprehensions, Tashi nodded and followed Yeshe down the winding path. They had taken less than ten steps forward when a sturdy net dropped over their heads without warning and yanked them off their feet, throwing them to the ground. Tashi's breath was knocked out of his body. His heart thudding against his chest, he looked up cautiously. Before he saw the nymph, her soft laughter rang out in greeting. Then his eyes fell on her. She was tall and slender, with a pair of silver wings sprouting from her shoulders. Against her complexion, silver as moonlight, her violet eyes were beautiful. A slim golden coronet sat on abundant mauve hair that fell to her waist in a braid. Tashi had never seen anything so beautiful in his life.

Suddenly, he heard Yeshe mumbling in the dark, her face pressed against the net, 'Nothing is working! I've tried a dozen spells, which would have taken this net off us in a trice, but simply nothing works now! I have truly lost my powers. What will we do now, Tashi?'

The nymph moved closer and said, 'I am the nymph, Serenee Na Nunaa, and you have trespassed on my land. I will release you soon, but you must promise to obey the law of the land. We do not allow trespassers here in Aggartha, but you are also the honoured guests of the sages. As such, it is my duty to escort you back to your camp. Dawn is not far off and you have an appointment to keep. But now that I find you here, I feel you should learn a lesson.' The nymph laughed gently before announcing, 'I will release you now.'

At a gesture from her, the net fell apart. Yeshe was instantly on her feet.

Serenee looked her over. 'The moment you got into the boat, we knew you were heading this way,' she said. 'Now that you are here, my father would like to speak with you. Our house is a short distance away. Follow me.'

'Do you own this island?' asked Yeshe.

'My father owns this island,' Serenee replied. 'It is known as Nee Nanarth and is home to our community of forest nymphs. Our forest island is famous in all of Aggartha for *nanarth*, the juice which derives its name from it. We prepare it from Nanarth blossoms that grow in abundance on trees. People in Aggartha do not drink wine and fruit juices are much valued among its denizens.'

The nymph led them off the main path and down a narrower, though well-maintained, trail that wound its way through the forest. The moonlight slanted through the branches, revealing clumps of tiny red flowers growing on the trees flanking them on either side. The deeper they went into the forest, the more Yeshe became aware of the forest sounds around them. Then a bright light cut through the darkness and as the road turned, Tashi and Yeshe saw the tree house. It had been constructed on the sturdy branches of an oak and light from a pair of windows peeped out through the branches. The nymph guided them forward and then led them up the tree.

'Follow me and welcome,' she said, leading them into the tree dwelling.

It contained a spacious room created out of branches that laced together overhead and was warmly decorated with hanging lanterns. A divan, piled with cushions, stood in the centre. Rugs were strewn on the floor and two high-backed armchairs with deep seats reclined in two different corners of the room.

'Make yourself comfortable,' Serenee urged. 'I will fetch Father.'

Yeshe settled herself on a huge cushion that lay to one side, while Tashi wandered around the room, looking out of the windows with interest.

'It is quite late, Yeshe,' he reminded her. 'Already, the moon is waning. Soon, dawn will break, announcing the hour of our meeting with the sages. Don't you think we should be getting back? There's an entire trek ahead of us.'

Yeshe reclined on the cushion. 'It is not quite as late as it appears,' she said. 'There is still some time before dawn. Besides, I am most curious to meet Serenee's father. As for the walk back you are anticipating, we are certainly not going to be walking, my dear Tashi. We will, most likely, have to run to be in time for the meeting! So eat and rest now and save all your energy for later.'

A strange luminescence filled the room as the nymph and her father entered. The latter was a tall man with an erect bearing and shining silver hair tied back neatly. A long, thick white beard flowed down to his chest. He was dressed in pajamas and a white shirt that came down to his knees. At the sight of him, Tashi sprang to his feet, while Yeshe remained seated, joining her palms together in the age-old greeting.

'Welcome, my friends!' the old man began. 'I can see that my daughter, Serenee Nu, has been looking after you. I am Raouf Ben Dalin. Your visit does me great honour. I was expecting you, of course. We had news of your presence here, Yeshe and young Tashi, as also of other members of your group. It did occur to me that the curious among you might venture into the forest and, perhaps, find their way to my humble abode.'

Raouf now gestured to Tashi, 'Sit, sit, my boy! You need to rest. You are both bound for the mortal world and rest will soon become a luxury for you. Serenee, pour them some juice and fill their plates. I can see they have not touched the refreshments laid out for them.'

'Raouf Ben Dalin,' Yeshe smiled, 'it is an honour to meet you. The forest that surrounds us is truly beautiful. Tell me, are you lord of the woods?'

Raouf, now seated on the divan, laughed heartily. 'And you, my dear,' he responded, 'are lovelier than the woods. Now to answer your question, I am no lord of these woods, but a mere citizen. Aggartha is a subtle realm, situated in a superior vibrational field. Supreme in its uniqueness, it has no lords, kings or kingdoms. We, its denizens, are united in oneness and ruled by the one omniscient power. All decisions in this realm are made with the speed of lightning through telepathic concurrence.'

'You have piqued my interest, Venerable One,' Yeshe admitted. 'Does Aggartha then have no government?'

'Imagine, my dear, a land that is really an energy field populated by thought forms fully aware of their nature. We do not have a government, but a council of twelve perfections. More will not be revealed to you now. All cannot be learnt in a single night, my child.'

'Surely, Raouf, this council of twelve perfections that you refer to is really the council of twelve sages?'

'Child, I will say no more on the subject!' Raouf laughed. 'The less you know, the better. Your concern should now be with the mortal realm. The subtle world of Aggartha is but a dream for you. Only the greatest effort – and grace – will allow you access to it. I knew you would be coming here tonight, Yeshe, and I have something to convey to you.

'The task you have all been entrusted with is very difficult one, but of paramount importance and your life, Yeshe, is now inextricably bound to it, as is your destiny. Know this, my child: your future lies in the fulfilment of this task. So embrace it with open arms. You who were the golden dakini, Yeshe, be on your guard against the dark prince. Beware of Asur royal blood. Beware!' Raouf's dark eyes glinted as he uttered these words.

A frisson went through Yeshe as her thoughts strayed to Arden and it was with conscious determination that she had to banish his image from her mind.

'Many trials await you,' Raouf continued. ' So choose your mate wisely and have your decision ready by the time you reach Mt Meru. Remember,

Yeshe, that when all else fails, the valley of the *sanjeevani* flower that lies in the shadow of Meru will offer you succour. Take refuge there, when all hope abandons you.

'Now here is something that I am entrusting to you,' he said, handing Yeshe a silver ring with a clear, shining stone in its centre that was of so pale a blue that it was almost white. Raouf looked at her intently. 'Take care of this ring, my child, and wear it at all times, for it will warn you of the Asur's presence. If they are anywhere within a radius of twenty miles, the stone will turn a bright red. Also, this ring will show you the path to the Alos valley, should you ever have need of it.'

Yeshe accepted the ring and slipped it on to the middle finger of her left hand. 'Raouf,' she said, 'I thank you for the gift of this precious ring. We have taken up a lot of your time. And now we had better leave, for night is on the wane and morning approaches. We have an arduous run ahead of us. Right, Tashi?'

'There is no need for that,' Raouf told her. 'I will transport you both to your campsite.'

As he held up his hand, Yeshe and Tashi felt a grey mist envelop them. For an undefined period of time, they felt suspended in a void. Then the wind rose around them and, within what seemed like moments, both found themselves landing on their feet at the campsite. Already, the camp was astir with activity. A-KarO was splashing water on his face and as Yeshe looked east, dawn sent its first magical golden ray shooting into the grey skies.

III

Tashi had run across to Lama Ozer and was now handing him a tumbler of water. The lama was seated on a large stone, his robes spotlessly clean and his hair brushed back in readiness for their meeting with the sages. After seeing to Ozer's needs, Tashi walked across to A-KarO, who was dressed and ready and busy grooming his long hair.

'Your Highness, should I brush it for you?' the boy enquired.

A-KarO shook his head. 'No, Tashi,' he replied, 'It is done. What you can do is fetch me some breakfast. Also call me by name or call me Master but not highness anymore.'

'Right away, Your Highness. It will take getting used to Lord,' Tashi replied.

Leaving the Lha, the boy scanned his surroundings to see if their morning meal had arrived. Sure enough, it was neatly laid out on a spread in one corner of the camp and Tashi's mouth watered at the prospect of the simple repast. Two jugs of milk stood next to a plate of flatbread and a dish of butter. A big platter of cut fruits had been set down alongside. Tashi poured out a tumbler of milk for A-KarO, arranged some food on a plate and laid them out for him.

'That is enough, Tashi,' A-KarO said. 'Now hurry and finish your own breakfast. It promises to be a long day. I expect the sages to be here very soon and we won't be getting our next meal until we reach Earth.'

Tashi had barely finished drinking his milk when there was a stirring in the air near them. A band of sharp, intense light appeared from nowhere, stretching like an arc before them. As the boy continued to gaze at it, he realized that the arc was not monochromatic, but glowed with rainbow hues.

A crisp, silent communication took place through a stream of thoughts. 'We are the Council of Aggartha,' it said. 'We are the twelve sages of light. That is all you are permitted to know. Do not seek to know more, for our mystery is impenetrable, inviolate. We are gathered here to assign you the sacred task for which the universe has been waiting for many aeons. The time has come for us to reveal your purpose and set you on the path on which depends the future of Earth, humankind and the wider universe. Your right actions in the mortal world could unleash the force that is destined to change the future of mankind for ever, shaping it in unimaginable new ways and making the universe evolve in so significant and creative a manner that even we cannot envision it yet.

'We understand that you have travelled long distances and been through much to reach this point. You have already had to undergo many sacrifices and surrender much that was important to you, but they are a trifle compared to what you must bear on Earth. Through our insight into your minds and hearts, we sense that you are ready for the challenges awaiting you.

'Now listen carefully to what is of primary and paramount importance. We, as guardians of this world and many others, assign you the task of creating the circumstances that will bring about the birth of a great symbol of purity on Earth, the birth of a messiah, the prophesied birth of Maitreya, the avatar. Only if you are able to meet the specific conditions set for it will this birth take place. Know this, all of you! The one who comes is veritable perfection, hitherto unseen on earth or in the subtle realms. If the child attains maturity, his contribution to Earth and the vast universe will be incomparable. You, as his appointed guardians on Earth, are to ensure the propitious conditions for his birth, protect him through his childhood and youth and, lastly, help create the age of purity that will follow – the Age of Maitreya, once known as Sat Yug. If your mission is successful, it will ring in this Sat Yug or the age of truth on Earth and in the universe.'

Minutes of silence ensued, followed by the announcement, 'Now my brother sage will address you.'

A quieter voice took over. 'Bringing about the birth of Maitreya promises to be a formidably difficult task,' it began, 'for even as I utter these words, the threat to the completion of that task continues to grow. This birth is to be kept a secret. None must know about it, other than members of your group and the wider group you will form when eighteen mortals approach you on Earth and help you achieve your quest. However, we fear that the Asur lie in anticipation of your descent to the mortal world, waiting to do their utmost to sabotage your mission. The moment you set foot on Earth, their search for your group and especially for the mother of the sacred child, Yeshe, will be set in motion. Their every effort will be focused on seeking her out and bringing her under their control. If she still manages to give birth without their interference, the Asur will concentrate their efforts on kidnapping the sacred child so they can use him for their own ends. So Yeshe, the prophesied mother, and the divine child she births, must be protected at all costs.

'Now to create the propitious circumstances for the birth, you must, first and foremost, travel to Mt Meru and reach it within six months of your arrival on Earth. This great mountain is easily accessed from the heavens and the subtle realms, but is invisible from Earth. It is said to have simply disappeared at the end of the Third Age and many have tried to search for it, but to no avail. So the quest to find Mt Meru, fraught though it will be with enormous difficulties, must involve an intensive search. But remember that you are not alone. You may seek help from the hidden communities of the Himalayas to guide you. Moreover, the eighteen pure mortals – men and women – I have mentioned will approach you voluntarily within the first six months of your sojourn on Earth. You will recognize them on sight and divulge your divine identities to them. You will also share with them the nature of your mission and include them in your group so that they can accompany you on your search for the mountain. Once you have found it, you are to climb to its upper reaches where lies the *sanjeevani* valley, also known as the Valley of the Golden Flower, named after the small shrub which grows in this place alone, bears tiny yellow blossoms and has immense healing properties. The valley was last accessed, many millennia ago, in the Sat Yug, but has remained beyond the reach of mortals ever since.

'It is here on the mountain that Yeshe, the prophesied mother of the sacred child, must announce her choice of mate. And it is here that the birth of Maitreya must take place. However, simply arriving in the valley with her guardians will not help the divine child's mother to give birth. She must subsist on a salt-free brew of *sanjeevani* flowers and milk and engage in the most intense meditation, especially in her ninth month. Now it is my brother sage's turn to address you.'

An energetic voice now made its presence felt in the group's collective consciousness. 'You will share the nature of your mission with the eighteen mortals who constitute a part of your group,' it said. 'It is on Mt Meru that A-KarO – no longer a celestial prince – will hold a *yagna,* leading to an amazing occurrence. The very essence of the universe will announce Yeshe's choice of mate. Now my brother sage will talk to you at length of the threats you face.'

A quiet communication made itself apparent in a pattern of thoughts. 'You have been repeatedly warned of the threat from the Asur. I need not underscore its gravity, but it is imperative that I share the information I have on their activities. I am told that their minions once again walk the

Earth and the Asur will now take greater risks than they ever have. I have reliable intelligence that they have descended on Earth in sufficiently large numbers to create utter chaos. They are like changelings and can adopt any guise. So beware of them and be forewarned that they will do their utmost to sabotage your mission and kidnap Yeshe. Child, you have already gone through that débâcle once. So you know what to expect.

'Unfortunately, our hands are tied. The extent to which our High Council and the Rigden's court can intervene in events on Earth is severely restricted. We are, however, keeping an eye on the Asur and will keep you informed of their possible whereabouts and movements from time to time. Also, when required, we will send you information through messengers, along with communications about tasks to be accomplished. On three occasions will one of us visit you, but this will happen only when required. Are there any questions?'

Silence descended on the group for a few moments. Then A-KarO spoke up.

'Venerable Sages, it is evident that we will face great danger in the mortal world for which we are bound. Yet we are being sent forth without any weapons to defend ourselves. During my days as a celestial prince, I engaged in combat with the Asur in many a celestial battle and it took all our great divine powers and superior weaponry to contain them. And now you are about to set us down on Earth, unarmed and unequipped but for our knowledge and wisdom. Is this a just and prudent decision? Should we not in all fairness be allowed a few of our weapons and powers, along with some Lha troops?'

The arc shone brilliantly and a voice answered, 'It is the collective will that you carry no celestial weaponry to the mortal world and completely forsake your vast powers when you set foot in it. As for the few Lha troopers you mentioned, A-KarO, with your skill, knowledge and innate wisdom, you yourself are equal to an army of warriors. We expect you to train the mortals who accompany you, use whatever weaponry you find in the mortal world and organize your own defence system through intelligent improvisation. You know the reason; we have no wish to transform Earth into a celestial battleground. Any more questions?'

There was a long silence.

'It is almost time for you to descend,' the voice reminded them. 'We have decided to set you all down in Qiang La, the silver fortress. This is where Lama Ozer and Tashi had left their mortal bodies and these will be restored to them. From western Tibet, you can make your way to Sikkim and acclimatize yourself through a brief stay there. Lama Ozer, of course, is needed at the monastery and will remain there to liaise with us and provide you with what support he can by monitoring the web of hidden communities across the Himalayas. He will be in touch with you and will serve as our messenger from time to time.

'Once again, be on your guard. Prepare yourselves for the descent to Earth, for the time has now come for us to begin the chant that will set it in motion. Any final questions?'

Tashi shyly raised his hand, then bowed low. 'Great One,' he murmured, 'if we are leaving now, I need to fetch my wind horse, Chetak. This will take but a minute.'

'Young Tashi,' the sage said, a smile in his voice, 'look behind you. Chetak is already here. And don't worry, he will travel with you to Qiang.'

Tashi spun around. There was Chetak, standing quietly behind the group!

The chanting began softly, then picked up, moving towards a crescendo. The band of light flashed brightly and, for a split second, Tashi saw the twelve sages seated there. Then he felt the wind rise and the world become a blur as everything around him began spinning at a frantic speed. He shut his eyes tight to counter the dizziness he was suddenly assailed by.

IV

When he opened his eyes again, the soft patter of rain and the familiar smell of Earth greeted him. He smiled. He was home. He was sitting in the darkened shrine room of the nameless monastery in Qiang La. The ancient figure of the Goddess Yum smiled coyly in the golden glow of candlelight and Lama Ozer was in the middle of a prostration before her. Tashi looked at his surroundings and laughed.

A-KarO was looking at him with a smile on his face. 'We'd better be on our way, Tashi,' he said. 'We have a long road ahead of us.'

Tashi smiled in response and even executed a little skip of pure delight as he made his way out of the shrine room and into the light rain. He stood outside for a moment, surrounded by the ruins of Qiang La, as the rest of the company filed out after him. A-KarO took the lead, with Lama Ozer walking alongside. Yeshe followed them with a dazed look and Tashi walked beside her, with Narasimha and Chetak bringing up the rear. The boy paused for a moment at the tinkling brook to wash his face and fill his canteen, peering into its depths to see if the nymph he had seen earlier was visible in the water. But she did not appear. Then he looked up again and found that his companions had almost reached the gates. Tashi ran to catch up with them and found Lama Ozer deep in conversation with A-KarO. The boy shivered a little as they moved out of the fortress complex and stepped on to Tibetan soil. As they made their leisurely way down the mountain, the sun began to come up over the hills, making the skies blush a vivid pink.

GLOSSARY

Amravati: Capital city of the Lha, of higher Gods.

Asur: Demons

Bodhisattva: Reincarnating Buddhas.

Bodhisattva Avaloketeshwara: The bodhisattva of compassion as per Tibetan Buddhism.

Chorten: Architectural reliquaries housing a relic are known as chorten in Tibetan.

Dakini: A wisdom goddess according to Buddhist tradition. Protectress of the dharma.

Goddess Tara: Principal Buddhist Goddess, the protectoress of the dharma. She has 21 forms including white Tara and green Tara.

Heruka: Enlightened beings who are wrathful or fierce deities in Tibetan Buddhism.

Inka: Asur world.

Inkala: Capital of Asur world.

Kalpa: Legendry capital of Shambala.

Kalki or Maitreya: The perfect one or the enlightened one. The messiah to come. Common to both Hinduism and Buddhism.

Lama: A Buddhist monk.

Lachen: A small hamlet located in Yumsamedong valley in Sikkim.

Lachung: A small hamlet located in North Sikkim near Yumsamedong valley.

Lha: Higher gods of light.

Mandala: Is a spiritual and ritual symbol in Buddhism and Hinduism representing the universe.

Mansarovar Lake: A holy lake in Tibet.

Nga Chung: A Tibetan rattle drum.

Qiang La: A legendary valley in western Tibet.

Rimpoche: A reincarnate Buddhist monk holding a position of great respect.

Rigden kings: Legendary dynasty of Shambala royalty.

Sprites: Lesser faeries.

Shambala: Legendary kingdom according to Buddhist myth.

Tangkha: A holy Buddhist painting done on cloth.

Tirthapuri: A religious town in western Tibet that gets many pilgrims.

Tummo: A breathing technique of Tibetan yoga through which intense heat is generated and which leads to advanced meditational states.

Vajra: A Buddhist weapon of power.

Yumsamedong valley: A high altitude alpine valley in the Himalayan state of Sikkim.

Yogi: A Hindu ascetic.

ACKNOWLEDGEMENTS

This book would not have been possible without the support and patience shown by my husband, Hardi and my son Suchet with their constant reminders to write. Also I have to thank my father for the dream he imbued me with, the dream to write. Thanks, Mom, for your encouragement and ideas.

My special thanks to the team at Hachette, especially to Nandita Aggarwal, without her advice and care this book would not have been in the shape it is today. My thanks also to the editor Mita Ghose and to Rohan Chhetri for their patience with this book.

Also Available from Hachette India

THE ARYAVARTA CHRONICLES

THE EPIC LIKE IT WAS NEVER TOLD BEFORE,

recreating the world of the Mahabharata and the lives of its characters through stunning imagination and powerful storytelling…

Book 1 GOVINDA

Book 2 KAURAVA

Book 3 KURUKSHETRA

PRAISE FOR *The Aryavarta Chronicles* series

'Suspense, vendetta, plots, counter-plots, gory scenes of torture and even a graphically described hallucinatory sequence is sure to give an adrenalin rush to those in need of one.' – *The Hindu*

'Strikes an intriguing balance between novelty and existing ideas… Surprises with retellings that are startlingly different.' – *DNA*

'Udayasankar takes the Indian fascination for magic, incarnation, renunciation, friendship, and of course, romance, to the next level.' – *Democratic World*

'Pick up the book(s) for a leisurely read and see how elegantly Udayasankar weaves tales in your head.' – *Mail Today*

'Thoroughly engaging...The drama, diplomacy and dispute in this reimagined version will make the book(s) unputdownable.' – *Straits Times*, Singapore

'Fast-paced…full of intrigue and guile.' – *Sunday Tribune*

The Aryavarta Chronicles Book I: GOVINDA

Ambition. Desire. Vengeance.

Aryavarta – the ancient realm of the Noble.

For generations, the Firstborn, descendants of Vasishta Varuni and protectors of the Divine Order on earth, have dominated here. For just as long, the Angirasa family of Firewrights, weapon-makers to the kings and master inventors, has defied them. In the aftermath of the centuries-long conflict between the two orders, the once-united empire of Aryavarta lies splintered, a shadow of its former glorious self. Now, the last Secret Keeper of the Firewrights is dead, killed by a violent hand, and the battle for supreme power in the empire is about to begin.

But who holds the key to the fantastic and startling knowledge of the Firewrights, which in the wrong hands will bring doom upon the empire? And does Govinda Shauri, cowherd-turned-prince and now Commander of the armies of Dwaraka, have it in him to confront the dark secrets of his past and discover the true meaning of being Arya, of being noble?

A format/Paperback/ Rs 199

The Aryavarta Chronicles Book 2: KAURAVA

Nothing left to fight for is nothing left to lose...

Emperor Dharma Yudhisthir of the Kauravas and Empress Panchali Draupadi rule over the unified realm of Aryavarta, an empire built for them by Govinda Shauri with the blessings of the Firstborn and by the might of those whom everyone believes long gone – the Firewrights.

Now the Firewrights rise from the ashes of the past, divided as before in purpose and allegiance, and no one, it seems, can stand in the way of the chaos about to be unleashed on the land – not the Firstborn, not the kings of Aryavarta, and not Govinda Shauri.

As sinister plans are put in play and treacherous alliances emerge, Aryavarta transforms into its own worst enemy. Dharma Yudhisthir gambles away his empire, the tormented empress is forced into a terrifying exile and the many nations of the realm begin to take up arms in a bid to fight, conquer and destroy each other.

His every dream shattered, Govinda is left a broken man. The only way he can protect Aryavarta and the woman in whose trusted hands he had left it is by playing a dangerous game. But can he bring himself to reveal the terrible secrets that the Vyasa has protected all his life – secrets that may well destroy the Firstborn, and the Firewrights with them?

B format/Paperback/384pp

[illegible]

[illegible] of the [illegible] over the [illegible] with the [illegible]

[illegible] from the [illegible] and [illegible] on this side [illegible]

As [illegible] into [illegible] and [illegible]

[illegible]